CROWN
PAPERS

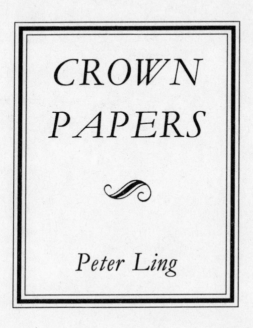

CROWN PAPERS

Peter Ling

WEIDENFELD AND NICOLSON
London

FOR JOAN M. LING
dearest aunt and best of friends

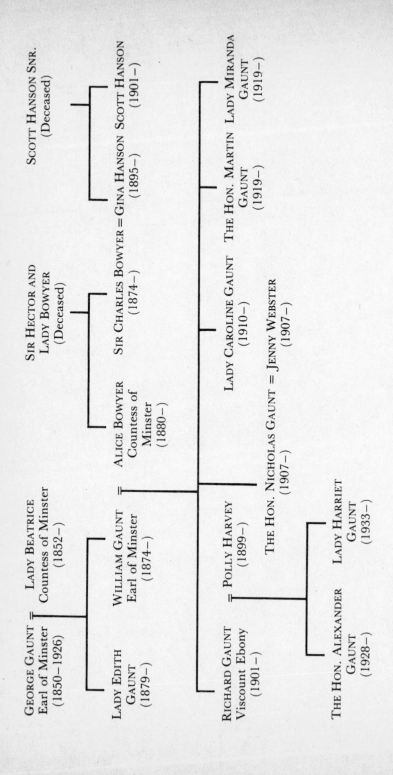

SCOTT HANSON SNR.
(Deceased)

SIR HECTOR AND
LADY BOWYER
(Deceased)

GEORGE GAUNT = LADY BEATRICE
Earl of Minster   Countess of Minster
(1850–1926)   (1852–)

SIR CHARLES BOWYER = GINA HANSON SCOTT HANSON
(1874–)   (1895–)   (1901–)

ALICE BOWYER
Countess of
Minster
(1880–)

WILLIAM GAUNT
Earl of Minster
(1874–)

LADY EDITH
GAUNT
(1879–)

LADY CAROLINE GAUNT   THE HON. MARTIN LADY MIRANDA
(1910–)   GAUNT   GAUNT
                       (1919–)   (1919–)

THE HON. NICHOLAS GAUNT = JENNY WEBSTER
(1907–)   (1907–)

POLLY HARVEY =
(1899–)

RICHARD GAUNT
Viscount Ebony
(1901–)

LADY HARRIET
GAUNT
(1933–)

THE HON. ALEXANDER
GAUNT
(1928–)

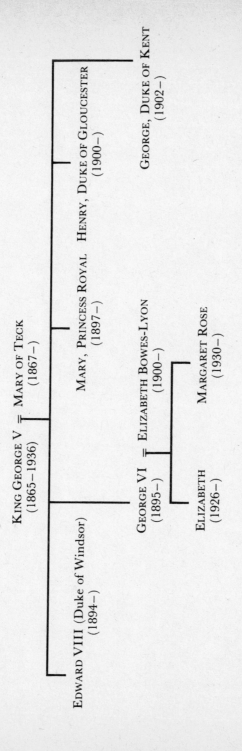

1

SUNDAY, 22 MAY 1932

'HELL!' Nicholas swore, as the train rattled over the points and the sleeping-car jolted, throwing them both off balance. Quickly, he apologized: 'I'm sorry, darling – did I hurt you?'

'No – not at all.' Suddenly, inappropriately, Jenny wanted to laugh. She bit her lip, then asked: 'What's the time?'

Nick stretched out a hand to his wrist-watch, which hung from a hook beside the berth, but the single blue bulb in the carriage roof was too dim for him to read the dial. He pressed a switch, and a shaded lamp above Jenny's pillow produced an amber glow that made them both screw up their eyes. The compartment had been in darkness for some time now, and this sudden brightness was uncomfortable.

'Just gone two-thirty ... Why did you want to know?'

'I just wondered.'

'I suppose you were wondering how much longer it would be before we – '

'No! Nothing like that. I simply thought ... It's long past midnight; this is my second day as a married woman,' said Jenny proudly.

'But we're not exactly married, are we?' he said quietly. 'Not yet.'

'After that beautiful service in St Peter's? The reception and the speeches – Richard reading out telegrams, and the twins throwing confetti – I don't think we could be more married if we tried.'

'That's just it,' said Nick. 'Perhaps I'm not trying hard enough.'

'Or perhaps you're trying too hard. Please don't worry about it, Nick. I love you very much, and I'm very happy.'

'I love you too – God knows what's wrong with me – I want you so much, and yet...' He pulled her closer, reaching for the light-switch, but she stopped him.

'Don't turn it out – let me look at you. I love looking at you.'

He loomed over her, taking his weight on his elbows, and she smiled up at him. Gently, she traced the tattoo on his upper arm, the single initial 'J' for Jenny. As she stroked his sunburnt skin, he began to relax a little.

'God, I do love you,' he whispered, and brought his mouth down to hers, kissing her again and again. Then the engine driver applied the brakes; the train jerked and lurched as it began to slow down and Nick's naked body rolled away from her yet again. *'Damn and blast!'*

She tried to suppress a sudden ripple of laughter, but it was too late. He frowned, averting his face.

'I'm glad it strikes you as comic,' he said bitterly.

'Oh, Nick – please don't be angry – I wasn't laughing at you: but perhaps an express train isn't the ideal place to make love... What time do we get to Paris?'

'Some time after seven, I think. You're probably right; this was a stupid idea. I'd better get back into the top bunk and let you get some sleep.'

He unfolded his tall, muscular body and rose to his feet. Jenny said, 'Dearest love – please don't feel badly about anything. Just because this is our honeymoon night, that doesn't mean we have to –'

'I know...' Nick's voice was muffled, as he climbed into the upper berth. 'But I wanted it to be perfect.'

'It will be – I promise. We've got a whole lifetime together, and it's going to be perfect for both of us.'

'Hmph...' He merely grunted, and the monosyllable suddenly reminded Jenny of Nick's aged grandmother: she smiled to herself at the memory of Lady Beatrice.

'Sleep well,' she said.

But it was a long time before either of them could get to sleep. Jenny lay awake, staring up into the darkness, aware of Nick's body above her – so close, yet so far away.

The train rattled off again, picking up speed as it left the station, and her thoughts raced with the pounding of the wheels. She thought back to that day – eight months ago, on an afternoon in late September – when he had come to find her in the gardens of Crown House, and had asked her to marry him.

No one could say that it had come as a surprise; the long, patient courtship – conducted principally by letter, since Lieutenant Nicholas Gaunt was away on board HMS *Norfolk* for months at a time – had been going on quietly for years. The family was fond of them both, and wanted them both to be happy – and yet ... It wasn't going to be an easy transition.

But then Jenny's situation had never been easy.

She first came to Crown House in 1910, when she was three years old, the daughter of an under-housemaid whose husband went off to seek his fortune in America and was never heard of again. In due course Mrs Webster was promoted to housekeeper, and Lady Beatrice, the Countess of Minster, left her to run the household in her own way.

The Minsters had one son – William Gaunt, Viscount Ebony, whose wife, Lady Alice, was an occasional lady-in-waiting to Queen Mary – and one daughter, Lady Edith Gaunt, who had never married and now would never do so, for she had made a contented life for herself with Grace Duncan, the Scottish teacher who ran the village school.

William and Alice had a large family of children, and these had been Jenny's daily companions when she was small. The eldest boy, Richard, was six years her senior, and she had hero-worshipped him a little. Next came Nicholas, exactly her own age; then Caroline – three years younger – and following a nine-year gap, the twins, Martin and Miranda, who were born soon after the First World War.

The old Earl was not an easy man to get on with, and eventually William decided that the only way to avoid continual family quarrels was for him to remove his wife and children to the Minsters' town house in Eaton Square. There they stayed for six years, with only an occasional courtesy visit to Crown House, at Christmas or in the summer holidays – so Jenny lost touch with her former playmates.

Then, early in 1926, the old Earl died, and William inherited the title, together with its obligations. He returned with his family to the manor-house in the weald of Kent, and Jenny tried shyly to pick up the broken threads of friendship.

Everyone had been very affable towards her, but somehow every-

3

thing had changed. She felt herself to be in a difficult position – *in* the family but not *of* the family. By now she had a job of her own, as an unqualified teaching assistant to Miss Duncan at the school on the village green, with special care for the kindergarten class. She left the housekeeper's flat within Crown House each morning and returned to it each evening; it would have been easy for her to withdraw from social contact with the Minster family altogether – except for one unforeseen development.

At nineteen, Jenny fell in love for the first time in her life, with her childhood hero, Richard – now a handsome young man of twenty-five, pursuing every pretty girl who crossed his path.

Once he became aware of Jenny's infatuation, he showered her with affectionate attention, and she was soon in his arms, embarked upon a love-affair which at first gave her deep joy – and then even deeper anguish, as she realized that she would never be anything more to him than a pleasing diversion.

He must marry a girl within his own class; she knew that. She accepted the inevitable end of the affair, when he became engaged to the daughter of a neighbouring squire, but her worst shock came when he jilted his fiancée at the eleventh hour, and instead married Polly Harvey, a bright, unpretentious chorus-girl from the revue at the London Pavilion.

For Polly had become pregnant; after a whirlwind engagement, Richard married her, and a few months later she presented him with an heir – the Hon. Alexander – red-faced and wrinkled, with a sturdy pair of lungs.

At first Jenny had been desperately unhappy, but her broken heart healed more quickly than she expected – thanks in no small measure to Polly's shrewd, sympathetic friendship. Slowly, she began to build a very different relationship; lovingly, Nicholas helped her to regain her self-respect, until she came to rely on this quiet, dependable young man, so unlike his elder brother. Nicholas had been in love with Jenny for some time; and in time she realized that he was the only man for her.

Time changed so many things. By then, Jenny's mother had been killed in a car crash, and her death left a gaping hole in the domestic hierarchy. When the Minsters offered her the job of housekeeper in her mother's place, Jenny did not hesitate for long. Her fate – and her feelings – were inextricably woven into the fabric of Crown House, and she could not refuse.

4

She gave in her notice at the village school, where her place was soon filled by an untrained, inexpert but extremely willing Lady Edith (who was overjoyed to find a role in life that would enable her to share every moment of every day with her beloved Grace Duncan), and took up the reins of Crown House with smooth efficiency. She continued as housekeeper for nearly eighteen months – until the day Nick asked her to marry him.

She could still remember how Lord and Lady Minster had looked, that September afternoon, when Nick dragged her into the Chinese drawing-room, with its greenish-yellow wallpaper and hangings, and the golden dragons whose twisted tails supported the chimneypiece.

'Ma – Pa – we've got something to tell you. Jenny and I are engaged; I've asked her to marry me.'

Of course they had not been surprised; indeed, the whole family were, in varying degrees, delighted. And yet Jenny was aware of the faintest possible shadow of anxiety, lurking behind those kind, welcoming smiles.

'Jenny, my dear – I'm so glad,' said Lady Alice warmly, as Lord Minster shook his son's hand. 'I don't know what I've done to deserve two such nice daughters-in-law – first Polly, and now ... you.' She put her arms round Jenny and kissed her with genuine affection; but they both knew there were a great many hurdles to be crossed before Jenny could be completely accepted into the family.

Only Lady Edith Gaunt had no reservations; her face shone with happiness – her nose, in need of a powder-puff, was pink with pleasure. 'Oh, Jenny – how lovely – it's what I'd been hoping for such a long time. I must go and tell Grace; she'll be as thrilled as I am. And you will come to supper with us, very soon, won't you? Nicholas as well – you must both come. It won't be anything very special, but I'll try one of my soufflés, and we must all hope for the best.'

Lady Edith had long since moved out of Crown House, into the lodge cottage at the gates, which had stood empty and unwanted for years until the two enthusiastic spinsters brought it to life again. Now they lived there in total happiness, half-way between the manor-house and the village of Ebony.

When Edith got home, she found Grace making tea, pouring boiling water into the pot.

'I heard you coming along the gravel drive,' she explained. 'Why, goodness gracious – you look as if you'd been running – what's wrong, for pity's sake?'

Edith struggled to get her breath back, laughing at herself for being so silly, and because she was so excited over her news.

'Jenny and Nicholas are going to be married!' she blurted out at last. 'Isn't that marvellous?'

'Ah well – I sincerely hope they'll be happy.' Grace's stern Scottish upbringing had made her cautious.

'Of course they'll be happy – I never saw two people so much in love,' said Edith, then touched Grace's hand apologetically. 'Any *other* two people, that is ... Why shouldn't they be happy?'

'I doubt your family would have preferred him to wed one of his own sort, if they'd had any say in the matter... No, Edith – don't pour the tea yet – give it a chance to mash! Will you never learn?'

'I don't care if it's weak – I'm dry as a bone,' insisted Edith, pouring out a cup that was ivory-pale when she added milk. 'And I think you're quite wrong about the family; everyone loves Jenny. They're not as snobbish as you think – look how they accepted Polly.'

'That's a very different matter.' Grace spoke thoughtfully. 'Polly Harvey came here as a stranger; she was Richard's fiancée before she ever set foot in Crown House. It's not the same for Jenny; she's been one of the staff, below stairs – only yesterday, she might have turned to and helped carry a tray of cutlery, if an extra pair of hands were needed. From this moment, the servants will be fetching and carrying for her... That could make problems all round.'

'I smell trouble,' sniffed Old Bea, irritably. The Dowager Countess had been listening to her wireless set, intent upon the news bulletin, which – even after all these years – she still assumed to be transmitted directly to her in some mysterious way, for her ear alone. When Lady Alice switched off the loudspeaker, she protested loudly.

'Don't interrupt the man!' Lady Beatrice banged her cane on the carpet. 'He was just telling me about the new arrangements for lighting Piccadilly – would you believe it, they're going to use electric street-lamps – I call it scandalous!'

'Mama – ' Alice tried to break in, but without success.

'I dare say they're hoping to keep it a secret, but I shall tell Minster about it. He must use his influence to get a question asked in the House – it's a waste of public money!'

6

Alice struggled to remain calmly reasonable: 'You can listen to your wireless later, Mama – this is much more urgent. Nicholas and Jenny are engaged to be married.'

There was a long silence, and then Old Bea snorted: 'Hmph ... I could see this coming.' She clawed at the rug across her knees with gnarled, arthritic fingers. 'Don't say I didn't warn you – but of course nobody ever listens to a word I say – you think you can overlook me, stuck away up here in this shoe-box of a room ... I've outlived my time, I'm well aware of that.'

At the age of eighty, Lady Beatrice – or, as Nicholas had christened her, the Old Bea – was determined to feel sorry for herself. She had retired to her own quarters when she was widowed and William's family moved into Crown House; she had chosen the warmest and sunniest suite of rooms, with the best views across park and gardens, to the summerhouse and the lake beyond. But Old Bea always had to have something to grumble about.

'They'll be up in a moment to tell you themselves, so do try to be nice to them.' Alice had thought it advisable to break the news first, just to be on the safe side. 'You know you're very fond of Jenny really ... And she's lived here since she was a baby – it's not as if Nick were marrying a total stranger.'

'Better for us if he were, in some ways,' said Old Bea stubbornly. 'Better for her too – I tell you, I smell trouble!'

'What on earth do you mean?'

'The staff won't like it. They'll resent having to treat her like one of us, when they know she's one of them ... It'll create bad feeling – mark my words.'

'Sssh – they're coming ...'

The door opened again, and Nick brought Jenny in, his arm around her waist. Finding his mother already there, he said; 'Ah – I suppose you've heard already, Grandmama. Well – are you going to give us your blessing?'

Old Bea's face softened slightly; she held out a bony hand, dry and brittle as a twig. 'Come here, child.' Drawing Jenny towards her, she pursed her lips in a grimace that was intended as a smile. 'Yes – you're a pretty thing ... You take after your mother in some ways – Webster was pretty enough, when she was a girl. And you're a hard worker; you've not let us down. Very well, Nicholas – you've always been a difficult lad – always gone your own way – but I dare say you've made a good choice, so I shan't scold you.'

7

She motioned imperiously, and Jenny leaned forward, to be rewarded with a peck on the cheek: an uncommon mark of approval. 'Just tell me one thing, miss –' the old lady added sharply. 'Where are you going to find us another housekeeper half as good?'

Polly's response was unequivocal. She gave Nicholas a smacking kiss and slapped him on the back, saying, 'You took your time, didn't you?' Pulling Jenny into her arms, she hugged her fondly. 'Thank goodness I won't be the only outsider in the family now – it'll be lovely to talk to somebody who speaks the same language!'

They had been having tea outside on the terrace; Richard hauled himself up out of a basket-chair, swallowed a mouthful of toasted teacake, and slapped his wife playfully on the bottom.

'Don't insult my friend Jenny Webster,' he told her. 'She's from good Kentish stock – not a fly-by-night cockney baggage like you, my girl!'

'Jenny knows what I mean,' Polly retorted, 'and you keep your hands to yourself... From now on I'll have someone to tell my troubles to.'

'What do you mean – troubles? What have you got to complain about?' Richard moved in closer, putting both hands on Jenny's shoulders, a mischievous gleam in his eye. 'Speaking for myself – I couldn't be more pleased to welcome our new sister-in-law. She's been jolly nearly one of the family for so long – I'm grateful to young Nick for making it legal at last!'

Like everyone else, he kissed Jenny. Only this kiss was unlike all the others, for there was something more to it than simple affection – something that stirred old memories, making her uncomfortably aware of days long gone when her lips had tasted his so often, and the same smell of tweed and tobacco and beer and shaving soap had pricked her nostrils. She managed to smile as she drew away from him; but something in the kiss disturbed her.

Nicholas, only a few feet away, looked from one to the other – and his face darkened.

'*That's* the sort of thing I'm complaining about – what a way to carry on!' Polly tried to pass it off lightly. 'And then he wonders what I mean by troubles...'

'Nonsense – it's my prerogative.' Richard turned to his brother for support. 'The best man always gets to kiss the bride – isn't that right?'

'I haven't asked you to be the best man yet,' said Nicholas.

'Ah, but you're going to – it's the traditional thing – who else could do the job for you? It will be my privilege and my pleasure to see you to the altar, old son; I wouldn't miss it for the world!'

Polly stepped in, changing the subject: 'Far as I can see, there's only one problem. We'll have to find ourselves a new housekeeper.'

'Yes, Old Bea was concerned about –' Jenny broke off and began again: 'Lady Beatrice was concerned about that too.'

'Call her Old Bea if you want to – you're one of us now,' Richard grinned. 'You'll call her a darn sight worse than that, if she ever gets her claws into you.'

'Actually – I was thinking of offering the housekeeping job to Lilian Brooks,' Jenny continued. 'You know, Polly – she's one of the vast Brooks family, from the village. She's been kitchen-maiding here for ages, but she'll never get any further until Cook is pensioned off, and that's not going to happen in a hurry. She might make a very good housekeeper, with a little training.'

'Lilian – yes, I know ...' Polly's stage experience came to the fore, as she transformed herself instantly into a rather heavily built, slow-moving countrywoman with a flat, Kentish drawl. 'Par'n me, yer ladyship, but Cook says you can't have no more strawb'rys 'cos Master Alexander's 'ad the lot!'

Jenny laughed: 'That's Lilian. She's slow but sure – and I think it would do her good to have a little responsibility. She's been under Cook's thumb much too long. I'll talk to Lady Alice about her.'

'Well, I leave all that to you ladies.' Richard shrugged it aside. 'I think I know the dear creature – about thirty, isn't she? – with a figure like a wardrobe and a face like an old boot. Still, there's one consolation – at least no Lothario is likely to follow Nick's example and carry her off as his blushing bride ...'

Nicholas had already talked to his sister Caroline about his feelings for Jenny, so she took the engagement in her stride – in fact, thought Jenny, Caro seemed to take most things in her stride these days.

The two girls came face to face in the library; they were almost identical in height, and the three-year difference in their ages that once seemed important had now ceased to matter. Caro was so confident and self-possessed – ten months as a junior reporter in Fleet Street, on the *Daily Argus*, had changed her so much, and Jenny compared Caro's sleek, dark fringe with her own soft blonde curls, feeling rather like a country cousin.

'Of course you'll put those boring old announcements in *The Times* and the *Telegraph*,' said Caroline. 'But couldn't I slip a para to our gossip columnist, the week before? I think I deserve a tiny scoop – seeing it's all in the family.'

And that only left the twelve-year-old twins. Martin was away at boarding-school; Miranda, released from an eternity of French irregular verbs with her governess, received the news politely, but without enthusiasm.

'Can I be a bridesmaid? And will there be champagne at dinner tonight? If there is, I shall tell Martin that he's missed out this time. It will be something to fill up my letter when I write to him.'

She was not exactly unfriendly – just a little cool and withdrawn. But then Jenny had never been able to break through that strange invisible shell the twins had built up around them, keeping the rest of the world at bay.

So much for the Minster family. Jenny had seen them all, and been welcomed by them all – all, that is, except one.

Quite correctly, Nicholas had broken the news to his parents before anyone else, and Lady Minster had responded just as Jenny hoped she would. But – looking back – she realized Lord Minster had said nothing in particular to her; nothing she could clearly remember.

He had shaken Nick's hand vigorously and congratulated him; he had kissed Jenny on the brow and murmured something about their future happiness. And the next time she had looked for him, he wasn't there. The french windows stood open, and William, Lord Minster, had slipped quietly away into the garden.

It was not until the following day that she spoke to him again.

She always tried to keep some time to herself in the middle of the afternoon, when lunch was out of the way, and it was still too early to worry about dinner. Sometimes she would take herself off to her room and write letters – but if she felt energetic, she would pull on her old gardening clothes and help Lord Minster, planting out seedlings in the herbaceous border or dead-heading the roses.

On this particular afternoon, she found him buried in the shrubbery, attacking an invasion of bindweed that threatened to strangle everything in sight.

'Come out, damn you!' he grunted, wielding a wicked pruning-knife. 'Who's that? Oh – Jenny...'

He emerged from a bush of fuchsia, and wiped his face with the back of his hand. Seeming oddly abashed, he muttered: 'You're the last person I expected to see. Why aren't you off with young Nicholas? Shouldn't you be choosing engagement rings, or something?'

'There's plenty of time for that. Richard challenged him to a game of tennis, so I decided to come and find you . . . I thought you might want a helping hand.'

'My dear girl – that's extremely kind. I'm engaged in a life-and-death struggle with this blasted convolvulus, and I'm sorry to say I'm not on the winning side.'

'Then it's time for reinforcements. Perhaps if I can follow it back to its roots . . .'

She got down on her knees and tried to trace the maze of tough, whiplash tendrils winding in and out of the red-and-purple fuchsia.

For a while they toiled in companionable silence, and Jenny sensed that Lord Minster's embarrassment – whatever might have caused it – was gradually being eased away. He was never so happy as when he was gardening; the grounds of Crown House were his pride and joy. When he first took possession of the estate after his father's death, he found the place run to seed – almost a wilderness. In the five years since then, he had worked wonders, clearing the lake, cutting down trees and opening up new vistas, planting, pruning, replenishing the beds with flowers of every kind.

Encouraged by the change in his mood, Jenny ventured at last: 'May I ask you something?'

'Of course you may.'

'Yesterday you congratulated Nicholas – you said you hoped we would be happy – but what do you really think?'

William continued to ply his knife for a while before replying; there was no sound but the slashing of leaf and stem. Then he said, 'You must know I couldn't want a better wife for Nicholas. Why do you ask such a question?'

'I thought you seemed a little – disconcerted, perhaps . . . And just now, when you saw me, you looked uncomfortable. Please tell me what's wrong; I'd rather know the truth.'

'My dear . . .' He put down the shining blade, and walked over to her. 'Surely you know how I feel? You should know – better than anyone.'

He came closer, and she looked up at him. The sun was over his shoulder, and although she shielded her eyes, she could not see his expression very clearly; but his voice was gentle, and a little sad.

'These last few years, when we worked together side by side, have meant a great deal to me. I thought you might have guessed how much. Of course I'm overjoyed that you are to marry my son, and become my daughter; but – yes, there's a touch of regret in my happiness too. I can't help thinking of the garden that we shall never make...'

'But we can still work together – I want to go on helping you –'

'I hope you will. But that's not what I meant.' He turned his face away, and the sun caught it, gilding his strong profile – so like Nicholas, yet so different, with the quiet, generous wisdom only age could bring; and she understood.

Neither Nicholas nor Jenny had wanted a long engagement, but that was the way it turned out.

First of all, she had to offer the housekeeper's post to Lilian Brooks, and then Lilian, who never made up her mind quickly about anything, had to take time to think it over. And after she accepted the offer, Jenny had to start training her; that could not be rushed either, for Lilian, thorough and painstaking, was a slow learner. For several weeks they shared the job between them, working in double harness; which meant that everything took twice as long as usual.

Then there was the question of finding somewhere to live.

To begin with, Nick had been very keen that they should have a home of their own, not too near Crown House. It wasn't that he wanted to turn his back on the family, but he cherished the idea of independence. Crown belonged to William – and to Richard... Nicholas was determined to make a fresh start, somewhere else; and he took Jenny house-hunting.

They saw big houses they could not afford, and tiny houses they could not fit into comfortably; very new houses with all mod cons and no atmosphere, and dilapidated houses with masses of atmosphere and no 'cons' at all.

At the end of November, Nicholas received a new posting, to a destroyer that was headed for a tour of the Far East, and that meant putting the wedding date off yet again.

'Of course I shall have to get used to you being away so much,' Jenny said, one afternoon in December, as they walked by the lake.

They were both well wrapped up, for the first frosts of winter had gripped the land overnight, turning it iron grey and iron hard. The reeds at the water's edge were trapped in a film of ice that crackled as the ripples shivered against them.

'You won't mind too much, will you?' Nick asked anxiously. 'After all, you must be used to it by now. I've been away more often than I've been at home, these last years.'

'I know – but I've never really been alone. I had my work – and my friends – your family all round me . . .'

He stopped and turned to her, searching her face: 'You're going to hate being alone, aren't you?'

'I'll get used to it – sailors' wives have to, I suppose . . . But – *do* I have to? Straight away?'

'What do you mean?'

'I was only thinking – we still haven't found a house we like; and it seems silly to buy somewhere in a hurry. Couldn't we leave it for a while, and stay on here? Then I'd have company while you're away at sea.'

He hesitated for a moment; but he could see she was right. It was by far the most sensible solution. There would be plenty of opportunities for house-hunting once he came home. So it was agreed: they would begin married life here, at Crown House. And the Minster family were absolutely delighted.

On one point, however, Nick was adamant. He did not want to spend his honeymoon in Paris.

The subject first cropped up one night after dinner. They were all in the Chinese drawing-room, having coffee. Richard swirled a snifter of brandy around the bottom of his balloon-glass, and said, 'Of course you really ought to go to Paris. Polly and I had a whale of a time there – didn't we, darling?'

'Oh, yes – marvellous. I used to think London was a bit of all right, but I didn't know the half of it till we went to Gay Paree. Those shops! . . . Oh, Jenny, get him to take you along the Rue de la Paix and down the Rue de Rivoli –'

'As for the cafés and the restaurants – you never had such food and drink, I promise you! And the nightlife – make him take you to the *Folies Bergère*, Jenny – it'll be an education for a quiet, respectable chap like our Nicholas.'

'Surely you didn't introduce Polly to the *Folies* on your honeymoon?' William raised an eyebrow.

'Only for her sake – she took a professional interest in the show –' Richard began. But Polly interrupted quickly: 'Take no notice, he's only pulling your leg… But seriously – it is a beautiful city, you'd love it. And it's not all streets and buildings – there's lots of parks and gardens – and the River Seine… I'm sorry to say it, but it knocks the poor old Thames into a cocked hat.'

'It does sound rather nice –' Jenny began, but Nicholas set down his coffee-cup with a clatter. 'We're not going to Paris. We're going to Scotland.'

Jenny stared at him. 'You never said anything about Scotland –?'

'It was going to be a surprise. I thought we should explore the Highlands. I only caught a glimpse of the mountains when I was up at Invergordon, but I've seen photographs. Magnificent scenery – you can walk for hours without meeting another soul.'

'Wouldn't that be rather lonely?' asked Alice, doubtfully.

'You don't want crowds of people around when you're on your honeymoon,' said Nick. 'You want to be alone together.'

'I think it sounds wonderful,' said Jenny loyally. 'I shall ask Miss Duncan to lend me some guidebooks.'

Only later, in strictest confidence, would she admit to Polly that Paris *did* sound rather fascinating… Still, perhaps they could go there another time.

Polly took the first opportunity to tackle Nicholas on his own. He had been out riding when the skies opened up, descending upon him in a shower of sleet; he was cold and wet, and very anxious to have a hot bath and a change of clothes – but Polly would not let him go.

'She'll never tell you so, but she's really dying to go to Paris, in her heart of hearts. Be a sport – give her a real surprise! I know you'll both love it – it's the most romantic place in the world. Those old mountains can wait; you should see Paris while you're young – with the one you love.'

Nicholas escaped to the bathroom as soon as possible, and lay and soaked in the tub for a long while, thinking it over. The next morning, he told Jenny briskly that he had changed his mind. He'd cancelled the tickets to Scotland; they would catch the night ferry from Dover, and the sleeping-car from Calais… She threw her arms round him: 'You must be a mind-reader! How on earth did you guess that was where I really wanted to go?'

Only Richard slightly spoiled things by saying casually: 'I'm glad you took my advice, old lad. Quite right – always listen to your elders and betters, and you won't go far wrong.'

The icy ground thawed out, and spring bulbs began to appear; snowdrops first, then crocuses, and then a golden sea of daffodils, in drifts beneath the trees. After that everything seemed to bloom at once, and the garden was rich with tulips, wallflowers and lilac, and riots of purple rhododendron... May was flying by: the wedding seemed to get closer by the minute.

Every post brought letters and cards, bursting with good wishes, many of them accepting invitations to the ceremony; and presents arrived from members of the Gaunt family scattered across the globe.

Jenny's own solitary background was thrown into sharp relief; almost all these messages and gifts came from friends and relatives of Nicholas – she realized more acutely than ever before how few friends she had of her own; and no family at all.

Grace Duncan joined with Edith to send her a bedspread of vivid crocheted squares that glowed like a stained-glass window. They had made it themselves, during the winter evenings, and Jenny was immensely touched by their kindness.

And there was another wonderful present, addressed as much to her as to Nicholas. From London, a very smart delivery-van brought a beautiful vase of lalique crystal, from the Duke and Duchess of York.

Nicholas knew the Yorks well, for his first posting had been on board HMS *Renown*, sailing to Australia and New Zealand with them on a State Visit – and Jenny had been on the point of taking a job as a nursery-governess to the Royal Princesses when her mother's death had forced a change of plan. Inside the parcel, the Duchess had added a handwritten note:

I hear you are planning a honeymoon in Paris. When you come back, please ring up and come to spend a weekend at Royal Lodge. The house is almost ready for visitors, though the garden still needs a lot of work. But we look forward to seeing you both very soon; Elizabeth and Margaret send their love. They are impatient to show off Elizabeth's own house, which she has recently acquired!

Of course there had been pictures of it in all the newspapers: the little cottage, with everything scaled down to a child's size – 'Y Bwthyn Bach'. It had been a present from the people of Wales to Her Royal Highness on her sixth birthday, in April.

Jenny felt nervous at the thought of a weekend at Royal Lodge, but she was excited too; with Nicholas at her side, she felt sure she could brave anything.

But before that could happen – there was the wedding.

Members of the family began to gather at Crown House, and Jenny found herself greeting people she had never met – remote aunts and uncles and second cousins twice removed. She would never remember all their names, but she did her best to respond to each one with a bright smile and a friendly handshake: 'How do you do? I'm so glad to meet you – Nicholas has told me so much about you' – which seemed to go down well, whether it was true or not.

Among the crowd of unfamiliar faces, there were some that she recognized.

'Jenny *darling*!'

The husky American drawl was unmistakable. Gina erupted from her car, draped in furs and glittering with jewels, followed by her husband, Sir Charles Bowyer.

'My sweet, you look simply heavenly – I couldn't be more thrilled that you and Nick are getting married at long last... Of course I knew it would happen, all along – the first time I saw you together, I said you were made for each other – didn't I, honey? And you know I'm never wrong about things like that.'

Sir Charlie opened his mouth to speak, but Gina did not wait for an answer, sweeping up the steps and into the house on a high tide of chatter. 'Where's the lucky bridegroom? I must give him a big kiss – he's always been my favourite nephew... And where's Alice? And William? I don't seem to have seen any of you in ages – it's been so long since we came to stay – why has it been so long, Charlie?'

He shook his head, unable to get a word in edgeways; and in any case he might have found it difficult to reply. There had been a slight coolness between the Minsters and the Bowyers for the last year or two.

Sir Charlie was Lady Alice's brother; a confirmed bachelor, he had startled everyone when, at the age of fifty-two, he had broken out of his regular routine and married glamorous Gina Hanson from Baltimore, twenty-one years his junior. At first it seemed to be a happy marriage, and Gina was thrilled to become Lady Bowyer, but soon they were in financial difficulties for she was chronically extravagant.

Her attempts to recoup some money had taken her into some

shady areas, and one of these ventures led indirectly to a rift with her in-laws. Since then, she and Charlie had not been such frequent visitors to Crown House.

But this was a special occasion. Sir Charles had to attend his nephew's wedding; naturally he had to bring his wife – and of course she had brought her younger brother.

'Scott's seeing to the baggage – we won't wait for him,' Gina announced, proceeding into the drawing-room. 'Alice, my angel – simply *too* divine . . . !'

Gina's elegant coiffure was a deep, burnished copper, while Scott's tousled red hair was frankly carroty – and they were also very different in character. Gina cared desperately about wealth and possessions, and her place in society; Scott was a struggling journalist on a left-wing weekly, whose only ambition was to tear down the pillars of society, and rebuild the whole thing on a more egalitarian basis.

Just at present, he was hauling bags from the boot of Gina's sports car, warding off the well-meant attempts of a footman to take them from him.

'Hell, no. I can manage,' he insisted.

'Let him have the luggage, Scott,' said Lady Caroline. 'He knows where it has to go, and you don't.'

Scott looked up in surprise; the footman grabbed his opportunity – and the suitcases – in both hands.

'Caro –' Scott stared at her. 'Hi there . . . It's good to see you.'

He was aware of the change in her at once. The young, fervent disciple of Scott's brand of social egalitarianism had grown up while he wasn't looking. Suddenly she had become a poised and beautiful young woman.

'Hello, Scott. I'm glad you could come,' she said. 'Let's go indoors – I want to hear what you've been doing.'

As they went up the broad stone steps, he said, 'I hope it's OK me being here. Gina said my name was on the invitation card, but I –'

'Oh, it was – I made sure of that,' Caro smiled.

She took him into the library, where they could talk undisturbed, and poured him a whisky from the tantalus on her father's desk.

'Now then!' She threw herself into the tall, buttoned wing-chair. 'Tell me about the magazine. You're still working for *Tomorrow*?'

'Sure. We struggle along from one crisis to the next. We're

generally being sued by someone or other – if it isn't the office landlord, it's the printers who haven't been paid – but we go on bringing the damn paper out somehow.' He sipped his drink, eyeing her. 'Let's talk about you. You look like working in Fleet Street kind of suits you.'

She shrugged. 'Oh, it's all such rubbish... I'm ashamed to be on a reactionary scandal-sheet like the *Argus* – but I remember you told me that's one way to fight the system ... from the inside.'

'Yeah.' He nodded sagely. 'It also pays better than working from the outside, I guess.'

Her smile faded. 'That wasn't why I chose to work for the *Argus*. It was the only paper that offered me a job. I suppose it's because my father met the chairman once, donkey's years ago – but since it was the only offer I had, I thought I'd better take it.'

'Oh, don't get me wrong – I'm not knocking it. As long as you enjoy what you do –'

'I suppose I must enjoy it really. I have to admit it can be rather fun. Part of me despises it, but... You meet a lot of people.'

'You don't meet me. How come you never call me, even though we both live in town these days?'

She looked at him for a moment, then said: 'Perhaps I was waiting for you to call me? You know where I live, at our London house.'

'Well, yeah – but Eaton Square is way outside my territory. If you're ever in Islington, why don't you look me up?'

'I might do that,' she said.

Another day, another night, and then – the wedding day itself.

Jenny woke at dawn, in the little guest-room of the lodge where she had been the guest of Grace and Edith for one night. Grace felt strongly that it would be so much nicer for Jenny to be married from their cottage, rather than the housekeeper's flat. Besides, she might have come face to face with Nicholas in one of the long corridors of Crown House, before the ceremony, and everyone knew that would be terribly unlucky.

From force of habit, Jenny sat up in bed and began to write in her diary:

Saturday, May 21st, 1932
It's strange to think that in a few hours I shall not be Jenny Webster any more, but the wife of the Hon. Nicholas Gaunt. By tonight I shall

18

*no longer be a single individual person, but one half of a married couple.
I do love him very much; I don't think I could have faced this ordeal
otherwise. The last few weeks have been like one of those nightmares
where you try to run faster and faster, desperate to get somewhere before
it's too late, but you can't remember what you're running to – or perhaps
you're running away from something ...*

*I am running away from loneliness. I am running into the arms of a
loving husband. That is why I am determined to remember every detail
of this day, as the most important turning-point of my life ...*

But of course she could not remember it all.

The day sped past like an express train, and the faces of her friends
loomed up and vanished again at intervals, like people glimpsed on
station platforms, as the train rushed by. She only remembered odd,
isolated moments ... Edith and Grace helping her into the car, with
its white ribbons ... Mr Hawkins, the butler, resplendent in a hired
morning-suit; he had volunteered to give her away, since she had no
father of her own to perform this function ... Lady Alice turning to
smile at her as they came up the aisle; the scent of flowers filling the
old, grey-stone church ... Nicholas and Richard waiting at the altar
steps ... The ring upon her finger – the words: 'Till death us do
part'.

And the photographs – Martin and Miranda shrieking with laughter as they flung handfuls of confetti – Lady Edith trying not to cry,
blowing her nose and being spoken to sternly by Grace.

The wedding breakfast and the telegrams – Richard's rather saucy
speech, and Nick's face, unamused – and the champagne. Then back
to her own flat, to change into her going-away dress. The drive to
Dover; the ferry crossing, and at last –

She opened her eyes. She must have fallen asleep after all, because
here she was in a real express train, rattling through France – and
there was daylight showing under the crack at the bottom of the
window.

She scrambled out of the bottom berth, and pulled the blind all
the way up.

'Hello – you're awake,' said Nick's voice, above her head.

'Yes – do come and see – there are lots of houses. Do you suppose
this is Paris?'

He glanced at his watch, then jumped down, joining her at the window. 'Must be – it's nearly seven o'clock. Did you get any sleep at all?'

'A bit. Did you?'

'Mmmm.' He pulled her to him, and kissed her gently. 'I'm sorry about – you know – last night . . .'

'Don't be silly, there's nothing to be sorry about.'

He was still naked, and as he embraced her, the smooth silk of her nightdress was cool against his skin.

'You're so beautiful,' he said.

'So are you.' She smiled back at him.

'I wish we . . .' Then he broke off: 'But I suppose we'd better get dressed. We're due in to the Gare du Nord in about fifteen minutes.'

They took turns at the miniature wash-basin, brushing their teeth and combing their hair in a dim square of looking-glass. By the time they were dressed, and Jenny was putting on a touch of lipstick, the train had slackened speed, and the buildings outside the window towered above them.

Criss-crossed girders flashed by. From a viaduct they looked down on glimpses of narrow streets, with unfamiliar posters on the walls: *Dubo . . . Dubon . . . Dubonnet . . .*

Suddenly they were engulfed by buildings – a tunnel, and then another – and at last the train pulled up with a squeal of brakes and a final flourish of escaping steam.

A porter in a peaked cap and a navy-blue blouse tucked into a stout leather belt with brass hooks on made light work of their luggage, leading them to the station forecourt. Once there, he spread his hands wide, and pointed expressively to an empty cab rank, making them understand that another taxi would be arriving at any moment, if they cared to wait.

But how could they stand there patiently when all Paris was spread out before them, waiting to be discovered?

Early as it was, there was a café already open for business across the open square. Jenny saw a waiter in black, a long white apron almost reaching his feet, setting out tables and chairs on the pavement.

'Couldn't we have a cup of coffee?' she suggested.

Nicholas summoned enough scraps of schoolroom French to inform the porter that they were going to have breakfast; pressing some coins into the man's hand, he entrusted him to keep an eye on their luggage – and they crossed the road.

The coffee was strong and black, and they added foaming hot milk from a second jug, and cubes of sugar that each had to be unwrapped individually. Hot croissants and butter – unsalted and deliciously creamy – completed the meal. They were both too impatient to eat anything more; there was so much to see.

Slatted window-shutters were opening up all along the street; a woman in a blue headscarf tossed a bucket of water from her front doorstep, sweeping down the pavement. Two schoolboys in baggy knickerbockers ambled past, carrying home long thin loaves of bread from the bakery; a clip-clopping horse pulled a cart piled high with fresh flowers. There was an extraordinary smell in the air – anthracite, and pungent foreign tobacco, the scent of lilies of the valley, new bread and hot coffee. Somewhere church bells were ringing, as the city came to life on Sunday morning.

They took a taxi to their hotel which was in a side-street off the top of the Champs Elysées; it was old-fashioned, but with a reassuring air of faded luxury. They were escorted by a pageboy in a buttoned uniform to their room on the second floor, ascending in a gilded lift like an abandoned bird-cage.

The room was spacious and cool, the windows shaded by closed shutters. The boy deposited their luggage, indicated the adjoining bathroom, accepted a tip, and left them alone.

'The bathroom's a bit antiquated – let's hope the plumbing functions properly,' said Nick, taking off his jacket and tossing it on the wide double bed. He prodded, and it surrendered under his pressure with a faint, satisfying sigh. 'Ah – a feather mattress...'

Jenny was already opening the double windows and unfastening the shutters. They swung outward, revealing a tiny balcony with a wrought-iron balustrade.

'Oh – Nick – you must come and look!' she called.

He went to join her. There was a view of another side-street, lined on both sides with leafy plane trees – more tall, sloping roofs of grey-blue slates – and above the rooftops, soaring up into a cloudless sky, a world-famous silhouette: the Eiffel Tower.

Jenny turned to him, her eyes dancing. 'This is really Paris – and we're in it!' she exclaimed.

Suddenly the years rolled away; she was no longer a young woman of twenty-five. She was completely and innocently happy, like a child – she was the girl Nick had grown up with – and he loved her with all his heart.

He took her in his arms, holding her tightly for a moment. Then, without any more words, he picked her up and carried her to the bed: and there were no more problems.

2

MONDAY, 23 MAY TO SATURDAY, 30 JULY 1932

From that moment, Paris was an enchantment.

The first day, they scarcely left the hotel: they passed the morning in each other's arms, upon that luxuriously soft bed, until pangs of hunger reminded them that they had had nothing to eat except croissants since the previous evening.

'We could ask for room service – get them to send up a tray,' Nicholas suggested, running a fingertip lightly along the smooth curve of Jenny's back.

'Oh, no! They'll think we're very peculiar, spending the day in bed,' she demurred. 'Let's get dressed and go out to look for a café. We need some fresh air; the walk will do us good.'

Nicholas smiled: 'You're a puritan at heart. We mustn't enjoy ourselves too much – it would be sinful... I promise you, the hotel staff won't be at all shocked; the French aren't ashamed about making love – they take it very seriously.'

'All the same, I should like to go out.' Jenny got up and walked over to the dressing-table. 'We can't stay indoors on our first day in Paris – it would be such a waste.'

Nicholas watched her pull her stockings on, her slim supple body outlined against the sunshine which streamed through the open windows.

'If you say so... What a pity we can't go out just as we are – naked and unashamed.'

'Even the Parisians might draw the line at that,' said Jenny. 'It's like a dream I have sometimes, where I'm walking along the street with nothing on.'

'I wish I were in that dream,' Nicholas teased her, getting out of bed. 'Do you ever dream about me?'

He put on a shirt, and began to button it; his eyes met hers in the speckled looking-glass on the wall.

'Often – especially when you're away at sea, and I'm missing you. It's awful when I wake up, because it seems so real at the time, and that makes the loneliness even worse.'

Her face was clouded, and he knew that she was thinking ahead to his next voyage.

'Let's not worry about that. We're together now, and I'll be with you every minute of the day – and the night.'

They lunched at an open-air café with a view of the river, on sweet cool melon and escalopes à la créme; and they sipped glasses of vin rosé, and Nick held her hand under cover of the tablecloth until they couldn't bear it any longer, and then they went back to their hotel.

The next day they agreed that they really must explore the city. They went to the Louvre, and gazed respectfully at the Mona Lisa, who sneered back at them; they visited Notre-Dame and put their tongues out at the gargoyles. Then they strolled along the boulevards, going nowhere in particular, until Nick asked Jenny what she would like to see next.

'Didn't Polly say something about parks – and gardens? I'd love to get away from buildings for a little while, and walk on grass – is that possible?'

Nick hailed a cab, and asked the driver to take them to the Bois de Boulogne.

When they reached it, they might have been in open country – there wasn't a building in sight, and no sound except the rustle of leaves and the hum of summer insects. They walked under the trees, and ran along winding woodland paths, then raced down a steep track that twisted and turned, and suddenly opened out on to a hidden sheet of water, fed from a little waterfall at the top end.

As they climbed up for a closer look, Nick wondered: 'Where do you suppose the water comes from? An underground spring?'

They scrambled through the undergrowth – and stopped. There, almost at eye-level, was another lake, set in higher ground; it seemed to be floating in mid-air, like the Hanging Gardens of Babylon.

'I wonder if Richard and Polly found this, on their honeymoon?' Jenny asked, bewitched.

'I hope not,' said Nick.

She glanced at him, surprised, and he explained quickly: 'I mean – it would be nice to think we saw it first. It's our private discovery.'

That night they dined in a restaurant at the top of the city, in Montmartre, almost under the shadow of the Sacré Coeur. It was growing dark by the time they left, and they strolled along the broad terrace in front of the Basilica. They were not alone; young men and girls stood near them in the gathering dusk, gazing out at the view. Twinkling street-lamps below came on one by one; as they watched, the city sank into darkness, and a myriad pinpoints of light appeared, glittering like diamonds scattered across black velvet.

Aware of the other couples around them, whispering and embracing in the soft night air, Nicholas put his arm around Jenny and drew her close, his lips brushing her cheek, his hands caressing her.

'Thank you for bringing me here,' said Jenny. 'I never imagined anything so beautiful.'

On their way back to the hotel, they passed a lighted theatre, and saw a poster with a portrait of a lithe black girl wearing nothing but a vestigial skirt of bananas.

'*Folies Bergère* . . .' Jenny read aloud. 'Isn't that where Richard said we –'

'Could we please stop talking about Richard?' said Nick.

Caro sat at her desk in the news-room, gazing into space and wondering what she should wear.

As a rule, she was not particularly concerned about fashion. In the winter she tended to wear jerseys and skirts; in the summer she wore blouses instead, or perhaps a dress in a bright floral print. She didn't really care about clothes, as long as they were serviceable and unfussy, and enabled her to do her job with the least possible inconvenience. Travelling expenses for junior reporters on the *Argus* were kept to a minimum, so she did a lot of running for buses, frequently incurring the conductor's wrath by jumping on or off a moving vehicle. And she had to be able to leg it at top speed up a street in pursuit of celebrities who had strong and sufficient reasons of their own for not wishing to be interviewed; so narrow skirts or tight, constricting waistbands were out.

She never bothered with a hat. A few years ago everyone had worn the pull-on cloche, and that wasn't so bad, but now brims had come back into style, hats were a positive menace.

All the same, she would need a hat for Ascot; that was certain.

She had been startled when the news editor, in passing, warned her to make a note of the Ascot dates in her desk diary.

'We're sending you with Chips Monahan,' he told her. 'He'll cover the sporting side, you can do the social notes. Your family connections might come in useful for once – spotting old friends in the Royal Enclosure.'

It was the kind of assignment she most disliked. Scott would despise her for it, if ever he found out: spending the day scribbling names in a notebook – the Honourable This, the Countess of That – for the benefit of the Great British Public who had never heard of these people anyway.

But the question remained: what should she wear?

It would have to be a summer dress – she had seen one in sea-green, with floating panels, in a shop-window in Bond Street. Frantically expensive, but for the sake of her job she had to enlarge her wardrobe, and it would come in useful for other occasions later.

The hat would be more of a problem. She loathed those ridiculous, broad-brimmed straws that people wore to the races – but a smart little pillbox, perhaps, with a tiny eye-veil in black net –

She came to with a start, when the telephone rang at her elbow. It was the news editor again.

'Caroline – forget what I told you. I'm taking you off the Ascot job. We've decided to send Daphne Matheson with Chips instead. Anyway, you'll be very busy that week; there's a series of protest meetings in Hackney about the Means Test, and we'll want you to cover those – righty-ho?'

'Righty-ho,' said Caro flatly, and put down the telephone.

In other words, Our Racing Correspondent would now be escorting Our Fashion Editress instead.

Of course, Ascot would have been a sheer waste of time and money, and the Means Test was much more socially relevant, but... She sighed, and began to draw pillbox hats on the cover of her notebook. Ah well, Scott would be pleased, anyway.

Spurred on by this thought, she flicked over the pages of her address-book, and picked up the phone again. 'Is that the *Tomorrow* office? Could I speak to Mr Hanson, please?'

A long pause, filled with some indistinct muttering, and then an American voice: 'Hello – Scott Hanson speaking – who is that?'

'Scott, it's me, Caro. I said I'd ring you, didn't I? Listen, I was just thinking – we never had the chance of a real talk at Nick's wedding, and I wondered if you'd like to come to dinner one evening?'

'Dinner? When? Where?' He sounded dubious.

'How are you fixed next week? Why don't you come to Eaton Square? I'll get them to lay on a cosy little supper; nothing grand – it will just be the two of us.'

Another pause, and then Scott said, 'I guess I'm old-fashioned, but I feel kind of awkward about being invited out by a girl. I'd like to see you, Caro – but only if it's clearly understood that *I'm* taking *you* to dinner.'

'Oh, goodness – I thought that went out with the Dark Ages!' she laughed. 'But if it makes you happy . . . All right then – I'd love to have dinner with you. Thank you very much.'

'It won't be anywhere smart. There's a little hideaway I know in Soho; cheap and cheerful – will that be OK?'

She wrote the time and place into her diary and rang off, feeling ridiculously happy.

On the appointed evening, she wore her best summer dress, a riot of peonies and roses. It was feminine, but it was practical, and she hoped Scott would like it.

The restaurant was in Greek Street; upstairs, with cramped tables too close together, and uncomfortable bentwood chairs, but that didn't matter. The food was Italian and unimaginative – minestrone, followed by plates of pasta in bolognese sauce – but that didn't matter either.

He called the waiter, ordering a 'fiasco', and she must have looked bewildered, because he explained: 'A flask of Chianti. In French it's a *carafe*: in Italian it's a *fiasco*. But don't worry, it'll be quite drinkable.'

She was impressed by his knowledge. They talked about politics; about the Soviet Union, which Scott admired, and Oswald Mosley's Union of Fascists, which he disliked intensely.

Caro found herself agreeing, and felt suddenly very young. She remembered the first time they had met, nearly five years ago, when she was still a schoolgirl. They had roamed the grounds of Crown House while he told her his life-story; he had outlined the steps of his career – how he got his first job in journalism back home in the States, and then threw up a lucrative post on a New York daily to take a badly paid job on a radical magazine.

She thought then that he was the most exciting man she had ever met. The surprising thing was that all these years later, older and wiser and a great deal more experienced in the ways of the world, she found no reason to alter her opinion.

She listened in silence, gazing at his red hair and his freckles; and the way tiny creases softened his eyes and mouth each time he smiled. When he called for the bill, she said, 'That was a marvellous dinner; thank you, Scott. I don't approve of you paying for it all – it's against my principles.'

He began to argue, but she forestalled him: 'But I'm prepared to let you do it – on one condition. You provided the dinner; come back to our house and let me supply coffee and brandy. Otherwise I shall insist on paying my share, and create an embarrassing scene, and you'll hate that.'

He grinned: 'OK – you win. A cup of coffee and a very small brandy – that would be terrific.'

Even so, he insisted on paying for the taxi to Eaton Square, and she had a pang of conscience, suspecting that he couldn't really afford it. But it was too late to back down now; she had made her plans, and would not change them.

A sleepy maid brought the tray of coffee, and Caro said, 'Thank you, Molly – don't wait up. I'll see to this; you can go to bed.'

Scott sprawled back along the sofa, and she sat on the white fur rug at his feet, gazing up at him. He was talking about Germany now and the policies of Adolf Hitler, but she wasn't really listening.

At last he glanced at his watch. 'Wow – it's after midnight – I had no idea. I'm sorry I kept you up; I must go.'

He made a move, but she stopped him.

'You can't go now; it's much too late. You'd never get back to Islington at this time of night; the tubes stop at twelve.'

'There'll be an all-night bus – I think they run one an hour –'

'That's ridiculous. You must stay here. The guest-room's all ready; the bed's made up and everything. We'll give you an early breakfast if you've got to dash off.'

He hesitated: 'What will your mother say?'

'She's not here; she's not on call at the Palace this week – she's got some time off. Anyway, I'm sure she wouldn't mind. You're one of the family.'

'Well . . .' He looked at his watch again. 'I guess it is kind of late, but I don't know . . .'

'You must stay here, Scott. I want you to.' She knelt up and took his hands, pulling him towards her. 'Kiss me.''

He embraced her – clumsily at first, and then holding her tenderly. Her heart pounded so loudly she felt sure he must be able to hear it. Her lips opened under his, and she felt weak with longing.

'You've taken me by surprise,' he whispered at last. 'I never expected anything like this, when you called me last week.'

'Didn't you? I did. It's what I hoped for – it's what I've wanted for a long time. You see – I hope you don't mind, but – I think perhaps I'm a bit in love with you.'

'You're crazy,' he said gently, and kissed her again.

'Mmm, that's nice,' she said at last. 'But it would be nicer still if we . . .' She stood up, drawing him to his feet. 'Let's go upstairs.'

'You mean – the guest-room?'

'If you like. Or you can come to my room. They're on the same landing.'

She led him to the door, but as she opened it, he caught her hand.

'Caro – maybe you shouldn't be quite so generous with your invitations.'

Something in his tone pierced her happiness, and she felt her excitement beginning to fade.

'What do you mean? I don't do this sort of thing as a rule, if that's what you're thinking,' she said defensively.

'I'm sure you don't, but it would be a mistake. You're very young –'

'I'm not, I'm twenty-two. I want you, Scott. Don't you want me?'

'Of course I do, but not like this – it's too sudden. You don't know what you're letting yourself in for.'

'No, I don't. But I want to know,' she said, with desperate sincerity.

'Then – I'm the first?'

'Of course. Oh, plenty of people have tried – some of the men I work with have asked me out once or twice, and they wanted to take me home afterwards and all that, but – I wasn't in love with them, so it was hopeless. It would be completely different with you.'

'No, Caro. You're a terrific girl, and I'm very flattered – honoured – that you should even –'

'Oh, shut up! Are you trying to tell me you don't love me at all? Is that it?'

'I don't know. And that's why it's not right. It wouldn't be fair to experiment . . . I really think I should go now – there could be a twelve-thirty bus from Victoria if I hurry.'

'Go on, then, if that's what you want.' She was suddenly furiously angry, and flung the door wide open. 'Go to hell if you like – I don't care!'

'Don't be like that. I'll call you tomorrow – we'll talk.'

'Don't bother! I'm busy tomorrow.'

'The day after –'

'I'll be busy every day from now on... Just go, why don't you? What are you waiting for?'

She knew she was behaving like a spoiled child who couldn't have her own way, and she hated herself. She saw the look on his face – troubled, hurt – and she hated him too for being so damn *nice* about it.

She didn't bother to see him out. She heard him stumble down the stairs, and a moment later the door banged behind him. The evening had been a total failure. Bitterly, she remembered the Italian restaurant: that pretty well summed it up... A cheap fiasco.

Jenny came out of the house, her arms filled with parcels, and Nicholas announced: 'Just a few little souvenirs from foreign parts.'

Alice and Polly were keeping an eye on Master Alexander, who sat on a plaid rug, building a tower of coloured wooden bricks. A yellow butterfly flirted with the honeysuckle along the west wall, and bees buzzed contentedly among the tubs of roses at the edge of the terrace.

'Presents for all of us?' asked Polly eagerly.

'Oh, you shouldn't!' Alice protested, but without conviction.

'We've had such a wonderful time, we wanted to share it with you,' Jenny said. 'This one's yours – and this is for Polly.'

She handed over two oblong packages in shining coloured paper, festooned with curls of gold ribbon. The ladies tore off the wrappings, exclaiming with delight at the contents – bottles of scent, in heavy frosted glass.

'Lovely – it's like having Christmas in June,' said Polly. 'I'm going to open mine right away and put a dab behind my ears for luck.'

'We've brought a doll for Miranda,' said Nick, 'and some cognac for Father – where is he?'

'Need you ask?' Alice smiled. 'Up to his waist in stinging-nettles – or knee-deep in mud, encouraging the new water-lilies. Miranda's in the schoolroom; you'll see them both at teatime, I expect.'

'I know Miranda's really too old for dolls, but I couldn't resist this one; it's the most sophisticated doll you ever saw.' Jenny sorted out some more parcels. 'We brought a stereoscope for Martin, with views of all the famous places in Paris. Shall we send it to him? Or wait till he comes home for the holidays?'

'That might be best,' Alice agreed. 'It would be awful if it got damaged in the post, and it's only a few weeks now until school breaks up. I don't know what's happened to this year – it's just whizzing by.' She broke off, as a thought struck her: 'Oh, by the way – the Duchess of York asked me to remind you that you've got to telephone her. She's very keen for you both to spend a weekend at Royal Lodge.'

Nicholas looked at Jenny: 'I don't know... Do you think we should? It seems a bit of an imposition...'

'My dear, she's already invited you! It's only a question of fixing a date,' said Alice. 'You'd like to go, wouldn't you, Jenny?'

'Well – yes – I'll be very nervous, but I would like to see them again,' said Jenny.

Polly interrupted them, waving and calling: 'There's Richard... Coo-ee! We're over here – come and say hello to the happy couple!'

Richard, walking across the park, waved back and quickened his pace. He had swung his jacket over his shoulder, as the sun was so warm, and his shirt was unbuttoned to the waist.

'Yes, you're quite right,' Nicholas said to his mother. 'We really must go to Windsor – it would be rude not to.'

'I've got their number in my book,' said Alice. 'The Yorks stay in Piccadilly during the week; they go down to the Lodge on Fridays. Would you like me to organize it for you?'

Richard came bounding up the steps to the terrace, two at a time. 'The return of the wanderers!' he exclaimed. 'You're both looking very well, I must say – married life obviously agrees with you. How was Paris?'

'Unbelievable – just like a dream,' said Jenny. 'But it's nice to be home again. Dreams are all very well, but real life is even better.'

'Look – we've got presents!' Polly showed her husband the scent-bottle. 'Don't you want to smell me?'

He nuzzled her cheek: 'Mmmm – delicious... Don't I get anything?'

'We brought you some cigars,' said Jenny, holding out another parcel. 'I think you told me once these were your favourites.'

Richard ripped off the paper and said: 'That's my girl – what a memory!' He took Jenny in his arms and gave her an enthusiastic kiss. 'Welcome home, Jenny.'

Over her shoulder, he smiled at Nick: 'You don't mind, do you, old son?'

'The problem must be solved. The Jews must go!'

A roar of approval greeted this statement, and Gina and Charlie exchanged glances. Sir Charles looked faintly uncomfortable; she merely smiled and nodded.

Together with the other specially invited guests, they were seated in reserved seats along the front row of a public hall, somewhere off Ladbroke Grove.

The speaker stood at the front of the platform; a small, bespectacled man who made up for his lack of stature by the impassioned fervour of his oratory. Behind him, at a long table, two other speakers awaited their turn. But Gina had eyes for one man only; the chairman, who sat with his hands folded on the green baize cloth, wearing a calm, gratified expression. The meeting was going well.

Gina joined the applause with enthusiasm, trying to catch his eye.

'Too wonderful,' she murmured, under cover of the noise. 'What an inspiration that man is!'

Charlie said nothing, though he too was clapping.

The Bowyers had been supporters of Oswald Mosley for the last eighteen months. Certainly he had had a spectacular political career; falling out of sympathy with the Conservative Party, he had crossed over and espoused the cause of Labour for a while; and when this too failed to satisfy his burning ambition, he had rallied a band of like-minded supporters – including some very famous names – to form his own political group, the New Party. Gina and Charlie had been founder members.

At first the New Party had flourished, but the economic crisis of 1931 undermined it, and they had made a disastrous showing in the general election last October.

In an attempt to revive their fortunes, Mosley had encouraged the younger generation to join them, creating a youth group – NUPA. Undoubtedly he was already an important figure in British politics; and in time Gina felt sure that he would become Prime Minister; or perhaps he might aspire to even greater heights. She visualized him as the man at the head of his country – the man of destiny, the man of power – and Gina found power curiously exciting.

Charlie agreed with a lot of Mosley's views; there was only one element in the party's ideology which worried him. Unfortunately, this was the very element that seemed to be dominating the entire movement.

'The Jews are behind the scenes, running our country. The British Government are blind to their sinister influence,' the speaker continued, and a fine spray of saliva showered upon the front row. Charlie winced, and dabbed his brow with his handkerchief. 'That is why we must deal with the problem now! The Jews must be removed from positions of authority. The Jews must be segregated –'

'How?' asked a sharp, clear voice from the body of the hall.

'What was that?' The speaker was momentarily disconcerted.

'How do you propose to remove the Jews? What are you going to do – throw them in gaol? Convict them of the crime of being Jewish? Sentence them all to death?'

'Sit down – be quiet!' shouted another voice from the platform.

'I'm asking you to tell us what your plans are. Are you intending to sterilize the Jewish people? Wipe them out altogether?'

The accent was American, and Gina thought she recognized it. She glanced over her shoulder. 'My God – Charlie, look, it's Scott.'

But her voice was drowned in the growing storm of anger from the audience. At a sign from Mosley, half a dozen brawny young men appeared as if by magic, and closed in on Scott Hanson. An approving cheer went up; Scott was still trying to make himself heard, but in vain. He disappeared in a flurry of arms and legs, and was dragged to the main exit.

'We must go to him – he might be hurt,' said Charlie.

Gradually the furore died down; Mosley brought the meeting under control, and the speaker continued his anti-Semitic harangue as Gina and Charlie slipped out through a side door.

In the street, they found Scott slumped against the railings, mopping his bloody nose, and trying to dust himself down.

'My dear chap – are you all right?' Charlie helped him to his feet.

'I guess so . . . No bones broken, anyhow,' said Scott breathlessly.

'For Pete's sake – why did you have to start a riot?' Gina wanted to know.

'I was only asking a question – is that so terrible?'

'Tom Mosley has to take a strong line with hecklers; he's been threatened by hooligans so often. That's why he trained the Biff Boys to act as his bodyguard.'

'And what are they if they're not hooligans?'

'Let's not argue about it now.' Charlie took charge of the situation. 'Gina's car is only just round the corner. I suggest we all go back to Curzon Street. You need a bath – and a clean shirt... And I think we could all do with a drink.'

An hour later, in a borrowed shirt, Scott sat on Charlie's buttoned-leather sofa with a Scotch on the rocks, and began to relax. They might have been a million miles away from that violent scene in North Kensington.

'Thanks,' he said. 'That feels a whole lot better.'

'What were you doing there anyhow?' Gina asked crossly.

'Covering the meeting for my paper, of course.'

'Of course... I suppose they sent you to stir up trouble deliberately?'

'Are you kidding? The trouble's already there – your friend Oswald glories in trouble – he's whipping up bigotry and race hatred –'

'Don't call him Oswald – nobody does,' Gina cut in scornfully, 'He's Tom to his friends.'

'Does he have any?' asked Scott.

Once again, Charlie tried to make peace. 'We shall never see eye to eye about politics, my boy; I suggest we change the subject... How are you keeping these days? We haven't seen you since the wedding.'

'I've been a bit out of touch with everyone,' muttered Scott.

'Not quite everyone,' Gina reminded him. 'Last time you called, you told me you were taking Caroline out to dinner – how did that go?'

Scott shrugged: 'OK, I guess.'

'God, getting information out of you is like drawing teeth! Come on, give – what's going on between you two?'

'Nothing,' he snapped. 'In fact – since you're so interested – I don't suppose I'll be seeing her again.'

'So that's it...' Gina smiled broadly. 'I should have guessed. You made a play for Lady Caroline, and you didn't even get to first base. Well, don't take it to heart, baby. Some of these Britishers can be so high-hat: you have to be a belted Earl at least – before you're allowed to unbelt.'

Scott drained his glass and turned to Charlie, ignoring his sister: 'Could I have a refill?'

It was very still, out in the garden. Jenny and Polly brought their coffee on to the terrace after dinner and sat talking quietly, while indoors William and Alice played a rubber of bridge with Nicholas and Richard. Polly had never mastered the rules of bridge, and Jenny didn't feel like playing, so they had come outside to gossip in peace.

'Isn't it nice when it stays light all the evening?' said Polly, admiring the sky which had shaded down from rose to apricot, with a green glow along the horizon.

'The sun's set at last; it will be dark soon,' said Jenny. 'And tomorrow's the longest day. After that, the days start to get shorter.'

'Oh, don't – I hate the winter. Always did, ever since I was a nipper. It was so perishing cold in the home; one of the big boys set fire to the dormitories once, and they said he was a wicked winner, wanting to burn the place down. But I reckon he was only trying to get warm.'

'That's terrible...' Jenny smiled, despite herself. The stories of Polly's childhood in an orphanage always fascinated her.

'I said two no trumps!' Within the house, Richard's voice was raised in protest.

'Oh, dear. When I realized Richie and Nick were going to be partners, I feared the worst,' continued Jenny. 'You don't suppose they'll come to blows, do you?'

'Not them. Richard can't help teasing Nick – but he doesn't mean anything by it. I bet they were the same when they were little – making everything into a battle and determined to win, every time.'

'I suppose that's true.' Jenny recalled boyish squabbles, long ago. 'But you'd think things would get better as they got older.'

'They're like big kids, the pair of 'em. I shouldn't worry about it.'

Then she turned her head, at the sound of a telephone bell. Jenny remembered the first telephone being installed six years ago, in the library. Now there were extensions in the drawing-room and the master bedroom too.

'I don't suppose it'll be for you or me... Come on – I feel like a bit of a walk,' said Polly.

They descended the steps and strolled across the lawn. In the fading light, the white flowers of tobacco-plants were almost invisible; only the rich, heady perfume identified them, blending with the smell of mown grass.

Jenny took a deep breath. It seemed only yesterday that she and Lord Minster had sat in the library, listing the new flowers he intended to plant; nicotiana, he said, was one of Lady Minster's favourites. Then he had broken down, fighting back tears. At that time Alice had left home and was living in London, and their marriage was going through a bad patch. Jenny had comforted him, holding him in her arms – until they had been disturbed by the telephone bell. It was the police, ringing with the news of Lady Minster's car crash, and Mrs Webster's death... The scent of the flowers – the pealing of the distant bell – brought it all flooding back to her.

'Penny for your thoughts,' said Polly.

'Oh – I was miles away ... Years away, I should say. I was thinking of the night my mother died, before I took over as housekeeper. It seems so strange now, looking back.'

'I'm sure it does. How do you like being one of the family?'

'Everyone has made it easy for me; you're all so kind. Though I still have to stop myself calling Nick's mother "my lady", the way I used to.'

'I know – it's tricky. I can't call her "Ma", like Richard does! And I don't like to call her "Alice". Generally I just settle for "you" ...' She laughed: 'It's nice to know we both have the same problem.'

They walked on in silence for a while, and then Polly asked:

'How was Paris – really? Was it as good as you said?'

'Yes, we loved it. Why? Did you think I was pretending?'

'I wasn't sure. Everybody's supposed to have a wonderful honeymoon, like everybody's got to enjoy Christmas, but its not always that easy, is it?'

'But you liked Paris, didn't you? You said you did.'

'Oh, yes ... But it was different for us. It's not every young bride who comes down the aisle four months gone! And Richard wasn't exactly the typical young bridegroom either, bless him.'

Jenny asked hesitantly: 'Did he really take you to the *Folies Bergère*? I know you said he was only joking, but –'

'Oh, you guessed that, did you? Well, yes, he did. Anyhow, I was quite keen to see the show. Gorgeous costumes – when they wore any – and the scenery takes your breath away – underwater ballets, fountains, staircases a mile high – it must cost a fortune; still they're sold out every night... Though if you ask me, it wasn't a patch on the Cochran shows. The numbers weren't up to much, and the comedy routines were pathetic... I don't suppose Nick took you to see it?'

'No. We went past one evening, but – no, he didn't.'

Someone was coming across the lawn; a pale dress shimmered through the dusk, and Alice's voice called: 'So there you are – I wondered where you'd got to.' She sniffed the air: 'Tobacco-plants – aren't they heavenly?... Jenny dear, I tried to telephone the Duchess of York earlier today, and she's just returned my call. We've fixed your visit to Royal Lodge: she suggested the last weekend in July – I hope that's all right? I asked Nicholas, and he says he'll drive you both down on the Friday evening.'

They could have driven straight across country to Windsor, but that would have meant arriving tired, hot and grubby. Instead, they went up to London, and lunched at Eaton Square.

Nicholas had telephoned Caro, inviting her to join them, but she said she was far too busy to trail all the way from Fleet Street to Belgravia – she would see them some other time.

'I thought she sounded a bit snappish,' Nick reported to Jenny. 'I don't know what we've done to upset her.'

'Nothing at all, probably. She must have a lot of work to do.'

So they lunched alone, and afterwards enjoyed the sunshine in Hyde Park and walked beside the Serpentine, and thought of Paris. Here too there were loving couples sauntering beneath the trees, or lying entwined on the grass, but this time Nick did not put his arm round Jenny.

They returned to the house to bathe and change, then drove out to the Thames Valley.

Having taken one wrong turning, they finally found the Royal Lodge on the eastern side of Windsor Great Park, half-way between the Castle and Virginia Water; a pink-washed country house, originally built in the eighteenth century, but with many features added during the next hundred and fifty years.

By the time Nick's car pulled up at the main entrance, it was six o'clock, and a manservant informed them that Her Royal Highness was at present engaged with the little Princesses, but would join them very shortly, if they cared to wait in the Tent Room?

The room was octagonal, with windows opening on to the

gardens. It was decorated to look like an outdoor marquee.

A moment later, the door was flung open, and a little girl dashed into the room. Lillibet, aged six, slowed down to a walk on seeing the guests. She was in her dressing-gown, but greeted them with a direct, friendly smile: 'Hello – I saw your house last year. I'm glad you came to see ours.'

She was followed by her mother, who wore a capacious white apron over her dress and had her sleeves rolled up, gently guiding Princess Margaret into the room – for the Princess, who would soon be two years old, still needed a little help with steps up or down.

'I'm so sorry to keep you waiting – how lovely to see you!' exclaimed the Duchess, crossing the room with one hand outstretched. 'I won't ask you if you're both well, because that's perfectly obvious... Say hello to our visitors, Margaret.'

Margaret said nothing, but regarded them solemnly.

'She doesn't remember you,' Lillibet explained. 'She was very small, last year.'

'You arrived in the middle of bathtime,' the Duchess continued. 'It takes rather a long while, because there's so much splashing, and I generally get soaking wet – but it's a sacred ritual. And so is a story before bedtime – only Lillibet pleaded to be allowed to come and say goodnight.'

After she had taken her daughters off to their nursery, the Duke of York joined them, and was equally welcoming. He had happy memories of his voyage on board HMS *Renown*, and talked easily to Nicholas, with only an occasional stammer.

He was a little shy with Jenny, whom he scarcely knew, but during a pause in the conversation, when he saw that she was studying the wall-hangings, he said: 'It's an odd sort of room – but I'm rather fond of it. I believe it was built for Great-Grandmama – Queen Victoria. She liked to drive over from the Castle to take tea here. Perhaps it reminded her of her tent at Balmoral.' Another pause, and then he added: 'I understand you know my brother David?'

Feeling equally shy, Jenny murmured: 'I can't say that I know the Prince of Wales, sir – I met him once, at a party. I shouldn't have expected him to remember.'

'He told me that you helped him to solve a difficult problem, and he is very g-g-grateful. In fact I had hoped he might join us this evening, but I understand he has g-g-guests this weekend too, at

Fort Belvedere – a Mr and Mrs Simpson. I suggested he should bring them over – the Fort is no distance away across the park – but unfortunately he had already made other plans. But he sends his good wishes to you both.'

The evening was very ordinary, and very pleasant. After dinner, they listened to the wireless, and looked through an album filled with snapshots of the voyage to Australia and New Zealand. When the clock struck ten, the Duke said: 'You won't feel offended if we have an early night, I hope?'

The Duchess chimed in: 'We've got a full day ahead of us, and we want to make an early start.'

'We were wondering whether you might c-c-care to join us in an assault on the wilderness?'

Seeing their blank expressions, Elizabeth smiled: 'Don't worry – we're not taking you on safari. The wilderness is Bertie's name for part of the garden that we haven't managed to tame yet. But we're getting there – gradually – and if you *would* like to lend a hand, we'd be simply delighted.'

Nicholas apologized, saying that he knew nothing about gardening, but that Jenny was more of an expert. The Duke grinned:

'You can't get away with it by pleading ignorance. We don't need experts, we need elbow-grease! Have you brought any old clothes with you? Don't worry, I can probably fit you up with some togs – we're more or less the same size.'

The following afternoon, Nick was wearing a baggy pair of khaki shorts and a threadbare tennis-shirt, flinging armfuls of brushwood on to a bonfire. He wiped away the sweat that ran down his forehead, looking up at Jenny who was perched on a stepladder, and said: 'I bet the family imagine we're sitting on gilded chairs in an elegant drawing-room, eating cucumber sandwiches . . .'

Jenny finished sawing off a branch of hawthorn, and flung it down to him, saying: 'Catch!' – and as he added it to the flames, she said: 'Personally, I think gilded chairs are overrated.'

Scrambling down the steps, she glanced at her once-white linen dress, now liberally streaked with grass, mud and leaf-mould, and sighed: 'This little outfit will never be the same again– but I don't care; I'm having too much fun.'

The wilderness was well-named; a hidden dell below the main garden, it had become completely overgrown with rhododendrons, and the Duke was determined to open it into a natural clearing among the trees. Lillibet now appeared, trundling a wheelbarrow full of leaves and twigs.

'Can I put these on the bonfire?' she asked.

'Let me help you,' suggested Jenny, and between them they emptied the barrow on to the burning pyre. The wind kept changing, enveloping them in thick smoke, and then Lillibet's quick ears picked up the sound of tyres on gravel.

'There's a car – more visitors!' she said, and dashed off to investigate.

Some minutes later she returned, hand in hand with two familiar figures. Jenny blinked at them through the smoke, and was rooted to the spot. Automatically, Nicholas sprang to attention.

'It's Grandpa and Grandmama!' cried the Princess joyfully.

Their Majesties stood at a wary distance from the bonfire, surveying the scene and looking rather lost; but their granddaughter rose to the occasion.

'These are our friends, the Honourable Nicholas Gaunt, and Mrs Gaunt,' she announced, in a high, clear voice; for she knew that her beloved Grandpapa was slightly deaf. 'And *this*, she added, with great *savoir-faire*, 'is the King and Queen.'

Somehow, Jenny managed to curtsey, and Nicholas bowed.

The Queen inclined her head, saying: 'How do you do? I feel I know you already, Nicholas – for your mother is one of my dearest friends.' Then she turned to Lillibet, asking: 'And where are your Mama and Papa, my dear?'

By way of reply, Lillibet dashed into a mass of rhododendrons, and after a lot of scuffling reappeared, leading two bedraggled figures in very old clothes, their faces blackened with soot from the bonfire.

'G-g-good afternoon, Mama … Papa,' said Bertie.

Queen Mary took one look at them and began to shake with laughter. She insisted on sending for a camera, and made them all line up – Jenny and Nicholas included – for a group photograph.

'This is a moment that must be seen to be believed!' she said, still highly amused.

The King mumbled gruffly: 'We should have warned you we were driving over, but your Mama suddenly decided she wanted to see this little Welsh cottage we've heard so much about. Where is it?'

A nursemaid brought Margaret Rose out to join the party, and Lillibet proudly invited her grandmother into the little play-house. It was completely furnished, on a miniature scale, down to the smallest chair and the tiniest saucepan. There was even running water in the kitchen taps.

The Queen insisted on entering every room – with some difficulty, for the ceilings were very low – and when she emerged with her flowered toque knocked awry she admitted that she had bumped her head in the doorway.

'But I am very pleased to have seen your house, Lillibet,' she said. 'There is nothing I enjoy so much as visiting other people's houses.'

That night, when they went to bed, Jenny said to Nicholas, 'I've enjoyed it too. I didn't think I would, but I loved being here. The Yorks are such a happy family – they make you feel at home right away.'

She stretched out luxuriously, like a cat, and Nicholas rolled closer, enjoying the touch of her soft, warm skin against his body.

'This has been the happiest day of my life,' she continued dreamily. 'Of course the honeymoon was wonderful too, but –'

He drew her closer still, saying, 'The honeymoon isn't over yet . . .'

They made love for a long time, giving themselves to each other and holding nothing back. Their bodies became one, and their feelings seemed to be interchangeable; desire passed between them, back and forth, doubling and redoubling, building to a height of passion they had never known before.

At last they lay back, physically spent. She took his hand, stroking it gently.

'Thank you,' she breathed. 'Oh, thank you . . . That was – I can't tell you – that was the best ever.'

Looking up at the ceiling, he asked: 'Was it better than – ' And then he stopped, unable to finish the question.

'Better than what?'

'Than – Paris . . .'

'Yes – you know it was . . . The very best.'

She nestled into the pillows, beginning to drift off into a deep, satisfied sleep. Nick's eyes were still open. He had not said what he wanted to say; and in his mind, one question remained unanswered.

3

SUNDAY, 4 SEPTEMBER 1932 TO SUNDAY, 1 JANUARY 1933

'WHERE'S Nicholas?' asked Old Bea, irritably. 'Why doesn't he come and see me any more?'

Alice, pouring a cup of tea for her mother-in-law, looked across at Jenny and shook her head in despair. 'You know very well that Nicholas has gone back to sea, Mama... Here you are. I've put in three lumps of sugar – will that be enough?'

'Don't you remember, he came to say goodbye to you before he went to join his ship?' added Jenny, handing the Dowager Countess a slice of Madeira cake. 'That was nearly a month ago.'

'It must have slipped my mind.' Old Bea gulped her tea noisily. 'What's wrong with the sugar nowadays? It's never sweet. Nothing tastes the way it used to.'

Jenny had not forgotten the day Nicholas left. They had been together for twelve whole weeks, and his absence left an emptiness in her life that was like a gaping wound.

'It's nearly time for the news bulletin, Mama,' Alice pointed out. 'Wouldn't you like me to switch on the wireless for you?'

'No, don't bother. The wireless isn't as good as it used to be, either,' mumbled Old Bea, with her mouth full of cake. 'It's not been the same since they went into that new-fangled building... I liked it better when they talked to me from the old place.'

For the British Broadcasting Corporation had moved out of their premises on Savoy Hill shortly before Jenny's wedding in May, to take possession of a splendid new building designed especially for them, at the head of Portland Place, where it rode above the traffic like an ocean-liner. Everyone acclaimed it as a landmark in broadcasting;

everyone, that is, except Lady Beatrice.

'They used to give me my very own news before, because I was one of the first subscribers. They sent it down here specially for me. But now I see from the newspapers that there are hundreds of strangers listening in as well – eavesdroppers, I call 'em ... It's not right at all. If that man Reith had any sense, he'd put up the licence fee, and keep out the riff-raff!' she concluded grandly.

Alice knew from long experience that it would be useless to try and explain, so she merely said, 'I believe I'm going to meet one of the gentlemen from Broadcasting House tomorrow, Mama. I'll try to pass on your suggestion, if I get the chance.'

Old Bea frowned. 'And why are you going to Broadcasting House, may I ask?'

'I'm not. I shall be at Buckingham Palace; I start another turn of duty this week. But Flora Kelso tells me the BBC are sending someone to discuss the possibility of His Majesty making a broadcast to the nation, on Christmas Day. Won't that be nice?'

'Broadcasting to the nation?' Old Bea was outraged. 'You mean to say every Tom, Dick and Harry in the country will be listening to *my wireless*? Is there to be no privacy?'

Lady Flora Kelso hurried into the anteroom, looking rather flustered. 'I've just seen the man from the BBC getting out of a taxi – and he's brought somebody with him! I told Their Majesties Sir Hartley Clowes would be alone, and now there are two of them. You know how the King hates it when plans get altered at the last minute ... Why do people have to be so difficult?'

'And I've ordered tea for three,' said Alice. 'Have I got time to send down for another cup and saucer?'

But there was no time at all, for almost at once the visitors were announced, and entered the room; Alice and Flora shook hands with Sir Hartley: a tall, distinguished-looking man in a wing collar, his weather-beaten face and rolling gait suggesting that he might have dropped anchor at Broadcasting House after a lifetime in the Royal Navy.

'And this is my assistant, who will take notes for me – Mr Weyman,' added Sir Hartley, bringing the younger man forward.

Flora shook hands with Mr Weyman, expecting Alice to do the same – and turned to find that Alice was standing quite still, looking steadily at the newcomer.

'Mr Weyman and I have met before,' she said.

'Yes, indeed,' said Paul Weyman, 'I served in Lord Minster's regiment during the war – we're old friends.'

'Well, that's wonderful,' exclaimed Lady Flora, immediately turning the situation to advantage. 'In that case I think perhaps it would be better if you stay here and talk to Lady Minster, Mr Weyman. You don't mind, do you? Their Majesties might prefer to see Sir Hartley on his own.'

'Quite right; I'll send for you if you're needed, Weyman,' said Sir Hartley.

Lady Flora took him into the adjoining room to be presented to Their Majesties, and Alice and Paul were left alone together.

'I had no idea you would be here,' he said. 'I didn't know I would be here myself until an hour ago. The old boy suddenly decided he needed someone to back him up, and I was dragged out of my office. I told him one doesn't just turn up at the Palace uninvited, but he wouldn't listen.'

Alice sat and folded her hands in her lap. 'When did you join the BBC?' she asked, studying her finger-nails.

'About a year ago. A chap at the club, who knew I was looking for some sort of regular post, said they were taking on staff. He was good enough to arrange an interview for me, and I went before a board... Rather to my surprise, I got the job.'

'What exactly do you do?'

'I'm a glorified office-boy at the moment. Mostly I fetch and carry for Sir Hartley, but I'm assured that they have a more responsible position in mind for me, so I must be patient. I've been working on outside broadcasts lately; I suppose that's why the old boy thought I might be useful today. He says the King is proposing to send his Christmas message from Sandringham. Is that right?'

'I believe so.'

'It's a long way from any of our transmitters. Still, I expect we'll organize something. It's just a question of getting the place wired up and installing a microphone. I suppose they'll let us go up there beforehand, to make some sound tests, and run a couple of rehearsals?'

'I shouldn't bank on it. His Majesty has a very full schedule; I doubt if he'll have time to rehearse.'

'Perhaps if you have a tactful word with him, you could explain that it would make the broadcast a lot easier... Will you be going

44

up to Norfolk with Their Majesties?'

'No. I shall be at home for Christmas – with my family.'

'Of course. Still, I expect we'll see each other before then. There are bound to be several more meetings before everything's fixed up.'

'I don't think we shall meet again, Paul.' Alice rose, and crossed to the fireplace, saying, 'In fact, I shall take care that we don't.'

She turned to face him at last, and his boyish smile faded – even now, in his middle forties, he still had an almost youthful air – and she wished with all her heart that he had never walked into her life, all those years ago.

'Alice – my dear – surely we can still be friends?'

She rang the bell by the overmantel, not answering his question directly. 'I shall order some tea for you; and when Lady Flora comes back, perhaps you can explain that I had a very bad headache, and asked you to excuse me ... I'm sure you understand.'

A fortnight later, with her duties as lady-in-waiting at an end, Alice went back to the country with relief. Every time she met Paul, things always went wrong; he still had the ability to unsettle her.

But if she expected Crown House to be a haven of peace and quiet, she was disappointed. William came to find her in their bedroom; she had just taken off her hat and was sitting at the dressing-table, doing her hair. He kissed the back of her neck, then broke the bad news: 'I didn't tell you over the telephone, because there was no point in worrying you while you were up in London. But I'm afraid Miranda is being difficult.'

'Oh, William – you should have told me. What has she been up to this time? Not frogs in the governess's bedroom slippers again?'

'Rather worse than that, alas. Miranda hasn't got a governess any more. Miss Warboys packed her bags and left, without even giving notice.'

'But that's monstrous! I shall complain to the agency –'

'The agency has already complained to us. They say that the last three ladies they sent all found Miranda completely uncontrollable. She's stubborn and argumentative, she always insists on having her own way, and she's extremely rude.'

'What nonsense. I admit she can be rather naughty sometimes, but –'

'She told Miss Warboys that she used too much face-powder and not enough soap, and that the resulting smell was very unpleasant.

And to underline her point, she turned the garden hose on her... The worst of it is, she was quite right; the lady's standards of personal hygiene left a lot to be desired.'

'How dreadful...' Alice tried not to laugh. 'What on earth are we going to do? Haven't the agency got anyone else they can send us?'

'They urge us very strongly to pack Miranda off to a good boarding-school. They say she needs discipline.'

'Ah, so that's it.' Alice put down her hairbrush. 'Ever since Martin went up to Eton, Miranda's been badgering me to let her go to school... Well, perhaps that's the answer. I'll get on to Roedean and ask them to send a prospectus.'

William put his arm round her shoulders. 'I'm always so glad when you come home, my dear.' He kissed her again. 'Did you meet that chap from the BBC – what was his name?'

'Sir Hartley Clowes – yes, he seems to be quite efficient. Aparently they're going up to Sandringham to test the acoustics in His Majesty's study.'

'They?'

'Sir Hartley and – his assistant.' Alice turned away. 'Christmas will be upon us before we know it. We must start making plans for a family party... Oh, darling, just look at those shoes – covered in mud!'

William sighed, and sat on the edge of the bed to unlace them. 'I suppose we'll have to ask Charlie and Gina?'

'Oh, yes, I think so. And Gina's brother, of course. He's a nice boy, even if he is a rabid socialist. Besides, Caro will be so pleased; she thinks the world of him. I must remember to tell her we've invited Scott, next time I ring her.'

When Fred Binns, the news editor, got into his office, he found a mug of steaming coffee waiting for him, together with a sticky Chelsea bun and a single rose in a glass of water.

'What the hell –?' he began.

Caro appeared in the doorway behind him. 'Good morning,' she said. 'I'm turning over a new leaf.'

'You certainly are,' he growled. 'I've never seen you here this early. What's the matter – couldn't you sleep?'

'Don't be beastly; it's all part of my campaign. This is "Be-Nice-To-Fred" week.'

She followed him into the office and perched on the corner of his desk. He eyed her dubiously: 'And what's it all in aid of?'

'You've got a nasty mind... As a matter of fact, I just want to ask you a little favour.'

'Let me guess. You want a day off?'

'Certainly not. It's about Christmas.'

'You want a week off! I can tell you right now, it'll take more than one lousy rose and a sticky bun to get that sort of –'

'Shut up and listen, Fred. I don't want any time off; I want to work over Christmas and New Year – right through the holidays. You can give me as many jobs as you like, I don't care.'

'Either you've gone barmy, or –' He bit into the bun. 'Hang on a minute... If you imagine you're getting double overtime 'cos it's the season of goodwill, you've got another think coming.'

'Don't be mercenary. I'm volunteering. Isn't that good enough for you? Put me on the roster; I'll work every single day.'

Still Fred regarded her with deep suspicion. 'There's got to be a catch in it somewhere.'

'If you must know, I spoke to my mother last night; she was talking about having a big family party at Christmas. Only I don't want to go.'

'Why not?'

'There'll be somebody else there, who –' She stopped. 'Never mind. The point is, I can't say I don't want to go home, can I? I need a cast-iron excuse; that's why I'm going to be terribly, terribly busy, and my cruel, wicked news editor won't give me any time off.'

'Well, if that's what you want, OK then.'

'You're an angel!'

She was half-way to the door when he called her back: 'Talking of Christmas, that reminds me. I see in this morning's *Times* that the King's going to broadcast a Christmas Day message to his people. Why weren't we told about this? You're supposed to be our source of Palace gossip; how come the Thunderer gets in first?'

Caro opened her eyes very wide. 'Sorry. Ma did mention something about it, but I didn't think it was much of a story, so –'

'When will you ever learn? Anything royalty does is news! Get on to the Palace – better still, get on to the BBC. I want to know all the details, my girl; that's what we pay you for.'

Dutifully, Caro rang Broadcasting House, and was passed from one office to another until at last a condescending voice informed her that, since the event was arousing a certain amount of interest,

47

they would be inviting a selected number of journalists to a small press conference on Friday morning at eleven.

It was the first time that Caro had been to Portland Place, and she couldn't help being impressed; it was all so beautifully shining and new. A uniformed commissionaire with white gloves tucked under his epaulette held open the massive swing doors as she walked in, and an earnest young lady at the reception desk asked her to wait for a few minutes.

She sat on a settee, watching the stream of callers going in and out. Flashing lights announced which floor the lifts were stopping at, from the basement right up to the roof; it was a very tall building. Then a secretary emerged, and led her to an airless room below street level, where a group of reporters sat on tubular-steel chairs round a polished table. Caro knew some of them by sight – the boy from the *News Chronicle*, the girl from the *Mirror*, and that chap with the stutter from the *Daily Mail*. Soon after eleven, the door opened, and a fair-haired handsome man walked in.

'Good morning,' he began. 'My name is Paul Weyman, and I have been asked to –'

'*Uncle Paul!*' exclaimed Caro joyfully, before she could stop herself. 'What are you doing here?'

Paul did not immediately recognize her; she had grown up so much in the last few years. But then he smiled briefly. 'Hello, Caroline – nice to see you. As I was saying, for those of you I don't already know, my name is Paul Weyman, and I've been asked to give you some information about the royal broadcast. It's something of an experiment for us, but if it's a success – and I'm sure it will be – we hope to make it a regular feature, every Christmas.'

As he continued, the girl from the *Mirror* whispered to Caro, 'Is he really your uncle?'

Caro scribbled a message on a page of her notebook. 'Just an old friend of the family. I knew him when I was little. "Uncle" is a courtesy title.'

She had been seven or eight when she first met Uncle Paul. In those days, she and her brothers were still living in London, in the same Eaton Square house. She remembered him vividly looking very dashing in his captain's uniform, dropping in to see them all when he was home on leave from the front line some time during the war. He used to bring them presents; she had a clear recollection of a soft, cuddly teddy bear which she had taken to bed every night for years, long after Uncle Paul himself had drifted out of their lives.

Then he turned up unexpectedly with the Bowyers at Richard's wedding, after they all moved to Crown House: he visited them several times after that – and then, inexplicably, vanished again. How odd that he should keep appearing and disappearing.

She looked at him sitting at the head of the table, explaining the BBC's plans to transmit the royal greetings to all parts of the Empire and Commonwealth. He was rather like the Cheshire Cat, she thought; when he wasn't there, it was the grin you remembered.

When he finished speaking, the reporters had a chance to ask questions, and Paul answered them clearly and helpfully.

'Yes, we shall certainly have photographs of the King seated at the microphone, since it will be a historic occasion. But of course those pictures won't be available to the press until afterwards, though I think we can safely promise that you will have them before New Year's Eve.'

The questions and answers continued, and Caro made some notes. After about half an hour, Paul wound up the meeting, and everyone rose to leave. Caro wondered if she should speak to Paul, or whether the others might resent her familiarity with this important person... But he was already beckoning her over.

'Caroline, before you go –' The rest filed out; she stayed behind. 'I'm so glad to see you. I didn't know you worked in Fleet Street?'

'I didn't know you were at the BBC.'

'Didn't you?' He seemed surprised, then shrugged. 'No, of course not. There's no reason why you should have known. Which newspaper are you with?'

'The *Argus*. I've been there nearly two years now.'

'Really? How interesting. I'm afraid I've rather lost touch with your family; we must have a long talk some time so I can catch up on all the gossip.' He glanced at his watch. 'I'd ask you to stay and have lunch, but unfortunately I've got to see one of our engineers from Daventry... How about tomorrow?'

'Tomorrow's Saturday.'

'So it is; I was forgetting. Well, why not come round to tea? Unless of course you're going home to Crown House?'

'No, I'm staying in town. Tea would be lovely. Where do you live?'

The following afternoon, at four o'clock, she made her way to the address he had given her; a block of solid, Victorian mansion flats on Primrose Hill. He lived at number fourteen, on the second floor, and he opened the front door himself, explaining, 'I do have a couple living in, who look after me, but they go away to their married daughter in Bushey every weekend, so you find me on my own. But I think I can just about manage to make you a cup of tea.'

The tea things were laid out on a low table in the sitting-room, and the pink-and-white china reflected the dancing flames in the fireplace.

'They call this flat number fourteen, but I'm afraid that's a cheat – the one before it is number twelve. I suppose they thought they'd never get an occupant for thirteen; however, I'm not superstitious, so it doesn't bother me.'

'It's a nice flat.' Caro walked to the windows, which looked across to the slope of Primrose Hill, and a sweep of trees, brilliant gold in the late afternoon sun. 'And you have a very good view.'

'You see the leaves are beginning to change colour already? I hope that isn't a sign of a hard winter.'

Somewhere in the distance there was an extraordinary sound; a high, undulating cry. Caro looked startled, and he hastened to explain: 'It's a baboon. The zoo is only just down the road; you can hear the animals when the wind's in the right direction. I often hear the lions roaring if I'm awake in the night.' He indicated an armchair. 'Come and sit down. There are two kinds of sandwiches: pâté and watercress, or apple jelly.'

'My goodness, you have been busy.' Caro sank into the low chair by the fire.

'Being a bachelor, I've had to learn some rudimentary skills in the kitchen.' The Cheshire Cat grin flashed out. 'Milk and sugar? Or do you prefer a slice of lemon?'

She looked round the room; like its owner, it was elegantly masculine. There were bookshelves on three walls, and very few ornaments. Only on the mantelpiece, some small porcelain figures in eighteenth-century military uniform stood guard over a French clock under a glass dome, and a pair of small silver cups.

'What are the cups for?'

'Rifle-shooting, I'm afraid. It's beastly bad form to show off, isn't it? But it seems silly to keep them shut up in a box. Not that I'm a champion marksman – I was lucky in a couple of competitions. Still, they're my only sporting accomplishment, so I make the most of them.'

'I suppose you learned to shoot in the Army? I don't think Daddy ever went in for it, though Richie goes out after pigeons and rabbits sometimes.'

'How are they all at home?'

'Quite well, I think. I don't get down very often; they keep me pretty busy at the *Argus*... But you haven't been to see us for ages!' she added. 'You really should. The family would love to see you.'

'I'm not so sure about that,' he said quietly.

'What do you mean?'

'Oh – the last time I was at Crown House, I think I said something that upset your parents. I got the impression that I wouldn't be very welcome there in future.'

'I'm sure that's not true. Daddy told me you were one of his best friends –'

'I used to be, but that was a long time ago. Not any more.'

'What ever did you say to upset him? I can't understand it. He's the most patient, easy-going man in the world –'

'I know he is. I – I think I was fairly insufferable, actually. Do you mind if we don't talk about it? It's not something I'm particularly proud of.'

'Yes, but surely –' She was about to argue, but he broke in once more: 'Except to say – when you do speak to them next, it might be as well if you didn't tell them you'd seen me. I suspect they wouldn't be best pleased about it.'

'Oh... Well, if you say so... But it does seem a pity.'

Looking across at him, his face suddenly illuminated by leaping flames, she saw the depth of sadness in his eyes, and added sympathetically, 'I'm sure it can't have been very dreadful, whatever it was. But I suppose when people grow older, they're liable to get funny ideas sometimes... Pa's quite a bit older than you, isn't he?'

'Quite a bit, yes.' He made an effort to break the mood. 'Are you ready for more tea?'

He went out to the kitchen for hot water, and while he was gone, Caro stood up for a closer look at the silver cups. There were several invitation cards along the mantelpiece, and she read them inquisitively. When he returned, she exclaimed, 'Gosh, you are lucky – going to the Chelsea Arts Ball!'

New Year's Eve at the Royal Albert Hall was one of the highlights of the season; Caro had heard some fascinating stories about this wild and wonderful party which always went on till dawn.

He glanced at the card, inscribed to 'Mr Paul Weyman and Friend –
Admit Two' – and said casually, 'Why – do you want to come?'

'Oh, I'd love to. But aren't you going with a friend?'

'I was hoping to, but she's cried off; the silly woman's got herself
engaged to some appalling bounder on the Stock Exchange, so I've
crossed her off my list! If you'd really like to go, I'd be delighted . . .
But won't you still be at home for the Christmas holidays?'

'Not this year. I'm working right through.'

'Really? What rotten luck.'

'No, it's not. I offered to work. I didn't feel like a family Christmas
this year.' She smiled. 'Perhaps that's something else we'd better not
tell them.'

He grinned back conspiratorially, and she suddenly felt enor-
mously fond of him. He had been such a favourite uncle when she
was little. She found herself wondering – what ever became of that
teddy bear?

'Christmas won't seem the same without Caroline,' said Lady Edith.

Alice looked at her; privately, she agreed with her sister-in-law,
though she wouldn't admit it. She and William were very sorry Caro
would not be with them this year, but they were determined not to
let her absence cast a cloud over the family party.

'Oh, she's got too much work to do,' Alice said. 'They must think
very highly of her at the *Argus*. They couldn't do without her, even
for a few days.'

'More likely it's because she's the youngest reporter on the staff,'
Richard suggested. 'Nobody else wanted to be on duty, so she got
saddled with it.'

With the exception of Caroline, the family would be complete:
Miranda and Martin, home from their respective boarding-schools,
had greeted each other cautiously at first, circling at a wary distance
like two cats; but within ten minutes they were back on their old
terms of easy familiarity, helping to put up paper-chains and hang
the kissing-bough of mistletoe in the main hall. Once the first
awkwardness had worn off, they seemed much younger than their
thirteen years.

Edith and Grace would not be staying in Crown House itself, for
their little cottage at the lodge gates was only ten minutes' walk
away; but Alice insisted that they must come over every day. Now
they sat at the card-table in the drawing-room, working on a jigsaw

puzzle of a three-masted schooner in a stormy sea.

Jenny looked over Miss Duncan's shoulder, admiring the half-finished picture. 'It's coming along very well. But how will you ever get all the masts and rigging sorted out?'

'Sheer perseverance,' said Grace Duncan. 'I remember Robert the Bruce, and try, try again . . . That's not part of the sky, Edith, it's a bit of sea . . . If the pieces won't fit, for heaven's sake, don't try to force them!'

Edith gazed at the mountainous, white-crested waves, and said, 'I'm so glad I'm not a sailor . . . But I suppose Nicholas must enjoy it, or he wouldn't do it. When do you expect him, Jenny?'

'Some time tomorrow, I hope.'

Tomorrow would be Christmas Eve. Today was Friday, and Gina had driven Charlie down from town after lunch to spend ten days at Crown House.

Mr Hawkins knocked and entered, bearing a steaming bowl with apples afloat in it: a traditional Christmas punch. Richard jumped to his feet saying, 'Thanks, Hawkins – I'll see to that.'

He made himself busy with glasses and a ladle, while Charlie sniffed appreciatively. 'Ah, that takes me back . . . This is how Christmas used to smell when I was a lad.'

'Much too rich for my blood, honey; could I have a gin and tonic instead?' asked Gina, and turned back to Alice. 'Do you mean to say we shan't see Caroline at all?'

'I'm afraid not.'

'What do we do with her present? If I'd known, I could have dropped it in at Eaton Square . . .' Suddenly Gina gave a throaty chuckle. 'Scott will be spitting mad when I tell him. You know he cried off at the last minute? He pretended he was too busy to leave town, but of course that's a load of baloney. I knew all along it was because he didn't want to face Caroline.'

Alice frowned. 'What do you mean? They've always been such good friends.'

'Yes – until my kid brother got a little *too* friendly! She had to slap him down, and serve him right. But my guess is, that's why he didn't want to spend Christmas here.'

'I had no idea,' said Alice. 'Poor Scott.'

'And poor Caroline.' Thoughtfully, William tasted the punch. 'I hope she won't be lonely, spending Christmas on her own.'

'She won't be on her own all the time,' Alice remarked. 'She's going out on New Year's Eve; some friends of hers have invited her to the Chelsea Arts Ball.'

'Shall I take some punch up to Lady Beatrice?' offered Jenny.

'No, I'll do it.' William stood up. 'She's always complaining that she never sees me. Pour another glass for your Grandmama, Richard – a small one!'

'There you are...' Richard glanced round the room. 'Look here, we're all much too prim tonight; let's get into a party mood. I vote we all play sardines. Any volunteers?'

Grace hadn't the faintest idea what he was talking about, so Edith explained as best she could: 'It's where one of you goes off and hides somewhere, say in a cupboard, and then the rest of you set out one by one to try to find him, and when you do, you stay there with him – or it might be her – and the next one goes and looks for you, and in the end there you are, all in the same cupboard...'

'I'm not sure I follow you entirely, Edith, but it sounds rather uncomfortable, and I think I shall stay here and finish the jigsaw,' said Grace firmly.

'Then I shall stay with you,' said Edith. 'I never liked the game very much. It can be quite frightening, walking round the house by yourself. I keep expecting someone to jump out at me.'

'I rather agree.' Alice pulled her chair closer to the card-table. 'Can I help with the storm at sea?'

So in the end it was Richard and Polly, Jenny and the twins who went off to play sardines. Polly was selected as the first to go and hide, and complained, 'Why does it have to be me? I know exactly what will happen. I'll pick a really good place, and none of you will find me, and after about three hours when you've all given up, you'll find my lifeless corpse in one of the attics, frozen stiff!'

But she trudged out all the same; the others counted to a hundred, then set off in pursuit, one at a time, until only the jigsaw players were left.

'I do wish Polly hadn't said that.' Edith shuddered a little. 'It really happened once, you know. I can't remember where it was, but I know some poor girl hid in an old oak chest and couldn't get out again, and they never found her for years and years, and by then of course she was only a skeleton.'

'I doubt if Polly will finish up as a skeleton,' Alice smiled. 'I was only thinking this evening, she's putting on a little weight.'

'Do you think so?' Grace searched through the jigsaw pieces. 'I thought myself she was looking very bonny.'

'Oh, she is. Those few extra ounces are very becoming.' Alice craned forward. 'Is this bit part of the taffrail?'

'What ever is a taffrail?' Edith wanted to know.

'I'm not quite sure. Isn't it that sort of balustrade thing at the end of a ship? We'll have to ask Nicholas when he —'

'Ask me what?' said Nicholas.

Startled, they looked up, then exclaimed with delight. 'Darling — we weren't expecting you till tomorrow,' said Alice, embracing him. 'Oh, you're like ice. Come and get warm — what a lovely surprise!'

'We docked this morning, and I managed to catch a train that connected at Waterloo. I'd been thinking I might stay overnight with Caro in town, but when I realized I could catch the Medford train with two minutes to spare, it seemed too good a chance to miss.' He looked round. 'Where is everyone? Where's Jenny?'

Jenny was upstairs, creeping through the darkened house. Though not particularly nervous as a rule, she found herself remembering what Lady Edith had said, and as she tiptoed along the empty corridors she held her breath, half expecting to be ambushed at every corner.

She saw that one of the bedroom doors was open; surely it had been closed when she went down to dinner earlier? It was Richard and Polly's room, so it could well be Polly's hiding-place.

She looked in; she couldn't see anyone, but then she noticed that the sliding door of the wardrobe was slightly ajar. She pushed it along tentatively — and gasped. '*Richard*!'

He put his finger to his lips, pulling her in to join him; they huddled together, ducking their heads under the hanging rail of Polly's dresses.

'But where's Polly? She was the first . . .'

'I found her in here, but then she thought she heard Alex crying and she was afraid he might be having a nightmare, so she's gone off to the nursery and left me all by myself . . . I'm glad you've come; I'd got bored with my own company.'

It seemed very odd to be alone with Richard in near-darkness. Jenny could smell the trace of Polly's scent on her clothes — the scent she had chosen for her in Paris. Richard moved closer still, and whispered in her ear, 'I was hoping you'd be the first one to find me.' And he put an arm round her waist, pressing himself against her.

'Richie – don't be silly!' she protested laughingly, trying to fend him off; she could smell the spicy punch on his breath.

'Oh, come on. It's the season of goodwill to all men, remember? I even grabbed a sprig of mistletoe on my way upstairs, so that makes it all right –'

He held up the sprig with his free hand, bringing his mouth down to hers . . . And then the wardrobe door slid back with a sound like a thunderclap.

'What the hell do you think you're doing?' asked Nicholas.

'I think that's the most beautiful sound in the entire world,' said Caro solemnly.

'What is?' Paul leaned closer. It was hard to pick out her words above the hullabaloo.

'The pop of the cork coming out,' she explained, carefully enunciating every syllable.

Champagne frothed down the neck of the bottle: swiftly, Paul refilled the two glasses.

'I'm surprised you could hear it with this racket going on,' he said.

The roar was getting louder all the time; it was as if a tidal wave of noise were rising, threatening to engulf the Albert Hall. On the platform below them a jazz band beat out a frenzied rhythm, almost drowned by the shrieks of excited guests, and the deafening cacophony of squeakers, toy trumpets, cowbells and klaxons.

Paul and Caro were in one of the boxes, looking down on the kaleidoscope of colour as it swirled continuously around, breaking up and reforming into different patterns: the spectacle of a thousand figures in gaudy costumes, anything and everything from Zulu warriors to Dresden shepherdesses.

'Chin-chin!' An *Arabian Nights* princess in spangled veils, Caro raised her glass and toasted him. 'Dear Uncle Paul, thank you for bringing me. I never dreamed it would be such fun.'

'Do you suppose we could drop the "Uncle"? It makes me feel very elderly indeed.' He wondered whether it had been a mistake to come as a pirate king; was he perhaps making himself a little ridiculous at his age, in a tricorn hat and gold ear-rings? 'I know I *am* very elderly indeed. That's why I don't need any reminders.'

'You're not elderly at all.' She gazed at him mistily over the rim of the glass. 'You're the youngest forty-year-old I ever met.'

'Nearer fifty than forty, in point of fact,' he said wryly. 'But let's not go into the sordid details. Do you want to go downstairs again, and join the throng?'

'Yes, please!' She stood up a little too quickly and swayed. 'Oops – oh, gosh, I feel quite dizzy. It must be the bubbles.'

'They've gone to your head, I expect.'

'I think actually they've gone to my feet.' She sat down, unsteadily. 'I'm sorry, Paul . . . I believe I shall have to . . . sit this one out . . .'

'Just as well. It's going to be sheer bedlam down there in a minute or two. It's nearly twelve o'clock.'

Now the lights were dimming, and a single spotlight picked out a huge silver globe bearing the date '1932', which hung above the platform. There was a roll of drums, and for a moment the noise abated, as an amplified voice boomed out, 'Ladies and gentlemen – it's exactly midnight! And a Happy New Year to you all!'

Then the silver globe split open like a bud bursting into flower, revealing a pretty girl, apparently nude, who held aloft a banner that said '1933'. The band struck up 'Auld Lang Syne', and a thousand voices joined in as the lights came up again, while from the top of the dome a huge cloud of coloured balloons floated down upon the crowd below.

'Bubbles . . .' murmured Caro. 'Lots and lots of bubbles . . .'

As Paul turned towards her, the door of the box opened, and several people rushed in – a Mickey Mouse, a comic policeman and a sea-nymph dressed in nothing but a few shells – all linking arms and chanting fervently that auld acquaintance should never be forgotten.

Paul held out a hand to Caro – and saw that her eyes were closed. She had turned very pale, and was slumped sideways in her chair, out like a light.

Ten minutes later, with the assistance of Mickey Mouse, he managed to get her into a taxi. He thought he had better not encourage gossip among the Eaton Square staff by taking her home in her present state, so he told the driver to go to Primrose Hill.

When she opened her eyes she did not know where she was. Then she saw Paul, holding out a glass of something fizzy . . . More bubbles.

'No, I think I've had enough champagne,' she whispered.

'It's Alka-Seltzer,' he said gently. 'It'll do you good.'

Obediently, she sipped it. 'What happened?'

'You passed out. I brought you back to my flat to sleep it off.'

She looked around; so this was Paul's bedroom. She was lying on his bed, with a soft, warm blanket over her. She tried to sit up. 'I must go. I'm terribly sorry I've been such an idiot... Could you call a cab for me?'

'Lie back and relax. You're not going anywhere,' he told her. 'You're staying here.'

4

SUNDAY, 1 JANUARY TO WEDNESDAY, 26 APRIL 1933

W HEN Paul knocked at the bedroom door and brought in a breakfast tray, Caro couldn't even look at it.

'Just have some coffee,' he urged her. 'And how about a slice of toast without any butter or marmalade?'

'I'm really not at all hungry. Just coffee, please – black.'

He poured it out for her, then sat on the edge of the bed and watched as she drank it.

'I feel simply terrible,' she said in a small voice. 'You must think I'm such a fool. I've never done anything like this before.'

'Don't look so miserable,' he smiled. 'You're not the first person to have one drink too many on New Year's Eve. I'm sure there are thick heads all over London this morning. And as for Scotland, it doesn't bear thinking about.'

She bit her lip. 'Yes, but – it's not only that... I feel so awful about turning you out of your own bed. Where did you sleep?'

'In the guest-room. That's no hardship; there's a pefectly good mattress, so you can stop feeling guilty about it. Spend the morning in bed; if you think you're strong enough to face lunch, I'll see what I can whip up in the kitchen. And after that, we might go for a walk, perhaps?'

There was one small crumb of comfort. At least she wouldn't have to travel across London in broad daylight, looking like a refugee from a sultan's harem. Paul had thought it wiser not to collect her from Eaton Square before taking her to the Albert Hall, so she had come over to Primrose Hill instead, and changed into her fancy-dress costume in his bathroom. Last night, before she fell asleep, she had taken off the seven veils – it seemed improper to spend the night in a strange bed attired as an odalisque – and had worn her petticoat as a nightdress. Now the rented costume lay in a heap on the floor while her own clothes hung over the back of a chair.

'All right . . . Thank you . . . You're very kind,' she said.

He leaned forward and kissed her on the forehead. 'A pleasure and a privilege, Lady Caroline,' he said.

She dozed for a while, then got up and ran a bath. At lunchtime, feeling a little stronger, she managed to eat a boiled egg and drink a cup of aromatic Earl Grey tea. He had made her some 'soldiers' – fingers of bread and butter – to dip into the egg; she felt as if she were back in the nursery and wondered if she should feel insulted, but on second thoughts she decided it was rather comforting. After lunch, they went out.

The zoo was open on Sunday afternoons, so that seemed the obvious place to go. It was a grey, chilly day, and there weren't many people about. They walked in silence for a time, looking at those animals who dared to venture into the open air. They thought of going into the lion house for warmth, but the strong, rank smell of the great cats was too much for Caro, and they had to retreat.

Even the polar bears looked a little disconsolate, their yellowing fur ruffled by the stiff northerly breeze; only the penguins were immune to the weather and toddled like a colony of Charlie Chaplins up and down the sloping ramps that encircled their pool, or raced each other through the water, dapper and sleek as seals.

Paul and Caro watched them for a while, and she suddenly realized that she was smiling.

'Thank goodness,' he said. 'Now you're looking cheerful again: I was beginning to think your headache might have come back.'

'No – what made you think that?'

'You've been so quiet.'

'Oh, I'm sorry. How boring of me. I didn't feel very talkative . . . Is that rude of me?'

'Not at all. Sometimes you can feel close to someone without having to say anything.'

'Yes . . . That's how I feel. I suppose it's because I've known you practically all my life.' She held out her hand, and he took it. 'Dear Uncle Paul – no, dear Paul – I'm so glad I've found you again.'

'And I've been thinking I never really knew you until this

weekend,' he said. Her fingers felt very cold. 'Let's go into the reptile house; that won't smell at all.'

It was comfortably warm indoors and quite dark, with brilliantly lit windows floating in blackness. A tree lizard sat motionless on a branch; only its eyes, swivelling in search of food, revealed that it was not an ornament carved out of jade.

After a moment Paul said, 'You remind me so much of your mother.'

'When she was my age?'

'No, no, she was already a married woman with a family by the time I knew her; your father and I came home on leave together from France, and he brought me to meet you all. I first saw you in the night-nursery; you had bunny rabbits on the pockets of your dressing-gown.'

'You gave me a teddy bear; I've never forgotten that.'

He smiled, and took her hand again. It didn't feel cold any longer.

Behind the next window a grey-green snake poured its coils lazily over a rock, basking in the heat. It seemed to stare directly at them; could it see them through the glass, Caro wondered? As if in reply, its tongue flickered in and out, like a black lightning flash.

Paul's hand tightened upon hers.

'Now we've found one another again, we must keep in touch. Would you come and have dinner with me one evening?'

'I'd love to.'

'Tell me your favourite restaurant,' he suggested.

'Anywhere – I really don't mind. We could eat at your flat, if you like...' She could see the line of lighted panels reflected in his eyes, like tiny stars. 'Can I ask you something?'

'Anything.'

'I can't imagine why you don't have a family of your own. You never got married, did you?'

'No. Perhaps I never met a girl I really wanted... No, that's not true; there was someone, but she was married already.'

Suddenly she guessed. 'You're thinking of my mother, aren't you?'

He tried to withdraw his hand, but she would not let go.

'I'm glad I remind you of her,' she said.

'Gina, my dear, we really must make a move,' said Charlie when they had finished tea.

61

'Sure, I'm all ready.' Gina stood up, then added, 'But I must finish telling Alice about Tom's meeting tomorrow. I know it's no good asking you to come with us, William darling. You never get up to town these days.'

'Quite right,' said William, politely rising to his feet to see his guests out. 'And in any case I doubt whether I should be entirely sympathetic to Sir Oswald's cause.'

'It wasn't so bad when he was with the New Party, but now he's running the BUF he really is going too far,' Alice agreed.

'What exactly is the BUF?' asked Edith, setting down her teacup.

'The British Union of Fascists,' explained Gina.

'Warmongers,' said Grace Duncan crisply, to no one in particular.

'Certainly not!' Gina was indignant. 'If you'd only listen to what Tom has to say, you'd understand. Fascism is going to save the world – it's the only alternative to the Red Menace. When the Fascists have taken control everywhere, there won't be any more wars. He told us that himself, didn't he, Charlie?'

'Well, yes, and of course I'm in favour of anything that stamps out Communism,' Charlie agreed. 'Though I confess I'm a little worried about some of the methods the BUF advocate...'

'Oh, you're such an old fuddy-duddy, sometimes!' Gina threw up her hands in mock despair.

'I'm not the only one,' Charlie pointed out, defensively. 'A lot of Tom's supporters have drifted away in the past year or so. Look at Harold Nicolson –'

'Well, *we're* certainly not going to rat on him... Alice, be an angel – change your mind and come with us tomorrow.'

'My dear, I can't possibly. I'm on duty all day at the Palace.'

'But not in the evening, surely? The meeting's at seven-thirty – we can all have dinner afterwards. I'm dying for you to meet Tom; I just know you'll adore him.'

'Oh no, I daren't make any arrangements for tomorrow; if Her Majesty has an afternoon engagement, there's no knowing when I'll get away... Some other time, perhaps.'

Charlie sensed that their hosts were becoming restive, and steered his wife towards the door.

'Come along, my love, we've got a long drive ahead of us and it's quite dark already.' He turned and nodded a farewell to Edith and Grace. 'Goodbye, dear ladies. It's been delightful, perfectly delightful.'

'Goodbye, Sir Charles... Lady Bowyer,' said Grace coolly.

As they crossed the hall to the main entrance, Gina remembered: 'Darn it, I never said goodbye to Nick and Jenny. Where are they?'

'I believe Nick went up to pack; he's leaving at the crack of dawn to rejoin his ship,' said Alice. 'I'll say goodbye to them for you, shall I?'

'Yes, do. I already saw Richard and Polly and that adorable little Alex up in the nursery... Thanks for everything, darling, it's been simply divine. Such a pity Caro couldn't make it this Christmas, but I guess we'll run into her in town some time.'

Their luggage was already in the boot, and as they climbed into Gina's car, Alice called anxiously, 'Drive carefully, won't you?'

William knew what she was thinking. Almost two years ago to the day, Alice had driven Mrs Webster up to London; that was the night of the accident. But he said nothing until the tail-lights of the little sports car disappeared, and they turned back into the house.

'Charlie's not so bad, but I must say Gina can be rather tedious. I can't honestly claim that I enjoyed the Christmas holiday very much. Did you?'

'No, not really.' Alice took his arm. 'There was something not quite right about it this year; everyone seemed to be a bit on edge, I don't know why.'

Upstairs, Nicholas wrestled with the locks of his suitcase. 'I can't get the damn thing to shut. Give me a hand will you?'

Jenny joined him, putting her weight on the lid. 'Is that better?'

'Got it. Thanks. I seem to have packed more than usual.'

'That's because you're going to be away such a long time.'

They looked at each other. This was to be a really long trip: first to South America, then on to China. He wouldn't be home again until the autumn.

'I wish you didn't have to go,' she said. 'I shall miss you dreadfully.'

'You know I hate leaving you.'

They sat side by side on the bed, and she added quietly, 'We've had such a short time together... And I felt you weren't enjoying it very much.'

'Of course I enjoy being with you, you know I do.'

'Yes, but the night you came home...' Her voice trailed away.

He frowned at the pattern in the bedroom carpet. He didn't want to think about that night: the quarrel with Richard – the argument afterwards, alone with Jenny in this room – the sulky silences – worst of all, the moment when they got into bed, and he had turned his back on her, unable to kiss her, unable even to say goodnight . . .

'I suppose – I was very childish,' he said at last. 'I'm sorry.'

'You didn't really think it *meant* anything, did you?'

'I didn't know what to think. Coming home and finding you – with Richie like that . . .' The words were torn from him. 'It was a nightmare.'

'Goodness, you don't suppose he was seriously trying to make love to me – in a wardrobe?' She tried to laugh, determined to make light of it. 'He was only playing the fool. I couldn't believe it when you got so upset.'

'Couldn't you? Well, now you know.' He got up and began to pace up and down the bedroom.

'Know what? I don't understand.'

'Just how stupid I am. You see, I can never forget that Richie was the first.'

She stood up quickly, about to interrupt, but he stopped her.

'No, let me finish. Perhaps it will be better if I get it off my chest . . . He was the first man you ever loved. And you're the first woman I ever loved . . . the only woman. That's the real difference.'

'Nick, that's not true! There were other girls before me. You told me yourself about that girl in London who looked after you when you were hurt during the strike. And there were other women sometimes, when you went ashore – women on the other side of the world –'

'That's not the same: I never loved them. Only you.' He looked into her eyes. 'But you really did love Richard. You adored him.'

'I was young then. I didn't understand what love meant.'

'Oh, but you did; you loved him with all your heart –'

'And now I love you with all my heart.' She flung her arms round him. 'Richie means nothing to me. You must believe that.'

'I want to believe it, I *do* believe it –' His voice broke, and he kissed her again and again. 'I don't know why I torture myself like this. It's just – sometimes I can't help remembering – you and Richie . . .'

She whispered in his ear, 'Wait till we have our first baby: it will all be different then. You and me and the baby – nobody else. You'll be happy then . . . Promise me you will.'

'I promise . . . Sometimes I think I must be crazy . . . Forgive me?'

'There's nothing to forgive.'

At six o'clock the next morning, when he had embraced her for the last time and gone off to catch his train, she lay in bed, happily confident. She was glad they'd been able to talk about it at last. It was going to be all right now... If only they could have the child they both wanted so badly, everything would be perfect.

And a month later, it seemed that her wishes had come true. She crossed her fingers, waiting and hoping – and soon afterwards she was able to write to Nicholas:

Darling –
Dr Parry gave me the best news I've ever had. The tests are positive:
we are going to have our baby, next October. Beautifully timed to coincide
with your next leave – it really couldn't be better, could it?
   I've already told the family – I couldn't keep it to myself. They are
as thrilled as I am. Your parents have been so sweet; they're going to
fuss over me like mad. Polly will be a tower of strength: she's already
sorting out the baby-clothes that Alex has outgrown – with blue
trimmings, of course, so our firstborn has just got to be a boy too!

She had never been so happy.

By the middle of February, Paul and Caro had dined together twice: once at a discreet little restaurant in Charlotte Street, with high-backed seats and pink-shaded lamps on each table, rather like a Pullman car on a train; and once at Primrose Hill, on a pleasant if unremarkable supper cooked by Paul's trusty Mrs Wheeler, and served by her husband. On both occasions, the evening finished early, and he sent her home in a taxi.

The third time was the last Saturday in the month, and they went back to Charlotte Street. Paul commented on the restaurant's resemblance to a dining-car, and Caro said, 'I wish we really were on a train – tearing through the night, on our way to Venice or Stamboul or somewhere... I wish we could go on holiday together.'

Paul smiled. 'I can't think of anything nicer. But I'm afraid other people might get the wrong idea.'

'Oh, do you think it would be wrong? I think it would be the right idea...'

Her leg brushed against his knee under the table; they were both aware of the instant physical excitement that passed between them like an electric current. Then the waiter approached with the bill, and Paul asked, 'Would you be good enough to order me a cab, please?'

The waiter bowed and withdrew. Caro said, 'You're not thinking of sending me home already?'

'Well, no – not if you don't want to go.'

'What I really want is to go back to your flat.'

He looked at her for a moment, then said. 'For coffee and a brandy, perhaps?'

'Perhaps.'

Since the Wheelers had gone away as usual, Paul made the coffee himself. It percolated into a round glass jug over a spirit-lamp, and they watched it bubble. A fire crackled peacefully in the hearth, and Caro switched out the lights, so they were illuminated by dancing blue and yellow flames.

'I love it here,' she said. 'I love being with you.'

She curled up on the carpet at his feet, like a cat, and he stroked the back of her neck. The room was very still; the only sounds were the bubbling coffee and a burning coal that settled in the grate.

'I know this is only a game we're playing, but it could be a dangerous game,' he said, after a while.

'It's not a game,' she said. She lifted her face to him, and put her hands round his neck, drawing him down to her; and they kissed. Briefly, she remembered that night at Eaton Square, with Scott. But she would not think about that.

'I love you,' she told him.

'My darling girl, this is all wrong –' he began. And then she kissed him again, silencing his doubts. He held her close, feeling her body move against him. 'We must stop,' he said at last; but he could not let her go.

Outside in the darkness, they heard the roar of a lion from Regent's Park, and Caro laughed. 'That's thrilling . . . It sounds so close.'

'You hear it more clearly at this time of night, when the traffic dies down.'

'It seems much nearer . . . Do you suppose one of the lions has got out of its cage? Perhaps it's escaped. It might be stalking its prey on Primrose Hill at this very moment . . . It could be right outside your front door.'

He chuckled. 'You really think so?'

'I'm sure of it. In fact I don't see how you can possibly turn me out now; it wouldn't be safe with wild beasts roaming the streets...I'm afraid I shall have to stay here – all night...'

He studied her face: love – trust – desire, all shining in her eyes.

'I want you – please,' she whispered. She blew out the flame beneath the spirit-lamp, and they let the coffee grow cold.

The next day, they stayed in bed till noon, sometimes talking and laughing, sometimes making love, revelling in their shared happiness. Then they got up and dressed, and went out to lunch. This was not an occasion for boiled eggs and bread-and-butter 'soldiers'.

Paul knew a Chinese restaurant in Camden Town which opened on Sundays, and they ate crispy noodles and shredded roast duck, bamboo-shoots and bean-sprouts. Caro experimented with chop-sticks for the first time, and soon picked up the knack. 'I'm learning a lot this weekend,' she said, with a gleam of mischief.

But Paul was not smiling. He pushed the rice-bowl aside, saying, 'Dearest child... This has been so wonderful. I shall remember it all my life, and I hope you will, too... But it must never happen again. We both know that.'

She was shocked. 'No! That's a terrible thing to say... And it's not true.' Leaning forward, she went on in a lower tone, 'I want it to happen again – often. I love you, Paul; don't you understand that?'

'But you must see this is completely impossible. I'm old enough to be your father –'

'That has nothing to do with it. When two people love one another, age doesn't matter. When will I see you again?'

'It's all too complicated. The Wheelers will be coming back later this afternoon –'

'Don't worry, I shall go home before then. But you said they go away every week. Can I come and stay next Saturday?'

He shook his head helplessly, not knowing what to say to her. But he did not say no.

When Caro got back to Eaton Square at four o'clock, a surprise awaited her. Her mother was in the drawing-room. Lady Minster looked up with a welcoming smile, saying, 'Oh, good. You're just in time for tea, darling. Ring the bell and we'll get another cup.'

Caro obeyed, then kissed her mother, her thoughts racing. She felt guilty for the first time, imagining that the events of the past twenty-four hours must be written in her face, transparently obvious.

'I thought you'd finished your turn of duty,' she began, stammering a little in her attempt to sound casual and innocent. 'I wasn't expecting you to be here.'

'I'm staying on to do one more duty tomorrow. Her Majesty asked me as a special favour, so I rang home and explained to Daddy... He sends his love, by the way.'

'Oh, thank you.' For some reason, the mention of her father made Caro feel even more guilt-ridden. She tried to show a polite interest in her mother's affairs. 'What are you doing tomorrow?'

'My dear, you'll never guess... The Queen is opening the new wing of our very own cottage hospital in Medford. I'm driving down with her and Flora Kelso; we've got to be there by ten-thirty.'

'*Two* of you, to wait on the Queen?'

'I'm going home afterwards; Flora's taking over, so she can attend Her Majesty on the way back. It will be my job to present all the local bigwigs – I just hope I remember all their names...' Alice changed the subject: 'I didn't realize you were going away this weekend. Miss Kendall tells me you didn't warn the staff either; they were quite worried when you didn't come home last night.'

'Were they? I suppose I should have let them know.' Miss Kendall was the housekeeper at Eaton Square; Caro cursed her silently – a born gossip, she must have gloated over this titbit of information.

'She said you didn't even take an overnight bag with you.'

'No, I didn't. I didn't plan to stay out, actually.' Caro improvised rapidly. 'I went over to have supper with a girl from the *Argus* – Muriel Beasley, I don't think you've met her. She lives in Hendon, and we were talking so much, I missed the last tube train. Wasn't that silly?'

She had seized upon the first name that came into her head; Muriel Beasley, who worked in the photo-library, was a dim, dreary girl. Caro had no idea where she lived, but Hendon seemed appropriate.

'So she put you up for the night? That was lucky. Has she got a flat of her own?'

'Yes, it's quite nice really – very small, just two rooms, kitchen and bath. I slept on the sofa.' Caro's invention was beginning to sound so convincing she couldn't resist elaborating on it. 'As a matter of fact, I was thinking – I might get a flat of my own, too...'

'Oh, surely not? It seems pointless, when you've got plenty of room here, and people to look after you...' Alice broke off: 'Which reminds me – nobody's answered that bell. Do you suppose the

68

wiring's gone wrong again? I'd better investigate.'

She went out of the room, and Caro breathed a sigh of relief; the danger was over. A moment later the telephone rang, and she picked it up, saying automatically, 'Caroline Gaunt – who's that?'

'Caro!' exclaimed Scott Hanson. Instantly, her feeling of guilt came rushing back, and she resented it.

'Hello, Scott.' Her voice was flat and unenthusiastic. 'How are you?'

'I'm fine. Hey, listen, I tried to call you this morning, but they told me you'd gone away for the night; they didn't seem to know where you were.'

'That's right; I only just got back.'

'Ah ... well, I was wondering – what are you doing this evening?'

'I don't know – nothing special. Why?'

'Great. How'd you like to see a movie? There's the new Garbo at –'

'No thank you, Scott. I don't feel like going out again; I'm a bit tired.'

'Oh ...' He sounded disappointed. 'Well, then, maybe I could drop by and have a cup of coffee? I mean, we haven't seen each other in quite a while, not since –'

'No, Scott. Not tonight.'

'OK ...' He took a breath and tried again. 'How about we make a date for some other –'

She cut in sharply. 'I'm very sorry, I've got a lot of work on at the moment. I really can't see you.'

'Well, if you're that busy ... Where'd you get to, last night, anyhow? Somewhere interesting?'

'I went out with a friend, that's all.'

A pause, and then, 'You mean, a boyfriend?'

Her patience snapped. 'Yes, I do mean a boyfriend. Does that surprise you?'

'No, of course not. I just didn't realize you –'

Then the door opened, and her mother walked in, saying, 'The bell was working, but Cook says the hot water – oh, dear, I didn't realize you were on the telephone.'

'Goodbye, Scott, I have to go now.' Caro hung up quickly.

Alice apologized: 'I'm sorry, I didn't mean to interrupt ... Was that *our* Scott? Scott Hanson?'

'Yes. He wanted to look in this evening, but I didn't feel like it.'

'What a shame. He's such a nice boy,' said Alice.

'Do you think so? I think he's a pain in the neck,' said Caro.

On the journey from Buckingham Palace to Medford, Alice was a little preoccupied. She sensed that something had disturbed Caro this weekend, but she could not decide what it was. The falling out with Scott Hanson had happened months ago, so that wouldn't account for it. And in any case, Caro did not appear to be distressed, exactly. But she was somehow different: her reactions were odd and unpredictable, and Alice felt uneasy about her.

As the royal Daimler made its way across South London, the suburbs of Lewisham and Catford fell away, and green fields began to spring up round the pleasant little town of Bromley. Her Majesty had been talking quietly to Lady Flora, and Alice – lost in her own thoughts – was startled when Flora addressed her directly: 'Alice, don't you think the car is behaving rather strangely?'

'Is it? I hadn't noticed.'

'It's going so slowly, and the engine keeps making funny hiccuping noises.'

Now it was brought to her notice, Alice had to agree that the Daimler was not purring in its usual confident manner.

'Wind down the window, Flora,' said the Queen, and raised her voice as Lady Flora lowered the glass panel that separated them from the chauffeur. 'Is there something wrong with the car, Humphries?'

'It's playing up a bit this morning, Ma'am. It could be the drive-shaft, I'm thinking,' said Mr Humphries over his shoulder.

'Or perhaps it could be the driver?' suggested Alice under her breath.

The Queen did not hear her, but Flora shot Alice a warning glance. Mr Humphries, an elderly and irascible man, had been in charge of the Queen's limousine for many years, and she would not hear a word against him though his driving was notoriously erratic.

'Oh dear, how tiresome,' said the Queen. 'I hope you can hurry up a little, Humphries; we don't want to be late, that would never do.'

She indicated to Flora that she might wind the window up again, and the car continued in a series of spasmodic jerks.

'I particularly wanted to get to Medford in good time today.' The Queen looked vexed. 'I was planning a little surprise for you, Alice.'

'A surprise, Ma'am?'

'This is the nearest I have ever been to Crown House. It's only a few miles from Medford, I understand?'

'That's quite right, Ma'am.' Alice's heart sank; she could guess what was coming.

'So I thought it would be a splendid opportunity for me to call in. Quite informally, of course; we won't disturb anyone.'

'Oh yes – that would be a great honour, Ma'am, but...' Alice tried not to show how she really felt.

Lady Flora bit her lip, guessing the agonies Alice must be suffering. It was all very well for the Queen to say she wouldn't disturb anyone; every visit by the King or Queen was an event of great importance, and preparations were usually made long in advance. The thought of Her Majesty dropping in on the family at Crown House, without warning, appalled her.

'But – but when – exactly? Your Majesty always has such a carefully planned schedule,' Alice continued, trying to find a straw to clutch at.

'We have to be at the hospital at ten-thirty, and the ceremony begins at eleven.' The Queen consulted her typed itinerary. 'Then a tour of the wards, and at twelve-thirty there is a reception in the Town Hall, and a civic lunch at one o'clock. I thought if we can get away promptly – by half past two, let us say – we might take tea at Crown House before we have to return to London.'

'Yes... That would be very – very nice...' Alice gazed out of the car window; clearly the Queen had it all worked out.

As they drove on through Kent, she did not see the rolling hills of the North Downs; she could only see Richard up to his ankles in farmyard manure, William in those dreadful old gardening clothes, Polly singing and dancing a music-hall song to entertain Alex, the house untidy and the servants disorganized. She shut her eyes and prayed for deliverance.

Never had her prayers been so promptly answered.

A few miles further on, the car coughed, spluttered, then swerved to a halt by the side of the road. Lady Flora opened the glass panel again. 'Well, Humphries? What seems to be the trouble?'

Humphries did not bother to reply; he was already out of the car, and opening the bonnet. They heard him swearing to himself as he poked about in the bowels of the machine. And they waited ... and waited.

At long last, he had to admit defeat. The motor had broken down, and he could not get it to start again. The car would have to be towed into a garage for repairs.

The ladies looked blankly at one another. The breakdown had occurred in open country, without a house or a telephone to be seen. The Queen looked at her watch. 'Dear me! It's twenty past ten already; we are going to be dreadfully late. Whatever shall we do?'

Alice volunteered to walk on till she came to the next village, and seek help; though there was no knowing how long that might take. Lady Flora would stay with the Queen until they were rescued.

Alice set out briskly along the road, and reached the brow of a hill; then saw with dismay that the road wound across empty fields. There were no buildings within sight. But there was a car coming towards her; a small family saloon.

Desperately, she waved at the driver. Obligingly, he pulled up.

'Excuse me,' she began, rather flustered. 'Are you by any chance going in the opposite direction?'

The driver – a mousy little man in grey middle age – stared at her as if she were raving mad, and said that he was on his way to Bromley. Alice explained the situation, throwing herself upon his chivalry.

'Would you mind giving the Queen a lift into Medford? She's supposed to be there almost at once. Her car's broken down, and it really is terribly important.'

'But surely – Her Majesty wouldn't let me drive her? I might be a Bolshevik for all you know!' objected the little man.

Alice said she felt sure that Her Majesty would be prepared to take that risk, and the Good Samaritan opened the passenger door. When they reached the immobilized Daimler, Alice went over for a private word with the Queen.

'He's a very respectable man, and he says he'll be proud to turn round and take Your Majesty to Medford. I'm afraid we shall be very late, but that can't be helped... Oh – and I should warn you he's a market-gardener, and the back of his car is full of onions.'

'Oh! Do they smell?' the Queen wanted to know.

'No more than usual, Ma'am.'

There really was no alternative; and the royal party proceeded a few minutes later, Her Majesty seated in front next to the awestruck driver, while Alice and Flora shared the back seat with a great many onions – and kept the windows open.

The Dowager Countess had struck up a friendship of sorts with Grace Duncan. Though there was a twenty-year difference in age – for old Bea had already celebrated her eightieth birthday – they shared a gritty, realistic view of life, and found that they got on surprisingly well. Almost every week, Edith and Grace would walk across from the lodge to share an early supper with the old lady, in her apartment within the east wing.

'I'm glad of your company,' the Countess admitted grudgingly. 'You're about the only faces I ever see nowadays. William keeps himself to himself, Alice is forever gallivanting off to London, and the youngsters don't want to be bothered with an old woman like me.'

'I'm sure that's not true, Mama,' said Edith. 'They're all very fond of you.'

'Then why don't they come and visit me? You've no notion how tedious it gets, stuck away here by myself. I don't like being overlooked and forgotten. But there – I suppose I've outlived my time. Nobody wants you when you're old and useless.'

'You must come and have supper with us at the lodge, my lady,' said Grace. 'It would do you good to get out more.'

'Out of the question.' Old Bea shook her head impatiently. 'It's as much as I can do to manage the stairs down to the drawing-room... I should have died years ago: it would have saved a lot of trouble all round.'

'We all have to face it – we're none of us getting any younger!' said Grace. 'I was sixty myself, on my last birthday.'

'That's no age at all,' snorted the old lady, refusing to allow anyone else to share her crown of thorns. 'You're still a spring chicken, compared to me.'

'All the same, I do think Grace ought to take things easier.' Edith took up the subject which had been exercising her a good deal lately. 'I keep telling her she works too hard – lots of teachers retire when they get to sixty. Don't you think she ought to give herself a rest? Let someone else take over the school?'

'Retirement?' Grace scoffed at the idea. 'They'll have to carry me out feet first. Teaching's all I know; what would I do if I gave it up?'

'You could go away with me, for a long holiday,' Edith suggested. 'We could travel – go abroad –'

'It's vastly overrated,' said Old Bea, in a tone that brooked no

73

argument. 'I spent some of the best years of my life in India, with Minster, and what good did it do us? I got sunstroke – and he ruined his liver. Nothing but heat and flies and smells . . . You'll stay here where you belong, if you've any sense.'

The door opened, and Alice came in, saying, 'How are you, Mama? I must sit down, I've been on my feet for hours.' She sank into a chair, adding: 'William's in the bath, and I have to tell somebody what a dreadful day I've had. Do I still smell of onions?'

She related the day's events, from the breakdown of the Daimler, through their late arrival at Medford, and their attempt to get through the planned schedule.

'Of course, we were nearly an hour late by the time we got there, and we never caught up. Everything went wrong, all along the line; we didn't sit down to lunch till half past two, and the food was atrocious because it had been kept hot so long – all dried up, and the white sauce on the chicken was like wallpaper paste. And when Humphries turned up with the car, it took ages to find a new spare part, so we were kept hanging about at the Town Hall for an eternity. But every cloud has a silver lining, and when they were able to drive back to London at last, I was graciously permitted to come home.'

'I wasn't expecting to see you,' said Edith. 'It was a nice surprise.'

'You nearly had another surprise,' Alice concluded. 'If it hadn't been for the Daimler, you would have had a royal visitation – Her Majesty decided to drop in for a cup of tea!'

Edith and Grace looked duly thunderstruck, but Old Bea grumbled: 'Speaking for myself, I should have enjoyed it. It's a long time since I saw the King or the Queen, and I don't suppose I ever shall again.'

'Yes, you will,' sighed Alice. 'When I left Her Majesty, she said: "I shall have to make a special visit to Crown House; we must plan it properly – and next time, I shall come to stay!"'

The months passed, and the year turned towards summer.

Jenny exchanged long letters with Nicholas, keeping him informed of every stage of her pregnancy. Although Polly had been generous in her offer of baby-clothes, Jenny was determined to provide some of her own, and began knitting. Grace gave advice on patterns and stitches, and Edith day-dreamed about the new 'little stranger' who would soon be joining the family.

Then, at the end of April, everything changed.

Jenny had some time on her hands; everyone else seemed to be busy – even Polly had gone off into Medford on some mysterious errand of her own. It was a lovely morning, and she decided she would try to find Lord Minster, to see if he needed any help in the garden.

She walked the length of the herbaceous border, but he was not there. She began to stroll towards the lake, and then suddenly – without any warning – she knew that she had to get into the house, quickly...

When she reached the hall, she stopped, wondering what she should do. None of the baby books had prepared her for this – nobody ever suggested something might go wrong. She must get Dr Parry, that was certain. It took agonizing minutes to get through on the telephone: her whole body was tense, in an effort to hold on to the tiny scrap of herself and Nicholas that was within her. The doctor was kind and reassuring, as always, telling her to put her feet up and wait until he arrived.

'Try to relax,' were his final words.

She made a conscious effort as she lay under the eiderdown, but the more she tried, the more the tension mounted. Perhaps if she breathed deeply... But the thoughts kept flooding back. If only she had followed the doctor's advice; he had told her to take things easily, but she had felt so well and happy, so full of energy... She longed for Nicholas's reassuring presence: did being a Navy wife mean having to face everything alone...?

Polly returned at lunchtime, looking very pleased with herself. As she entered the house, Alice was crossing the hall, and Polly hailed her.

'I suppose Richard's in the farm office?' she asked, breathless. 'I ought to tell him first really, but I can't keep it to myself a minute longer. 'I've been to see a new doctor – a lady doctor in Medford – she's ever so good. I got fed up with old Parry; he's such a fusspot. Well, I didn't want to say anything till I was sure, but now she's told me it's definite... We're going to have another baby – isn't that marvellous? So Jenny's not the only one!'

Alice looked at her, frowning as if she couldn't take in the news. 'You're pregnant...?'

'That's right – I can't wait to tell Jenny – where is she?'

'She's in her room, lying down. I shouldn't disturb her; not now.' Alice held Polly's hand, and kissed her. 'Forgive me – I do congratulate you. I'm glad you're going to have another baby, my dear – but I'm afraid Jenny isn't... Not now.'

5

MONDAY, 17 JULY TO SATURDAY, 14 OCTOBER 1933

It was a difficult time for Jenny. Losing the baby was a terrible blow, though she tried to tell herself that it would have been even harder to bear if it had happened later in her pregnancy. She made three separate attempts to write to Nicholas before she found a way to break the news gently – without self-pity, yet reaching out to him in their shared loss.

He was not due to come home until the autumn, and the summer seemed to drag on interminably.

Jenny tried hard to feel happy for Polly and Richard. For their part, they sympathized with her disappointment and said all the right things – but now Polly was in a world of her own; a world of blissful serenity, where nothing could touch her.

The weeks passed, and she became prettily plump, content to sit about, sometimes playing with Alex – until he became too obstreperous, and then Jenny had to come to the rescue and carry the little boy away to work off his energy in the garden. Polly was cushioned and cocooned in motherhood, all her thoughts devoted to the great day in November.

As for Richard – the prospect of another addition to the family did not overwhelm him. Their first baby had been a very special event, and he had shared all Polly's enthusiasm; but now they already had a son and heir, he could not take the same interest. If anything, he slightly resented Polly's absorption in her pregnancy, feeling himself excluded.

He began to grow restless, and spent more time at the home farm, often staying out until dark. Polly saw less of her husband, but accepted this placidly enough: summer was a busy time on the farm – he had a lot to do.

But Richard remembered the old saw about 'all work and no play' – and he could not tolerate a life of dullness.

One July morning, Jenny was dead-heading the roses, with Alex's help – for he had been particularly boisterous at breakfast, and Polly needed time to rest. They were making slow progress; Alex delighted in using the cut flower heads as confetti, tossing them into the air and laughing as the petals fluttered down around him.

'You're a rascal,' Jenny reproved him mildly. 'Now we'll have to fetch a broom to clear up the mess.' She broke off as the housekeeper came across the lawn.

'Excuse me, madam – could I have a word with you?' Lilian Brooks looked flushed and a little embarrassed.

'Of course – what's wrong?'

'Well . . . It's difficult to say at the moment, madam. Little pitchers have long ears,' said Lilian, with a meaning look at Alex, romping on the grass.

'Really?' Jenny was puzzled, but continued smoothly: 'Alex – why don't you go and look for a broom? Ask one of the gardeners; then you can help me sweep up.'

Glad to have an errand, Alex rushed off, and Lilian said; 'Thank you, madam. I couldn't very well speak out in front of the boy – it's about his father, you see . . . I don't know what to do for the best.'

Jenny frowned: 'I don't understand – what's happened?'

'Well – it's like this. One of the maids came to me this morning; Eileen Fennell – she lives over Peachey way, and generally comes to work on her bicycle. Well, last night she was going home, wheeling the bike along the farm track, when his lordship called her in to the stables . . .'

'Richard –?' Jenny busied herself picking up petals, so Lilian would not see her face. 'Go on . . .'

'Seemingly he asked if she wanted a lift home in his car. She said no, 'cos she couldn't leave the bike, see. And then he got a bit silly, larking about, she said, and then he made advances to her . . . Pawing her around, trying to kiss her, and that. She was real upset about it. She's only a slip of a girl, but she's been properly brought up – her mum and dad are both strict Baptist – she won't have that sort of carry on, and no more would I.'

Jenny reflected that plain, stolid Lilian had probably not been

78

subjected to 'that sort of carry on' very often; but she forced herself to deal with the situation sensibly.

'Has she given in her notice?'

'No, madam – not yet. But she will, if he tries it on again. And if she goes, there'll be talk – and we wouldn't want that, would we?'

'Certainly not. Thank you for telling me, Lilian. I don't think it will happen again, if she made her feelings clear. I should advise her to try and forget about it ... Though perhaps she might find a different way home in future.'

Jenny was almost sure Richard would not pester the girl a second time, after this rebuff. All the same, it was an unfortunate echo of the past. Since his marriage, she had assumed that he was a changed man; if he were to revert to his old ways, there could be nothing but trouble and misery for everyone concerned.

At lunch, Alice noticed Jenny's unhappy preoccupation, and misinterpreted it.

'It's wretched for you, having to be so brave and patient; I do wish they'd let Nick come home on compassionate leave.'

'Oh, no – I'm perfectly all right.' Jenny smiled quickly. 'Really I am.'

'I know, but I think you need a change of scene. Why don't you come up to town with me for a couple of days? I'd be glad of your company. Caro never seems to be at home – that wretched newspaper keeps her so busy, and she goes to stay with one of the girls in her office every weekend.'

Jenny accepted the invitation gratefully, pleased to be able to put aside the problem of Richard for the moment.

She spent three happy days in London. Lady Minster had two engagements with Her Majesty, while Jenny amused herself with window-shopping, and a matinée of *Richard of Bordeaux*: a young man with a strange name – Gielgud – was fascinating in the title-role. On the last afternoon, Alice took her to tea at 145 Piccadilly, with the Duchess of York.

'Jenny dear – I was thinking about you and Nicholas only the other day. Alice told me your sad news; I do hope you're not too miserable about it. I'm sure next time things will go according to plan. After Lillibet was born, I was afraid I might not be able to have another baby – but when darling Margaret arrived, everything was perfectly straightforward, so you see one must never despair.'

She was interrupted by the entrance of the two Princesses: seven-year-old Lillibet guiding Margaret Rose, who would very soon be three.

'Lady Minster – and Mrs Gaunt!' exclaimed Lillibet joyfully. 'We've brought Dookie to meet you!'

A small dog raced round them on stumpy, short legs, wagging a brief but energetic tail.

'Is Dookie a new addition to the family?' asked Alice.

'His official name is Rozavel Golden Eagle – but that's a bit of a mouthful,' said the Duchess. 'So he became known as Dookie, short for "The Duke's puppy".'

'He's lovely – I've never seen a dog quite like him,' Jenny said, as he licked her hand.

'A friend of ours has one, and when the girls saw him they fell in love with him at once, so of course we had to have one too!'

The Princesses asked for a biscuit from the tea table, as they wanted to teach Dookie to sit up and beg, and their mother said with a twinkle in her eye: 'Just this once, then ... In fact we're thinking of buying another – Rozavel Lady Jane – so he won't be lonely. I don't blame you for not recognizing the breed; they're from Wales, and not very well-known – he's a Pembroke corgi.'

London was always quiet in August. Once the schools had broken up, the people who could afford holidays departed in search of sunshine and sea breezes. Those with money motored down to the south of France, while families from Stepney or Rotherhithe packed into charabancs for day-trips to Southend, returning home late in the evening with crates of empty beer bottles at their feet, and sleeping children on their laps.

The West End seemed strangely deserted when Paul and Caro came out of the cinema. There were few people about, so it was particularly unfortunate they they should have collided with a young man hurrying along the pavement.

'Goodness, that was thrilling,' Caro was saying. 'I almost screamed as loudly as Fay Wray when King Kong – oh – sorry ... !' She turned to apologize to the passer-by, then stopped dead.

'Hi there,' said Scott. 'Long time no see.'

'Yes – hello.' Caro glanced from Scott to Paul, and back again. 'I don't believe you know one another. Scott Hanson – Lady Bowyer's brother ... Paul Weyman – an old friend of the family.'

'How do you do?' Paul smiled politely.

'We have met, at Richard's wedding,' Scott reminded them. 'But only briefly.'

'Ah yes, of course,' Paul cleared his throat. 'I'm sorry if I seem unsociable, but we've booked a table for dinner, so . . .'

'That's perfectly OK. I'll see you around, Caro,' said Scott.

'Yes, I expect so. Goodbye.'

She hurried away, on Paul's arm; Scott stood watching them until they were out of sight.

At lunchtime the following day, he made his way to the *Argus* office, asking for Lady Caroline Gaunt at the reception desk. Ten minutes later, Caro hurried out of the lift, looking mystified.

'Hello again – this is a surprise.'

'I've got to talk to you, Caro. Maybe we could have lunch or something.'

'Oh, I wish you'd telephoned first – I don't bother with lunch. I usually grab a sandwich at the Milk Bar down the road.'

'I tried calling you at home, but you weren't there – at any rate they said you weren't . . . Come on: I'll stand you a sandwich and a milk shake.'

Clearly he wasn't going to take no for an answer, so Caro accompanied him to the Moo-Cow Milk Bar. It was crowded and noisy, but Scott managed to find two vacant stools by a corner shelf. She sipped her chocolate milk shake through a straw, then asked: 'What is it you want to talk about?'

'You . . . And that guy you were with last night – Weyman.'

'What about him?'

'Last time we spoke, you told me you'd been going out with a boyfriend . . . I remember you stayed out all night.' Scott spoke loudly enough to make himself heard above the chatter of the other customers.

She glanced round quickly: 'That's got nothing to do with –'

'Just tell me something. Is he the one?'

To her annoyance, Caro felt herself blushing, and retorted angrily: 'Mind your own business!'

'My God – so it's true. You and that old man . . .'

She put down the half-empty glass and left the sandwich untouched, slipping off the high stool.

'I didn't come here to be cross-examined. Goodbye, Scott.'

He grabbed her arm: 'You must be crazy – goddamit, he must be fifty at least. How could you –?'

Pulling herself free, she turned on him, aware that by now everyone was listening and staring. 'You've no right to pester me!' she
exclaimed. 'In future – just leave me alone!' And she walked out
quickly, without looking back. With as much dignity as he could
muster, Scott followed. He could see her some yards ahead, but he
did not try to catch up with her. There was no point now.

When they finished work, Paul and Caro often met for a drink at
a pleasant bar in Margaret Street, near Broadcasting House. Tonight,
he thought, she was unusually quiet.

'You've got something on your mind,' he said. 'Has it been a bad
day?'

'Not specially... Except for a stupid scene at lunchtime.' She
told him about Scott's unpardonable behaviour, only omitting his
references to Paul's age. 'Anyway, it really doesn't matter what Scott
thinks. He's an absolute pest – not worth bothering about!' She tried
to smile, shrugging off the incident, but Paul could not dismiss it so
easily.

'He is a member of your family, by marriage. Suppose he tells
your parents?'

'Oh, he won't do that. I know he's behaved like an idiot, but he
wouldn't sneak on us.'

'You can't be sure. If he feels jealous enough –'

'He's got no reason to be jealous; he made it quite clear he's not
in the least –' She stopped, and began again. 'In any case, what do
we care? We love each other; that's nothing to be ashamed of, is it?'

Paul looked at her, unsmiling. 'I'm not ashamed. But there'd be
a hell of a row if your family ever found out. We must avoid that,
at all costs.'

'Why? They're bound to find out sooner or later; they'll probably
be a bit shocked at first – the thought of their little girl having an
affair – but they'll just have to get used to the idea. I think we should
tell them, actually. I'd like to move into your flat, then there wouldn't
be any more lying or pretending –'

'No!' He spoke more sharply than he had intended to, and she
stared at him. Pulling himself together, he continued: 'I'm sorry, my
darling, but that's out of the question. Your mother and father
would never forgive me... I beg you not to say anything to them –
or to anyone else. And I just hope that confounded American keeps
his mouth shut.'

Lord Minster was supervising a squad of men as they unloaded slabs of rock from the back of a lorry, parked at the end of the lake.

'Careful now – carry the boulders to the bottom of that slope, and build them up one at a time. I'll show you exactly where they have to go.'

It was a golden afternoon; still very warm for mid-September, and the workmen shone with sweat as they lugged the heavy rocks over the grass. At William's elbow, Jenny said: 'I was going to ask you if you needed any help – but I don't think I should be much use at manhandling lumps of stone.'

'Don't worry – you and I will have plenty to do later, when the rocks are in place, and we've added the right kind of soil in between the crevices. I shall want your assistance then, to plant out the alpines before the weather breaks.' He stood back, eyeing the scene with satisfaction as each rock was set into place. 'I'm using East Sussex sandstone – more expensive than the local Kentish ragstone, but that takes too long to weather, and it must blend into the landscape.'

Creating a rock garden was William's latest ambition, and he was taking immense trouble over it, carefully preparing a mix of soil – four parts of loam, two parts of leaf-mould and garden compost, and one and a half of grit.

'These alpines are sensitive beasts; they won't tolerate a sour mix. And they won't thrive if the soil gets waterlogged – that's why we need the grit, for drainage.'

'Well, I can see you're very busy; I won't disturb you.' Jenny turned to go, but he stopped her.

'Don't run away. As it happens – I'd been hoping to have a word with you.' He took her arm and led her across the lawn, to a white wrought-iron bench beneath the trees. 'Can you spare a moment or two? We shan't be disturbed here, and I can keep an eye on things.' He hesitated, choosing his words carefully. 'Polly seems very happy these days, doesn't she? Positively glowing with health.'

'Yes, she is indeed.'

'It must be difficult for you, seeing her so contented, after – well, you know what I'm trying to say.' He patted her hand lightly. 'I mustn't embarrass you ... But it strikes me that Richard may not be quite so dedicated to the idea of fatherhood, for the second time? Correct me if I'm wrong.'

'I know what you mean ...' Jenny wondered what he was leading up to.

'My son is a man of abundant energy; he has to occupy himself with something – or someone – all the time. He has never learned to be patient.'

A long silence: Jenny said nothing, but waited for him to continue. When he spoke again, he seemed to have changed the subject.

'Do you know the Morrisseys, over at Fallowfield? Joe Morrissey's a JP – sits on the Bench at Medford – and a gentleman-farmer, as they call them. Decent enough chap; he's made a good thing out of that farm of his. He's got a pretty little wife – Helen, I think her name is. I've run across them a few times, at dinner parties, charity balls and so on. Have you met them at all?'

'No, I'm afraid not.'

'I just wondered. Morrissey's a good deal older than she is, and he puts in a lot of hours on his farm ... They say she feels rather neglected.'

Jenny frowned: 'Are you afraid Richie might be neglecting Polly too? He has been working late at the farm office recently.'

'No, no, I wasn't making comparisons. Besides, Joe Morrissey has other calls on his time; apart from his duties as a magistrate, he's on several charitable committees. He's away from home a good deal, I believe. And Mrs Morrissey finds time hanging heavy on her hands ... or so I'm told.'

'I don't quite follow ...'

'Sometimes I hear the gardeners talking among themselves ... There's a certain amount of gossip going round – probably nothing in it, but I do feel a little anxious. You see, although I've been over to our farm office several times in the evenings, I've never found Richie there ... As I say – people are beginning to talk.'

'Oh, no – surely not ...' Now she understood, only too well. 'He wouldn't be such a fool.'

'I hope not. I tried to talk to him – tactfully, you know – but it was useless; he wouldn't discuss it with me. But he might listen to you.'

Jenny took a long time to decide what to do. She wished that her father-in-law hadn't asked her to intervene in this situation, though she understood why he had done so. Richie might play the injured innocent with Lord Minster; she would not let him get away with it.

All the same, she was reluctant to interfere. She knew instinctively that if Nick were here, he would not let her involve herself with Richie's problems. But he could have tackled his brother instead, man to man.

Still she couldn't make up her mind. Then she saw Polly sauntering through the orchard, under the ripening apple-trees, hand in hand with Alex; seven months pregnant, she moved like a galleon in full sail, on a high tide of happiness.

For an instant, Jenny almost hated her; how dare she be so blissfully serene that she didn't even notice that her husband was unfaithful to her?

This feeling was followed instantly by remorse; if Richard's stupidity should create a scandal, how could Polly cope with it?

That settled it. Jenny made her way to the farm without any more delay.

'Hello, old dear!' Richard, slipping on his jacket, looked round in surprise as she walked into his office. 'What an unexpected pleasure; I can't remember when you last came to visit me.'

'Can't you?' Jenny moved across to the chair by the desk. 'May I sit down? I won't keep you very long.'

'Unfortunately you've caught me at a rather bad moment – I'm just on my way out.' He straightened his collar, and passed a hand over his curly hair. 'And I don't know when I'll be back – probably not till late.'

'Are you paying another call on Mrs Morrissey?' Jenny asked.

Richard already had his hand on the door. After a moment, he shut it again, then asked: 'Who's been talking?'

'A lot of people, apparently. Don't you know how quickly gossip travels? That's what I had to tell you: it's not a secret any longer.'

His face darkened, and he lit a cigar, giving himself time to think. 'I suppose Pa put you up to this? The dear old boy had a go at me the other day. Why can't he stop meddling in other people's business –?'

'He's terribly worried, and so am I. For goodness sake, Richie, what happens when Polly finds out?'

'She won't find out. Unless of course you're kind enough to tell her.'

'Don't be stupid. She's not deaf or blind; at any moment she –'

'Oh, yes, she is.' Richard turned to face her. 'That's exactly what she is – deaf and blind to everything except young Alex and that other child inside her. She doesn't see or hear or care a damn about anything else; she lost interest in me long ago. I can't help it if I've got to take my fun elsewhere; I'm an ordinary sort of chap – I need a bit of excitement – a bit of loving... Good God, you should understand that, better than anyone! Your husband's away for months on end. How the hell do you put up with it?'

He came closer, and she looked up warily. 'We're in the same boat, you and I,' he went on. 'You ought to be more sympathetic – you must know how it feels, not having anyone to...'

He put his arms round her, forcing his mouth upon hers. This time he was not playing games. She struggled against him as he fumbled with her dress, his fingers upon her breasts.

'I was lying when I said I couldn't remember the last time you came here. I've never forgotten those days – the good times we had together... You loved me then, Jenny Webster – I believe you still do...'

He was not prepared for the force of the blow as Jenny slapped his face, and he recoiled, letting her go. 'Bloody hell!' He put his hand to his stinging cheek. 'Don't be like that –'

'I was trying to bring you to your senses.' She adjusted her dress, determined to stand up to him. 'If you act like a spoiled child, I shall treat you like one. That's the way Alex behaves – when he sees something he wants, he makes a grab for it without stopping to think, but he is only five years old... Isn't it time you grew up?'

The mark of her palm was crimson on his face, and he turned away sulkily. 'I thought you were still fond of me... I didn't mean any harm.'

'I don't suppose you did, but you'll stir up endless trouble and unhappiness if you go on like this. First it was one of the maids, and now this woman at Fallowfield –'

'She's a darling; that husband of hers is a brute... It's not my fault if she's fallen in love with me.'

'It's your fault if you encourage her. Oh Richie, you've got a wife and a family – they're your responsibility. Marrying Polly was the best thing you ever did; don't throw that away just for a bit of fun.'

'Helen's more than that... I tell you, she loves me.'

'And do you love her?'

Richard did not answer. Slowly, he took his jacket off again, and hung it up; then sat at his desk. 'I don't know,' he said at last. 'It's all so difficult – you don't understand... But I'll think over what you said.'

'Please do.' She left him sitting there, staring blindly at the papers

86

spread out before him. She had done all she could; she only hoped she had not made the situation any worse.

In the weeks that followed, Jenny could not decide whether Richard had changed his ways or not. Certainly William never referred to their conversation again, and seemed totally absorbed in the building of the rock garden. Nor did Jenny hear any rumours from below-stairs, though she felt sure Lilian would have been quick to carry tales about Richard, if they were circulating in the servants' hall.

On the other hand, he still disappeared for hours at a time, and frequently stayed out on unexplained business until late in the evening, just as he had done before. Jenny felt uneasy, but there was nothing more to be done. He must solve his own problems now. Only Polly sailed on triumphantly, unaware of these troublesome undercurrents; counting the days on her calendar, supremely confident.

Disaster struck on a Saturday morning.

Over breakfast, William asked Richard if he had any plans for the day. Alice was in London, and would not be home until late.

'I wondered if you and Jenny would care to give me a hand? I'm planning to divert a little stream from the lake, and build a miniature waterfall into the rockery. It'll be a muddy, messy business, but I remember how helpful you were when we cleaned out the drainage channels, some time ago.'

'I'd love to,' said Jenny. 'How about you, Richie?'

'I'm afraid I can't – I've arranged to do something else,' said Richard.

They both looked at him. 'You're going out?' William asked.

'No, I'll be at the farm: I've promised the stable lads a morning's shooting. We've been troubled with a plague of rats in the barns, so I said the boys could take a few pot-shots at them.'

As soon as he had finished his toast and marmalade, he pushed back his chair and left William to explain his scheme to Jenny.

It turned out to be as messy as he had predicted, and she was glad she had put on her oldest clothes. Kneeling at the water's edge, she dredged out the mud, encouraging the water to run among the small stones and trickle down the rocks.

'Not that way, my dear – we'll have to dig out a deeper gully on the other side first; you can't make water run uphill!' He broke off, as a volley of shots rang out in the distance. 'It sounds as if Richard and his lads are waging a full-scale war!'

Jenny saw that his hands shook as he lifted his spade, and she looked up with concern. 'What's the matter? Have you caught a chill?'

'No, no – I'm perfectly well. That noise gets on my nerves, I'm afraid. I've never enjoyed shooting as a sport. I had enough of it, fifteen years ago... More than enough.' His eyes were unfocused, looking beyond her and seeing a different view: a grey landscape where no tree grew, and no flower bloomed. Then he squared his shoulders and got down to work, trying to ignore the next fusillade.

There were still sporadic cracks and bangs going on when Edith came to join them a little later, and she jumped nervously.

'I wish they wouldn't do that...' She turned to her brother: 'William – I thought I should tell you – there are some people at the other end of the garden.'

'People? What people?'

'I don't know – two girls and two young men – I saw them as I walked over from the lodge. They've spread out a tablecloth on the grass, and they're having a picnic.'

'You mean trespassers?' William asked indignantly.

'I suppose they must be. I didn't like to say anything – they seem to be enjoying themselves; they've got thermos flasks and sandwiches and pork pies on paper plates... But I felt you ought to know.'

'Damned cheek!' Another shot rang out, and William let the spade fall from his hands. 'As if we hadn't enough to worry about... I suppose I shall have to say something...'

Jenny rose to her feet, knowing how much her father-in-law hated to meet strangers. 'I'll speak to them if you like. Perhaps they don't realize this is private property.'

'That would be very kind.' William sounded relieved.

'I expect they came in by the footpath behind the churchyard.' Edith tried to make allowances for them. 'There isn't a notice-board there – no gates or fences. It would be a natural mistake.'

'I'll see them off diplomatically.' Jenny turned to Edith: 'Could you show me where they are?'

As they set off together, Edith began gratefully: 'I'm so bad at this sort of thing. If Grace had been with me, she'd have dealt with them – but she was rather tired this morning. I think her leg's been troubling her; I told her she ought to rest it.'

'Oh, dear – is it her rheumatism again?'

'I'm afraid so.' Edith sighed. 'She drives herself too hard. I can never get her to sit down and put her feet up, even at weekends. And on schooldays, she's busy from morning to night.'

'She's always been the same, ever since I can remember,' smiled Jenny.

'Yes, that's why she ought to start taking things easily now. I've talked to her about retiring, but she won't listen... I don't suppose you'd have a word with her...?'

Jenny shook her head. 'I really don't think it would do any good. Once Miss Duncan makes up her mind about something, that's that!... And sometimes it's a mistake to try and interfere in other people's lives...'

'Do you think so?' Edith looked crestfallen.

They turned the corner of the walled vegetable garden, and found that the picnic party was breaking up. They had finished their meal, and were packing things into a wicker basket. The two young men looked up as Edith and Jenny approached, and a girl in a striped blouse and beach shorts said aggressively: 'What do you want?'

'I'm afraid these grounds aren't open to the public,' said Jenny. 'This is a private garden.'

'There's no signs up,' said the girl, defensively. 'How are we supposed to know?'

'All right, Gladys – never mind that,' said the older of the two men. 'We were just going anyhow.'

'In that case I'd be grateful if you would take these bits and pieces with you.' Jenny pointed to some greasy paper plates and an empty paper bag on the lawn.

'Yeah – OK.' He picked them up and turned to his companions: 'Come on – let's get back to the motor.'

'What about Molly? Our friend's gone to look for a convenience,' explained the younger man.

'She can catch us up – she knows where the car is.' The first man seemed anxious to get away. 'Sorry about that – we didn't know.'

'I told you all along it was daft, having a picnic. I'm sure that grass is damp.'

Gladys continued to grumble as they hurried off along the path, in the direction of the village church. Edith breathed a sigh of relief: 'What dreadful people!'

'Oh, they weren't so bad.' As they began to retrace their steps, Jenny said: 'About Grace – I didn't mean to sound unhelpful... I'll speak to her, if you think it will do any good.'

'Would you really – oh, good gracious!' Edith jumped violently as another girl appeared suddenly from behind a bush; she wore a white sun-dress with blue polka-dots, and appeared equally startled.

'Your friends have gone back to the car,' Jenny told her.

'Where –?' She looked round helplessly as if she were lost.

'You see the church spire? Go along that path; you'll soon catch them up.'

'Oh – yes – thank you.' She followed Jenny's instructions, and soon disappeared among the trees.

'I suppose I'd better get back to the rockery. I'm supposed to be helping Lord Minster to build a waterfall,' said Jenny. 'It will be a surprise for Nick, when he comes home.'

'You must be looking forward to that. When is he due to arrive?'

'I don't know exactly; but quite soon.'

She worked for another hour, getting covered in mud, and was rewarded at last when a trickle of water chattered over the stone outcrop, draining away among the pebbles at the foot of the rockery. William patted her on the back.

'Well done! I only hope the channel doesn't block up, when the leaves start to fall.'

'And if it does?'

'If it does – that means wellingtons and waders, and another cold, messy job!'

Jenny laughed, and went off to wash and change. Half-way to the house, she was stopped by one of the stable boys, who mumbled sheepishly: ''Scuse me, ma'am – I bin looking for you all over. Master give me this note for you; he said as I was to hand it to you personal – nobody else.'

She took it from him: a plain buff envelope, used for farm business. As the boy hurried away, she tore it open; inside was a single sheet of paper.

Dear Jenny,
I did not forget what you said. But it isn't as simple as you seem to think. Please come and see me as soon as you can – alone. I must talk to you.

Yours – R.

She hesitated: she was filthy dirty, and it was almost lunchtime. Something in the tone of the letter suggested that it was urgent, but

90

she did not want to keep the family waiting. She took a few steps towards the house – then stopped, seeing Polly and Alex upon the path ahead. Polly waved to her cheerfully.

She was suddenly very conscious of the letter in her hand; Polly would recognize the handwriting on the envelope, and might wonder why her husband should be writing to Jenny.

She screwed the letter up, and called out: 'I'll be in presently! I shan't be long!' Then she walked away, towards the farm buildings.

There was no one in the office. Richard's jacket hung on the back of his chair, so he could not have gone very far. In the corner, an old-fashioned iron stove smoked and spluttered: Jenny levered up the lid, tossed the crumpled letter inside and watched it burn. Then she waited for Richard to come back.

After some minutes, she walked out into the yard. There was nobody there, either. She called Richard's name, but there was no reply.

She crossed the yard and looked inside the stables. The loose boxes were empty, too; the horses must be out in the paddock. A wooden ladder led up to the loft – and at the sight of it, her heart beat faster. This was where she used to meet Richie, years ago. She tried to put the thought from her mind ... The trapdoor stood open now. Could he be up there – waiting for her? Was it some sort of trick? She was tempted to turn and walk away, but something drove her on.

Slowly – cautiously – she climbed the ladder, scrambling up into the hay-loft.

He was there, lying on the straw, with his back to her. Somewhere a drowsy bluebottle buzzed.

'Richie – what are you playing at?'

She took a step towards him: for a moment she thought he was asleep – but she saw that the straw covered his head ... Then she saw the bluebottle, and the pool of blood ...

Dropping to her knees, she pulled the straw away frantically, pulling him towards her. His eyes were open, wide and staring; there was blood everywhere.

And Richard was dead.

6

SATURDAY, 14 OCTOBER 1933

At the same moment, in their Curzon Street flat, Gina put down the phone and turned to Sir Charles. 'That was Alice. She asked us to excuse her this afternoon; she's finished her duties at the Palace earlier than she expected, so she's going straight back to Crown House.'

'I'm sorry; I was looking forward to seeing her,' said Charlie.

'Never mind. Now we can do what I wanted all along.' Gina took out her compact and lipstick, and crossed to the mirror. 'We'll drive over to Chelsea and sign up with the BUF.'

'Oh, no, Gina – I don't think that's a good idea . . .'

'What are you so jittery about? We go to all their meetings; it's time we took out membership. I'm going to support Tom all the way.'

'I'm not sure about that.' Sir Charles Bowyer fingered his tie nervously. 'A lot of people are having serious second thoughts about Mosley; I think we'd be well-advised to refrain from any definite commitment.'

Gina applied the final touch of lip-gloss, and turned to her husband. 'How do I look? I want to make a good impression; Tom's friends are always so stylish.'

'Didn't you hear what I said? I have no intention of joining the Fascists – not yet, anyway. Perhaps in time, when things settle down –'

'Honey, you do what the hell you like – I don't give a damn,' said Gina crisply, putting on her hat and taking one last look at her reflection. 'If you won't come with me, I'll go by myself.'

The BUF had taken over a building in the Kings Road as their headquarters, but the enquiry office on the ground floor was not quite as stylish as Gina had anticipated. The furniture was severely functional; some boldly lettered posters on the wall proclaimed 'Britain First!' and 'Action – Now!' and a sour-faced lady in tweeds sat at a wooden table, sorting through piles of leaflets. She might have been the headmistress of an old-established girls' school.

'Yes?' She ran her eye over Gina's fashionable two-piece in yellow and black silk, looking with disfavour at the long yellow feather that quivered above the shiny black straw. 'Can I help you?' Her inflection implied that this would be highly unlikely.

Gina flashed a brilliant smile and explained that she was Lady Bowyer – that she wished to become a member of the party – and that she had been an ardent follower and a close friend of darling Tom for several years.

'Really.' The lady was not impressed. 'We require rather more than that as qualification for membership. This is not a social club.'

'Oh, but I'm terribly keen on the movement; you only have to ask Tom – he'll tell you.'

'If you are referring to Sir Oswald Mosley, I must tell you that Our Leader does not take any active part in recruiting members himself. You must fill up a form and apply through the usual channels; your application will be considered in due course by the committee, and *if* you are accepted – which would of course depend entirely on the committee's decision –'

An inner door opened, and a masculine voice said: 'All right, Constance – I'll take over, shall I? It must be almost time for tea; would you like to put the kettle on?'

'Oh... Very well... There's a person here enquiring about membership.'

'So I gathered. Thank you, Constance; you can leave this to me.'

Constance raised her eyebrows and disappeared into the other room.

The newcomer grinned at Gina; and her spirits, which had begun to nose-dive during the last few minutes, took an upward turn. He was a young man in his early thirties, with blond, wavy hair and the build of an athlete – shown off to advantage in the smart BUF uniform of black shirt and trousers.

'Dear Constance has a heart of gold, but rather an unfortunate

93

manner sometimes,' he said. 'My name is Roland Voss; how do you do, Lady Bowyer?'

They shook hands, and Gina said: 'I've seen you at meetings – sometimes you've been on the platform, sitting near Tom.'

'And sometimes I stay in the body of the hall, helping to deal with trouble-makers.' When he smiled, a dimple appeared at the corner of his mouth. 'It's good to know you're a loyal supporter: I'm sure you're just the sort of recruit we need in the party. I can promise there will be plenty for you to do.'

'I'm more than happy to help you – in any way I can,' said Gina.

By the time she got back to Curzon Street, she was feeling very cheerful, and told Charlie that she had had a very satisfactory afternoon. 'Some snooty bitch tried to choke me off, but she soon realized she'd made a mistake. I always believe in going straight to the top, and Roland was so friendly –'

'Who?'

'Roland Voss – you must remember him; he's at all the meetings – practically Tom's right-hand man. He says I'm going to be a really useful member – look!' She pointed to the badge on her lapel – the lightning-flash Fascist emblem – and added proudly, 'He pinned it on me himself – isn't that cute?'

When Alice walked into Crown House, she already knew something was wrong, for she had seen the police car parked in the drive. Lilian Brooks was at the foot of the main staircase, talking to William; her eyes were wide, and she looked very frightened. A uniformed police constable stood nearby, as if he were on guard. As soon as he saw Alice, he walked towards her.

'Excuse me, madam,' he began, but William was there before him.

'This is my wife,' he said, putting his arm round Alice as if to protect her.

'What is it? What's happened?' she asked.

He did not reply, but began to lead her away, saying, 'It was just before lunch, when Jenny . . .' His mouth was dry; he moistened his lips and continued: 'I tried to get hold of you – I telephoned the Palace, but I was told you had already gone. Then I tried Eaton Square, but you'd left there too – and Caro wasn't at home.'

'No, she's with her friend, Muriel somebody – what's happened to Jenny? She's not hurt?'

'No, no, Jenny's perfectly all right.' William opened the drawing-room door, then stopped, seeing Edith and Grace were in the room.

At the sight of Alice, Edith burst into tears, and buried her face in her hands. Grace tried to calm her, murmuring, 'There, there, my dear – don't give way.' Then, to Lord Minster: 'Is there anything I can do to help?'

'Perhaps if you could take Edith to another room . . . I should like to be alone with my wife.'

'Yes, indeed. Edith – come now – we must not intrude.'

They moved to the door. At the threshold, Edith turned and sobbed: 'Alice – I'm so sorry – so very sorry . . .'

Then Grace led her away, and the door closed behind them. Alice gripped William's hands; her face was white. 'For God's sake tell me! It's Nicholas, isn't it? His ship –'

William helped her into a chair and knelt beside her. 'You must be very brave, my darling. It's not Nicholas . . . It's Richard. This morning, he was out shooting with some of the stable lads, and –'

Alice felt the breath rush from her lungs. With an effort, she heaved a deep sigh, gulping in air, before she could form the words: 'He's – dead – isn't he?'

William nodded, and she clung to him. The world had fallen apart, and without William's strength, she would have collapsed.

'How –?' She was still fighting for breath. 'How did it happen? Some stupid accident – with a gun –?'

'We don't know exactly how it happened. The police are still asking questions. But –' William too found it hard to get the words out. 'The worst thing is – they say it wasn't an accident.'

Jenny faced Inspector Rudge across the desk in the farm office, and tried to answer his questions clearly and calmly.

She was still numb from the shock of finding Richard's body in the stable-loft; she wanted to help the police, but she felt as if she were recounting a bad dream: it all seemed unreal and impossible. The events immediately before and after the discovery were blurred and jumbled together, and it was difficult to make them coherent.

'Take your time, Mrs Gaunt; there's no hurry.' The inspector was a heavily built man in late middle age, with a kind smile; but his eyes were shrewd. 'Let's go back to the very beginning, shall we? You say you received a message from Viscount Ebony when you were on your way in to lunch?'

'Yes – it was given to me by Pearson – one of the stable lads.'

The inspector made a note, then asked: 'What time would that have been, exactly?'

'I'm not sure – I'd been working on the new rockery with Lord Minster; we'd just finished making a waterfall...' Her voice shook; it sounded absurdly trivial, in the light of what had happened at the stables. 'When I looked at my watch, I think it was about a quarter past twelve.'

'Yes, His Lordship told me you were with him all the morning.'

'Except for about twenty minutes, when I had to go with Lady Edith – she was rather upset because there were some trespassers in the garden, having a picnic, so I offered to go and speak to them.'

The inspector was immediately interested. 'These people were strangers, then? Can you describe them to me?'

Jenny did her best, and he made several more notes.

'So you were with Lady Edith Gaunt throughout this period? What time would that have been?'

'About eleven o'clock – I really can't remember... Does it matter?'

'It might do. According to the doctor's preliminary report, death probably occurred between ten-thirty and eleven-thirty.'

'I see.' Jenny shivered, involuntarily. 'I remember hearing some shots when Lady Edith came to find us... But that couldn't have had anything to do with – Viscount Ebony's death – could it? He was with the other men, shooting rats in the barns –'

'He had been. But at some stage he left them taking pot-shots with a rook-rifle, while he went back to the stables carrying his own gun. One shot more or less around that time would not have attracted any attention. He was using an old service revolver, apparently; it had been issued to Lord Minster, during the war, and it was kept at the farm as a protection against vermin... You didn't happen to see it, did you?'

'A revolver? No, I've never seen it.'

'I meant – you didn't see it this morning, in the loft? It was only a few feet away from the body, among the straw.'

'No!... I didn't stop to look – when I saw Richard was dead, all I could think of was getting help... I went down the ladder and out into the yard, calling somebody – anybody... I'm sorry, it's all so confused – I really don't remember.'

'So if you didn't see the gun, you certainly couldn't have wiped any fingerprints from it?'

'Of course not.' Jenny stared at him. 'What do you mean?'

96

'Someone did. Not very efficiently – there are still traces of half a dozen prints, because the shooting party had been taking turns to use it. They're too smudged for any positive identification... But that was the weapon which killed Viscount Ebony; and I think we can assume it was wiped by whoever pulled the trigger.'

Jenny closed her eyes, but that did not help. She would never be able to blot out the image of the dead face, the sightless eyes, the small round bullet-hole...

'Forgive me for putting you through this ordeal, madam, but I'm afraid it is necessary,' the inspector went on. 'I'd like to get back to this message you were speaking about, the one given you by Mr –' He consulted his notebook. 'Pearson... What did the letter say, exactly?'

Jenny tried to recall the words: 'Something like – "*I haven't forgotten what you said. It's not as simple as you think. Come and see me – alone – I must talk to you.*" And he signed it with his initial – "R".'

'Just the letter R? No "yours truly" or anything like that? "With love", perhaps?'

She looked up quickly, sensing a hidden meaning in his tone. 'I think it said "*Yours – R.*" I only read it once; then I screwed it up.'

'Why did you do that? The message annoyed you, did it?'

'No, but...' Jenny tried to think; she wanted to tell the truth, but she wouldn't say more than she had to. 'I suppose it was silly of me – I saw Polly walking towards me – Richard's wife. I didn't want her to see his handwriting on the envelope; she might have wondered why he wanted to see me.'

'And why did he want to see you?'

'I don't know. When I got there – he was dead ... I told you.'

The inspector stroked his chin. 'You said just now that the message began with the words: "*I haven't forgotten what you said.*" What did that refer to?'

'Oh – it was a domestic problem we talked about a few weeks earlier – nothing important.'

'But important enough for you to conceal it from Lady Ebony?'

Jenny stammered slightly: 'I – I didn't want to trouble her with it – she is expecting a baby very soon, so –'

'Quite so.' He held his hand out. 'May I see the letter, Mrs Gaunt?'

Jenny wondered why she had ever thought his expression was kindly. The eyes that looked into hers were as cold and hard as steel.

'I'm sorry. I haven't got the letter now. I burnt it – in the stove.'

There was a long silence and then the inspector said, 'I'm afraid I shall have to insist that you tell me the exact nature of the domestic problem you had been discussing with Viscount Ebony.'

The evening really went wrong when Scott noticed the badge on his sister's lapel.

'What in hell is that?' he asked, angrily.

Scott had called in for drinks at the Bowyers' flat, after supper. He was aware of a slight strain in the atmosphere as soon as he arrived. Gina was in high good humour, if a little over-excited, but Charlie was very subdued and seemed to have something on his mind.

Gina kept the conversation going, talking at length about her best friends ('Did you ever meet Wallis Simpson? Oh, you really should – she's such a sweetheart, you'd be crazy about her: I met her when she first came over – she goes around with Thelma Furness – that's how she met the Prince of Wales; I hear she and that dreary husband of hers are regular guests at Fort Belvedere these days . . .') and then moved on to the Minster family ('Isn't it strange, even with their connections with the Royals, they never seem to move in the right circles? They will stay buried alive in the country where nothing ever happens – wouldn't you go totally insane with boredom?') and she couldn't resist a little dig about Caroline: 'Such a pretty girl – so attractive – I don't blame you for chasing her, sweetie. But I guess you handled it badly – and now of course she's got the pick of all the best young men in London . . .'

'You could have fooled me,' growled Scott. 'Judging by the guy she's hanging around with . . .' Too late, he decided to change the subject. 'Did you ever see *King Kong*?'

Gina hooted with laughter: 'You mean to say she's having a passionate romance with a giant ape?'

'Lay off, will you? I happened to think of it, because I saw Caro coming out of the movie-house one time, with her new beau.'

'She has a beau? Who is it? Anyone we know?' Gina was all agog.

Scott cursed himself for saying too much; but at that instant his eye fell upon the lightning-flash badge, and he found an outlet for his feelings. 'I don't believe it! You're not seriously joining Mosley's bully-boys?' he demanded. 'Charlie – is this true? You've actually enlisted in that band of thugs?'

Quickly, Sir Charles replenished Scott's drink. 'Certainly not – I wouldn't dream of it,' he said. 'Though I admit there's a good deal of sense in Sir Oswald's views upon the economic system. But like all political theories, the good ideas are mixed with the bad – so I prefer to remain an interested onlooker. Unlike Gina, I shall not become personally involved.'

'I swear to God, Charlie, when you die I'll have you buried half in and half out of the churchyard – and on your tombstone they'll put: "Here lies Sir Charles Bowyer – still on the fence"!' exclaimed Gina, tinkling the ice-cubes in her glass. 'Don't I get a refill too?'

Sir Charles, who was twenty years older than his wife, was not amused by this flight of fancy, but poured her another drink without a word while she continued: 'Anyhow, I'm not scared to stand up for Tom – one of these days he'll be the leader of this country, and then you'll see I was right. He's Britain's only hope; that's why I joined the BUF.'

'You want Britain to become another dictatorship? Are you out of your mind? Don't you see what's happening in Italy? in Germany?'

The argument rolled on, and both sides became more and more heated. Sir Charles said nothing, but occupied himself by pouring more drinks. When the gin bottle was empty, he announced that he was going to bed.

'Good night, Scott,' he said. 'I think it's a mistake to get into an argument about politics or religion; it always creates bad feeling.' Turning to Gina, he added, 'Don't sit up too long, my dear.'

When they were alone, Gina said, 'Poor darling – he hasn't any opinions of his own, so he hates it when I do... Hey, listen – if we're fresh out of gin, there's probably some brandy in the decanter – how about a snifter?'

Five minutes later, when Scott was sitting on the floor at her feet, a balloon-glass cradled in his hands, she brought the conversation round to Caroline again.

'I almost forgot – you were going to tell me about the new boyfriend, and we got side-tracked... What's he like?'

Scott stared into his glass, inhaling the fumes. 'I wouldn't call him "new" exactly. "Ancient" would be a better description...' He couldn't resist telling her now. 'He's a friend of the family – and a friend of yours... And he must be twice her age – probably more.'

'What are you saying? She's having a fling with a friend of mine? Scottie, do tell!'

He blinked up at his sister, trying to focus upon her. 'Promise you won't say anything? He's a guy called Weyman – Paul Weyman.'

He shut his eyes, and swayed a little. 'Every time I think of it, I want to throw up . . .'

Alice and William had been sitting in silence for a long time. He had his arm round her shoulders; there was nothing more that either of them could say.

A respectful knocking at the door roused them. William looked up and said, 'Come in.'

The young policeman entered tentatively. 'Excuse me, my lord – Inspector Rudge's compliments, and he'd be pleased if you could spare him a few minutes, in the farm office.'

'I see . . .' William looked at Alice. 'Will you be all right?'

She nodded, but he was still doubtful. 'I don't like to leave you on your own. Perhaps if Edith and Grace –'

'No.' Alice stood up, suddenly conscience-stricken. 'Where is Polly? I must go to her. How terrible – all this time, I've thought of no one but myself – I must see Polly. How is she?'

'Doctor Parry has been with her. She may be asleep by now.'

'I shall go to her anyway.'

Alice made her way to the bedroom which Polly and Richard had shared ever since their marriage. It was dark outside, and the light-brackets in the upstairs passages threw unexpected shadows. Everything seemed alien and unfriendly; in the space of a few seconds, life itself had changed out of all recognition, and Alice felt like a stranger in her own house.

Dr Parry, a balding, red-faced man with horn-rimmed spectacles, had his hand on Polly's wrist, checking her pulse rate. Seeing Alice, he came over to her, saying softly, 'I gave Lady Ebony something to help her sleep. She'll have a peaceful night, at least.' He cleared his throat, then added, 'May I say how extremely sorry I am – you know you have my sympathy in this tragic loss –'

'Yes – thank you –' Alice cut in quickly. 'That sleeping-pill you gave her, or whatever it was – it couldn't harm the baby in any way, could it?'

'No, no; you may take my word for that.' He glanced at his watch. 'Dear me – it's getting rather late – I think, if you will excuse me . . .'

'Of course. I shall sit with Polly for a while. Good night, Doctor.'

When he had gone the room seemed very quiet. Alice took his place beside the bed, looking at Polly; her face was calm, but a little shadowed by sadness. For a moment, Alice had the horrifying impression that Polly too had passed from this life and was looking down at the unhappy world from another plane altogether, with gentle pity for our human frailties... She pulled herself together; she must not entertain such fantasies – the girl had a good colour; her breathing was slow but regular.

Then Polly stirred, turning her head upon the pillow, and opened her eyes. She did not appear to recognize Alice at first, and seemed to be still half-asleep. Her words, when they came, went straight to Alice's heart.

'Richard... I dreamed he was dead.' After a pause she continued, in the same tone, 'But it wasn't a dream, was it?'

She spoke like someone in a trance. Alice struggled to find an answer to her question, and said at last, 'Try not to worry about it now. Try to rest. Things will be better soon... Think about your new baby.'

Polly studied her gravely for another long moment, then said, 'Yes – that's right. My baby... I must think of my baby. He's the only thing that matters now.' And she closed her eyes, sinking back into a deep sleep.

The creak of the bedroom door made Alice look round, and she caught her breath. A small figure in striped pyjamas was peering into the room, trailing a teddy bear.

'Mummy... I want Mummy,' said Alexander.

Alice went to him immediately, gathering him up in her arms.

'Sssh, darling – Mummy's asleep; we mustn't wake her,' she whispered. 'Just look at poor Teddy! He's sleepy too. Let Grandma take you both back to the nursery...'

Inspector Rudge stood up as William entered the office.

'Ah, come in, my lord – take a seat, would you? I'm sorry to have to trouble you again; I've taken statements from various people, and there are just one or two minor details I'd like to clear up tonight, if you wouldn't mind.'

'Certainly.' William took the chair that was offered to him. 'Though I don't quite see what else I can tell you; as I said before, I did not see my son again, after breakfast.'

'No, sir. But this is more in the nature of background information. The question I have to ask you is rather a delicate one, I'm afraid.' The inspector laced his fingers together, regarding them thoughtfully. 'Would you describe the late Viscount Ebony as a man of principle, as far as women were concerned?' He glanced up to see the effect of his words upon Lord Minster.

William frowned, taking his time before framing a reply. 'That is certainly a very difficult question for me to answer. My son was a healthy young man, with normally healthy appetites. He was fond of women, certainly; but he had also been happily married for the last five – nearly six years. He and his wife were devoted to one another.'

'Yes, sir.' The inspector's face was expressionless. 'But before his marriage, I gather he had something of a reputation as – shall we say – a ladies' man?'

'He sowed his wild oats, no doubt.' William shifted in his chair. 'I'm afraid I don't see the relevance of this line of enquiry.'

'But it might be relevant, sir, if we could establish that in recent months the Viscount had begun to kick over the traces again . . . ?'

William gazed straight ahead of him, at a calendar on the wall. 'Have you been listening to rumours, Inspector? Idle gossip and speculation?'

'I have here a signed statement made by your other daughter-in-law, Mrs Gaunt, in which she explains the reason for her visit to the farm this morning, and also on another occasion a few weeks ago. She had some cause for concern about His Lordship's behaviour, seemingly.'

William's shoulders sagged a little. 'She told you that? Yes, of course – she had to tell the truth.' He passed a hand over his face, realizing suddenly how tired he was; he had felt exhausted ever since lunch, but had tried to fight it off. 'God forgive me, I had no right to involve that poor girl in Richard's problems . . .'

'*You* involved her?' The inspector's face changed. 'Now that's something I didn't know. She implied that she had acted on her own initiative.'

'Did she? . . . Dear Jenny . . .' William closed his eyes for a moment. 'I must be absolutely frank with you: I had heard the same rumours myself, and I was very concerned about them. I tried to speak to my son, without much success, and then – I suggested to Jenny that she might succeed where I had failed. I wish to God I had not meddled . . . But he has always been – he had always been extremely fond of Jenny.'

'Yes, sir. I believe that there had in fact been a romance between them at one time?'

'You have done your work well, Inspector. Yes, it's no great secret – but of course that was all over long ago, before either of them was married.'

'Has it ever struck you, sir, that it might not have been over? That when Mrs Gaunt began to make these clandestine visits to the stables – there might have been another reason for them? That possibly the affair could have started up, all over again?'

Jenny was in the drawing-room with Grace and Edith; they had both been very kind; and yet their sympathy did not touch her. It was as if she were protected within a hard shell, which kept out every kind of emotion.

When Alice returned, Grace said, 'We'd best be getting back to our own place. We all need some sleep, I'm sure of that.'

As soon as she had taken Edith off to the lodge, Alice sighed, and dropped into a chair.

'Sleep . . . It would be a blessing, but I wonder if I shall . . . My thoughts keep racing round and round – it's all so unthinkable, I still haven't really taken it in . . . William's with the police inspector again; goodness knows what they're talking about.'

'How's Polly?'

'She is asleep, thank heaven. Dr Parry gave her some kind of sedative. I sat with her for a while, and then Alex came in; I had to carry him back to the nursery, poor little mite. We shall have to look after him; Polly won't be in a fit state, I'm afraid.'

'I'll help; we can take turns with Alex. I'd like to.'

'Thank you, dear. I know you were very fond of Richard; this must have been a terrible shock for you – especially as you were the one who – who found . . .' She could not finish the sentence.

Jenny stood up. 'I think, if you don't mind, I'll look for something to read. Perhaps if I take a book up with me, I might get to sleep eventually.'

Jenny went to the library. She did not particularly want to read, and sleep seemed impossibly far away – but above all, she wanted to be on her own. She had not been alone all day, ever since she went to the stables to look for Richie . . .

She sat in one of the wing-backed library chairs, trying to analyze her mental paralysis. Perhaps this was the normal after-effect of shock, this cold, numb feeling. The family were treating her like a piece of fragile porcelain that might easily be shattered. Everyone knew that she and Richie had been lovers, and they assumed she must be suffering unbearable grief.

But she could not grieve. It was too sudden; and she had not loved him for a long time. Lately, she had found him selfish and thoughtless, concerned only with his own pleasures, never giving a thought to anyone else. She could not shed tears for Richie – not yet.

She tried to think of him as he had been, seven years earlier; so young and handsome, so full of life and excitement... But she still felt curiously detached; that carefree young couple, loving and laughing together, were like two strangers, people she could scarcely remember.

The library was lit by one green-shaded lamp on the desk, so it was startling when the door opened, and someone switched on the overhead light.

'They said I'd find you here,' said Nicholas. 'What in God's name has been going on?'

She gave an inarticulate cry, and ran to him: now the tears she had held back all day burst through her defences, and she wept helplessly in his arms. He talked to her softly, holding her very close, until she stopped crying and was able to tell him what had happened.

'...But the police say it couldn't have been an accident,' she finished at last. 'I still don't understand it – they believe Richie was killed deliberately – murdered...'

'There is something else I don't understand.' She was on his lap, and she could feel his muscles, hard and tense, against her. 'You say you went to the farm this morning, to see Richard. But you didn't say why.'

She looked at him in bewilderment: 'Yes, I told you, he sent me a note by one of the stable lads –'

'Asking you to meet him in the hay-loft? Alone?'

'No – it wasn't like that! Nick, for heaven's sake – what are you saying?'

'I'm not saying anything. I'm simply asking why you went to meet my brother – in the same old place you used to go, whenever he wanted to –'

Pulling free, she scrambled to her feet. 'How can you say such a thing? You must be mad – Richie's dead, and you don't even seem to care – all you can think of is your insane jealousy –'

The door opened again, and Inspector Rudge walked in, without knocking.

'Good evening, sir – Lieutenant Gaunt, I believe? My name is Rudge. Medford Police. I was on my way home when my men told me you were here; I've been looking forward to meeting you ... You'll forgive me interrupting like this, madam?'

'Yes – of course.' Jenny felt isolated and utterly lost, not knowing what to say or what to think.

Nicholas stood up, erect and imposing in his naval uniform. 'How do you do, Inspector? I'm afraid I can't be of much assistance to you, as I only arrived a few minutes ago.'

'Yes, sir, quite so. And that's the very point I wanted to bring up. You see, I made enquiries earlier today, and I gather that your ship docked at Portsmouth some time yesterday evening – over twenty-four hours ago, in actual fact.'

Jenny stared at Nick: 'What? You didn't tell me –'

'It was late; I'd missed the last train to London,' said Nick.

'You could have phoned me.'

'I wanted to surprise you,' he said.

'Do I take it you decided to stay overnight in Portsmouth and travel down today, sir?' the Inspector asked politely. 'But then surely you would have arrived at Crown House long before this?'

'I – I stopped off in London.' Nicholas's voice faltered slightly. 'I had some personal business to attend to.'

'Indeed, sir?' The inspector turned from Nicholas to Jenny. 'As I was about to enter the room, I fancy I heard you mention the word "jealousy", madam. Quite a coincidence, because that's a word which has been at the back of my mind all the evening.'

He walked up to Nicholas. 'Let me put a hypothesis to you, Lieutenant. If you left Portsmouth by an early train this morning, and got a good connection at Waterloo, it strikes me you could have been in Medford by ten a.m. Then you would have arrived here some time between ten-thirty and eleven-thirty ... Isn't that so?'

7

SUNDAY, 15 OCTOBER TO TUESDAY, 17 OCTOBER 1933

Nobody had told Old Bea. William should have done so; but Saturday afternoon and evening had been taken up with emergency action in the face of the crisis, and he had kept putting this unpleasant duty aside, to be dealt with later. By the time the inspector and his men had left Crown House, the old lady had retired for the night, so he had to postpone it once more. Early the following morning, he went up to her bedroom.

She took the news surprisingly well. Once the initial shock had passed, she remarked, 'I am exceedingly sorry – but I can't pretend that I'm surprised. There was bad blood in that poor boy; he got it from his grandfather's side of the family.'

William began to defend Richard: 'He was a little wild, perhaps, but he meant no harm –'

'Of course he didn't mean it – but the fact remains, he has brought disgrace upon the family – lack of discipline, lack of backbone. He'd begun sporting with young women again; I suppose you didn't know that?'

Not for the first time, William was startled by his mother's perspicacity.

'Yes, Mama, I knew it; I didn't expect that you would.'

'I keep my ears open,' said the Countess, grimly. 'None of you ever tells me what is going on, so I have to scrape my news together from the servants' gossip. They're always in the know.' She leaned back against the pillows, asking, 'And when is the funeral to take place?'

'We can't fix a date yet; there has to be an inquest first.'

'Ah, yes... It's all very disagreeable – bound to cause a great deal of talk, but that can't be helped... Send for Lilian Brooks; I want to get dressed. I shall come to church with you this morning.'

'Are you sure you feel strong enough, Mama? You haven't been out of the house for a long time.'

'There hasn't been a death in the family for a long time. And since there's no knowing when the boy's funeral will take place, we must pay our respects – and we must be seen together, a united family.' She threw back the bedclothes. 'Pass me my dressing-gown, and help me out of bed.'

William lifted his mother up and set her on her feet; small and bird-boned, she weighed next to nothing.

'And we must pray for your grandson,' Old Bea continued. 'You realize that child is now Viscount Ebony – your heir...? God help us all.'

Nicholas and Jenny were alone in the breakfast-room. Polly was still asleep upstairs, and Alice had gone to supervise breakfast in the nursery. Jenny broke the silence.

'I said I would take Alex for a walk later on.'

Nicholas glanced at the grey sky through the windows. 'It looks like rain.'

'Then he can put on his mackintosh and wellingtons and splash in the puddles.'

They spoke to one another politely, relieved to have found a topic that could be discussed without anger or resentment. Last night had been a hideous experience for them both. Nick began by losing his temper with the inspector, objecting violently to being under suspicion, even hypothetically. Like Jenny, he had an alibi for the time of Richard's death; his personal business in London had been a visit to a jeweller in Hatton Garden, which had taken up most of the morning.

'My wife's birthday is less than two months away; I was ordering a small gift for her,' he explained gruffly. 'So much for my hopes of surprising you, Jenny.'

She took his hand and squeezed it, touched by this token of his love.

But when they went up to their room, the questioning began again.

'Why did you go to see Richard at the stables? Why did you have to see him secretly? Why didn't you want Polly to know? What were you trying to hide?'

She was torn between pity and anger; pity because he was torturing himself with these suspicions – and anger that he was not able to trust her, even now.

'I keep telling you – Richard had been making a fool of himself. There was some trouble about one of the maids; then he started going further afield. Your father asked me to speak to him, and I said I would: I hoped it might bring him to his senses, but I don't think it did any good. Yesterday morning he asked me to go and see him – it sounded as if he was in some sort of trouble, so I went . . . But by the time I got there –'

The sentence hung in the air, as she saw it all happening again, like a film that ran forever in her brain; the body rolling over, the head lolling towards her, the staring eyes – the bullet-hole . . .

Nick read the horror in her face, and his heart went out to her. 'Dear God – I'm sorry – I keep flying into a rage . . . What's the matter with me?' He took her in his arms. 'Forgive me: I can't help it.'

'I know.'

Even so, when they got into bed, they both lay awake for a long while in the darkness: together, but apart.

Now, as they stood at the breakfast-room window, Jenny said, 'You were right.'

'Right?' He echoed the word sharply.

'It's begun to rain already.' Big drops spattered the stone flags on the terrace. 'What a miserable day.'

William walked in, saying, 'Mama's getting dressed. She's determined to go to church this morning.'

Nick frowned: 'Do you think she's up to it?'

'I tried to dissuade her, but she insists we must all go – we must be seen to face the situation, not run away from it. I hope you'll both come with us?'

'I suppose so . . . She may be right.' Nick turned away. 'Anyhow, it might do the old girl good. The excitement's probably set the blood pounding through her veins.'

'Nick!' Jenny put a hand on his arm.

'Sorry. But you know what I mean.' Nick walked away to the console table, where the Sunday papers were laid out, still unread. 'I suppose next we shall have the newspaper reporters ringing up.'

'Hawkins tells me he's already taken calls from the *Medford Gazette* and the *News of the World.*' William sat on the deep window-seat, next to Jenny. 'He told them I wasn't available to come to the telephone; they won't got much change out of Hawkins.'

'But how did the news get out so quickly?' Jenny asked.

'Goodness only knows. I tried to speak to Caroline again, but she's staying with this girl friend of hers – she's not expected back till teatime.' William sighed. 'Thank heaven Martin and Miranda are away at school; they will have to be told, of course – at least they've been spared the worst of it.'

'I keep thinking of Polly – what she must be going through...' Jenny went to the door. 'I'll just slip up and see how she is. Are you coming, Nick?'

'No, you go ahead. I want a word with Pa.'

As soon as she had gone, Nicholas turned to his father. He spoke quietly, but there was no mistaking the raw pain in his voice. 'Jenny tells me you asked her to get mixed up in this filthy business about Richard. How could you do such a thing?'

William looked up as Nick came towards him, and asked simply, 'Do you suppose I haven't reproached myself with that ever since? All I can say is that it didn't seem unreasonable at the time. I was desperately concerned about Richard –'

'You didn't spare a moment's concern for Jenny, I suppose? You never thought what it might do to her? Or to me?' Nick stood over his father, struggling to contain his anger. 'I would never have believed you could be so selfish.'

William accepted the accusation: 'I did what I thought was best. I did it for the sake of the family ... I couldn't have guessed it would turn out as it did.' He rose to his feet, meeting Nick's gaze directly. 'If you think that was selfish of me – you may be right. But perhaps you should examine your own reactions a little more closely. Isn't there a certain amount of selfishness there, as well?'

Somehow the dreadful day wore on. The weather remained bleak and cheerless, and when the church party set out, they were huddled under umbrellas. William and Alice accompanied Lady Beatrice in the car for the short drive to St Peter's; all the family wore black except little Alex, who was in a sailor suit. The villagers stood in the churchyard, sheltering under the yew trees and whispering; they fell silent as the party from Crown House walked up the mossy path, and then the Minsters heard the whispers beginning again.

Polly, of course, remained at home; still in bed, suspended in limbo, somewhere between sleeping and waking.

Before they left the house, Jenny had brought Alex in to see his mother, saying, 'We thought he might like to come to church with us – will that be all right?'

'If you like.' Polly sounded apathetic.

'And this afternoon I could take him to tea with Edith and Grace, perhaps?'

'Whatever you think. I don't mind.' The only time Polly showed any interest was when Jenny was about to leave, and then she asked suddenly: 'How many days is it now?'

'Days?'

'Till the baby's due. I seem to have lost track of time.'

'It's almost exactly three weeks, isn't it? Twenty-one days, more or less.'

'Yes...' Polly put a hand out and touched Alex's hair. 'That's something to look forward to – twenty-one more days, and you'll have a baby brother.'

'I'd rather have a puppy,' said Alex.

Jenny scooped him up: 'Come along, love – we mustn't be late for church.'

As they were going out, Alex asked, 'Is Daddy coming to church as well?'

'No – not today,' said Jenny quickly, glancing back at the bed. But Polly's eyes were already closed, and she did not appear to have heard.

Caro rang home at five, as soon as she got back to Eaton Square, and William broke the news over the telephone. By eight, she had reached Crown House. On the journey down, alone in a first-class carriage, she had had time to dry her tears and make her plans.

'Have you had any more calls from the press?' she asked her parents.

'Two more – the *Sunday Dispatch* and *Reynolds News*. But Hawkins wouldn't put them through to me,' William told her.

'Good. From now on, if anyone calls, I'll speak to them,' she said. 'I've rung Binns at the *Argus* and he told me to cover the story, so they're getting an exclusive. I'll stay here as long as you need me.'

Alice hugged her. 'Bless you – you don't know what a comfort that is. I still can't imagine how everyone found out so quickly.'

'You can't keep these things quiet.' Caro explained. 'Probably someone at the police station in Medford got wind of it – a clerk in the office, one of the cleaners, even – then it got to the *Gazette*, and they'd pass it on to Fleet Street right away.'

'Surely not?' Alice was dismayed. 'I always thought Mr Palfreyman was so nice.'

'Oh, not the editor!' Caro corrected her. 'Dear old Palfrey wouldn't dream of it – but there's a drunken reprobate called Mac in the newsroom – he's the stringer for half a dozen national papers. He'd sell his own granny for the right price.'

'That's disgraceful! You used to work at the *Gazette* – isn't there any loyalty?'

'Provincial hacks have to earn a living; it's the same everywhere. Don't worry – we'll keep the jackals at bay.'

But the press would not be fobbed off by Hawkins's stonewalling tactics for long. On Monday morning, the reporters began to arrive in person. At eleven o'clock, Hawkins reported to Lord and Lady Minster that there were several uninvited guests from Fleet Street outside the house.

'I explained that your lordship had important matters to attend to, and told them you were not seeing anyone, but they won't go away. They're out there on the terrace, waiting. Some of them found their way round to the tradesmen's entrance, trying to get the younger members of the staff to talk – promising them their pictures in the paper and suchlike. I packed 'em off pretty smartly, I can tell you.'

'Oh, dear...' Alice looked at William in despair. 'How long do you suppose this will go on?'

'It's outrageous – I refuse to be a captive in my own house!' grumbled William. 'Surely the police could do something?'

So far the actual press coverage had been comparatively restrained. Due to a lack of any real information, the more conservative newspapers only carried small items in the Monday morning editions ('Tragic death of Peer's eldest son' – 'Shooting accident in Kent') while the popular dailies asked provocative questions ('Who is mystery assassin?' – 'Why did Viscount die?').

Alice had taken one look at the papers and pushed them aside, sickened; but Caro read them carefully, then stood up, saying, 'I think Pa's right. It's time the inspector took a firm line. I shall go and speak to him.'

Half an hour later, to their surprise, the pressmen were invited to enter Crown House. They were shown into the drawing-room and provided with coffee and biscuits, as Caro introduced herself.

'Some of you know me already – but for those who don't, I'm Caroline Gaunt – I work for the *Argus* – and it's my brother Richard who was killed on Saturday. This is a horrible situation for my family; we're all trying to come to terms with it, but it's not easy for any of us. My sister-in-law, Lady Ebony, is under medical supervision, and much too upset to talk to anyone. My mother and father have nothing to say either at this stage, because police investigations are still in progress. That's why we have asked you in to meet Inspector Rudge, who is in charge of the case.'

The inspector took over. He did not take long to explain that at this stage of the enquiry, it would not be in the public interest to give out any details. He expressed his opinion that Viscount Ebony's death had not been – despite reports in some of the papers – accidental: but added that he could not say whether it should be regarded as manslaughter or murder. In either case, the motive had yet to be established. He regretted that he was not able to answer any questions, and advised them all to go back to London until such time as further information could be released to the press.

Some of them tried to argue, but the inspector and Caro disappeared rapidly, and they all found themselves being escorted outside once again by Mr Hawkins and a pair of stalwart footmen.

They did not, however, take the inspector's advice and return to London, but hung about in the drive, waiting for something to happen.

Just after mid-day a little van drove up, and they besieged it hopefully; it took ten minutes before the delivery-man could get through to the house. When Lilian Brooks eventually handed over a large bouquet of red roses, the paper wrapping was crumpled, but Alice didn't notice that. She tore open the accompanying envelope and read the enclosed card, which said simply, 'Thinking of you all.'

Alice turned to Nick, and her voice shook a little. 'They're from the Duchess of York... She really is – very kind.'

Nick nodded: in some ways, the messages of sympathy already coming in from friends and family were harder to bear than the intrusive curiosity of the press. You could arm yourself against rough treatment; never against kindness.

'Where's Father?' he asked. 'Don't tell me he's out there gardening today – with all this going on?'

Alice shook her head: 'No – though I expect he wishes he could. He's down at the farm office; the work has to go on, and – there's no one in charge of things now.'

'He's not planning to try and run the farm, on top of everything else?' Nick knew it would be an enormous task for one man to take over the management of the entire estate. 'He'll wear himself out . . . I mean – let's be realistic – Pa's not getting any younger.'

'I know. But who else is there to do the job?'

Nick said nothing. This was a question he had been trying not to think about.

'I must put these roses in water . . .' Alice looked round. 'Where's Jenny? She's so good at arranging flowers.'

'That damned inspector sent for her again; it's something to do with one of the housemaids, apparently.'

Since Lord Minster was occupying the farm office, the inspector had taken temporary possession of the housekeeper's room, just off the servants' hall. He wanted to put some questions to Eileen Fennell – but the girl was almost speechless with terror, so he had asked Jenny if she would mind sitting in on the interview, in the hope that this might put her at her ease.

'There's nothing to be afraid of,' Jenny told the girl, and remembered how scared she herself had felt under the inspector's searching examination.

'Yes'm,' whispered Eileen.

'Of course you know I'm here in connection with Viscount Ebony's death?' the inspector began.

'Yes, sir.'

'Then you know it's my job to find out all I can about the events leading up to his death. I have to find out what sort of man he was – what he'd been doing lately – that sort of thing.'

'Yes, sir.'

'Very well, then. What sort of man do *you* think Richard Ebony was? How would you describe him?'

'I – I dunno.'

'Well – was he cold and stand-offish? Or would you call him more the friendly type?'

Eileen looked appealingly at Jenny, unable to speak.

'I think the inspector wants to know if he ever tried to kiss you,' said Jenny quietly. 'Did he?'

'Oh, yes'm.' Eileen seemed relieved to be asked a direct question. 'He did try – only I wouldn't let him, see.'

'Good girl,' said the inspector. 'And did you tell anyone about it?'

'Yes, sir. I told Miss Brooks – the housekeeper – and I told Miss Brooks's cousin Norman.'

The inspector's eyebrows went up. 'Why was that? What had it got to do with the housekeeper's cousin?'

'Me and Norm are walking out together. We're both in St Peter's choir, and he always sees me home Thursday nights, after practice.'

'And what did Norman say when you told him the Viscount had tried to kiss you?'

Eileen gave a small but gratified smile: 'He told me if he ever tried it on again, he'd break his perishing neck, Viscount or no Viscount.'

'Really?' The inspector and Jenny exchanged glances, and his eyebrows rose even higher.

'Only of course he didn't really do it, if that's what you're thinking,' Eileen chipped in quickly. 'He wouldn't never have done nothing like shooting him – and even if he'd wanted to, he couldn't have, 'cos he works at the Old Forge Garage along the Fallowfield Road, and he was on duty all day Sat'day.'

'Ah . . .' The inspector's eyebrows settled down again, and he made a note in his book. 'The Old Forge Garage – Mr Norman –?'

'Brooks, sir.' Eileen sat back with a knowing look, and commented: 'The garage men say you oughter go over to Fallowfield and ask questions round there . . . You could try Morrissey's farm for a start.'

'Morrissey? You mean Mr Joseph Morrissey – the magistrate?'

'That's enough, Eileen,' said Jenny. 'The inspector doesn't want to hear a lot of silly gossip, and I'm sure Miss Brooks has plenty of work for you to do.'

'Yes – very well – you can go. Thank you for your help, Miss Fennell.' The inspector watched her as she scuttled from the room, then remarked, 'You'd be surprised how interested I am in silly gossip, Mrs Gaunt. It was silly gossip which put me on to that young lady in the first place – and now she's given me another lead. Judging by your expression, I take it you'd heard tales about the Morrissey family yourself?'

'Yes, I had,' said Jenny shortly. 'But if you're going to follow up every woman who'd ever been involved with Richard –'

'I follow up everything, Mrs Gaunt; it's part of the job. For instance, those picnickers you told me about – we managed to track them down. They came from South Croydon; they'd been having a jaunt into the country – and their story tallies with yours in every particular. They'd never visited this part of Kent before, and they'd never even heard of Viscount Ebony – so I think we can rule them out of our enquiry... But as for Mr Morrissey –' He made another note. 'We can't afford to overlook anything.'

The press siege of Crown House continued all day. In the entire family, only Lady Edith managed to carry out her routine as usual. She and Grace opened the village school on time, and the round of lessons, morning milk, playground breaks and trips to the lavatories carried on unchanged. Unchanged, that is, except for one or two awkward questions.

'Please, miss, why are all them policemen up at the big house?'

'*Those* policemen,' said Grace, firmly. 'They have their work to do, just as we have – and I want all your sums finished before going-home time.'

'Please, miss, my mum says there's somebody bin murdered over at the farm... Please, miss, is it true they cut his head off with a chopper? ... Please, miss, my bruvver works in the stables, and he says there was blood everywhere...'

Edith thought for a terrible moment that she might be going to faint, but she pulled herself together. She must try to be strong and brave, like Grace.

'Now we're all going to paint pictures of fireworks today, because it will soon be Bonfire Night,' she announced in a high, bright voice, ignoring everything else.

She was more grateful than ever to have her job as teaching assistant; at least she could put the tragedy from her mind for a while, and concentrate on her work. But she was relieved when the bell rang at last, and it was time to help the infants into their hats and coats, to tidy the classrooms, and to lock up.

It was still drizzling when she and Grace walked over the village green, and along the main road to Crown House. Today they kept close to the high wall that encircled the park, under overhanging trees, then turned the corner by the entrance gates.

A car was parked near the lodge cottage, and as Grace turned her key in the lock, they heard doors slamming and hurrying feet behind them. A moment later they were surrounded by men in caps and raincoats.

'Lady Edith Gaunt? I'm from the *Mirror* –'

'We were told we'd find you here – the deceased Viscount was your nephew, I understand –'

'My card – Mullins of the *Daily Sketch* – I'd like you to give me your impression of the late Viscount Ebony –'

Edith lost her head and dived into the cottage, whimpering. The reporters would have followed her, but Grace barred their way, her arm outstretched across the doorway.

'How dare you come here, tormenting that poor soul? Lady Edith has nothing to say to you – take yourselves off, the pack of you, and leave her in peace!'

Grace Duncan's blood was up, and her eyes flashed fire; but she was outnumbered. One man leaned against the door as she tried to shut it – another planted his boot firmly across the threshold; they all talked at once, and she began to get flustered.

'Get away – do you hear me? Do I have to summon the police?'

This threat had no effect. Grace realized that if she tried to retreat, they would invade the cottage without any hesitation. She gripped the door with all her might, and prayed that her bad leg wouldn't let her down.

Then another voice broke in; loud, clear and feminine. 'You're all wasting your time – did you know that?'

The men turned, taken off-guard. A dark girl with a smart Eton crop stood watching them, a faint smile on her lips.

'Oh – it's you,' said the man from the *Sketch* ungraciously. 'What do you want?'

'Nothing; but I just picked up a nice little titbit from one of the coppers on guard at the house,' she said. 'He's the only one left on duty; all the others have gone whizzing off to some place called Fallowfield.'

'Eh? What's going on?' The man from the *Mirror* sounded suspicious.

'How should I know? But from what I heard, I get the feeling they're just about to make an arrest . . .'

The men looked at one another; then with one accord they all raced across to the parked car, jumped in, and drove off at top speed.

'Poor dears – they didn't even stop to ask the way, and now

they're going in the wrong direction,' said the girl cheerfully. 'Still, at least that's got them off your hands for a while.'

Grace narrowed her eyes. 'Are you a reporter as well?'

'I'm afraid so. But I work on one of the Sundays, so I don't have to fight like a wildcat to meet a deadline every day. I try to be a little more civilized.'

'So I'd noticed – and I'm thankful for it.' Grace began to relax. 'But aren't you going to rush off to Fallowfield as well? Didn't you say something about an arrest?'

'As a matter of fact – I hate to admit this, but I made that part up. The inspector *did* go to Fallowfield, but its probably nothing to do with this case. For all I know, he's been called out to trace a missing bicycle... I just thought you needed a little breathing space.'

Her grin was infectious, and Grace found herself smiling back. 'You never said a truer word, Miss –?' She hesitated.

'Lane. Brenda Lane, from the *Sunday News*... I'm glad I was able to help – good afternoon.' With a wave of the hand, she began to walk away.

Grace called after her, 'Miss Lane – stop a bit... I'm about to put the kettle on – would you care for a cup of tea, maybe?'

Brenda Lane turned, and her face lit up. 'How did you guess? I'm dying for one.'

Over tea, she met Lady Edith, and entertained her hostesses with some amusing anecdotes about life in Fleet Street. After tea, Edith brought out her portfolio, and Miss Lane admired some of her recent water-colours; they all got on wonderfully well, and Edith felt the dark clouds that hung over them begin to lift for the first time.

Impulsively, she invited Brenda Lane to stay to supper; a stewpot had been cooking slowly in the oven all day, and there would be more than enough for an extra guest. Brenda was overwhelmed by the invitation, and accepted gratefully; and they all enjoyed an unexpectedly delightful evening.

By the time she left, Edith and Grace felt that they had made a new friend.

On Tuesday, the papers were full of the Crown House story. There was no longer any suggestion that Viscount Ebony's death might have been an accident; the word 'murder' was printed in bold black headlines. The *Mail* carried a small item framed in black: 'Flowers from Duchess for Tragic Family'.

'The van driver was bribed,' said Caro. 'I hope he gets the sack.'

There was of course no speculation as to the identity of the murderer, or the motive behind the killing, and no word of any arrest. A statement issued by the Medford police merely said that the investigation was taking its normal course.

'What's normal about it?' asked Nick, when he had read this item aloud at breakfast. 'The whole thing's a nightmare.'

'I don't think our lives can ever be normal again,' said Alice, putting down her teacup. On her plate, a slice of toast remained untouched, though William tried to persuade her to eat something.

'Perhaps later,' she said, pushing back her chair. 'I want to go up and see how Polly is – and Alex.'

'Alex needs new shoes,' said Jenny. 'I told Polly I'd take him into Medford this morning... It was rather strange; she seemed to be more concerned about Alex's shoes pinching him than anything else.'

'I'd try Maidstone if I were you,' Nick advised her. 'It's further to go, but you might not get gawped at. With any luck nobody will recognize you there.'

'Oh, come on – it's not that bad,' protested Caro. 'You make it sound as if we were social outcasts –'

'We might as well be,' said Nick bitterly. 'Thanks to your precious colleagues – and thanks to Richard – we've all become part of a freak-show... Something to entertain the great British public over the breakfast table –'

'*Stop it at once!*' William rapped out the words. Then he continued more quietly, 'Your brother is dead; nothing we say or do can change that. But we have to learn to go on without him. We have to look to the future.'

He walked slowly to the window, looking out at the green vista of lawns and trees, and they heard him say, 'The farm must go on – the garden has to be remade, year by year... Just as we have to rebuild our family.' Then his voice changed, and he added, 'The inspector is here again. It looks as if he's coming to see us.'

When Inspector Rudge joined them, he came straight to the point. 'I have some disturbing news; but you will be relieved to know that the major questions have now been answered.'

In the pause that followed, the clock on the wall seemed to be ticking more loudly than usual.

'Yesterday afternoon I paid a visit to Mr Joseph Morrissey and his wife, and put certain questions to them. Their response was not altogether satisfactory, and I warned them that I should want to see them again ... In the early hours of this morning I was summoned by a telephone call from Mrs Morrissey. She is suffering from a nervous breakdown and has been taken in to the new wing at the cottage hospital.'

Alice felt for William's hand and gripped it tightly.

'She admits that she embarked upon a liaison with Viscount Ebony during the last few months. On Friday evening, Mr Morrissey intercepted a letter from the Viscount, addressed to his wife, asking her to meet him the following day. When he demanded an explanation, she collapsed and admitted everything. On Saturday morning, her husband went to keep the appointment instead. He was beside himself with jealousy.'

Sitting beside Nicholas, Jenny longed to look at him, but dared not take her eyes off the inspector.

'They met here in the stable-loft, and a violent quarrel broke out. Richard Ebony had his revolver with him, and in the struggle that followed, the gun went off. Mr Morrissey left immediately; but after I interviewed him yesterday, he realized that the game was up. He had a gun of his own. Sometime before dawn, he left his house and walked out into the little copse at the end of the garden. Mrs Morrissey was woken by the sound of a shot, and found him there a few minutes later. The gun was still in his hand.'

Inspector Rudge looked at them all in turn – each one tense and still.

'When I arrived, I found the letter Joseph Morrissey had left for me, making a full confession. Under these circumstances, I think you may take it that the case is now closed.'

8

FRIDAY, 20 OCTOBER TO TUESDAY 7 NOVEMBER 1933

AFTER that, everything happened very quickly. The inquests on Richard Ebony and Joseph Morrissey were little more than a formality. The police presented their evidence, and a doctor confirmed that in both cases death had been instantaneous. The coroner took the opportunity to deliver a short public homily on the lax morals prevalent in society, which had brought the lives of two men to such a tragic and futile end. He wound up by expressing his condolences to the unhappy widow, Viscountess Ebony, who was expecting the arrival of her second child in the very near future.

Nobody spared much sympathy for Mrs Helen Morrissey, who was also under heavy sedation at this time in the cottage hospital.

Polly was not well enough to go to her husband's funeral. It was a very quiet ceremony, attended only by members of the immediate family. Lady Beatrice had hoped to be there, but at the last moment complained that her arthritis was too painful.

'I couldn't manage the walk up the aisle,' she told William. 'And I don't intend to make a spectacle of myself, propped up like a helpless cripple. I paid my respects to the boy's memory last Sunday; that will have to be sufficient.'

So in the event only Richard's parents, together with Nicholas and Jenny, Caro and Aunt Edith, were present to mourn his passing.

When they got back from church, Jenny and Nicholas went up to Polly's room, and sat with her for a while.

'It was a very simple service,' said Jenny. 'I think that's how Richard would have wanted it.'

'I suppose so... Will there be a piece about it in the papers tomorrow?' asked Polly.

'A few paragraphs perhaps; nothing more,' Jenny assured her. 'And no photographs – Nick took care of that.'

'There was one chap with a camera at the church gate,' Nicholas explained. 'I had a quiet word with him. I said if he tried to take any pictures, I'd break his camera first and his neck afterwards.'

'Good for you.' Polly sighed: 'It's funny – before I got married, I thought it would be wonderful to get my name in the papers... But now I've seen the sort of muck they've been writing about us, I've changed my mind.'

Apprehensively, Jenny glanced across at Nick: 'You've seen the newspapers –?'

'Course I have. I had to know what was going on, didn't I? I was beginning to feel like Old Bea – "*Nobody ever tells me anything!*"' She mimicked the old lady's voice with such wicked accuracy that Jenny couldn't help smiling. It was good to catch even a brief glimpse of the old Polly Harvey.

Polly continued calmly, 'It's OK – I know all about the other woman, if that's what you're wondering. She was asking for trouble, wasn't she? Well, perhaps the silly cow's learned her lesson by this time... It can't be much fun for her now – all on her own.'

Nicholas frowned: 'It's no more than she deserves.'

'Oh, come on – don't be too hard on her. I dare say she got carried away; it wasn't all her fault.'

'No – it wasn't,' he retorted stonily.

'And it wasn't all Richard's fault either. Women were a weakness of his – that's the way he was, and nothing would ever change him. I found that out soon enough.' Polly's voice was drowsy; too much talking exhausted her. 'You and him never really got on, did you?'

'I don't know – sometimes we did. I looked up to my big brother when I was young. But later on – we had our quarrels, certainly.'

'You don't have to tell me! I was the one who put the wych hazel on his bruises, after you'd knocked each other about... It seems a long time ago, now.'

There was a silence, broken by Nick who said quietly, 'I really hated him sometimes. But now he's gone, I shall miss him like hell.'

'So shall I.' Polly closed her eyes. 'But he's not gone altogether – there's still something of him left... Let's hope the new one's going to have his looks.'

'And you've got Alex,' added Jenny.

'Yes – poor little perisher. He's looking forward to having a brother – I tried to explain he won't be big enough to play with for a year or so, but he can't really take it in.'

'Polly...' Jenny had been trying to find a way to bring up a difficult subject, and this seemed to be a good opportunity. 'Talking about Alex... You haven't told him about Richard, have you? He keeps asking when he's coming back.'

Polly shifted uncomfortably. 'I know I ought to tell him, but I can't face it at the moment. Later on, perhaps...' She opened her eyes, looking straight at Jenny. 'I don't suppose you'd tell him for me, would you? He'd take it better from you than anybody else ... I'd be ever so grateful.'

Afterwards, as they walked away from Polly's room, Nick burst out angrily: 'She had no right to ask you! What's wrong with everyone in this family? Pa asked you to talk to Richard – Polly asks you to talk to Alex – it's unfair to load their responsibilities on to you.'

'It's not a question of being fair. Polly's not well enough to do it herself; it would be a terrible ordeal for her. And it's not right to pretend to Alex that his father's just gone away for a few weeks – he's got to be told the truth... I don't *want* to do it, but I suppose I'm the obvious person.'

'Why can't Ma tell him? She's his grandmother.'

'She's been under a lot of strain herself. She might break down and cry – that would frighten Alex more than anything.'

Nick gave her a sidelong look. 'How do you know you won't cry?'

'I shan't do that,' replied Jenny. 'It's simply a question of deciding the best way to break it to him.'

She found the little boy in the nursery with his nanny, and said. 'I'll stay with Alex for an hour or so – why don't you slip downstairs for a cup of tea?'

The uniformed nursemaid bobbed gratefully, saying, 'You be a good boy now, Master Alex – and do what your Auntie Jenny tells you, mind.'

Alex had been looking at a picture-book – an old favourite, judging by the finger-marks and the dog-eared pages.

'Will you read to me?' he asked hopefully. 'It's *Robin Hood and his Merry Men*. When I get a baby brother, he's going to be Little John. Daddy's promised to make us bows and arrows.'

Jenny lifted Alex on to her lap. 'We'll ask Uncle Nicholas to make them for you instead,' she told him.

'Why can't Daddy do it?'

'Because Daddy won't be here any more.'

'I know, but when he comes back –'

'He isn't going to come back. We shan't see Daddy again for a long time,' said Jenny carefully, making her way through the minefield one step at a time.

'Oh... Where's he gone?'

'He's gone to heaven,' she said. 'People don't come back when they go to heaven – it's much too nice.'

'Where's heaven?'

'I'm not really sure. Sometimes it seems to be a long way away, and sometimes it seems quite close. But he's having a lovely time there, wherever it is.'

Alex seemed to lose interest. He fiddled with a button on Jenny's blouse, and said nothing for a while. Then he asked, 'What's lovely about it?'

'Oh, goodness – I don't really know that either.' She racked her brains. 'It's the nicest place of all – everbody wants to go there.'

'Will I go there too?'

'Of course – one day.' She was on safer ground now. 'And when you get there, Daddy will be waiting to meet you. And so will Jesus – and all the other people who've gone there already.'

'Oh...' He seemed to be quite content with this, and twisted the button again, loosening the cotton that held it. Then, as an afterthought, he added, 'What other people?'

'The people who used to live here on earth, then died and went to heaven, like your great grandpapa – and Queen Victoria –' In the library there was a photograph of the old Queen with a group of courtiers, taken at the time of her Diamond Jubilee, and Alex had often had Great-Grandpapa Minster pointed out to him. Jenny cast about for further inspiration, and her eye fell on the picture-book. 'And lots of old friends too – like Robin Hood, and King Richard the Lionheart, and –'

Suddenly the button came off, as a terrible wail brought this litany to a halt. Overcome by grief, with tears streaming down his face, Alex struggled to say something, but could not get the words out.

'Darling – what is it? Don't cry –' Jenny tried to calm him. 'What's the matter?'

'*I never knew Robin Hood was dead!*' sobbed Alex, and howled again.

Jenny had to comfort him for a long time before he finally stopped crying.

By the end of the week, Crown House appeared to be settling down. Richard's absence left an aching gap, but William was doing his best to carry on the work at the farm, and as long as Nick was home on leave, there was still a young man around the house. Life might have started to run smoothly once more – but then the Sunday papers arrived.

The *News of the World* had a photograph of the stables on the front page ('Scene of Shooting Scandal') with as many grisly details as they dared to print, and the history of the unhappy Morrissey marriage on an inside page.

This was bad enough; the *Sunday News* was far worse. Now there was no longer any mystery to titillate its readers, the *News* had decided to fill in the background of the Minster family, and with painstaking efficiency they had collected every scrap of gossip they could find.

One after another, the family read the article with mounting horror.

Even Lady Beatrice was not spared. Somehow the journalist had discovered the late Lord Minster's appetite for servant-girls and shopkeepers' daughters, both in England and in India; there was even a veiled hint that as a young woman, Lady Beatrice had once run away from her husband to take refuge with another man.

'Nothing but a pack of lies!' The Dowager Countess sat up in bed, peering short-sightedly at the newspaper. 'I *never* left Minster . . . I may have taken a short holiday without him – no more than that. Call my solicitor; I shall sue the editor for libel!'

But the article had been carefully vetted by legal experts, and there were no positive allegations that could be challenged; only an overall tone of sneering innuendo.

Richard's sexual freebooting was already public knowledge, but for the first time the *Sunday News* revealed that he had broken off his engagement and jilted his fiancée to marry a Piccadilly chorus-girl – who had given birth to their first child remarkably soon after the wedding.

Polly dropped the newspaper on to the bedroom floor, and turned away. 'Who cares? We loved one another – that's what matters. And soon now – very soon – we're going to have another son. I can feel him kicking – he's impatient, like his Dad; he won't wait much longer.'

It was suggested that the Hon. Nicholas Gaunt had also brought shame upon the family, by marrying the housekeeper's daughter; while Lady Caroline had run away from home some time ago, and now lived alone in London as a 'bachelor girl'.

And Lady Edith Gaunt was also unmarried. The author of the article described the little cottage at the park gates; it had two bedrooms, though only one of these was ever occupied; the other was kept as a guest-room. But guests were a rarity at the lodge, since Lady Edith found all the love and friendship she needed in the person of her constant companion, Miss Grace Duncan ... a strong-minded, almost masculine lady who ran the tiny village school (with Lady Edith's assistance, for the happy couple were inseparable) and instilled the principles of moral behaviour into her infant charges. The writer also mentioned in passing that among the novels on the bookshelves she had noticed copies of Radclyffe Hall's study of inversion, *The Well of Loneliness*, and Virginia Woolf's *Orlando* – 'an unusual story about a young woman who suffers a change of gender'.

Not one phrase in the entire piece was actionable; but every word implied something discreditable. And it appeared under the by-line of the newspaper's special correspondent, Miss Brenda Lane.

William's immediate reaction was: 'Burn it. Thank God they only take the *Sunday Times* at the lodge – there's no need for them to know this rubbish has ever been printed.'

Nicholas and Jenny agreed, but Alice said, 'I think we ought to show it to them.'

The others stared at her, and William began: 'Why on earth –?'

'Because other people will see it. I'm sure there are a lot of *News* readers in the village. Talk will soon get round – Grace and Edith ought to be prepared for it.'

After some discussion, they agreed that Alice was probably right.

'In that case, I shall take the damn thing to them myself,' said William.

He folded the paper up carefully, tucked it under his arm, and went striding off down the drive. He dreaded the scene that would inevitably follow, but he would not shirk it.

In the lodge parlour, Grace and Edith read the article together, side by side. There was a long silence, and then Grace lowered the newspaper. She and Edith turned to one another in despair and disbelief.

'Brenda Lane –?'

'She couldn't – she would never have done such a – she was so *nice*...' Edith clasped her hands to stop them shaking.

'My first thought was that you should never know this vile stuff had been printed.' William's face was flushed and his jaw set, but he continued doggedly: 'Then Alice pointed out that other people were bound to read it, and you might have to face some sort of – public reaction.'

Edith looked at Grace helplessly: 'What ever shall we do?'

Grace's Scottish burr was more pronounced than usual as she replied in a low voice, 'We carry on. We ignore it. We continue to live our own lives.'

'If you think that's best...' Edith felt sick and dizzy; her head was spinning – but she must say something to her brother. 'Thank you, William – thank you for telling us. I'm so very sorry if we have caused you any embarrassment –'

'*We do not apologize*!' Grace's voice rose defiantly. 'We have done nothing we are ashamed of.'

'Quite so.' William nodded, then rose to his feet. 'There is no reason for any apology on your part. This disgraceful example of gutter journalism attacks us all; we shall treat it with contempt. And as Mama reminded me last Sunday, it is important for us to stick together as a family. You know you have our loyalty, and our love.' Awkwardly, he stopped to kiss Edith on the cheek, and touched Grace's hand lightly, before he left the cottage.

'I approve of your brother.' Grace took a long breath. 'But as for that evil little witch, Miss Brenda Lane –'

'I still can't believe it – she was so – understanding...' To her surprise, Edith found that she was crying.

'She understood us well enough, and that's a fact.' Grace put her arms round Edith. 'Don't cry, my dearest. We've come through worse than this before now... But it won't be easy. Make no mistake about that.'

In the Primrose Hill flat, after lunch, the Sunday papers lay strewn upon the carpet.

'If I ever come across that Lane woman, I shall kill her with my bare hands,' Caro threatened.

'I do hope you won't,' said Paul with a wry smile. 'Otherwise the Minster family will hit the headlines all over again.'

'How can you joke about it?' Caro rounded on him. 'Don't you see what this will do to them all? They'll be crucified!'

'My darling, you know as well as anyone – this time next week, somebody else will be on the front page; by next month, the Minster story will be utterly forgotten.'

'It won't be forgotten at Ebony. The villagers will remember this filth for the rest of their lives. Aunt Edie's never going to live it down.'

'Don't exaggerate. I'll bet you fifty pounds none of the good burghers of Ebony has even heard of *Orlando* – or Radclyffe Hall. They won't pick up the implication.'

'Somebody will explain it to them. Of all the sneaky things to do!' Raging, Caro walked across to the window and threw up the sash. 'I need some fresh air... When I read things like this, I begin to think I'm in the wrong job. I wish I did something clean and wholesome – like being the attendant in a ladies' lavatory.'

Paul laughed: 'I think on balance I prefer you as you are. Besides, I'm sure that lady lavatory attendants have their problems too. In this life, we all have our crosses to bear.'

'You don't. You enjoy every minute of your life.'

'I do as a rule – at least, since you walked into it. But I've had hell's delight at the office this week.'

She looked round to see if he were still teasing, but he appeared to be perfectly serious.

'You never told me,' she said.

'It's all supposed to be desperately secret – but I shall be indiscreet for once. You remember what a huge success the King's broadcast was, last Christmas Day?'

'Of course, and no wonder. He sounds like an absolute duck.'

'He sounds what he is – the archetypal Edwardian country gentleman. That's why the entire nation loved the broadcast, and why my lords and masters have arranged to repeat the experiment this year.'

'From Sandringham again?'

'Naturally; from a small office built under the staircase, to cut out any extraneous sounds. And with a very thick chenille cloth on the table to stop the paper rustling, because His Majesty was rather nervous last time.'

'So what's the problem?'

'The problem is that the dear old boy has suddenly decided he doesn't want to do it again. He says last year the ordeal upset his digestion, and completely ruined his Christmas.'

'Oh ... Well, you can't blame him—'

'I don't. On the other hand, we don't want to disappoint listeners all over the world who are looking forward to it. And Whitehall are frightfully keen on a repeat performance. The Prime Minister tried to persuade the old man by saying: "Wouldn't it be interesting if we had a recording of Good Queen Bess at Tilbury?"... To which the King is reported to have replied: "Damn Good Queen Bess!" ... But we're still working on him; I've sent him a selection of all the letters that poured in last time, hoping he'll change his mind...' Paul saw that Caro's attention had wandered. 'Here I am, telling you secrets of state, and you're not even listening to me.'

'I'm sorry.' She had been watching the yellow leaves fluttering down from the plane trees outside. 'I was miles away.'

'At Crown House, no doubt?'

'I was thinking – I really ought to ring home and say I've just read that beastly *News* thing. There might be something helpful I could say – or do –'

Paul's smile vanished. 'But you can't ring from here!'

'Don't worry; if they ask, I'll say I'm with Muriel in Hendon... Oh, gosh, I do *hate* all this lying...'

There was one further development a few days later, although it might not have had any direct connection with the *Sunday News* article.

Soon after Richard's death, Alice had received a letter from Her Majesty's private secretary, expressing the sincere condolences of both the King and the Queen. On Tuesday morning, she was a little surprised when an identical envelope appeared by her place at the breakfast-table.

As she opened it, William remarked gloomily, 'Don't tell me they're asking you to go back to work already?'

'Perhaps the Queen thought it would help Ma to take her mind off things,' suggested Nick.

'That might be a very good idea –' Jenny began, but Alice shook her head.

'No, it's not that – quite the opposite, in fact.' She read a few sentences aloud: '"I am instructed to inform you that Her Majesty is deeply conscious of the great loss you have suffered, and the strain which you must still be under. She therefore wishes you to know that she will be happy to release you from any further duties at Court this season. She has no doubt that a period of rest and recuperation will be most beneficial to you, and looks forward to the pleasure of your company at some time in the future…" In other words, I'm not wanted!'

'For this relief, much thanks,' grunted William, munching toast.

'Well, I call that damned selfish!' Nicholas cut the top off his boiled egg with such vehemence that the yolk ran down the eggcup. 'I thought the Queen was such a good friend of yours?'

'Yes, she is, in a way –'

'That's not my idea of friendship,' he retorted, shaking salt angrily over his egg. 'She knows you've had family trouble, and what does she do? Turns her back on you!'

'Nick – that's not fair!' Jenny tried to intercede. 'You heard what she said: rest and recuperation –'

'Tommy rot! It's all because of that bloody journalist. The Royal Family don't wish to mix with the kind of people who get their names in the Sunday papers.'

'I'm sure that's not true.' Alice was on the defensive. 'Her Majesty has been very thoughtful. I should like more time at home; especially now your father has so much extra work to do. It will give me a chance to help him – if I can.'

'Somehow I can't picture you milking cows, Mama,' said Nick, with his mouth full. 'Ugh – too much salt.'

'I might be able to do some of the office work,' Alice persisted. 'Would that be useful, William?'

'Eh? Oh – yes, certainly.' William put his napkin to his lips. 'I'm grateful for anything that allows you to spend more time at home.'

'I'm sure that's what the Queen had in mind,' said Alice. But in her heart of hearts, she wasn't so sure. The unpleasant publicity concerning the Minster family was exactly the kind of thing the Palace deplored, and she thought she felt the chilly wind of disfavour blowing in her direction.

Grace and Edith, too, noticed a change in the social climate. As they walked across the green on their way to school, they passed some of the Ebony women gossiping outside the general store.

'Good morning,' said Grace pleasantly.

She expected a little chorus of 'Good mornings' in return – but was met with silence. The women fixed their eyes on one another, refusing to look round or to acknowledge her greeting.

'They must have seen us,' whispered Edith as they walked on.

'They saw us all right. I suppose we can expect a certain amount of foolishness.' Grace tried to be philosophical. 'No doubt they'll come round, in time.'

But that was small comfort, especially when they picked up half a dozen handwritten notes which had been slipped through the school letter-box. Grace read them quickly.

'They're all much the same,' she said. 'The little darlings are far too ill to come to school today – they've got coughs or colds or nasty wheezes, so they're being kept at home for the time being ... It's a positive epidemic!'

She tried to make light of it; but when Edith walked across to the shop at mid-day to buy some chocolate biscuits, she returned empty-handed.

'I don't understand it,' she said. 'Mr Wilkinson was really quite brusque – he told me the shop was shut, and I've never known him to shut at lunchtime before, have you? And I'm sure other people were being served ... It doesn't make sense.'

'It makes no sense at all,' said Grace quietly. 'But I understand it.'

That evening, she spent some time composing a letter, and eventually showed it to Edith. Addressed to the local education committee, it was a letter of resignation. Miss Grace Duncan announced that for personal reasons she had decided to retire from her post at the school sooner than she had anticipated, and suggested that the committee should find another head-teacher to replace her at the earliest possible opportunity.

'But – but you said you'd never retire –' Edith was dumbfounded.

'Then I was wrong, wasn't I?' Grace managed to smile. 'We can't go on like this; it's not fair to you – and it's not fair to the children. They're already beginning to stare at me, and whisper behind my back. Heaven knows what the parents have been saying ... Well, we can't have that. I'd sooner give up the job.'

Edith replaced the letter carefully on the table, and said, 'I can't imagine the school going on without you ... I can't imagine you without the school, either.'

'It's what you've been nagging me to do, isn't it? You kept telling me to retire and put my feet up. Now I shall go and do precisely that!'

'You mean – go away?'

'Why not? It's time we set out to look for that dream of yours, before it's too late. We've a little money put by; we must start making plans – and the sooner the better.'

'But where would we go?' asked Edith.

'Somewhere by the Mediterranean – somewhere you can get on with your painting – somewhere in the sun!'

At the same moment, a baby Austin was churning up the gravel at Crown House; it stopped, and Dr Hilliard jumped out.

Polly had chosen Dr Ruth Hilliard in preference to old Dr Parry, to deliver her baby; and when the pains began to come at regular intervals, the doctor had been summoned from Medford, together with the midwife.

It was very different from the birth of Alexander, five years earlier. That had been a long, hard struggle, and Polly had battled her way through it, gripping Richard's hand, determined not to let him down.

This time there was no Richard. But Dr Hilliard had taught her some breathing exercises to do, and helped her to push with the contractions, instead of fighting them. The delivery was swift and comparatively easy. Polly could scarcely believe it when she heard the sound she had been longing for – the high, piercing cry of a newborn child.

'Already?' she panted, as Ruth Hilliard wiped her face with a damp cloth. 'I'm getting better at it! That was like shelling peas.'

'Congratulations,' said the doctor. 'You can be proud of yourself – you have a beautiful, healthy daughter.'

'What?' Suddenly, the sweat on Polly's body turned to ice; a cold fear touched her heart. 'What are you saying? It –it's a *girl*?'

'That's right. And she's a little darling.'

The midwife held her up for Polly to see. For a long moment there was no sound except the baby's cries, then –

'No.' Polly shut her eyes. 'Richard wanted another boy – it had to be a boy . . . Take it away.'

The midwife shook her head, clucking, 'What a thing to say – just hold her in your arms, my lady –'

'I said *take it away*!' Polly's voice was harsh, and she turned her face towards the wall. 'That's not my baby . . . I don't want it.'

9

MONDAY, 7 MAY TO SATURDAY, 23 JUNE 1934

'This house is dead. The life has gone out of it.' Old Bea sat at her window, looking out over the lush green of early summer, but found no joy in the prospect.

Jenny pulled aside the lacy shawl that shaded the baby's face, and said quietly: 'She's fast asleep.'

'We're all asleep,' grumbled the old lady. 'Poor wretch – what a world she has come into. Anyone would think our lives had stopped too, the day her father died.'

Jenny touched one tiny hand, and in her sleep, the baby stirred and grasped her finger. A surge of happiness swept through her, and she wanted to say: 'It's not true – life goes on – look at this little miracle!'

But there was a bitter truth in Lady Beatrice's words.

The Dowager Countess had made a great effort when she went to church with the family, to pray for her grandson's soul. Perhaps it had been too much for her; certainly she had never left her rooms since that day. Arthritis enfeebled her, twisting her cruelly; she listened to her wireless, and looked contemptuously through the newspapers – and that was where her contact with the outside world began and ended. She complained that nobody came to see her, yet she didn't care much for her great-grandchildren. She found Alex too noisy and exhausting, and as for the baby –

'She's a pretty thing,' she conceded grudgingly. 'But what possessed them to saddle her with that absurd name?'

For the little girl was known to everyone in the family as 'Harry'.

When it was time for the baby to be christened, Alice asked Polly what name she had chosen.

'Who cares?' Polly shrugged off the question. 'Richard expected me to give him another son. He'd set his heart on a boy – he wanted to call him after the first Earl, the one who was a sea-captain or a pirate or something – Harry Gaunt. But now it doesn't really matter, does it? Call her Harry if you like; it might make Richard laugh, wherever he is. He'll know I did my best.'

'Harry? You mean – Harriet?'

'Harry or Harriet – I don't really give a damn.'

So Alexander's sister became Lady Harriet Gaunt, and Polly put the subject – and the child – out of her thoughts.

The family summoned Dr Hilliard for a consultation. What was to be done? Lady Ebony had rejected her daughter; she would not feed her, or bathe her. She took no interest in her at all. They had never heard of such a thing.

Ruth Hilliard assured them that it was not in the least unusual. Of course, Richard's death had been a terrible shock to Polly, in the last stages of her pregnancy, but she had sustained herself with the thought that he would somehow live on through the son who was to be born. When that son turned out to be a daughter, she felt cheated of her last hope, and could not forgive the child who had disappointed her. In time, perhaps, the wound would heal, and one day she might accept Harriet; but for the moment they must be patient.

In these circumstances, Polly could have clung possessively to Alex – but she did not. Alex was already a person in his own right, not a re-creation of his father; she had lost a man – the man she loved with all her heart – and the child was no substitute.

So she ignored both her children, while Alice and Jenny did their best to make up to them for this lack of affection. Alex was a bright, lively boy with an enquiring mind, and it was easy enough to keep him happy.

And Jenny adored Harry.

After her miscarriage, Jenny and Nicholas told themselves that they would be luckier next time; but the more they wanted a child, the more impossible it seemed.

When Nick's leave ended, and he went back to sea, Jenny would have felt lost and lonely if it had not been for Harry. Her maternal longings were channelled into her feelings for the baby; now she held her up for Great-Grandmama's approval, saying,'It's her six-month birthday today, so I've given her a new dress to celebrate – do you like it?'

'Broderie anglaise – yes, very suitable,' sniffed the old lady, then waved her away. 'No, I don't want to take her. To be perfectly frank, small children bore me.' She looked bleakly at the parkland beyond her windows, and added, 'Most things bore me, these days. Nobody comes to see me. Richard's gone – and Edith's got this crazy notion about living abroad... All my family are deserting me.'

Edith's departure was a great upheaval. Grace worked out her notice, staying on until Easter, but it was with a heavy heart that she closed the school door behind her for the last time.

Then the two ladies – who hardly ever disagreed – almost fell out over choosing a place for their retirement. Edith had always dreamed of a villa in Provence with whitewashed walls and a mimosa in the garden; while Grace felt strongly that Spain would be more exciting. There was something about that proud, passionate land which appealed to her.

'Oh, but Grace dear – they're such a cruel people – think of those dreadful bullfights!' Edith shuddered.

'Think of Carmen – think of the wild, beautiful gypsies, and flamenco dancers!' Grace had once seen a travel film about Seville and Granada which made a great impression on her. 'Think of picking oranges from our own trees!'

'It's not as if we were particularly fond of marmalade,' objected Edith.

In the end they settled on a compromise. Grace found a book about Catalonia, the ancient kingdom with its own language and traditions that ran from Perpignan in the north-east to Barcelona in the south-west, still proud of its own identity, however the boundaries might be redrawn.

'We'll go to the French Pyrenees,' she concluded, 'and find somewhere near the Spanish border – that should suit both of us. Mimosa for you – oranges for me!'

They packed up their furniture, their books, china, glass and bed-linen, and left everything, crated and labelled, to be sent on after them once they found somewhere to live; and early in May they set out.

The ferry crossing from Dover was not particularly rough, but

Edith was convinced she would be seasick, and Grace only managed to avert disaster by persuading her to recite all the poems, songs and hymns she could remember. Some passengers passing along the deck looked askance at two maiden ladies taking turns to declaim verses from 'The Wreck of the Hesperus' at the tops of their voices, in the teeth of a stiff sou'westerly – but it did the trick, and they reached Calais without any ill effects.

They boarded a train for Paris, and stayed there for two nights; it seemed silly not to look round the capital of France while they were passing through. But the weather was unusually warm for May, and they found it sticky and oppressive. They visited the Louvre, and Grace declared that Monet's water-liles weren't a patch on Edith's (*The Lake, Crown House, at Sunset* was one of Lady Edith Gaunt's most successful efforts) – and they got cricks in their necks gazing up at the Eiffel Tower, though naturally Edith's vertigo made an actual ascent out of the question.

But neither of them really enjoyed city life, and they were glad to get on their way again, heading south.

On the journey the weather broke, and there were thunderstorms at Bordeaux and sheet lightning at Perpignan. When the train reached the last stop before the Spanish frontier, at Cerbère, they climbed down on to the platform (Edith turned her ankle as she alighted, and complained that French trains were much too high up) to find themselves in the middle of a cloudburst.

An ancient taxi took them to their destination: a tiny fishing port a few miles along the coast, called Collioure. Grace had seen a picture of it in a guidebook; it had looked so charming, with an old pink lighthouse guarding the little harbour, and yellow sands beside a brilliant blue sea.

Today everything was grey, and practically invisible through a curtain of driving rain that half-blinded the travellers. They paid off the taxi – Grace felt sure that the driver overcharged them, but she was in no state to argue, even if her French had been up to the task – and he drove off, leaving their luggage on the wet pavement. They blinked at the grey, narrow street, now running with water like a mountain stream – at the grey, cheerless houses, with their windows shuttered against the storm – at the grey-green trees that dripped mournfully under a leaden sky . . .

'I *think*,' said Grace cautiously, 'those might be your mimosas.'

Edith's face puckered up: 'Have we come all this way for *that*?'

'Excuse, please.' A deep voice with a thick Catalan accent broke in, and they were assailed by the odour of garlic. 'You look for good hotel – yes?'

They looked in dismay at the speaker; he had a walnut-wrinkled face and several gold teeth, and he held aloft a large, inviting umbrella.

'I am the Baron. I show you best hotel in all France. You come with me.'

The weather in Kent was much better. Jenny only wore a light cotton frock as she worked her way along the herbaceous border, tugging out weeds. Beside her, little Harry lay back on a rug, shaded by a parasol, kicking her feet in the air and gurgling happily.

'My – don't you make a pretty picture?' exclaimed Gina, ducking under the wistaria on the pergola. Alice and Sir Charles followed her.

Feeling rather foolish, Jenny scrambled to her feet. She and Gina had never liked one another, but she smiled politely: 'Lady Bowyer – Sir Charles – what a nice surprise. I didn't know we were expecting visitors; you must forgive my gardening clothes.'

'But darling, you look simply divine!' cooed Gina. 'And as for that cunning little cherub – who's a sweetie-pie then?'

She swooped down, bringing her face very close to the baby girl. Not unreasonably, Harry took exception to this, protesting loudly; Jenny picked her up, making soothing noises.

'I shouldn't worry – it's probably wind.' Gina settled herself on a garden bench and lit a cigarette. 'Charlie and I were at a loose end, so I said why don't we motor down and drop by?'

'I told her we should telephone first,' said Charlie apologetically.

'It's lovely to see you,' said Alice. 'William's over at the farm, but he might join us for tea. I hardly ever see him these days; that wretched estate office keeps him busy from morning to night.'

'He never has a chance to get into the garden – that's why I promised I'd keep up the fight against the dandelions,' Jenny explained. 'We must get them out before the flowers seed.' She added mischievously, 'There is a spare trowel, Lady Bowyer, if you feel like helping –?'

'Oh, honey – I wouldn't know the difference between a dandelion and a dahlia!' Gina pronounced it 'darlia', in the American manner. 'I guess I'll just sit here in the sun and relax. You're so lucky to have this beautiful garden.' She looked round, then asked, 'But where's Polly? I thought she'd come running the minute her little precious started to yell.'

Alice said quietly, 'I thought you knew . . . Polly doesn't take much interest in the children at present.'

'You mean that's still going on – after all this time?' Gina looked suitably appalled. 'What is it – some kind of mental crack-up?'

'Emotional exhaustion, according to the doctor,' said Alice.

'It's been a terrible time for you all.' Charlie patted Alice's hand. 'I must say I think you're all bearing up magnificently, under the circumstances.'

'Oh, sure!' Gina agreed. 'And you're so wise not to listen to all those malicious rumours . . .'

'Rumours?' Alice frowned.

'You know how people talk. Just because the Queen crossed you off her list – it's so cruel –'

'I'm only being rested, temporarily.'

'Yes, that's what I'm telling everybody . . . But the Royals never forgive – remember how the Prince of Wales cut me dead that time at Thelma Furness's party? Just because I'd been seen with Prince George at some night-club . . . Mind you, David's no angel! People are saying terrible things about him these days. I bet the King and Queen are spitting mad.'

'Gina dear –' Alice tried to stop this flow of gossip, but her sister-in-law never even paused for breath.

'I knew all about it from the very start, because Thelma's one of my dearest friends. It all began when she had to go back home to the States in January, on some family business. Before she left, she lunched with me and Wallis Simpson, and she told us she was anxious about leaving David alone in London – well, you know they'd been a twosome for simply ages. Thelma turned to us girls and said: "I'm so worried about the little man – will you look after him for me, Wally?" Because David and the Simpsons were real buddies by that time – he was always asking them down to the Fort at weekends.'

Trying to build up her own role in this drama, Gina continued, 'The way it turned out, she'd have done better to ask *me* to keep an eye on him – but ever since that little misunderstanding over Prince George, I've been *persona* definitely *non grata* with David . . . Anyhow – when she got back in March, she discovered her darling friend Wallis had got her hooks into him! I'll never forgive Wally for double-crossing Thelma like that...'

'I don't imagine Mr Simpson was exactly overjoyed about it either,' murmured Charlie.

'Oh, Ernest Simpson had nobody but himself to blame – he's such a snob, he practically pushed Wally into David's arms... But I guess he's regretting it now; everyone's talking about –'

She broke off with a cry of delight, as Lord Minster appeared. 'William darling – how ever are you? My, you look tired – what have you been doing?'

'Working,' said William shortly. 'But I thought I'd done enough for one day... I've come to give you a hand, Jenny.'

'Nonsense – you'll wear yourself out!' Gina sprang to her feet. 'Come and sit down – you need a break. In fact, that's why we're here; Charlie and I want you and Alice to come up to town for a few days. We're inviting you to Olympia – as our guests.'

'Olympia?' Alice looked mystified. 'Is there something on? Not another Ideal Home Exhibition?'

'Tom Mosley's having a mass meeting – it's going to be the biggest political shindig of the year. Everybody will be there; it's something you simply cannot miss!'

'The BUF are holding a rally on June the second,' Charlie explained. 'I'm not a party member myself but I agree with Gina; it should be an important occasion.'

William sat down on the grass. 'It's extremely kind of you to ask us,' he said. 'Unfortunately I have a prior engagement.'

'Oh, no – that's too bad!' Gina wailed. 'The very same day?'

'That day – and every day. I have such a full engagement-book,' William smiled. 'What with the milking – and the pig-swill – and the chickens, and the horses, and the goats – not to mention the haymaking... I'm afraid the British Union of Fascists will just have to struggle along without us.'

When Lady Edith was a child, she had once been taken to see a Christmas pantomime at the Lyceum theatre; and she had never forgotten the breathtaking magic of the transformation scene, when a wintry landscape dissolved into a glittering fairyland.

She thought of it on the first morning after their arrival in Collioure, when she opened the shutters of the hotel room. The grey, wet weather had disappeared overnight, as if it had never existed; and there was the little harbour, with its fishing boats bobbing on a sparkling sea, and warm, generous sunshine bathing the red-tiled roofs, the creamy walls, the tossing plumes of palm trees: flowers, flags, light and colour everywhere. This was the moment when Edith and Grace began to fall in love with France.

Things had begun to cheer up as soon as they booked in to the hotel. It was half-way down the street that led to the fishermen's beach, facing the medieval citadel, once a stronghold of the Knights Templar. Inside, the walls were covered in oil paintings, for the bar was a favourite haunt of artists, and many of them preferred to settle their bills by leaving a picture or two by way of payment. Many of these works were in a very modern style: there was one by a Spaniard called Picasso which Edith particularly disliked.

Surrounded by pictures, they had ordered hot soup and plates of grilled sardines, and shared a bottle of local red wine which put new heart into them. Once or twice the Baron, with rainwater dripping off his long nose, had looked in to make sure that all was well, and assured them that the sun would shine tomorrow.

Now Edith called Grace to come to the window: 'The Baron was quite right – look at the sunshine!'

Grace agreed that his forecast had been accurate, though she was not altogether convinced that he was a Baron. 'He seems to be employed to tout for customers – I'd say "Baron" was a courtesy title, myself.'

But on such a morning, Edith could believe anything was possible. They would set out after breakfast and find that little whitewashed villa; she felt sure of it.

Over the next week or two, they explored Collioure and the foothills surrounding it; this was where the Pyrenees met the sea, and the village was encircled by a line of crags and pinnacles, jagged and sharp as a child's drawing. On one peak, a single watch-tower – the Tour Madeloc – dominated the scene.

They enquired about properties for sale or to let, but without success. They saw some hideous modern bungalows like shoe-boxes; they saw some decaying mansions in need of repair; they saw an apartment above a restaurant, which smelled of fish, and an empty studio once let to an artist who had left behind unpaid bills and a mountain of rubbish – and that smelled worse than the fish.

But they never gave up hope. They stayed on at their hotel, and learned to eat sea-urchins, and to enjoy bouillabaisse. They strolled down to the harbour each evening at dusk, to watch the little flotilla of boats setting out to sea; each one carried a bright acetylene lamp that hung over the water to lure the fish up to the nets. They stood in the shadow of the old lighthouse, which served as the tower of the little church by the beach, and saw the winking lights of the *lamparos* reflected like stars in the calm sea... And they knew that this was where they would make their home. There was no hurry.

The warm, dry weather and the regular exercise helped Grace's bad leg. One hot afternoon they set out to climb up to the Tour Madeloc; they found it slow going, picking their way up a rough, stony track that gradually dwindled to a footpath and then petered out altogether in rough scrub and coarse grass.

Edith mopped her brow, panting, 'I'm not sure I'll be able to climb all that way.'

'Look back and see how high we've come already,' Grace encouraged her.

'Yes, but look how much further we still have to go!'

Either way, it was a glorious view. There was the huge panorama of blue sea, and the long curve of white beach stretching away towards Perpignan; near at hand, the rocky coastline was broken into tiny bays and headlands, with secret valleys running deep between the hills... And in one of those valleys, they looked down on the chimneys and roof of a building, half hidden among a grove of trees. Then they looked at each other.

Though it was downhill, it was still a difficult walk; and when they reached it at last, Edith wondered whether they had made a mistake.

The signboard at the gate bore the name 'Mas-Lou'. It had been a smallholding, though now the land was overgrown, smothered in nettles and briars. The little farmhouse stood empty; semi-derelict, with a gaping hole in the roof and window-panes missing. Even the front door had come off its hinges and hung drunkenly askew. As they pressed on through the undergrowth, following the remains of a path, a small goat ran out of the doorway with a startled bleat, and took refuge among the brambles.

But there was an almond tree beside a well; and an overgrown jasmine smothered one of the walls in sweet, white flowers. Between the trees, there was a glimpse of the sea, shining in the distance.

'We could always plant our own oranges – and mimosa,' said Grace. 'And buy some whitewash...'

'Oh, but – there's so much to be done – could we ever –?' asked Edith, uncertainly.

'Remember the state the lodge was in, when we first saw it?' Grace prompted her. 'We've done it before – we can do it again!'

Although it was eight years since Alice and William had moved into Crown House and made it their home, some ties with London had never been broken. One of these was the family dentist; Alice still went up to Mr Pleach in Wimpole Street for her annual check-up, and this year he found a small cavity which had to be filled.

Nobody enjoys dental work, and afterwards she cheered herself up by dropping in to Fortnum's. She had intended to buy some chocolates for Alex, and treat herself to tea and an éclair before catching the train back to Medford. But her plans changed when she was hailed affectionately beside a display of preserved ginger.

'Alice, my dear – *what* a coincidence!' The Duchess of York, in periwinkle blue exactly matching her eyes, kissed her on the cheek. 'I'm so pleased – you're the very person I wanted to see, but I didn't know you were in town. Are you staying in Eaton Square?'

'No, I'm catching a train as soon as I've had tea.' Alice explained about her dental appointment.

'Take a later train and have tea with me instead,' urged Elizabeth. 'I've only got to pick up some biscuits – Bertie has developed a passion for shortbread, and I told him there's nothing like real Scottish petticoat-tails... The car's waiting outside, so we can be home in a twinkling.'

Alice could not resist the invitation, and half an hour later she was in the Duchess's sitting-room, nursing a cup of tea and eating a home-made scone. A mass of cottage-garden flowers gave the room a country-house air; on a side table there were framed photographs of the two Princesses.

'Such a shame you've missed them – they've gone for an outing in the park, to make the most of the weather,' Elizabeth explained. 'Actually, I wanted to ask your advice about the girls.'

'Really?' Alice couldn't imagine what advice she could possibly give the mother of such a happy family.

'Bertie and I are both very keen for them to learn to swim,' Elizabeth went on. 'And I seem to remember, when you lived in London, your children took lessons at the Bath Club – is that right?'

'Absolutely right. We took them all when they were quite young.'

'I thought so. I've been told at the Palace that the instructors at the Bath Club are very good – Bertie's sister Mary was taught there and so was Princess Arthur of Connaught... But I wondered whether the teachers might be a little too strict? I don't want the girls to feel nervous about it; I do think swimming ought to be fun, don't you?'

'Don't worry,' Alice reassured her. 'Mine all had a wonderful time. Let me think – how old are the Princesses now?' She looked at the photos; Lillibet's pleasant, serious face, with the merest hint of a smile, and Margaret's impish grin.

'Lillibet's eight – and Margaret's nearly four.'

'Of course.' Alice thought for a moment. 'It will be ideal for Lillibet, but Margaret is a wee bit young, perhaps? If she could wait for another year or so –'

'Oh, dear, I hoped it was something they could share. It's so difficult, trying to be fair to both of them. Perhaps I should wait a little longer, so they can begin lessons together.' Elizabeth refilled Alice's cup. 'Help yourself to another scone... And tell me all about your family. You had such a ghastly time last year; I do hope things are a little easier now.'

'Oh, yes – we're beginning to come to terms with it... William's working twice as hard. I try to help him, but I don't seem to be a very good organizer. Still, I think he's pleased to have me there. Between ourselves, he was rather relieved when I gave up my occasional duties at Court.'

Elizabeth refilled the teapot with hot water, and replaced the lid carefully, then said, 'Alice... I wondered whether you might have felt a little hurt when the Queen decided to rest you?'

'No – not really – I know she meant to be kind.'

'Yes, she did. We were talking about it at the time.' Elizabeth's expression, normally so full of humour, was serious now. 'She wasn't afraid of the gossip, if that's what you thought. She was more concerned for you. You would have been so much in the public eye on royal occasions, and with those awful newspaper stories still in people's minds, you might have found it embarrassing... She really was thinking of you – I'm sure of that.'

Alice was touched. 'Thank you for telling me.'

'I know she wants to have you with her again, very soon.' The smile, when it reappeared, was radiant. 'I expect you've missed your jaunts up to town, haven't you?'

'Oh, I have – and I've thought of you all so often. I hope the King and Queen are both well?'

'They're looking forward to the Jubilee next year – just think, twenty-five years already! And David...' The Duchess broke off, then began again. 'I don't see him very often; he has his own circle...' She glanced at Alice. 'You've heard about Mrs Wallis Simpson, I suppose?'

'I know Mrs Simpson and the Prince are – great friends,' said Alice, carefully.

'*Very* great friends. He makes no secret of his feelings for her. Every time they go out together, she seems to be wearing some new jewellery he's given her.'

'He's always been generous; if it pleases him to buy her presents –'

'My dear, that wouldn't be so bad! But when old Queen Alexandra died, she left a lot of her most valuable pieces to David, thinking that in due course, when he married, they would go to his wife... And that's where it's coming from – diamonds, emeralds, rubies – you can imagine, Their Majesties are not at all pleased!' Then Elizabeth bit her lip: 'Oh, I'm sorry – have I put my foot in it? Isn't Mrs Simpson a friend of yours?'

'I've only met her once or twice, very briefly. She's a friend of my sister-in-law, Charlie's wife. I can't really say I know her.'

'Thank goodness. I've met her several times, but don't know her either. I've tried to like her, but I simply can't – there's something about her I don't trust, and how can you make friends with someone if you don't trust them?'

There was a knock at the door, and a young woman entered the room.

'Excuse me, ma'am,' she said; her voice was bright, with the hint of a Scots accent. 'We're back from the park; I wasn't sure if you'd wish me to bring the Princesses in to tea, as you have a visitor?'

'Oh, yes, let them come in,' said the Duchess. 'They'll want to see Lady Minster. Alice, I don't believe you've met Marion Crawford? She's not only a nursery-governess – Crawfie's become a very dear friend.'

It was said that fifteen thousand tickets had been sold for the BUF rally; certainly Olympia was filled to capacity, and there was an air of mounting excitement as people took their seats.

'I recognize quite a few Conservative MP's' said Sir Charles, looking around. 'And there's Aldous Huxley – the tall chap, with spectacles – and Vera Brittain –'

'It's simply too thrilling for words,' said Gina. 'Look – there's Roland.'

'Who?'

'Roland Voss. Right there on the platform.'

At the front of the stage, Mosley's most trusted lieutenants were drawn up in a single line, surveying the scene with obvious satisfaction. They all wore the same uniform – a black jacket like a fencer's tunic, a broad black leather belt, and black trousers tucked into shining jackboots. Above them spotlights converged upon a vacant place on the rostrum, awaiting the Leader himself.

Down in the body of the hall, Caro too felt the tingle of anticipation; somehow it reminded her of the Albert Hall. This time, there would be no balloons and no champagne; she was here to work. The *Argus* had sent her to cover the rally – as a social occasion, as well as a political meeting.

If there was excitement in the hall, there was even more tension outside, where more than a thousand Communists had set up a counter-demonstration – only to be held back by a posse of seven hundred policemen, on foot or on horseback. Shouting and booing broke out and scuffles developed, as the police drew their batons, ordering the crowd to 'Move along there.'

Inside no police were on duty. Order was to be kept by the black shirted stewards; for in addition to the phalanx on the platform, each aisle was monitored by a squad of men, deployed with military precision.

When Sir Oswald Mosley took his place at the centre of the stage, the roar of welcome completely drowned the faint sounds of protest from outside. His supporters leaped to their feet, cheering and applauding.

He smiled upon them benignly, letting the noise continue for several minutes, before raising his right arm in the Fascist salute. Most of the audience returned the salute; and then he stilled them with a single authoritative gesture. Even Caro, hating him and hating all that he stood for, had to admit that his control of the crowd was masterly.

When he began to speak, his words were blurred and hard to understand; there were twenty-four loudspeakers around the walls, and the sound reverberated in overlapping echoes.

Perhaps the first interruption came from a member of the audience who could not hear – but no one ever knew what he was trying to say.

Instantly, a battery of mobile spotlights were swung round and trained upon the unfortunate man, completely dazzling him. As he stopped and stammered, putting up a hand to shield his eyes, the blackshirt brigade moved in. They raced down the aisle, grabbed him, struggling and yelling, dragged him out of the auditorium, and threw him out.

It was a brilliantly simple manoeuvre, and it was repeated so many times that Caro lost count. Someone would try to interrupt and would immediately be ejected. Someone else would stand up to protest at this rough treatment, only to be manhandled from the building in the same way.

Sir Oswald's voice, amplified and impervious to any interruption, rolled on. Only once did he refer to the activity in the hall, saying: 'As these interruptions go on, the process of interrupting becomes increasingly painful – not for us, but for the interruptors.'

And he was still smiling.

One young man near Caro tried to make himself heard, and the Biff Boys swung into action. Sickened and incredulous, she saw them punch him in the face, knock him down, and kick him in the ribs and the groin; she heard him scream with pain as they dragged him away. She never meant to get involved, but suddenly she was on her feet, shouting: '*Stop them – someone will get killed – you must stop –*'

She got no further. White light blinded her; half a dozen thugs grabbed her, lifting her up, and she was tumbled roughly from hand to hand; her dress was torn, her arms and legs bruised and bleeding, and she finished up in the street, like all the rest.

From their vantage-point, Charlie and Gina recognized the latest victim with dismay.

'Dear God – it's Caro! ... We must do something!' Charlie was trembling.

'Don't be a fool – we can't interfere.' Gina was frightened too – but her fear was mingled with another emotion. She was breathlessly elated, like a spectator at a prize-fight, and her heart beat faster. 'We'd never find her now...'

'It's an outrage – this is a massacre!' Charlie had to raise his voice above the continuous background of noise. 'We can't stay here, it's too dangerous.'

He stood up, but Gina remained where she was, staring with shining eyes at the figures on the platform as if she were hypnotized.

'*Come along!*' exclaimed Charlie, desperately. He had to grip her by both arms before he could make her tear herself away.

Outside, the situation was even worse. The police were still trying to move the crowds on, ignoring the battered victims who had been thrown out, and threatening others who went to their assistance.

Sir Charles told a police sergeant to send his men inside the building and put a stop to the violent scenes taking place there, but the sergeant shouted him down, threatening to arrest him for causing an obstruction. Eventually they managed to force their way through the angry crowd and were lucky enough to pick up a cruising taxi.

Some time later, in the Curzon Street flat, Sir Charles poured a stiff whisky and soda, and said: 'That settles it. I'll have nothing more to do with Mosley and his bully-boys... The man's a political maniac. I shall write to *The Times* about it.'

Gina hardly heard him. She kept thinking how splendid Roland Voss had looked, standing on the platform like a young god, above the tumult... Tomorrow, she would telephone party headquarters. She had to meet him again....

Charlie, too, wanted to make a telephone call: he rang the Minsters' house in Eaton Square, but was informed that Lady Caroline was not at home.

'Do you suppose she's all right?' he asked Gina. 'What can have happened to her?'

'I guesss she rushed off to her boyfriend,' said Gina dreamily. 'Paul will take care of her – don't worry.'

'I didn't know she had a boyfriend... Did you say Paul?'

'Oh, didn't I tell you?' Gina went to the drinks cabinet to replenish her gin and tonic. 'She's having an affair with Paul Weyman; it's been going on for quite a while. But don't breathe a word – it's a deathly secret.'

Caro's article for the *Argus* had to be heavily subbed, and all the more inflammatory comments deleted, but it aroused a good deal of interest. Disapproval of the Fascist Party was widespread; the directors of the White City, where another BUF rally was due to be held later in the summer, cancelled the booking, and Sir Oswald announced that he would hold an open-air meeting in Hyde Park instead. The police offered no objection to this.

At Ebony, life was uneventful. Crown House seemed to be under a spell, like the castle in the story of the Sleeping Beauty. The long days of June were stifling; the scent of roses and meadowsweet hung heavy on the air, and when Old Bea was being settled for the night, she complained to the housekeeper, 'I can't breathe – leave the windows open, wide open.'

'It's that sultry tonight,' said Lilian Brooks. 'There could be a thunderstorm, my lady.'

'Let's hope there is; it might clear the air ... Tell me – what day is it? I lose all count of time.'

'Twenty-third of June, my lady. Midsummer day tomorrow.'

She took a last look round the bedroom, and turned out the lights, leaving the old lady propped up in bed.

It was not quite dark, even now; the last traces of day still glimmered in the sky. Somewhere in the woods, a nightingale began to sing.

So this was midsummer eve ... Old Bea had a hazy recollection of a play she had once seen – about some fools who went into a wood on midsummer eve, and got into all kinds of mischief; there was a boy called Puck, a wary, wicked youth with tousled hair ... Or had they fallen asleep and dreamed it all? She couldn't really remember; it was too long ago.

She closed her eyes, but sleep would not come. She longed for sleep; she found no pleasure in her waking life.

What was the good of being alive at eighty, if you couldn't enjoy it? What was the point of having a large family, if they never came to see you? She had not particularly enjoyed her daughter's company, but now Edith had taken herself off to foreign parts with her schoolmarm friend, Old Bea found that she missed them both. She had had a postcard this morning from somewhere in the south of France, a picture of green hills and blue sea, and an 'x' marking the spot where they had found a little house ... But she would never see it ...

She looked back over her life, trying to remember the good times; the parties and the dancing partners, the ball-gowns and sparkling jewels ... Well, that was all over long ago, never to return. Pretty faces and pretty frocks didn't last; only the jewellery remained, and that was locked up in boxes which she kept under her bed (for the

Countess didn't trust banks). She would never wear it again.

She felt very sorry for herself. The hours crawled by, and an owl hooted beyond the open windows. Her life was over; she was old and crippled and alone, and she longed for death.

Still she could not settle. The night air was alive with little sounds – the rustle of leaves, the crack of a twig – and then she heard another sound, much closer... The sound of a handle turning slowly – slowly – and the creak of a door swinging open.

Old Bea opened her eyes in the darkness. She held her breath, listening to the unmistakable sound of a stealthy footstep. Who would dare to creep into her bedroom in the middle of the night? Moving as silently as she could, she reached out, groping for the bedside lamp. She heard another footstep, a little nearer – and pressed the switch...

'Who are you?' asked Old Bea indignantly. 'What are you doing in my room?'

The intruder stood transfixed at the foot of her bed, like a rabbit caught in the glare of a car's headlamps... A wary, wicked youth, with tousled hair.

10

THE silence was broken by a distant clock striking twelve.

'Midnight,' said the intruder, brightly. 'It's getting late – I'd better be on my –'

'*Don't move!*' Old Bea's voice had eighty years of authority packed into it. The boy froze again. 'I asked you two questions,' she continued. 'Who are you? And what are you doing here?'

'Um – it's a bit awkward-like.' He tried an engaging smile. 'I come in to the wrong room – sorry about that.'

Once again he edged towards the door, but Old Bea stopped him in his tracks.

'If you take another step, I shall scream for help. I also have a bell and a police-whistle within reach, and I shall use both, if necessary. I wish to know how you come to be in this house at all.'

'I was – er – looking for a friend of mine,' he said. 'She works here. In the kitchen – she's one of the maids.'

'Ah... It may interest you to learn that none of the kitchenmaids lives in the servants' wing; they all sleep out.'

'Is that a fact? Fancy me not knowing.' He was the picture of innocence. 'I must've made a mistake – sorry to have disturbed you – I'll just –'

Before he could move, she raised an imperious hand. 'Your name,' she repeated. 'I am waiting to be told your name.'

After a short pause, he said confidently, 'Ronald Colman.'

'Come here, boy.' She crooked one bony finger. 'Closer – I'm not going to eat you... Ronald Colman, indeed! I may not visit the picture palace myself, but I have my wireless – I keep in touch...'

149

He stood by the side of the bed; the smile was still fixed on his freckled, impish face, but there was a sheen of sweat on his forehead.

'You're afraid of me, aren't you?' she asked. 'Quite right too; I could send you to prison for breaking and entering these premises. Now begin again and this time you will tell me the truth. First – your name.'

'Norman,' he mumbled. 'Norman Brooks.'

'Brooks, eh? I know the family; my housekeeper is a Miss Brooks –'

'Yeah, she's my cousin Lilian. You won't tell her you seen me, will you?' he asked urgently.

'I take it she doesn't know you're here?'

'Not her – she'd half kill me. I told you, I come in looking for Eileen Fennell –'

'You're lying again.'

'I'm not! She's my girlfriend, ain't she? Her and me goes to choir practice, Thursdays –'

'In that case I'm sure you know where she lives; and you did not expect to find her in my bedroom. Suppose you tell me what you were really looking for.'

'I – I dunno what you mean... I don't know what you got in here, do I?'

'Unless your cousin Lilian happened to mention my jewellery, perhaps? So you decided to come in and help yourself – eh?'

'I never!' He was beginning to shake, and she thought he might be about to faint. 'I – I only –'

'Pull up that chair, and put your head between your knees.' She watched with grim satisfaction as he obeyed her. 'You're a poor sort of burglar, I must say – nervous as a scalded cat, for all your bluster... How old are you?'

'Seventeen ... and a bit.'

'And do you know anything about jewellery, Norman Brooks?'

He shook his head dumbly.

'I suppose you'd have taken the lot into the first shop you came to, and asked how much they'd give you for it. You'd have been locked up within minutes. No doubt you're short of money?'

He licked his lips. 'I want to buy a garage ... a place of me own.'

'A *garage*?'

'That's my trade, see. I work at the Old Forge, on the Fallowfield Road. But it's a dog's life – I don't get nothing but the mucky jobs to do, and I'll never have anything better, 'cos the boss's son works there too, and he gets all the perks... If I had a bit of cash behind me, I'd buy me own place – and me own car...'

His eyes glistened; for a moment he was transported by the glorious vision of his own future, and he turned to the old lady appealingly: 'You could set me up in business, couldn't you? It wouldn't cost you much.'

'Do you take me for an imbecile?' asked the Countess. 'I see no reason why I should do you a kindness, when you came here with the intention of robbing me, and murdering me in my bed, as like as not.'

'Ooh, I wouldn't have!' he protested, deeply shocked.

'So you say. You certainly came after my jewels... Well, perhaps I should let you see them.' She leaned back, rapping out orders. 'You'll find half a dozen boxes under the bed. Fetch them out, and open them up. We'll go through the lot. I always enjoy looking at them.'

As if in a dream, he did as he was told; she began to show off her treasures, turning over the contents of the jewel-cases. He gazed at them unbelievingly, and suddenly asked: 'How d'you know I won't knock you over the head and run off with 'em?'

'You can try – you won't get far. And I'm not afraid of dying, I can promise you that... All right – put them away, and get out – preferably without being seen.'

'You're letting me go? You're not going to call the coppers?'

'We've had enough policemen in this house lately. You may go, Norman Brooks – but on one condition. You will come back on Monday morning, at ten o'clock; I shall have something to say to you then. And I advise you not to be late.'

He put the last of the boxes under the bed, then looked at her. 'What are you up to?' he asked.

'You'll find out,' she replied. 'And I'll thank you to call me "my lady" the next time you address me.'

'How d'you know there'll be a next time?' He grinned suddenly, and she thought of Puck again. 'I could walk out now and do a bunk – you'd never see me again.'

'The police would soon pick you up, once I told them what you'd done.'

'You said you wouldn't call the police!'

'And I shan't – provided you do as you're told and return here on Monday morning. If you try to run away, I shall have the law on you.'

'But I ain't done nothin' –' he began.

'You can hardly expect anyone to believe that, when your finger-prints are all over my jewel-cases,' she pointed out, with quiet satisfaction. 'Off you go now; I'm feeling quite tired. And shut the door behind you – anyone would think you were born in a barn!'

Sir Charles Bowyer was bored. Sunday afternoons were a dreary desert at the best of times, especially without his wife to keep him company; Gina had gone off to some meeting at the BUF headquarters, leaving him on his own. He didn't know when she would get back.

He leafed through the Sunday papers, trying to find something to entertain him – but the news was particularly depressing. He looked at a photograph of Adolf Hitler shaking hands with Benito Mussolini; they had met a week earlier, in Venice: two unprincipled rascals, Sir Charles suspected, and neither of them a gentleman.

At first Charlie had rather admired the changes Mussolini was making in Italy, but he had never cared for Hitler – a jumped-up, hysterical little creature. Now he had become disenchanted with the Fascist movement, he felt extremely irritated, as if he had backed the wrong horse in an important race. It aggravated his annoyance that Gina should be so completely besotted with Mosley and his henchmen.

Turning a page, he noticed a reference to the BBC and their Outside Broadcasting Department; the name Paul Weyman caught his eye, mentioned in connection with the improved cricket coverage this season.

He winced, as if he had bitten on a sore tooth.

Ever since Gina had told him about Caroline's liaison with Weyman, Charlie had felt distinctly uncomfortable and more than a little angry. The man must be a complete bounder, seducing the daughter of his old friends – and the difference in age between them made it particularly repellent.

And Sir Charles felt guilty; his conscience told him it was his duty to warn Alice and William, but Gina had made him promise to say nothing to the Minsters.

'It's no concern of ours, honey-lamb,' she told him. 'Let the girl have her fling – what's the harm in it? She's got to grow up some time; you can't expect her to stay a schoolgirl for ever.'

All the same, Charlie resented Paul's conquest of his favourite niece, and the more he thought of it, the angrier he became. According to Alice, Caro stayed with some girl from her wretched newspaper every weekend; according to Gina, she was actually with Paul Weyman . . . No doubt they thought themselves very clever, laughing at the family behind their backs . . . It was insufferable.

Charlie decided that something must be done. He looked up 'Weyman, Paul' in the L to Z volume of the London telephone directory, and found that he lived in Primrose Hill.

At five o'clock, he rang the bell of Paul's mansion-flat. When Caroline opened the front door, she caught her breath.

'Uncle Charlie!' She looked uncertainly at him, then stepped back to let him in. 'What are you doing here?'

'I came to see Mr Weyman. I imagine he is at home?'

'Yes, he is . . . We're just having tea – would you like some? I can easily fetch another cup –'

'Thank you, no.'

She showed him into the sitting-room. Paul stood up, his face taut with anxiety.

'Sir Charles – this is my day for pleasant surprises,' he began quickly. 'I met Caroline at the zoo, so naturally I invited her back for tea. Do sit down . . .'

'Don't bother, Paul,' said Caro. 'He knows. It's written all over his face. I suppose Scott told you?'

'Then he told Gina, and Gina told you – that must be it,' Caro guessed. 'It couldn't be anyone else.'

'That's beside the point.' Charlie found it embarrassing to look at Caro, and addressed himself to Paul. 'The fact remains – I know what has been going on, and I am extremely shocked. Caroline is my niece, and I feel a sense of responsibility towards her – which you obviously do not share. You should be ashamed of yourself.'

'Look here, can't we talk this over sensibly?' Paul tried to sound friendly and reasonable. 'We shan't get anywhere if we take up high moral attitudes – I really think you had better sit down.'

'I will not sit down! You call yourself a friend of the Minsters – and this is the way you repay that friendship. You know as well as I do, Alice would be distressed and horrified if she found out –'

'Then don't tell her,' said Caro. 'And she won't be upset.'

The argument went round and round in circles for a long time;

Charlie found he was getting tired of standing up, and perched on the edge of an armchair. After a while he sat back and accepted a cup of rather stewed tea.

As Caro pointed out, there was really nothing he could do about the situation. He did not wish to cause Alice and William any unhappiness, so he promised not to inform them that Paul and Caro were having an affair; but equally, he could not persuade them to give one another up.

'I love Paul, and he loves me, and quite honestly, it's none of your business what we do,' said Caro. 'I know you mean well, Uncle, but you won't do any good by coming here and giving us a lecture.'

Charlie snorted with frustration: 'Perhaps you'd be kind enough to tell me what your plans are? I take it you're not contemplating marriage?'

'We might – we haven't decided,' said Caro, airily.

Paul said nothing, but Charlie detected a flicker of embarrassment in his eyes, and followed it up quickly.

'You'd be laying yourself open to ridicule if you did,' he assured them. 'How would it look – a girl of twenty, marrying a man of fifty?'

'I'm twenty-four,' exclaimed Caro, 'and Paul's forty-seven. What's that got to do with it? We sleep together because we love one another, and whether we get married or not, it's nobody's business but –' She broke off, seeing too late that the sitting-room door had opened.

Paul's domestic couple, Mr and Mrs Wheeler, stood in the doorway. Carried away by the long, unresolved argument, Caro had not noticed the time; she had always been careful to leave the flat by five on a Sunday afternoon and to remove every trace of her occupation from Paul's bedroom before the Wheelers returned.

But it was too late now – and too late for any kind of pretence. From the expressions on their faces, it was clear that Mr and Mrs Wheeler had heard every word.

Just before eleven o'clock on Monday morning, Alice and William met on the main staircase: Alice had been called from the drawing-room, where she was writing letters, and William had been urgently summoned from the farm.

'What's it all about?' he wanted to know. 'Is Mama ill?'

'I don't think so – but Lilian says it's something important.'

William turned to the housekeeper who was hovering on the landing, but she could give him no explanation.

'I don't know any more about it than you do, sir,' she told him fretfully. 'Her ladyship wants me to go with you – eleven sharp, she said; not a minute before or after.'

'What the dickens is she playing at?' demanded William. 'I was in the middle of the dairy accounts. I hope this won't turn out to be another of her whims...'

Upstairs, Lady Beatrice sat on the edge of her bed, fully dressed and more cheerful than she had been for months. She wore a spot of rouge on each cheekbone, and had sprayed herself with perfume; and she was concluding an exhaustive discussion with Norman Brooks.

He too was dressed for the occasion, in his best black suit, and he had plastered his hair down with brilliantine. At first he had looked scared, then bemused, but finally the grin reappeared.

'You think you can manage that?' the old lady asked him.

'I'm certain sure I can, mum – I mean, my lady,' he said. 'When do I start?'

'As soon as possible. You have all the necessary qualifications, I hope? I hear from my wireless that they are introducing something called a driving test – and a speed limit of thirty miles per hour as well. Are you aware of that?'

'Don't you bother about such rubbish, my lady – they gave me my licence on my seventeenth birthday, and I got a clean record.'

'Apart from a little matter of attempted robbery... But we have agreed to draw a veil over that. One more question: are you strong?'

'Yes, my lady. I may not be heavy-like, but I'm wiry.'

'Excellent. Because I shall require you to carry me, from time to time. Come and pick me up, then take me into the sitting-room.'

Norman blinked. 'Now, my lady?'

'Now, boy.'

He was relieved to find how light she was, and carried her as easily as if she were a child: he was half-way across the sitting-room, with the old lady in his arms, when William and Alice entered, followed by the housekeeper.

'Mama!' exclaimed Alice in amazement.

'*Norman!*' Lilian Brooks was scandalized.

'Put me down in the chair by the window,' said Old Bea, unruffled. 'Gently, boy, gently. I bruise easily.' As soon as she was settled, she nodded at her visitors, well pleased. 'I'm glad you're so prompt,' she said. 'I have to tell you of some new arrangements I have made. This is Norman Brooks; I shall be employing him as my chauffeur and personal footman.'

They stared at Norman who went bright red, so that his freckles almost disappeared.

'But Mama – we already have a chauffeur; Dennett is perfectly reliable,' William began. 'We don't need –'

'Dennett is your chauffeur, and drives your car. Brooks is my chauffeur, and will drive mine,' the Countess informed her son.

'But you haven't got a car,' said Alice.

'I shall have. The boy will set about buying one today. I've been stuck in these rooms far too long, like a cabbage in a cabbage-patch; it's high time I got out and about, and Brooks will enable me to do so. I understand he is well qualified. He will provide a satisfactory reference from his present employers, at the Old Forge garage.'

Lilian broke in: 'I don't understand, my lady – he's my cousin Norman, and he's been a real trial to his poor mother from the day he was born – how did you ever come across him?'

'It was a lucky accident,' said the old lady firmly, and changed the subject. 'I shall also require him to live on the premises, so that I can call him whenever he is needed. You can find a spare bed in the servants' quarters, I'm sure... William – I leave you to organize details of wages and suchlike... Alice – he will need a uniform. Brass buttons, I think, and a peaked cap... Very well; that will be all.'

William cleared his throat. 'You don't think perhaps you're rushing into this rather too hastily, Mama? I don't wish to say a word against the Brooks family, but we know nothing about this young man. We must make sure that he is trustworthy and reliable –'

'I've gone into all that, William.' Old Bea cut him short. 'And I know I can rely on Norman Brooks absolutely. He will do *exactly* as he is told – isn't that right, boy?'

Norman swallowed once, then answered, 'Yes, my lady... Whatever you say.'

That evening, Caro met Paul in their usual bar in Margaret Street. She saw at once that he was a worried man.

'I'm sorry about yesterday,' she began as she sat down. 'I was furious with Uncle Charlie for coming in and throwing his weight about like that... Though I suppose he thought he was doing his duty, poor old thing. It's really Gina I'm angry with – and her loathsome brother... Were the Wheelers frightfully shocked?'

'They were.' Paul took a drink, then said: 'I tried to calm them down, but without success. They're old-fashioned creatures, and they must have sat up half the night, discussing it. The result was, when Wheeler brought in my early-morning tea today, he informed me that they wish to give in their notice.'

'But that's ridiculous!'

'Apparently they feel very strongly about it. They couldn't possibly stay in an establishment with what Mr Wheeler described as "goings on"...'

'What ever will you do?'

'Set about finding new staff, I suppose,' he sighed. 'It's all very unfortunate – and it means we shall have to be doubly careful in future.'

Caro put down her glass. 'Not necessarily,' she said.

'What do you mean?'

'I've got a much better idea. I shall move in with you. We don't need anyone else; I can keep the flat clean. Just think: we'll be together all the time – won't that be wonderful?'

Paul's brow was furrowed. 'My darling girl – what on earth would people say? Your parents would never forgive me.'

'They won't know. I'll tell the family Muriel and I are taking a flat together; I'll move my things out of Eaton Square... Of course I'll go back for the odd night when Mummy's up in town, to keep her happy – not that she spends much time in London nowadays, since she stopped being a lady-in-waiting.'

Paul still looked far from happy. 'I foresee endless complications. It's a lovely idea, and of course it would be a joy to have you with me, but I'm afraid we –'

'Don't be afraid.' She put her hand on his. 'And stop looking so worried. I'm a very good cook – you said so the other night.'

'But we usually eat out at weekends. I admit you sometimes make the odd omelette or do a bit of finnan haddock, but –'

'I shall put them together; that's what they do at the Savoy... And that's only a beginning; I shall buy a cookery book.' Her eyes were dancing. 'It's going to be terrific fun – you wait and see!'

The long hot summer was like a calm sea: towering white clouds were galleons sailing across the blue. Jenny watched little Harry growing day by day, crowing with delight as she discovered daisies in the grass, or the pattern of leaves in the trees above her perambulator. Everyone came out of doors, making the most of the fine weather. Only Polly shut herself up in her room, seeing no one and wanting no one's company.

Even Old Bea began to explore the world beyond the walls of Crown House.

Norman Brooks had done all she asked of him. He found a very suitable Lanchester saloon, with maroon upholstery and a walnut fascia, and polished the paintwork to a dazzling shine. Every morning he presented himself, to be given his orders for the day; sometimes she would send him out alone on an errand, but nearly always she announced that she wished to go with him. Then he would pick her up and carry her downstairs to the car.

At first she contented herself with brief trips round the nearby lanes, or into Medford, but then they ventured further afield, to Maidstone or Sutton Valence. One day she decided she would like to visit Sevenoaks, and arrived uninvited at Knole just as the Sackvilles were about to begin luncheon. They assured her they were very glad to see her, and she joined them for salmon mayonnaise, followed by strawberries and cream.

When she returned home, she asked speculatively: 'How many miles is it from here to Windsor?' And Alice had to talk her out of it.

But the excursions were doing the old lady good; she began to look livelier and younger, and the family welcomed the change in her. Even William admitted that his mother's decision to have her own transport was not a bad idea, adding privately to Alice: 'I'm in favour of anything that gets her out of our way for a few hours . . .'

He was less happy about Caroline's continued absence, and complained that they scarcely saw her at all these days.

Alice explained: 'I expect she's very busy, getting settled in to her new flat with Muriel Thingummy.'

'I suppose so . . . Whereabouts did you say it is?'

'Somewhere near Primrose Hill. Quite a nice area.'

'But you haven't actually been there yourself?'

'No, not yet. Caro says there's still so much to be done; she doesn't want me to see it till it's completely finished. Bless her, she's so thrilled to have a home of her own.'

'And she's not on the telephone? That seems odd – in her line of business, I'd have thought a telephone was essential.'

'She does all her telephoning from the office. Muriel's got an elderly aunt who stays with them; apparently she's very highly strung, and the telephone bell might bring on a nervous attack. But Caro promised she'll be coming down for a weekend very soon.'

With this, William had to be satisfied.

When Gina and Charlie heard that their niece was sharing a flat in Primrose Hill with a young lady from her office, they said nothing. Gina smiled; Charlie did not. He was bitterly disappointed by Caroline's devious behaviour, and felt the deepest possible resentment of Paul Weyman; but he had promised to say nothing, and kept his word – against his better judgement.

Gina told him not to be so old-fashioned; he was only sixty, for heaven's sake – anyone would think he was a hundred and sixty, the way he carried on.

But Caro was not the only subject on which they held opposing views. Charlie had severed all connections with Sir Oswald Mosley; but Gina was being drawn more and more closely into the Leader's inner circle.

She went to party meetings regularly, and began to wear her own version of the blackshirt uniform: a beautifully tailored black skirt, with the enamelled Fascist badge pinned to her black silk blouse.

When, at the beginning of September, Sir Oswald rallied his supporters in Hyde Park, she could not persuade Charlie to go with her – but she said she didn't care. She was perfectly happy to go on her own.

She arranged to meet Roland Voss at headquarters, then drove him to Kensington, leaving her car parked near the Serpentine.

As usual, Mosley had organized the event well, and two and a half thousand Blackshirts assembled at the rallying-point. This time, the authorities were taking no chances, and the BUF members were heavily outnumbered by a cordon of six thousand uniformed police, who enclosed the area completely. Outside the police perimeter, a much larger crowd of Labour and anti-fascist demonstrators held meetings of their own.

In consequence, despite a battery of microphones and loudspeakers, the Leader's words were drowned by a continuous roar of protest, chanting and booing.

When Gina and Roland drove away under the watchful protection of the police, the young lieutenant was in a very bad temper.

'It's not that bad, honey!' Gina tried to cheer him up. 'Look how many people turned out; that's really encouraging.'

'I'm thinking of that mob of lefties and yids who tried to wreck our meeting,' said Roland. 'I'd like to get my hands on those bastards –'

'You'll have your chance, one of these days,' Gina soothed him. 'Listen, where am I supposed to be taking you – back to the Kings Road?'

'No – there's no one at headquarters now; it'll be shut up. I'll just go home. Drop me off anywhere. I can pick up a taxi.'

'You'll do no such thing! It's too risky to wander round on your own when you're in uniform; some idiots might gang up on you.'

'Just let 'em try!' He clenched his fists. 'I'd give a pretty good account of myself, I reckon.'

'I'm sure you would – but I'm taking you home. Tell me where you live.'

Roland had a studio flatlet in Maida Vale, not far from the Edgware Road, and they were there within fifteen minutes. When he got out of the car, he said awkwardly, 'Well, thanks a lot... I'd ask you in for coffee, but I'm in a foul mood – I wouldn't be very good company.'

'That won't bother me one little bit,' smiled Gina. 'As it happens, I'm in a terribly good mood myself – maybe some of it might brush off on you? And I'd simply adore a cup of coffee.'

The flatlet was small and untidy; an unmade bed seemed to take up a disproportionate amount of space. Roland had obviously left home in a rush, and cast-off clothes still littered the floor.

'Sorry about the mess.' He filled a kettle and put it on a gas ring in the corner. 'That's the worst of being a bachelor – one stops bothering. I keep saying I'll get a little woman in to do for me, but somehow I never get around to it.'

'A little woman to do – what?' Gina's eyes opened very wide.

Going to the cupboard which served as a larder, he found that the milk had gone sour in the hot weather.

'Bloody hell!' he exclaimed, tipping it down the sink. 'Sorry about that...'

'That's OK. I like it black – and strong,' said Gina.

'You must forgive me. I still feel steamed up – I really should take a three-mile run, or go swimming or something to work off some energy.'

'Don't bother, Roly.' Gina sat on the bed, and kicked off her shoes. 'I'm sure we can find some other way...'

The fourteenth of October was the anniversary of Richard's death, and everyone at Crown House was very much aware of that fact. William got up early and walked in the gardens before breakfast, though he did not go near the rockery. He had abandoned his new rockery, leaving the gardeners to do what they liked with it, since that Saturday morning one year ago when he was called away to go to the stables.

Today he picked an armful of golden chrysanthemums, and took them to Polly's room. He did not say anything; there was nothing to be said.

She held out her arms and hugged him, whispering, 'I've been a real wash-out, haven't I? I've got to pull myself together – I know that – and I will... Soon now... Very soon – I promise.'

He patted her shoulder, and kissed her. Later, over breakfast, he said to Alice, 'I'm still very worried about that poor girl. We really should spend more time with her. She's alone far too much.'

'But if that's what she wants...' Alice was skimming through a letter from Buckingham Palace, and now broke off to exclaim: 'William! Her Majesty has asked me to go up and help her, before the wedding... You won't mind if I'm away for a few weeks, will you?'

There had been a lot of talk about the forthcoming wedding of Prince George. According to the gossip, Queen Mary originally hoped Princess Marina of Greece might make a suitable bride for her eldest son; but David was hopelessly enthralled by Wallis Simpson and would not even consider the idea.

George, too, had given rise to a good deal of anxiety within the palace. His escapades had been notorious, and there were whispers of unconventional sexual exploits. Some people said George's parents had given him an ultimatum: this outrageous behaviour must stop. He had to settle down to a respectable, domestic life. He had to get married.

He was introduced to Marina; a stylish, intelligent girl, amusing and sophisticated – he was immediately charmed by her. After a whirlwind courtship, they announced their engagement; the wedding was to take place at the end of November.

When Alice presented herself at the Palace, she found the King and Queen sitting together in His Majesty's study; the Queen welcomed her warmly, and pressed her hand with unspoken sympathy. His Majesty grunted something about being pleased to see her again, and busied himself with a sheaf of papers on his desk.

'I can't make out half the names – why can't people write a decent fist nowadays? All these damned lists . . .'

'There are a great many invitations to be sent, dear,' the Queen pointed out.

Alice thought that the King looked much older; it was only a year since she had seen him, but he seemed to have aged a great deal. The Queen was unaltered in appearance, holding herself very erect in her chair, her coiffure and her style of dress the same as ever. But Alice found a change in Her Majesty, when she ventured to ask:

'I imagine you will entertain visiting royalty, Ma'am – from abroad?'

The Queen looked momentarily puzzled, then her face cleared. 'Yes, indeed – the people's loyalty is very gratifying; at home, and in the Commonwealth too.'

Alice realized that the Queen's slight tendency to deafness had worsened since they last met.

The King was trying to sort out two different lists. The longer of the two included all those who would be present within the Abbey; the second, which he examined carefully, was more selective: these were the guests who would be invited to the reception at the Palace a few nights earlier.

'Did you know Lillibet is to be the principal bridesmaid?' Her Majesty asked with a smile. 'She's looking forward to it so much. Of course Margaret is too young; I only hope she can be persuaded to sit still throughout the ceremony.'

Suddenly the King gave a snort of annoyance, and ran his pen through two names. 'No, no – out of the question,' he muttered to himself. 'Completely unsuitable.'

They were still checking the lists at four o'clock, when they were joined unexpectedly by the Prince of Wales.

'The Duchess of Dillwater, as I live and breathe!' David greeted Alice with the nickname he had given her, and she thought that here at least was one member of the family who never changed. Then he turned to his father: 'Papa, I hear you're approving the guest-list – may I cast an eye over it?'

The King seemed inclined to protest, but David was already leaning over his shoulder, checking the names. After a moment he spoke again, in a different tone. 'Why have Mr and Mrs Simpson been crossed out?'

'Go away, David; we have a lot of work to get through, and if you keep interrupting –' the King began irritably.

'I asked why you had crossed the Simpsons off the list. Surely you know they are close friends of mine?'

'They are not the kind of people I wish you to cultivate, and I won't have them here.'

The King folded up the guest-list, as if that was the end of the matter – but his son snatched the folded paper, saying angrily: 'I'm sorry, Papa – but if the Simpsons aren't invited, you needn't expect to see me here either . . . I mean that.'

King George looked as if he were about to explode, and the Queen rose. 'Alice, my dear, perhaps we should be more comfortable in the other room – would you be kind enough to ring for tea?'

The two ladies waited in the adjoining room, and Alice did her best to make conversation; but it was obvious that Her Majesty had her mind on other things. At first there was no sound from behind the closed study door, but then His Majesty lost his temper, and Alice heard him roar:

'How dare you give me orders! You are a cad, sir! You dress like a cad, and you act like a cad! Get out!'

Shielded by deafness, the Queen was unaware of this; perhaps David asked his father to lower his voice, for Alice could not hear what followed, though a little later the King asked loudly: 'Will you give me your solemn word that this American woman is not your mistress?'

The Prince's reply was inaudible, but Alice presumed that it must have satisfied His Majesty, for there were no more angry exchanges, and after a few minutes the Prince walked out. He nodded briefly at the Queen, threw a curt 'Good afternoon' to both ladies, and took his leave of them as the tea-trolley was wheeled in.

So he had changed too, Alice thought, and not for the better.

'Would you ask His Majesty if he will join us?' said the Queen.

Alice knocked, and entered the study. The King was still at his desk, with his back to her. Hearing the door open, and assuming his wife had returned, he said bitterly: 'It seems we shall be forced to receive that woman after all . . . I tell you this, May – when I'm gone, David will ruin himself within twelve months.'

11

MONDAY, 6 MAY 1935

On the day of the Royal Jubilee celebrations, William was up and about early, for although this was a national holiday his work had to go on as usual. As he walked along the path that led to the home farm, he was astonished to come face to face with Polly. It was the first time she had set foot outside the house for over a year.

She looked very pale, but she had put on her lipstick and dressed with some care, and she managed to smile at his obvious surprise.

'It's all right – it's only me,' she said. 'It looks like being a lovely day, so I thought I'd come out for a breath of air. Doesn't it smell good, outdoors?' She took a deep breath, determined to appear calm and relaxed. 'Where is everybody?' she went on. 'I thought I might take Alex for a walk later on. Where's Alice? And Jenny?'

'Alice is in London; she's on duty at the Palace today – it's a great occasion.'

'Is it?' Polly looked puzzled, then said vaguely, 'Oh, yes, the Silver Jubilee – I think I saw something about it in one of the papers.'

William nodded: the newspapers had been anticipating this historic event for weeks.

'And where are you off to?' continued Polly.

'To the farm. I think I'm beginning to learn how it's run, at long last; at first I rather suspect that the farm was running me!' he said. 'Would you like to keep me company? Have a look at our livestock?'

'No, thanks,' she said. 'I'm going the other way – round by the lake.'

Belatedly, William realized he had been thoughtless. As far as

Polly was concerned, the farm was still Richard's territory; he should not have reminded her of it.

But then she smiled and waved, as Jenny came out of the house with little Harry in her arms, and Alex running round them in circles like an eager puppy. Jenny looked startled, but quickly recovered and walked across the lawn towards them.

'Ah – here comes the family,' said William. 'I must be getting along. I'll see you later, I hope.'

He set off once more along the path to the farm, as Jenny approached with the children. When Alex saw his mother, he slowed down, hanging back. For a long time now, he had been accustomed to the idea of Mummy as a permanent invalid, spending her life in her room, and he looked up doubtfully as she bent to kiss him.

'What a nice surprise!' Jenny held Harriet out, expecting Polly to take her; but she made no move to do so.

'Isn't this a gorgeous day?' Polly ignored the baby completely. 'I thought I'd take Alex for a walk round the lake. We could go paddling, p'raps – would you like that?'

Alex's face crumpled with disappointment, and he turned to Jenny. 'Do I have to?' he asked anxiously.

Polly's smile faded. 'Not if you don't want to.'

'Actually – I promised I'd take the children into the village,' said Jenny. 'There's a special Jubilee fête on today, with a party for the schoolchildren. They said Alex could join in the fun – I think he's rather looking forward to it.'

'I see: Grace and Edith put in a word for him, did they?'

Jenny stared at her. 'They moved to France last year. There's a new teacher now.'

'Yes, of course – I remember.' Polly tried to laugh. 'All right then; off you go, Alex – have a good time.'

'Why don't you come with us?' Jenny suggested. 'It should be fun.'

Polly shook her head. 'Into the village? I don't think so. People would want to come up and talk . . . I'd sooner stay here. See you when you get back.' She did not look at her children again, but set off alone towards the lake. It felt so strange, being in the garden after all this time. It felt particularly strange because she was on her own. She couldn't remember walking here by herself; Richard had always been with her . . . But she mustn't think about Richard.

Jenny watched her as she walked away, and sighed.

'Can we go now?' Alex was impatient.

It took a little while to get the children ready. Harry had to be settled into her pushchair, and Alex – after only ten minutes in the garden – had to have his face and hands washed all over again. But at last the little party was ready to set out.

So was Lady Beatrice. As they came down the front steps, they saw Norman Brooks, spick and span in his peaked cap and uniform, carrying the old lady across to her car. Jenny took the children to say good morning to their great-grandmama.

'We're going to the Jubilee,' said Alex, in the hushed voice of one passing on a state secret.

'Are you indeed?' Old Bea smiled a crocodile smile. 'So am I.'

'To the village fête?' said Jenny. 'Oh, good, we'll see you there –'

'No, no – I'm going to the proper Jubilee, in London.' The Dowager Countess tossed her head, showing off her feathered toque. 'Don't I look grand enough for a royal occasion?'

'You look splendid,' Jenny assured her. 'I didn't realize – nobody told me you'd been invited.'

'I haven't. People always think they can overlook me, but I won't be overlooked. Norman will drive me up to St Paul's, and if I can't get inside, I shall see the King and Queen going by.'

'Oh ... Do you think that's a good idea?' Jenny foresaw all kinds of difficulties. 'It's a long drive to London; you'll be very tired when you get there.'

'In that case I shall go to Eaton Square first, for a cup of tea and forty winks ... All right, boy!' Old Bea snapped her fingers imperiously at her young chauffeur. 'You may start the motor; we haven't time to hang about chattering.'

Norman touched his cap respectfully, but he looked perplexed. 'Beg pardon, my lady, but I ain't never been to London. I don't know the way.'

'What an extraordinary boy – there are signposts, aren't there? Just follow the signs saying "London", and when we get there I shall direct you myself. I know London like the back of my hand ... Drive on!'

The day turned out to be a real scorcher. Outside Buckingham Palace, the roads had been cordoned off, and policemen kept the huge crowds under control. By ten o'clock, the mass of sightseers was so thick, and the heat so oppressive, that many people fainted and had to be lifted up and passed back over the heads of the crowd; they were laid out on the grass in Green Park or beside the Mall, to recover.

Within the Palace, tension mounted as the cavalcade prepared to set off. The Duke and Duchess of York kept a firm grip on the two little Princesses. They looked angelic in pink dresses with straw bonnets decorated with ribbons and rosebuds, but they were so excited it was impossible to keep them quiet.

'Would you like me to tell them a story?' Alice suggested.

'My dear, that would be an act of true heroism,' said Elizabeth gratefully. But she was interrupted by Lady Kelso who came into the anteroom, looking for Alice.

'I'm so sorry – but there's a telephone call for you, from Lord Minster,' Flora explained.

'At a moment like this?' Alice felt a chill of apprehension. 'Someone must be ill... I'll be as quick as I can,' she explained to the Duchess, and hurried off to the telephone.

'William? What's wrong?' she asked breathlessly.

'I shouldn't trouble you when I know you're so busy, but – it's Mama.' William's voice sounded thin and unreal. 'I'm rather worried about her.'

'Not her heart again?'

'No, no, she's not ill – she's disappeared. I've only just heard; apparently she took it into her head to drive up to town, without telling me. She suddenly decided she would like to see the procession; according to Jenny, she's making for St Paul's.'

'Good heavens... But she'll never get through – all the roads are closed.'

'I know. She also announced her intention of going to Eaton Square first, and I feel someone should keep an eye on her. She doesn't realize the staff have totally changed since her day; there'll be nobody there who knows her. They'll probably think she's some dotty old woman suffering from delusions, and turn her away.'

'Very well – I'll ring up and warn Miss Kendall.' Alice heard voices calling along the corridor, and glanced at her watch. 'Darling, I must go – the first carriages are due to leave at any moment. I'll talk to you later.'

'Of course. Good luck; I hope all goes well.'

Silently cursing her mother-in-law, Alice got through to Eaton

Square and explained the situation to the housekeeper, then dashed out to join the royal party.

The Yorks left in the first landau, and were lustily cheered by the crowds; the Princesses waved back as they ascended the gentle slope of Constitution Hill to Hyde Park Corner.

They were followed by the Duke and Duchess of Kent (for Prince George had been given this title at the time of his marriage), then by Prince Henry and the Prince of Wales. All of them were given an enthusiastic reception as they drove by, but the cheers reached a thunderous climax as the royal carriage turned out of the Palace gates. The King and Queen bowed graciously to left and right, acknowledging the ovation.

'Do you see that, May? A lot of 'em are holding up their arms in that damned foreign salute!' exclaimed the King. But then he saw the flashes of reflected sunlight and corrected himself: 'No, they're not – they're holding up mirrors!'

He was quite right; the crowds were so tightly packed that the people at the back could not see the procession, and many of the women had pulled out their handbag mirrors, holding them up as makeshift periscopes.

The royal progress continued – along Piccadilly, through St James's, Pall Mall and Trafalgar Square. At Temple Bar, the King was greeted by the Lord Mayor of London who presented him with a ceremonial pearl sword as a mark of the City's allegiance; and so on to St Paul's Cathedral, where the service of thanksgiving was to be held.

The streets were jammed with people; of these, only a small number were Londoners. Some had travelled up to the capital from remote corners of the British Isles, and many came from further afield: there were visitors from all over the world. They screamed and shouted and roared the national anthem; they waved pennants and threw streamers; and every street along the route was garlanded with royal emblems, flags and flowers.

The King found himself unexpectedly stirred by this expression of love and loyalty. Before his illness, a few years earlier, the nation had regarded him as a cold, aloof man; not a jolly, roguish uncle like his predecessor, King Teddy. Only when George was at death's door did his people discover how much they loved him, and now they showed their feelings in no uncertain manner.

When the procession began the return journey, by way of Blackfriars and the Embankment, the King spoke – so quietly, the Queen could hardly make out his words through the sound of cheering.

'Do you know – this is the greatest number of people in the streets I have ever seen . . .' He sounded completely astonished. 'I am beginning to think they must like me – for myself.'

When they had reached the Palace for a late lunch, His Majesty was in high good humour, and chucked Lillibet under the chin, then hoisted Margaret on to his lap, saying with a beaming smile, 'I suppose you think those flags and things were hung out for your benefit, eh? Well, let me tell you – they're all for *me*!'

Then he and the Queen led their family out on to the balcony, waving an acknowledgement to the crowds.

Alice took the opportunity to slip away to the telephone, and rang Miss Kendall at Eaton Square again, enquiring after Lady Beatrice. The housekeeper sounded rather aggrieved.

'I'm afraid there has been some mistake, my lady. I waited in specially – I had intended going out to try and catch a glimpse of the procession, but then I thought I should be here to welcome the Countess, so I waited all this time . . . But she never turned up.'

Immediately, Alice's imagination ran away with her. She put the telephone down, thinking that Lady Beatrice's car must have been involved in an accident; those things happened so fast, so unexpectedly. She remembered that dreadful night when her own car had overturned on a patch of ice, and Jenny's mother had been killed . . . Should she start ringing round the hospitals and police stations? But there was no time for that, while she was on duty.

Then she had a brainwave. Caroline would be at the *Argus* offices, preparing the special Jubilee edition for tomorrow morning; she was a resourceful girl, and would know what to do. Alice dialled the Fleet Street number, and waited.

Someone in the news-room told her Caroline had been given the day off; Lady Minster might find her at home perhaps – why not telephone her there?

'Oh, but she isn't on the telephone –' Alice began.

'I'm sure she is. Haven't you got her number?'

'No, I haven't.' Alice thought fast. 'Could you put me through to her friend Muriel –' in the nick of time, she remembered not to say 'Muriel Thingummy' – 'Muriel Beasley, in the photo-library?'

A moment later, a female voice came on the line. 'Good after-noon – can I help you?'

'Oh, yes – this is Alice Minster speaking. I'm Caroline's mother. I'm sorry to bother you, but we have a little family crisis, and I gather Caro may be at home today, so –'

'Caroline? Caroline who?'

Alice frowned. Really, the girl was remarkably dense. 'Caroline Gaunt – my daughter! She told me you weren't on the telephone at home, because of your poor aunt, but perhaps since then –'

'I'm sorry, I don't know what you're talking about. We do have a phone at home – but I haven't got an aunt.'

'Oh, I'm so sorry... I thought you were – how silly of me.' Alice began again. 'I want to speak to Miss Muriel Beasley. She's the young lady who shares a flat with my daughter, at Primrose Hill.'

'I am Muriel Beasley – but I don't live at Primrose Hill and I don't really know your daughter – just to say hello to. I live at home with my Mum and Dad, in South Norwood. I think somebody's been pulling your leg.'

'Oh... I see... Thank you.'

Stunned, Alice replaced the telephone receiver. It was hard to believe that Caroline had lied to her; but there was no other expla-nation. The story about her move from Eaton Square had been a fabrication from start to finish... But why?

Clearly, she had moved into a flat with someone else; someone she did not want her parents to know about.

Alice pushed a wisp of hair back from her forehead, with fingers that trembled. Caro was over twenty-one, and had a life of her own. If she chose to go and live with some young man, that was entirely up to her... But why couldn't she have been honest about it?

With a great effort, Alice wrenched her mind away from Caroline. The immediate problem was of greater urgency. She must do some-thing about Lady Beatrice. If she had been injured in an accident – or worse – the police would probably get in touch with the household at Eaton Square, and there was no one there capable of dealing with such a crisis. Quickly, she made up her mind.

She found Queen Mary in her private sitting-room; the King was with her. He looked very tired, but very happy, lying on a sofa with a rug over his legs.

Alice hesitated in the doorway: 'Your Majesties – I'm so sorry to disturb you –'

'Not at all – come in, come in.' The King sounded positively cordial. 'I'm just taking a short rest. It's all been wonderful, but the day's not over yet – not by a long chalk.'

'I told him he should put his feet up,' explained the Queen. 'He has to make his broadcast to the Empire at eight o'clock – and after that he must go out to light the first of the Jubilee beacons in Hyde Park, so he needs to take things easily while he can.'

'But I'm enjoying it all – much more than I expected.' The King smothered a yawn. 'Everyone's been very kind ... And Bertie and Elizabeth have been such a help – even my grandchildren have done their best to make this a happy day for me ... Such a splendid family ...'

He closed his eyes, but continued to speak in a low, dreamy voice – talking as much to himself as to them, Alice thought.

'I pray to God that my eldest son will never marry and have children – and that nothing will come between Bertie and Lillibet, and the throne ...'

Alice glanced quickly at the Queen, but Her Majesty made no reaction to these last remarks; perhaps she had not heard them. She looked up at Alice with friendly interest, and said: 'You came in to ask me something, I think? What is it, my dear?'

Alice outlined the situation briefly; she was very worried about Lady Beatrice, and felt so helpless here in the Palace. Would it be possible for Her Majesty to excuse her from her duties for the rest of the day, so that she could go back to Eaton Square and take charge of things there?

'Of course, Alice. It is an emergency – you must go.' The Queen was very understanding. 'I hope you hear some good news of the Countess soon.'

'Thank you, Ma'am.'

Alice looked across at the King, but he was fast asleep. The Queen held out her hand: Alice curtseyed and kissed it before leaving the room.

She slipped out of the Palace by a side entrance, through the Royal Mews, and into Buckingham Palace Road, where a police escort saw her safely through the cordon and into the crowds beyond.

Now she was on her own; alone, and surrounded by a thousand people. It was hopeless to try and find a taxi: she would have to make her way home on foot.

The press of sightseers was overwhelming, and by now the temperature had risen to the upper seventies. A steamy heat arose from the packed crowds, and Alice fought her way through, step by step, trying to get into the side-streets where there might be room to move.

Her hat was knocked sideways, she was jostled and shoved; someone trod on her feet. The journey was only half a mile from door to door, but it took her nearly an hour to get home.

She tried to concentrate on Old Bea, praying that her mother-in-law would be found, safe and well... But again and again her thoughts returned to Caroline. She felt as if she had lost two members of her family today; her mother-in-law had disappeared, and so had Caroline. Where was she now? Who was she with? Why had she lied about it? Why couldn't she tell her parents the truth?

Polly was sitting under a willow tree at the far end of the lake. She liked it out here – it was so peaceful. All around her, there were green leaves, as fresh and shining as springtime, and tiny ripples lapped against the pebbles at the water's edge. It was so gloriously hot; she was tempted to take off her blouse and skirt and lie in the golden, glowing sunlight – nobody would see her here; a grove of elms concealed her from the house.

But she was too comfortable to move; she couldn't be bothered. She shut her eyes lazily, enjoying the drowsy insect hum and the far-off chuckle of doves in the trees.

'Polly – darling...'

She wasn't surprised to see Richard walking towards her. This was his place; he belonged here. He looked just the same as ever; his curly hair untidy, his shirt unbuttoned, and the joyful, generous smile lighting up his face – the smile that said: 'I am yours and you are mine, and nothing can ever come between us.' It was the smile she had fallen in love with, the first time she saw him.

'Where have you been?' he asked. 'I've been looking all over the place. Dearest Polly – there's never been anyone like you, and there never will be.' He held out his arms: she stood up, and ran to him.

And now they were in the lake, thigh-deep in the water; and she realized that they had no clothes on. He held her in his arms, and they were floating together, weightless and effortless, gliding through the still, cool water...

'Polly –?' A different voice; another hand on her shoulder.

She opened her eyes. William stood looking down at her, concerned.

'Are you all right?' he asked.

'Oh – yes – I must have nodded off.'

'You didn't come in for lunch,' he said. 'I wondered where you'd got to.'

'I wasn't hungry. It's so nice out here.' She stood up, and they began to stroll back together, towards the house.

'The place has been deserted today. Mama's gone on one of her crazy excursions – up to London, if you please, to try to see the Jubilee! I hope she's enjoying herself.'

'I'm sure she is. And Jenny took the children off to some party or other, didn't she?'

'The fête on the village green: we'll all have tea together when they get back... I must telephone London; I want to make sure Mama's all right.'

She slipped her arm through his. 'You look after us all. What would we do without you?'

The elms gave way to an avenue of chestnuts; emerald-green fingers spread out, balancing cream-and-pink candles. As they walked along the line of trees, stepping from patches of shade into brilliant sunlight, William said, 'They've had perfect weather for the celebrations – royal weather.'

'It's been a bit of a celebration for me too,' Polly smiled. 'My first time outdoors – I really enjoyed it. I can feel it doing me good.'

'I'm very glad.'

Across the broad expanse of grass, they saw Jenny wheeling the pushchair with three balloons tied to it, one red, one white and one blue, in fine patriotic style. Alex, walking beside Jenny, spotted his mother and grandfather, and waved frantically, calling to them, 'Look what I've got!'

He was carrying a precious souvenir. All over the country, schools had given their pupils Jubilee mugs with portraits of the monarchs in linked medallions, surrounded by roses, thistles, daffodils and shamrock.

'Look!' he repeated, starting to run. 'They said I could have one too!'

'Isn't that lovely?' Polly quickened her pace.

Then, when he was only a few yards away, Alex's foot slipped on a soft patch of turf, and he fell headlong. The mug went flying, landing with an ominous crack, and the handle came off.

'Never mind – I'm sure we can glue it together again,' William began, but the mingled shock and disappointment were too much for the little boy, and he let out a howl of grief. He had grazed his knees, and needed instant comfort.

'Alex – darling . . .' Polly ran to pick him up, but he scrambled to his feet, dodged her outstretched hands, and headed in another direction, wailing: 'Jenny – Jenny –!' He threw himself into Jenny's arms, and she hugged him until he stopped crying.

'Well . . .' Polly made herself useful by picking up the broken mug, and handed it to William. 'Perhaps you could do something about this. I think I'll go to my room.'

'So soon? Aren't you going to have tea?' he asked.

'They'll bring me up something presently, I expect. I'm a bit sleepy after all this fresh air.'

She walked quickly into the house, eager to get back to bed – impatient to dream again.

Sir Charles Bowyer entered the drawing-room at Eaton Square, and was met by Alice, looking distraught.

'Charlie . . . Thank you for coming over so promptly – I didn't know who else to call . . .' She waved him into an armchair. 'Would you like some tea? Or is it too late?'

'Much too late. A whisky and soda would hit the spot very nicely.' He watched her as she went over to the drinks table. 'Not too much soda – don't drown it.'

She poured herself a sherry, and they clinked glasses; he took an appreciative swig.

'That's better. Now then – what's the problem?' he asked.

'There are two problems, really; but the urgent one is Old Bea – Lady Beatrice, I mean. She's vanished.'

Charlie stared at her. 'How d'you mean – vanished?'

'She set off to drive up to town this morning, and that's the last anyone saw of her. I don't know what to do. William rang me at half-past five, and I had to break it to him. He took it pretty well – he says she's bound to turn up sooner or later, but I keep thinking of all the dreadful things that might have happened. I mean – if the car broke down, she'd have told the chauffeur to telephone us – or call the police – or *something* – wouldn't she?'

'Have you spoken to the police yourself?'

'No. I was going to, but – they must have had so much to cope with, today of all days... Do you think I should?' She had begun to shake again, and he patted her shoulder.

'There, there – don't upset yourself, old girl. I'll call Scotland Yard if you like. One of the Commissioner chappies is a member of my Club.'

'Would you really? Oh, Charlie...' Her voice broke. 'It's such a relief to have you here. Being all alone was the worst part.'

'Glad I was able to help. I was alone too, as it happens; Gina's gone off to another of those damned rallies – they're holding a torchlight procession this evening, as their contribution to the festivities... Let's see, I shall need the telephone number for Scotland Yard –'

'I think it's Whitehall one two, one two,' Alice remembered. 'They're always saying that on Mama's wireless set... Oh, I do hope she's all right.'

Charlie was lifting the receiver when they heard raised voices from somewhere below, and Alice hurried to the door. The harsh domineering tones of the Dowager Countess were unmistakable.

'Announce me to Lady Minster immediately! Norman – carry me upstairs. And afterwards you can go down to the servants' hall – I dare say they'll find you a glass of beer. No more than one, mind: you've had quite enough today.'

She looked a little tired when Norman carried her in to the drawing-room, but she was still indomitable.

Alice greeted her with relief: 'Where on earth have you been, Mama? We were simply frantic.'

As soon as she was comfortably settled in the best chair, Lady Beatrice told her story. Norman had managed to get as far as the outskirts of London, then got completely lost somewhere near New Cross, and finished up in Bermondsey.

There they had found a great many roads closed to traffic – not on account of the procession, as they first supposed, but because the entire district was celebrating with street-parties.

When she realized that she was never going to get to St Paul's in time, Old Bea decided they might as well stay where they were – and the residents of Bermondsey had given them a warm welcome.

'Most hospitable people – and so obliging. One couple brought out an armchair for me, and we were given home-made cake, and plates of trifle, and there was an endless supply of milk-stout –

and something called saveloys... It was all highly enjoyable. After luncheon, the children ran races, and they asked me to present the prizes; then someone played a piano – it needed tuning, but that didn't matter – and a lot of people danced, and sang songs. There was one about a ghost walking round the Tower of London with its head tucked underneath its arm – quite inappropriate for the occasion, no doubt, but rather entertaining...' She paused for breath and gazed round the room, with considerably less enthusiasm. 'I can't say I care for the way you've redecorated this house. Too much chintz – what have you done with Minster's portrait? And I don't recognize any of the staff downstairs – they're all total strangers.'

'It's a long time since you were here, Mama.' Alice tried to appease her. 'There are bound to be changes... But I'll tell Miss Kendall to prepare the guest-room for you – I expect you'd like an early night, after so much excitement –'

'Good gracious, Alice – I'm not staying! I'm much too old to sleep in a strange bed. No, no – I won't impose on you – the boy will drive me home.'

Her mind was made up, and Alice could not persuade her that she needed to rest. Half an hour later, Lady Beatrice summoned Norman, telling him she was ready to leave. As he carried her downstairs, she was humming tunelessly to herself. Alice could not recognize the melody, but she thought she heard something about the Bloody Tower.

Once the Countess had gone, the atmosphere relaxed. Alice rang Crown House to tell William he could expect his mother's return in two or three hours.

'And that's that,' said Charlie comfortably. 'I must say, she's a game old girl – she'll see us all out, I shouldn't wonder.'

Alice sat down. 'There's something else,' she said. She told him about the conversation she had had with Muriel Beasley, finishing, 'I don't know what to do about it; I haven't said anything to William yet – he'll be absolutely horrified. But I had to tell somebody... You won't breathe a word, will you, Charlie?'

She looked at her brother; he was frowning at the empty glass in his hand, and she expected him to ask her to refill it, but he said quietly, 'I'm glad you know. I've had this on my conscience for some time – they made me promise not to tell you.'

'They? What do you mean? I don't understand.'

'It was Gina who heard about it. Caroline's been having an affair with this man – someone totally unsuitable – it's been going on for more than a year, apparently.'

'Oh, God – you should have told me . . .'

'I couldn't. But now you've found out, I do think you should speak to Caroline yourself.'

'I don't even know where she's living –'

'I can give you the telephone number. She might be there now.'

Alice did not know what she would say to Caro, but she felt Charlie was right. Anything was better than the awful barrier of pretence and deception which had grown up between them. She gave the number to the operator and waited. At last she heard the sound of a receiver being lifted.

'Hello,' said a man's voice. 'Paul Weyman speaking – who is that? . . . Hello?'

After a very long moment, Alice put down the telephone.

12

MONDAY, 6 MAY TO SATURDAY, 31 AUGUST 1935

GINA had not enjoyed the Silver Jubilee very much. She didn't like going on marches at the best of times. There were a lot of other things she enjoyed as a member of the BUF – going into pubs and cafés to sell copies of their newspaper *Blackshirt* could be quite fun, especially as it was considered unwise for female party members to undertake this duty alone, and she usually contrived to get Roland Voss as her escort. She enjoyed being with Roly very much indeed, both on duty and off.

This evening there was to be a torchlight procession, but she was prepared to put up with that as she had arranged to go on to supper with Roly as soon as it was over. Then she heard that their Leader had called a meeting of senior officers immediately after the march, and of course Roly had to attend... So that knocked their private plans on the head.

She promptly developed a very bad blister on her heel, which prevented her from going on the march, and returned to Curzon Street in a nasty temper – only to learn that Charlie had gone out to visit his sister.

Gina arrived at Eaton Square half an hour later, saying, 'Well, I certainly wasn't going to spend the evening on my own, with the radio! So I jumped into a cab, and here I am... You two look like conspirators – what have you been up to?'

Sir Charles glanced at his sister in mute enquiry; Alice nodded. She was very pale, and kept wiping her palms with a lace handkerchief, then twisting it into a knot.

Having been given permission to speak, Sir Charles told his wife,

'Alice has just found out about Caroline – and Paul Weyman. It's been a dreadful blow to her.'

'My angel – how ghastly for you!' Gina made herself comfortable on a *chaise-longue*, putting her feet up. 'Who spilled the beans? I certainly didn't tell a single, solitary soul – I swear it. It must have been my fool brother –'

'No, I found out quite by accident.' Wearily, Alice recapitulated the story, concluding, 'And when I rang the number, Paul answered himself.'

'What on earth did you say to him?'

'Nothing. I just put the telephone down.'

'I thought she was going to pass out,' said Charlie. 'It must have been the most terrible shock.'

'Yes, it was.' Alice could not look directly at either of them; she concentrated on tiny details, like the pearl links in Charlie's cuffs, or the buckles of Gina's snakeskin shoes. 'I didn't know what to do. I've got to do *something*, but . . . I still don't know.'

'What do you want to do?' Charlie asked.

'I want to go to bed, and sleep . . . I want to go on sleeping for days and days – and when I wake up, I want to find out it's all been a nightmare, and it never really happened.'

Gina ran a hand through her long red hair, then tossed it back in a gesture she'd seen Garbo use in some movie. She had started to let her hair grow longer; Roly said it suited her.

'Charlie – do you think you could fix me a teeny-weeny drink? I'm dry as a bone.' Her husband got up obediently, and she turned back to Alice. 'Sweetheart, I do sympathize, believe me – but don't you think maybe you're making too much of all this? I know it's been a shock, but let's face it – it's not the end of the world.'

'Gina!' Charlie said reproachfully, adding ice-cubes to her gin and tonic. 'Paul Weyman's totally unsuitable – he's twice her age –'

'A difference in age isn't necessarily such a bad thing, is it?' Gina raised the glass he handed to her, gently mocking. 'Cheers, honey-lamb . . .'

Wounded by this sly reference to his own age, Charlie turned away, and Alice broke in, 'It's not just a question of age, Gina – there are a hundred reasons why Paul's the wrong man for Caro. William and I have known him for donkey's years – he used to be one of our closest friends . . .'

'So what? Would you be happier if she'd gone off with a total stranger?'

Alice looked down at her hands, and said, 'I must find another handkerchief; this one is too sordid for words . . . I don't know – it's just – I'd rather it had been anyone in the world than Paul . . . I can't explain it.' She got up, moving to the door. 'All I know is, I've got to break it to William – and I'm absolutely dreading it.'

'Could be he won't feel so deeply about it. You never can tell.'

Alice shook her head. 'He'll feel even worse – I'm sure of that.' And she left the room quickly.

She could not possibly tell William over the telephone. The Court calendar kept her fully occupied in London until Wednesday night, and then it was too late to travel down to Ebony; so it wasn't until nearly noon on Thursday that she found her husband in the rose walk, busy with secateurs and raffia.

'I looked for you at the farm,' she said, as she kissed him.

'I was there most of the morning, but I'd noticed this poor brute needed first aid, so as soon as I could spare the time, I slipped away.' One end of the rustic pergola had collapsed, bringing a mass of rambling roses down with it. 'There was a high wind in the night, and these wooden arches were always pretty flimsy. Our best American Pillar has snapped half-way up the main stem: I'm trying to cover the gap by training the Dorothy Perkins across – you see?'

Alice tried to smile. 'However hard you work at the farm, the garden is still your first love, isn't it, William?'

He looked at her, then threw down the secateurs and took her hands. 'My darling – whatever is the matter? You look quite ill – what's wrong?'

'I'm not ill – it's just – I haven't been sleeping very much lately . . . I've got to talk to you.'

'Come and sit down.' He led her to a wooden bench, under a flowery arbour at the end of the walk. 'Now tell me about it.'

So she told him.

She had never seen William so angry. He stood up, walking back along the pergola with strange dragging footsteps, then seized the wooden poles which still supported the roses, and gripped them: the entire structure shuddered, and she thought he would bring it down on top of them. But the moment passed, and she realized that he would never do that; even in his fury, he was incapable of destroying any living thing. Instead, he began to swear: quietly, under his breath, but with bitter, poisonous anger, heaping the worst names he could think of on Paul Weyman's head.

At last he pulled himself together and came back to her, saying huskily, 'I'm sorry... That was a kind of madness; I had to get rid of it... Why is he doing this to us? Is he trying to hurt us – deliberately?'

She put her arms round him. 'You mustn't think that. He didn't want us to know – he never meant anyone to know. Charlie thinks he feels ashamed.'

'As he should be.' She could feel William's body against her, rigid as steel. 'It must be stopped.'

'Stopped? How?'

'I don't know yet. But it's wrong, Alice; it's so terribly wrong – it cannot be allowed to go on.'

They began to walk slowly back, William's arm about her shoulders. Near the house they met Jenny, sitting on a nursery-rug patterned with teddy bears, feeding Harriet spoonfuls of mashed potato and gravy. The little girl gurgled happily on seeing her grandparents, and a dribble of gravy ran down her chin.

'Oops!' Jenny wiped it off in the nick of time. 'I thought I'd get Harry's lunch over before we have ours.'

'Oh – is it lunchtime already?' asked Alice vaguely.

Jenny looked up at her in surprise. 'It's nearly one o'clock... Oh, by the way – there was a call while you were out. Caro rang up, and left a message.'

'Caroline?' William and Alice looked at one another.

'She says she'll be coming down this weekend – won't that be nice?'

After lunch, Polly walked out on to the terrace; the weather remained fine, and she felt stifled indoors. She found Jenny and the children, about to climb into the family Daimler. Jenny hailed her cheerfully.

'Hello! We were just talking about you, weren't we, Alex?'

Alex nodded and smiled – a familiar smile, with too much of Richard in it to be bearable. Polly looked away.

'I thought I'd go for a walk,' she said, about to move on.

'I've got a better idea,' suggested Jenny. 'Dennett's driving us in to Medford, to do some shopping; Harry's growing so fast, she needs some new dresses. Why don't you come and help me choose some pretty things? Then afterwards we can all have tea at the Copper Kettle.'

Polly glanced at the little girl in Jenny's arms. Harriet stared back at her, unsmiling, as if she were an extraordinary stranger.

'No thank you,' said Polly. 'Another day, p'raps.'

There were two cars waiting at the foot of the steps; behind the Daimler, the Lanchester stood with its doors open. Polly heard footsteps approaching, and turned to find Norman Brooks coming out of the house, carrying Lady Beatrice.

'Aha! And where are you all going?' the old lady wanted to know.

'To do some shopping,' Jenny explained. 'I've been trying to persuade Polly to come with us, but –'

'Not today,' said Polly firmly. 'I don't feel like trudging round shops.'

So Jenny and the children drove off without her, and Norman settled Old Bea into the back of her car. He was about to shut the door when she called out, 'Polly! If you don't fancy shopping, you can come with me instead. It's a pleasant afternoon for an outing.'

'If you don't mind, I'd really rather –'

'But I do mind. It's a long time since you and I had a talk; I shall enjoy your company.'

It was virtually a command, and Polly could not refuse. Reluctantly, she climbed in beside the Countess, and the car moved away.

'You used to enjoy shopping, once upon a time,' remarked Old Bea, as they drove between hedgerows bright with early summer. 'Where was Jenny off to – did she say?'

'Into Medford – the baby needs some new dresses. She asked me to help choose, but she's much better at that sort of thing – they don't want me hanging round.'

'Hmph...' Old Bea sat in silence for a while, and when they reached the next village, she leaned forward and tapped Norman on the shoulder. 'Stop the car, boy. I want you to buy some stamps.'

Norman obeyed, pulling up at the General Store which was also the village post office.

'How many shall I get, my lady?' he asked.

'Oh, I don't care – a dozen, I suppose – twelve penny stamps.' She fumbled in her handbag and produced a half-crown. 'And be sure you bring me the correct change.'

As Norman disappeared inside the little shop, Polly said: 'I never think of you as a letter-writer.'

'I'm not. But I expect Alice can use the stamps... I didn't want Norman listening to what I have to say.' She cleared her throat. 'I must be frank with you, Polly. You neglect your children: it's not right that you should leave everything to Jenny.'

'But she enjoys it – and they both love her. Anyone can see that.'

'That's not the point. You're their mother, and it's your duty –'

'I'm sorry, I don't agree.' Polly refused to be browbeaten by the old lady. 'Jenny's ten times better with them than me. If I took them away from her now, she'd be miserable, and so would I, and the kids would hate me – so what's the use of that?'

'Quite apart from anything else, it would do you the world of good. Just look at you, mooning around the place all by yourself. What sort of life is that for a young woman? Looking after the children would give you something to do.'

'There's nothing for me to do at Crown House. I only came here 'cos of Richard – without him, I'm a fish out of water. I don't belong here any more, and you know it.'

Old Bea frowned, and thought for a moment, then continued in a different tone, 'I'm not saying I agree with you, but – if that were true – perhaps you should think about making a different life for yourself... What would you be doing now, if you hadn't married my grandson? You'd still be in London, I dare say, following a theatrical career?'

'Yes, I expect so.' Polly sighed. 'But how could I do that now? You and the family – you'd never forgive me, if I went back into the business.'

'Don't talk rubbish, child. If it's what you want, then you must do it. I'm quite sure William won't try to stop you. Anything would be better than to have you drifting round the house like a ghost...' Lady Beatrice broke off to add crossly: 'What on earth is that boy doing? He's taking a long time to buy a few postage stamps. Go and find out what he's up to!'

Inside the shop, Polly found Norman flirting with the attractive young lady in charge of the post-office counter. He was saying loftily, 'Oh, yes – I get about a bit – the old girl and me buzzed up to town the other day, to see the Jubilee –'

'Norman – you're wanted,' said Polly, and he jumped to attention.

During the rest of the drive, Polly was hardly aware of the Kentish weald unfolding around them; instead, she saw Shaftesbury Avenue and Piccadilly Circus, stage-doors and dressing-rooms... She wasn't too old – she could still get back into that world, couldn't she?

As soon as they returned to Crown House, she took her address-book to the drawing-room, looking up a telephone number: the office of Mr Charles B. Cochran, the best guv'nor she'd ever worked for. He'd been down to Crown House, on her wedding-day; since she had no father, he had given her away at the ceremony, and made a witty and graceful speech at the reception afterwards. She felt sure Cockie would help her now.

But he wasn't in his office. Icily polite, his secretary – new, since Polly's day – informed Lady Ebony that Mr Cochran was heavily involved in rehearsals. *Anything Goes*, a new American musical, was about to open at the Palace Theatre in a few weeks, and he couldn't possibly be interrupted.

Polly turned back the pages of her address-book and began to work her way through a series of old friends – stars she had known – managers, agents, even chorus-girls like herself. But it was nearly eight years since she had hung up her tap-shoes, and everything had changed so much; old friends had gone abroad, some had given up the business, others had moved away leaving no address . . . An hour later, she put the telephone down.

It was no good. The stage-doors were shut against her now; she would never get back into that world. She would have to stay at Crown House, where there was no place for her; haunting it like a ghost, as Old Bea had said . . . Searching for another ghost, and never finding him.

Caro came home on Friday evening, but she did not arrive until after ten o'clock. When she entered the drawing-room, William and Alice greeted her warmly, and she hugged them both.

'Sorry I'm late – it's been a pretty hectic week. Still, that's better than sitting in the news-room, twiddling my thumbs.'

'But I thought you'd had some time off?' Alice could not help saying. 'I mean – last Monday . . .'

Caroline wrinkled her brow: 'That's right – how did you know?'

'Oh – I rang you at the *Argus*, and someone said you were away.' Her mother went on quickly: 'There was a nasty moment when Grandmama got lost in the Jubilee crowds, and I wanted to talk to you – but in the end she turned up again, as bright as a button, so it didn't matter.'

They told Caro the story of Old Bea's expedition to London, and she laughed, then stretched and yawned: 'I do feel a bit sleepy, actually – that beastly train stopped at every station. I think I'll go straight to bed, if you don't mind.'

'Of course not. We'll see you at breakfast.'

As soon as she had gone out, William said quietly, 'I still can't believe it. She's the same as ever – the same old Caro . . .'

'Do you think so?' Alice shook her head. 'I think she's changed. She's grown up.'

The following morning, the sun shone, and it was warm enough for breakfast outdoors. Jenny was just finishing her last slice of toast by the time Caro came out to join them.

'I slept like a log. Hello, Jenny. How lovely to see you – it's been ages.'

Jenny kissed her, saying, 'I must slip up to the nursery: we can talk presently.'

Caro took an empty chair, and said, 'Goodness, it's quite hot already. This is something I miss in London – meals out in the garden.'

'I imagine you don't have a garden, where you live?' asked William.

'No, I don't.' Caro helped herself to a boiled egg which had been kept warm under a knitted cosy. 'You'd hate it.'

'Yes, I expect I should.' William had been glancing through *The Times*; now he folded the newspaper carefully, and put it aside. 'Your mother and I want to talk to you – about your life in London.'

'Oh?' Something in his tone arrested Caro. 'What do you mean?'

Alice began, 'When I tried to ring you at the *Argus*, they told me you were at home – so I asked to speak to Muriel Beasley.'

A blackbird in one of the chestnut trees began to sing joyfully. Slowly, Caro put down her egg-spoon.

'Damn . . . I should have thought of that. She told you –'

'She told me you weren't sharing a flat. She suggested someone must be playing a joke on us. But it wasn't a joke, was it?'

'No. I'm sorry.' Caro thought for a moment. 'Actually – I'm glad you know. I hated having to lie to you . . . I'm living with Paul – Paul Weyman.'

'Yes, we know that too,' said William.

'You *know*?' Caro pushed aside her plate. 'I suppose Uncle Charlie told you?'

'Not exactly,' said Alice. 'But he gave me your telephone number,

186

and when I rang up, Paul answered.'

'Paul never said a word about –'

'He doesn't know. I hung up without speaking.' Alice was fidgeting with her napkin, folding and unfolding it endlessly. 'Darling – why couldn't you tell us?'

'I knew you'd be shocked... But you don't understand: it's not something to be ashamed of. Paul and I love one another; you should be happy for us.'

'I wish we could.' William gazed out over the treetops, unable to look at her. 'I wish you had told us about it, right from the beginning. We might have been able to advise you – to help you.'

'Help?'

'We might have persuaded you to think again. Paul Weyman is not the right man for you,' he said flatly.

'How can you say that? I've just told you – I love him –'

'We are asking you to give him up. Surely you can see this affair is completely impossible?'

Angrily, Caro slid back her chair and stood up. 'I suppose you mean that he's too old for me.'

'That comes into it, certainly.'

'Do you think so? Then you don't know the first thing about love. I love him for the man he is – not because he's old or young, or rich or poor. I'd marry him tomorrow if he'd let me –'

'Why won't he let you?' Alice broke in.

'Because he has old-fashioned principles – like you... I suppose he doesn't want you to be hurt.'

'That's very considerate of him. It's a pity he couldn't have been equally considerate before he embarked on the affair,' said William.

'Don't say it like that – as if it were something furtive and horrible. We *love* each other – can't you accept that?'

'I will never accept it.' William's tone was implacable. 'I find the idea totally repugnant, and I'm asking you – begging you – to leave the man.' He looked at her at last, adding gently: 'It's for your sake, my dearest – believe me... If you go on like this, it can only end in heartbreak for you.'

'It's not for my sake at all!' Suddenly Caro's temper flared up. 'How can you be such a hypocrite? You're worried about the disgrace to the family – you're afraid of what people will say...'

She took a few paces across the terrace, then turned to face her parents. 'I'm happy with Paul – happier than I've ever been in my life – and if you don't want me to be happy, I don't want any more to do with you. I'm sorry I came home this weekend; it was a bad mistake. I shall send for a taxi, to take me to the station... I won't come here again.'

Then she walked away quickly. William stood up and put out a hand as if to stop her – but it was useless. He sank back into his chair; his whole body was tense, and a muscle in his arm had begun to ache. Caro walked into the house, and was gone.

A month later, Alice went to London for her next turn of duty at Buckingham Palace. She had lived through four long, unhappy weeks. Not only did she suffer agonizing regret over the way she and William had parted from their daughter, she was also burdened by a deep sense of guilt. In her heart, she felt sure William blamed her for what was happening now – that this was only an extension of the wrong she had done him, seventeen years ago, when for a brief moment she and Paul had become lovers... She was glad to get away from Crown House, away from the accusation she read in William's eyes whenever he looked at her.

But London too had unhappy associations. She was continually aware of Caroline, working in Fleet Street or living at Primrose Hill – she only had to hail a taxi to be with her daughter in a matter of minutes. But that was impossible; she felt that she would never be close to Caroline again.

For the first three days, Her Majesty had a series of engagements, and Alice was kept busy; she was grateful to be fully occupied, since it enabled her to put her private problems aside for a while.

On the fourth day, the Queen informed her that a projected visit to an exhibition of handicrafts had been cancelled at the last moment, and they found themselves, unexpectedly, with time on their hands.

'We shall have a peaceful afternoon to ourselves for once,' said Her Majesty. 'I shall get on with my petit-point – perhaps you would care to read to me while I am working?'

Returning to Queen Mary's private sitting-room, they made themselves comfortable. The Queen had begun a new novel which had been highly recommended to her – *National Velvet* by Edith Bagnold.

'She's Lady Jones, you know – rather an unconventional person, I believe, but such a clever writer. It's about a girl who has a passion for horses, and she rides as a jockey in the Grand National – but it's not at all improper,' she hastened to explain. 'I shall pass it on to

Elizabeth when I finish it; of course she loves horses – and perhaps Lillibet will like it when she's older.'

'I think most little girls enjoy riding lessons,' Alice agreed, finding a marker in the book. 'Shall I begin the next chapter, Ma'am?'

'If you would.'

So Alice started to read; and as she read, she couldn't help thinking of her own daughter. She remembered Caro on her first pony – and the day she entered her first gymkhana... Suddenly, to her dismay and embarrassment, she felt a prickling behind her eyes, and then tears trickled down her cheeks.

'My dear – are you unwell?' The Queen rose, putting aside her needlework.

'No, I – I'm quite well, thank you... But I – oh, I'm so sorry.' Humiliated, Alice fumbled for a handkerchief. 'It's very silly of me, but – something reminded me of Caroline – my daughter...'

The mention of Caro's name set her off again. Concerned, the Queen patted Alice's shoulder.

'Something has happened to Caroline? Why didn't you tell me?'

'It's just – a family matter...' Alice dabbed her eyes, trying to control herself. 'I think you know Caroline has left home... We found out the other day that she is living with – with a man... Of course she believes she is in love with him.'

'I see.' The Queen looked sad. 'They live together – but they do not intend to marry?'

'It would be a very unsuitable match; he is considerably older than Caroline. We tried to make her see that she is ruining her life, but she wouldn't listen to us. There was an awful scene, and she walked out of the house. She says she never wants to see us again.'

Alice's voice was choked with tears, and the Queen took her hand.

'Try not to give way, my dear – I understand how you must feel. I have been through something very similar. I suppose it happens to us all, at one time or another.'

'Surely not, Ma'am –'?

The Queen nodded. 'I think you were once present when the King quarrelled with David? They are hardly on speaking terms now; he wants nothing to do with us. And we are thinking only of him...' Slowly, she went back to her own chair; but the moment of intimacy had removed the barriers between them, and she continued: 'He doesn't realize how reckless he is being... The other day he attended a British Legion rally at the Albert Hall, and in his speech he made some very unfortunate remarks about Germany – suggesting that we should stretch forth the hand of friendship, and so on. . It was as if he were inviting the men to join in his admiration of Hitler! And today I am told that the American woman has been invited to dine at the German Embassy – and she has accepted the invitation . . .'

Her back was ramrod-straight as she gazed ahead, looking into the future. 'It is *her* influence that takes him away from us. I have always been so close to David; we used to be such good friends . . . But now he is a stranger to me.'

When Alice returned to Eaton Square that evening, a surprise awaited her. William – who detested coming to London at any time – was waiting in the drawing-room.

'Darling – I had no idea – you never said you were coming up to town!' she exclaimed, putting her arms round him.

'I didn't plan it in advance,' he said. 'I'd been thinking about Caro so much, and suddenly I couldn't stand it any longer. I decided something had to be done – things can't be allowed to go on like this. So I told Dennett to get the car out, and we drove up this afternoon.'

They sat on the sofa, and she held his hand; they looked at one another, and Alice couldn't help smiling.

'It seems so strange, being here with you again,' she said.

For they had lived in Eaton Square with their growing family for many years, before and then after the war. They had been so much in love when they moved into this house; now it seemed that time had rolled back, and she felt as if they were a young married couple, all over again.

'Yes – we were happy here,' said William, with a half-smile. 'It was another life altogether, but I haven't forgotten . . . I remember you standing at that window, in a pale blue dress, with lace at the neck.'

'Alice-blue, they called it. There was a song –'

'You looked beautiful, in your Alice-blue gown.'

'Until Caro was sick at her birthday-party, sitting on my lap – and that was the end of that!'

'Caro – yes . . . I'd forgotten that birthday-party . . .' His face changed. 'I know she's a grown woman, but I still can't think of her – with Paul . . . I have to put things right.'

'How can you? We tried to talk to her –'

'I shall speak to Paul. I decided – I shall go and have it out with him tomorrow.'

'At his flat?'

'No, Caro might be there; I must see him alone. I shall go to his office at – what do they call it? – Broadcasting House.'

The following morning he presented himself at the reception desk. He explained that he did not have an appointment, but hoped Mr Weyman might spare some time to see him. The receptionist, impressed by Lord Minster's title, asked him to take a seat for a few moments. William looked round the imposing, pillared hall; the décor did not appeal to him.

After ten minutes, he was informed that Mr Weyman would see him now. He was ushered into the lift by a uniformed commissionaire, who escorted him to the fourth floor. Paul's office door had a small sign on it, which read: 'P. F. Weyman – Special Project Development.' Inside, a meeting had been in progress; three men in dark grey suits rose to their feet, rolling up blueprints and gathering sheaves of typescript.

Paul greeted William with wary affability, introducing him to his three colleagues, although their names went out of William's head immediately.

'I see I am interrupting your work,' he said – but did not offer to leave.

'Not at all; we had a planning meeting, but it's over now. Do sit down, my dear chap.'

The other gentlemen murmured politely and eased themselves from the room, leaving William and Paul alone. It was not a large office, but reasonably pleasant, with a beige carpet and battleship-grey walls. Three tubular-steel chairs – which William hated on sight – were provided for visitors; Paul himself sat in a swivel chair behind the desk, upon which stood not one but two telephones.

'Sorry I had to keep you waiting,' Paul began. 'The fact is, I'm pretty busy these days. I've been seconded from Outside Broadcasts, dividing my time between this place and Alexandra Palace. We're building some studios there – the new television service, you know.'

William, who had not the faintest idea what he was talking about, said: 'No, I didn't know. I came here today because –'

But Paul was not to be put off. 'It's all at an exploratory stage so far, of course – test transmissions and so on – but we're aiming to put out the first regular television broadcasts some time next year; it's an exciting prospect. Just an hour or two each day to begin with, but eventually we hope to extend –'

This time William interrupted him successfully: 'I did not come here to discuss your work, Paul. I have to talk to you about Caroline.'

Paul put out a hand to one of the telephones, and for a moment William half-expected to be shown out, but Paul merely asked: 'Would you care for some tea? My secretary can easily –'

'No, thank you. I want to take up as little of your time as possible – but this situation has to be resolved.'

Paul let his hand drop to the desk. 'Yes . . . Of course. Ever since Caro told me what happened last weekend, I knew we should have to talk about it.'

'Then you agree it cannot be allowed to continue?' William had not expected so little opposition. 'You admit that the circumstances make the whole thing intolerable?'

'I didn't say that. I know you and Alice must be feeling very distressed, naturally.'

'I should prefer to leave my wife out of this. It's bad enough that I should have to come to you on such an errand; I don't wish to be reminded of – any relationship which may have existed in the past.'

'No. I realize that makes it much more difficult; I need hardly say that Caroline knows nothing of – any previous relationship.'

William gripped the steel arms of his chair. 'Am I supposed to congratulate you on your forbearance and good taste?'

Paul stood up and walked to the window, gazing out over the rooftops and spires that surrounded the building.

'I am more sorry than I can tell you, to be the cause of your unhappiness. I never expected this; Caroline came into my life by chance, and we fell in love. She is the best thing that ever happened to me.'

'And how would you describe yourself?' William's question had an edge of steel. 'As the best thing that ever happened to her?'

Paul turned to face him. 'I can't answer that. I can only say that we are both very happy, and that I will never give her up. You can't expect me to.'

They went on talking for some time, but William soon realized that he was wasting his breath; there was nothing more to be said, on either side. Paul was sincerely sorry, but he remained adamant – and despite himself, William felt an unexpected twinge of respect for

the man: he was determined to remain loyal to Caroline at all costs . . .
If only, William thought, it had been anyone but Paul Weyman . . .

The pulled muscle in his arm was hurting like hell: more than anything, he wanted to be at home, in his own place.

He did not spend a second night at Eaton Square. He reported the failure of his mission to Alice, then drove back to Ebony as soon as possible.

In the weeks that followed, he tried not to think about his daughter; but at night in his dreams he saw her again and again, in Paul's arms. Sometimes she turned her head and smiled at him defiantly; and in the worst nightmare of all, he recognized that the radiant girl was not Caroline, but Alice.

During the day, he blotted out these images by throwing himself into his work. He rose early each morning to put in a full day at the farm, and spent every spare moment in his beloved garden, toiling away like a labourer – hoeing, digging, pushing a mowing-machine – deliberately making himself dog-tired, hoping that he would fall into a deep, dreamless sleep at bedtime . . . But his dreams were always lying in wait for him.

He had never felt so much alone. Alice had to be in London a great deal at this time, for the Court was busy with preparations for the second royal wedding within a year. Prince Henry had fallen in love with another Lady Alice – Lady Alice Montagu-Douglas-Scott, a daughter of the Duke of Buccleuch – and they were to be married in the autumn.

One afternoon at the end of the summer, William closed the farm office door behind him and went into the garden as usual; but today he found himself in a part of the garden he had not visited for a long time: the rockery, which he had been building on the day Richard died, nearly two years ago.

The gardeners had done a little more work after that, planting out some alpines among the crevices, but since then it had been untended. Now the plants were choked by weeds, presenting a picture of neglect.

William took his jacket off and rolled up his shirt-sleeves. Coming to it with a fresh eye, he could see now that his original design had not been completely realized, and he set to work.

Some time later, a voice broke in upon his thoughts: 'Why didn't you ask me to help?'

Jenny was walking round the lake with Alex; the boy had taken his sandals off, and was paddling at the water's edge. Rather out of breath, William said cheerfully, 'That's all right – I can manage perfectly well.'

'Those rocks must weigh a ton – shall I call some of the men to give you a hand?'

'No, no – it's not necessary; I've almost finished. Where's little Harriet? Isn't she with you?'

'Harry's having her afternoon nap, so Alex and I came out to explore the lake.'

'Jenny knows where the culvert is, where the water comes in,' Alex said excitedly. 'She's promised to show me.'

'I helped to clean it out, years and years ago – soon after you came here to live.' Jenny smiled at William.

He remembered that sunlit day... Richard had been with her then, splashing through the green water, clearing the mud and weeds... Richard was alive – and Caro was only a schoolgirl –

Jenny saw his expression change: suddenly he stared at her with enormous surprise, his eyes widening.

'I must – I –' Then he made a strange choking sound, and collapsed, face down in the grass. Jenny ran to him, falling to her knees.

'What is it? What's Grandpa doing?' Alex asked in a frightened voice.

'Alex – be a good boy – run to the house as fast as you can, and tell them to call a doctor – *quickly*!'

13

SUNDAY, 1 SEPTEMBER TO FRIDAY, 25 DECEMBER 1935

CROWN HOUSE
Sunday Sept. 1st

Darling Nick,

When you are away, I always look forward to Sunday morning, as my regular appointment with you – on paper, at any rate. When we come home after morning service, I generally start this weekly letter, and finish it after lunch; in the summerhouse, if the weather's fine.

I think today will be fine; though it is still very early in the morning, before sunrise. I didn't get to sleep until late, and then I had a restless night, so I decided to get up and begin this letter instead.

I'm afraid I have some unhappy news for you. If only I were with you now, wherever you are, so I could put my arms round you; I wish I could be close to you, when I tell you this.

Yesterday afternoon, your father was working in the garden, when he collapsed. Luckily I was there at the time, with Alex. I sent Alex to fetch help and stayed with him, hoping he would come round – but he didn't. He looked so ill – he was horribly pale, and covered in sweat. I was very frightened, but I held his hand and kept telling him he was going to be all right. I don't suppose he could hear me; perhaps I was trying to reassure myself, as much as him.

Alex was wonderful; he found Hawkins, and told him what had happened, and the doctor was here within fifteen minutes. Some of the men from the farm helped to carry your father indoors, and get him up to bed, and he soon regained consciousness.

Dr Parry says it was a heart attack. Apparently it could have been brought on by overwork – he has been putting in an awful lot of time at the farm, and then gardening as well – but it might have been aggravated by worry.

I telephoned Eaton Square and your mother came home on the next train; it must have been terrible for her. She wanted to send for a specialist and get a second opinion, because Parry is a bit doddery nowadays, but the Harley Street men go away at weekends, and we can't call anyone till Monday – so we shall have to be patient.

I'm glad Miranda is here; she doesn't go back for the new term at Roedean until next week; but Caro is in London as usual, and Martin is staying with schoolfriends in Devonshire. It makes everything seem even more alarming, when the family is scattered. I even found myself wishing Lady Edith were here; not that she would have been much help in the crisis, but Grace Duncan is always level-headed and practical.

Thank goodness, your father seems to be recovering gradually, though of course he is still very weak. Dr Parry says he must have complete rest: he's been given sedatives, and sleeps a great deal – he is not allowed to talk too much, or get agitated at all. As far as I can see, he is not in any immediate danger, but if his condition should get any worse, of course I will send you a cable immediately. For the time being, we must simply wait, and pray, and hope for the

Jenny looked up from the green leather writing-case; she thought she heard footsteps in the corridor. She glanced at her watch – who could be walking round the house at six o'clock in the morning?

She opened the bedroom door: Alice looked over her shoulder, startled by the sound.

'Oh – Jenny!' She came back to join her, knotting the sash of her dressing-gown, and speaking in a whisper. 'You're awake too...'

'Yes – what's happening? He's not any worse?'

'No, he's asleep. But I woke up because – well, I suddenly realized I never had anything to eat last night after I got home, and I'm simply famished. I thought I'd forage for myself in the kitchen.'

'What a good idea – may I join you? I'm feeling quite peckish myself.'

They invaded the servants' hall, and Jenny made tea and toast.

'It's a good job I know my way around. I remember where everything's kept,' she smiled, offering Alice the marmalade.

'Thank you, dear – you're a great comfort. Couldn't you sleep either?'

'On and off. When it got light, I thought I might as well start a letter to Nick; he ought to know as soon as possible.'

'Yes. I sent a wire to Edie before I went to bed. I told her not to come home; it may turn out that we've been worrying unnecessarily ... But I thought she should be warned.'

'That's more or less what I told Nicholas. What about Caro? And Martin?'

'I telephoned Caroline last night too.'

'Oh, good – is she coming this morning?'

'She wanted to, but I told her not to. She has her work to think of; I expect William would say we're making a fuss about nothing.'

'But surely – if she wants to see him –'

'He must be kept very quiet; we can't risk disturbing him.' Seeing the puzzled look in Jenny's eyes, Alice continued quickly, 'If he thought the family were rushing to his bedside, it might alarm him ... And Martin's due back this weekend anyway, so that's all right.'

Jenny sipped her tea. 'Do you think it was moving those heavy rocks that brought on the attack? I keep thinking I should have helped him –'

'I'm sure it wasn't that. William had been complaining about pains in his arm – he thought he'd pulled a muscle, but that was the first warning sign, apparently. And of course he's been working himself to a shadow for months now.'

'That's true. And Dr Parry said anxiety might have made it worse. When he went up to London a few weeks ago, I couldn't help wondering: *has* he been worrying about something?'

Alice finished her tea and poured a second cup, before she replied, 'We've been having problems with Caro. She's got herself involved with a man in town – someone we don't quite approve of. We tried to make her see that it was a mistake, but – she wouldn't listen to us. I'm afraid it upset William very much.'

'I wondered why she only stayed one night.'

Alice nodded. 'That's why I don't think it would be a good thing for William to see her – not just now.'

In the bedroom at Primrose Hill, Caro stared at the ceiling and waited for morning. Beside her, Paul slept heavily. He refused to admit that he snored, but he did – a little. It didn't bother her as a rule; she rather liked the gentle growl. It reminded her of the teddy bear she had when she was little; if you prodded it in the middle, it produced a noise very like Paul's low rumble. But it wasn't Paul who had disturbed her; she had been lying awake half the night, thinking about her mother's phone call.

'... I honestly don't believe there's anything to worry about now; Dr Parry seems very confident that Daddy will make a good recovery. I'd rather you didn't come down, darling – not yet, anyway. You do understand, don't you? We can't risk upsetting him again.'

Caro thought bitterly: What you really mean is – if his darling daughter hadn't upset him in the first place, this might never have happened... Am I supposed to blame myself for his heart attack? It's so unfair! Is it my fault he's old-fashioned and narrow-minded?

But she kept imagining him on his sick-bed, his eyes closed, fighting for breath. She pictured him surrounded by the rest of his family, all supportive and sympathetic – all except one...

Suddenly she turned to Paul, flinging her arms round him. He woke to find her kissing him passionately, and he tasted the salt tears on her cheeks.

Alerted by another telephone call Sir Charles arrived some time after lunch on Sunday. Alice met him in the drawing-room, and embraced him.

'Charlie – thank you for coming.'

'How is he now? Is there any change?'

'He's better; he had a little consommé at midday. But he gets tired so easily, the least thing exhausts him. I'll take you up to him later, when he wakes.' Alice looked round. 'Isn't Gina with you?'

'I'm afraid not. She had to go to a party meeting; they're planning another damned rally. I'm sure they would have excused her, under the circumstances, but she said she couldn't let them down.' He frowned, looking out at the smooth green lawns beyond the terrace. 'I didn't realize you had visitors this weekend. How very awkward.'

Alice looked blank. 'But we haven't got anyone staying – what do you mean?'

'There's someone walking towards the lake – a pretty blonde girl, in a beach-wrap.'

Alice joined him at the window, then laughed: 'Oh, Charlie – that's not a visitor – it's Miranda!'

'Good heavens!' He adjusted his gold-rimmed spectacles. 'The last time I saw her, she was a schoolgirl in a gym-slip – now she's a young lady.'

It had turned out to be another hot day, ushering in a golden September. Finding it was too stuffy indoors, Miranda had decided to go for a swim.

She took a towel with her, and the book she had been reading. A girl at school had lent her *Vile Bodies* by Evelyn Waugh; she found it fascinating but mystifying. Such extraordinary people, so different from anyone she had ever met. They were shockingly unconventional – they drank something called Black Velvet for breakfast, and went to bed together as casually as if they were brushing their teeth. Did men and women behave like that in the real world?

She walked to the far end of the lake, knowing she would be alone there. Sometimes at Roedean, with so many girls surrounding her, she longed to be on her own; but now she would be glad to get back to school. It would have been different if Martin were at home. She resented the fact that her brother had friends of his own to go and stay with, a life of his own, that she could not share.

That was the worst of being a twin. When she was away from Martin, there was always something missing; she longed for him to be close to her, making her feel complete again. Yet he didn't seem to feel the same way; he could be perfectly happy without her.

She found her chosen bathing-place, dropped the towel and book on to the grass, then slipped out of her wrap. She looked very lovely in her sea-green swimming-costume: still a child, lively and impulsive, but with the generous promise of womanhood, on the threshold of life.

She hesitated at the edge of the lake, testing the temperature with her toe; this was always the worst moment. There was only one way to tackle it. She stepped back, braced herself, and took a running dive into the water.

The first shock took her breath away: but after that it was wonderful.

She swam happily for several minutes, then turned over, floating on her back. The sun was hot upon her skin, and drops of water slipped from her body like beads of mercury. Suddenly a voice from the bank hailed her.

'Mandy! Hi! What's the water like?'

Her heart leapt: Martin stood on the bank, waving to her. She stood up, treading water, and called back: 'Gorgeous! You should try it!'

He laughed: 'Why not? Race you to the other end and back again!'

As he spoke, he began to tear off his blazer, his open-necked shirt and flannels: within seconds he was completely undressed. Naked, he jumped in, swimming underwater.

'God – you're a liar!' he gasped, surfacing beside her. 'I thought you said it was gorgeous – it's bloody freezing!'

She felt wildly happy; they were together again, as if they had never been apart. They raced one another, splashing each other, and playing silly, childish games. At last they pulled themselves up on to the soft green turf, and lay in the sun to get dry.

He rolled on to his side, facing her, and laughed breathlessly.

'You're right – it is gorgeous,' he said. 'By the way – how's Pa?'

Miranda looked away, suddenly conscious of his body, close beside her. 'Mummy says he's going to be all right. I only saw him for a few minutes this morning. He looks – I don't know – older, somehow.'

'Ma told me as soon as I arrived. I haven't seen him yet – she says he's taking a nap, so I thought I'd come and find you first.'

Miranda reached out for her towel, and offered it to him.

'You'd better cover yourself up,' she said. 'Somebody might see you.'

'Who cares?' Martin grinned. 'That's something I learned pretty quickly at school – you soon stop feeling shy about taking your clothes off!'

He stretched his arms and legs to the sunlight, exulting in his youth and masculinity. Miranda felt confused and uncertain; instinctively modest herself, she did not want him to guess that she felt shy. But with the inexplicable telepathy which linked them, she sensed that he was aware of her embarrassment – and that he was enjoying it.

He spread his legs wide, laughing at her.

'You ought to take off that stupid costume – get yourself a sun-tan all over!' he teased. 'What are you afraid of?'

'I'm not afraid – I just...' She could not look at him, and edged away as he moved closer. She wanted to get dressed, but at the same time she felt mysteriously excited. 'Don't you think – perhaps we ought –'

But he wasn't listening. Raising himself on one elbow, he looked past her, into the undergrowth; suddenly he jumped up and plunged into the bushes.

'What the hell do you think you're doing?' he asked, dragging Norman Brooks from his hiding-place.

Red-faced and apprehensive, Norman was the older by nearly two years, but Martin – only just sixteen, and unashamedly naked – was in command of the situation.

'You dirty swine – how long have you been spying on us?'

'I never – I didn't mean to – I was just walking past, like –'

'You lying bastard – you were watching us behind those bushes – I've a good mind to beat the daylights out of you!'

Miranda threw her towel over her shoulders, pulling it round her body. 'No, Martin – don't – let him go . . .'

'I didn't mean no harm, sir –' Norman began to shake.

'You ought to be horsewhipped.' Martin let the boy go, pushing him away contemptuously. 'Go on, then – and if I ever catch you up to those tricks again, I'll have you gaoled as a peeping tom . . . Now shove off – before I change my mind!'

Sir Cuthbert Wandell, the eminent physician, drove down in his Rolls Royce on Tuesday afternoon, and gave William a very thorough examination, while Dr Parry hovered in the background.

The prognosis was reassuring, though Sir Cuthbert explained to Alice that they could not rule out the possibility of further attacks in the future. For this reason, Lord Minster had to be kept under close observation for some months. He would have to spend much of the day in bed: he must not think of returning to work, either at the farm or in the garden; above all, he must be kept quiet, and free from worry.

'And how are we supposed to manage that?' Alice asked Jenny, after Sir Cuthbert Wandell had departed. 'William can't bear the idea of being an invalid; he's impatient to be up and about again already.'

In the end it was William's mother who persuaded him to behave himself. Old Bea had already been told of his illness, and when Norman reported to her for his orders on Wednesday morning, she said, 'I don't want to go driving today, boy. I wish to visit my son. Pick me up and carry me to his room.'

Norman obeyed, and they found Lord Minster sitting on the edge of his bed, making a determined effort to pull on a pair of trousers over his pyjamas.

'What are you thinking of, William?' asked the old lady, crossly. 'Put me down in that chair, boy – and then help his lordship back to bed.'

'I was thinking of going out for a breath of air –' William began.

'You'll do no such thing! You are under doctor's orders, and you will do as you are told!' snapped his mother.

While Norman removed his trousers and lifted him on to the bed, William tried to protest: 'Someone has to look after the farm, Mama. It won't run itself...'

'Oh, yes, it will – and if it doesn't, we'll hire a manager for the estate. One thing's quite clear: you mustn't think of going back to work until you're completely cured, or we shall have another funeral on our hands...'

'But it's my job!' William persisted. 'The farm is my responsibility.'

'Thank you, Norman – you may go. I shall send for you when I want you.' Old Bea dismissed her chauffeur, and when the door shut behind him, she turned on William briskly. 'Your responsibility is to your wife and family – and your job is to stay alive. Don't you understand that? I'm not going to let you kill yourself because you're too proud to admit you have weaknesses like the rest of us. If you disobey your medical advisers and end up in the churchyard along with your father and your son, I'll never speak to you again!'

William could not help smiling. 'Is that a promise, Mama?'

'Don't be impertinent. Nobody is indispensable, William; and it's time you stopped driving yourself so hard. Think of your wife and children, and stop being selfish!'

William blinked, but said no more. When Old Bea was in this mood, it was useless to argue with her. There was a grain of truth in what she said, much as he hated to admit it. To Alice's amazement, he stopped kicking against his enforced inactivity, and accepted it – for the time being, anyway.

'When I'm well enough, I shall get back to work,' he added. 'You wait and see.'

'Of course you will, darling.' Alice tucked in the bedclothes. 'But until then – do try to rest.'

The house seemed unusually quiet. Once the school holidays were over, Martin and Miranda disappeared again, and a new routine was gradually established. William spent the mornings and evenings in bed; every afternoon, he would sit in a chair by his window with gardening catalogues on his knees, making plans for next season. He did his best to direct the farm and the gardeners from a distance, using Alice as a go-between, and tried not to show his irritation when the directions were misinterpreted, and the plans went awry.

A few weeks later, Nicholas came home. As soon as he received

Jenny's letter, he had applied for compassionate leave, and sent a cable to Crown House, telling them he was on his way.

Jenny was in the nursery giving Alex and Harriet their tea when he arrived. He stood in the doorway for a moment, enjoying the cosy domestic scene: Harry was on Jenny's lap, and Alex sat at the table, eating a poached egg and getting dollops of yolk on the tablecloth.

'Try to be careful, there's a dear,' Jenny was saying. 'Then after you've had your bath, it will be time for a story. Which one shall we have?'

Nicholas felt a sudden pang: if only the children had been Jenny's children – *his* children . . . But he pushed this thought from his mind, and asked: 'Can I be the storyteller tonight?'

Three faces turned to him with delight, and Alex exclaimed: 'Uncle Nick! Nobody told me you were coming home!'

'Well, now you know.' Nick walked in, throwing his cap and greatcoat over the rocking-horse, and smiled at Jenny. 'Hello, my love . . .'

She lifted Harry into the playpen, then opened her arms wide: 'Nick – darling – welcome home!'

After dinner, they had a long discussion with Alice. Nicholas explained that he was in the Indian Ocean when the news came through, and had been flown home from an airfield in Ceylon.

'I promised I'll return to duty as soon as Pa is well enough,' he said.

'It won't be long, darling – he's getting a little stronger every day,' said Alice. 'And he's so happy you're here; I haven't seen him so cheerful for a long time.'

'He's looking a lot better already – don't you think so?' Jenny asked.

'Is he? I was pretty shocked when I saw him tonight. Tell me one thing, Ma – I want you to be absolutely honest with me . . . Do you really think he's ever going to be strong enough to take on the farm and the garden – the way he used to?'

There was a moment's silence, and then Alice replied, 'I wish I could say yes – but the doctors say he shouldn't. I suppose we shall have to do as your Grandmama suggested, and advertise for an estate manager. I haven't mentioned it to your father; he's going to hate the idea.'

'Would he hate it quite so much if I took the job on?' Nick asked.

'You? I don't understand.'

He stretched out, taking Jenny's hand. 'As soon as I saw him tonight, I realized that's what I must do. It's what I should have done a long time ago ... I'm going to stay here, with my wife, where I belong; I'm going to resign my commission, and come home.'

When Alice informed the Palace of her husband's illness, she was relieved of all duties until further notice; and it was not until the beginning of October that she went to London again.

Queen Mary was delighted to see her, and insisted that she must stay to tea. This was a particular pleasure for Alice since the Duchess of York had also been invited. Both ladies wanted to hear the latest news of William.

'He's making very good progress, according to the doctors,' Alice told them. 'And I'm much happier about him now, although...'

She hesitated, and Elizabeth prompted her: 'Although?'

'He's not as strong as he used to be; I have to get accustomed to the idea that he will never be really strong again.'

The Queen said softly, 'We all have to grow old, my dear; it's a hard lesson to learn – and watching the ones we love growing older is the hardest part of all.'

'How is His Majesty these days?' Alice ventured to ask. 'Judging by the reports in the newspapers, he seems to be in very good health.'

'He keeps up appearances wonderfully well,' agreed the Queen. 'If it wasn't for those wretched bouts of bronchitis – he can't seem to shake them off.'

Elizabeth tried to lighten the conversation by saying: 'I expect he's looking forward to Henry's wedding, next month – I know his granddaughters are!'

It had been decided that both Princesses should officiate as bridesmaids, and Margaret – aged five – could think of nothing else.

The Queen shook her head: 'Between ourselves, I don't think the King is looking forward to it very much. After George's wedding, and then the Jubilee, he feels these public celebrations are becoming a little too frequent... But that reminds me, my dear – the King would prefer the girls not to wear long skirts. He says he likes to see their pretty little knees.'

'Oh, dear...' Elizabeth sighed. 'How ever will I break it to them? They've set their hearts on full-length dresses – they're dying to look grown-up.'

Her Majesty turned to Alice: 'I suppose it's no good asking you to attend us at the wedding, my dear? You'll be at home with your husband, no doubt?'

'Well ... I can't be sure, Ma'am. But if he continues to make good progress, I might be able to leave him for a few days. My son Nicholas has resigned his commission in the Navy, and is going to stay at home to help his father.'

'But Nicholas enjoys his life on board ship so much!' Elizabeth looked dismayed. 'Won't it be a terrible wrench for him to give up the sea?'

'I presume he sees it as his duty to remain with his family,' said the Queen firmly. 'And I'm quite sure that he –'

At this point she was interrupted, for the door burst open, and the King marched into the sitting-room. He carried a cardboard file of documents, and when he saw his wife was not alone, he stopped short, and a few pages of typescript fluttered to the carpet.

'I beg your pardon, May – I didn't know you were entertaining visitors,' he grunted. 'But I had to come and tell you ...'

Alice knelt to pick up the papers the King had dropped; as she handed them back, she could not help noticing Mrs Wallis Simpson's name, together with a list of dates and places – Hong Kong, Shanghai, Peking ...

'Thank you.' His Majesty stuffed them back into the file. 'You remember what I told you, May? About the report that was being prepared for us on the American woman? I've just been going through it: I won't show it to you, because some of it makes damned filthy reading – but there's no doubt that the rumours are perfectly true. That is why I have to tell you –' He swung round to include Alice and Elizabeth. 'I have to tell you all – that we shall never receive Mrs Simpson again, here at the Palace or anywhere else. She is not fit to be my son's companion ...'

He spoke so emphatically that he became short of breath, and started to cough. Alice saw his face becoming drawn and mottled, and could not help thinking of William.

After His Majesty left the room, there was an embarrassed silence. The Queen busied herself with the tea things, trying to appear calm after the interruption.

'He worries so much about David; it's all very unfortunate ... Let me see – what were we talking about when –'

'We were discussing my son, coming home to live at Crown

House,' Alice reminded her.

'Ah, yes – certainly. You must be very proud of him.' The Queen refilled the silver teapot with hot water. 'You are fortunate to have a second son who is able and willing to take up his father's burdens.'

The Duchess put down her cup, averting her face; but Alice caught a glimpse of the sadness in her eyes, and heard her murmur, under her breath, 'Poor Nicholas...'

It was not a happy time for anyone. Even the celebration of Prince Henry's wedding on 6 November was diminished by mourning, for Lady Alice's father, the Duke of Buccleuch, had died after a long illness. Under these circumstances, the ceremony, which would have been at Westminster Abbey, was held quietly and privately at Buckingham Palace, in the Chapel Royal.

On the same day, the red tape surrounding Nicholas's departure from the Navy was finally unravelled, and Lieutenant Gaunt, RN, relinquished his commission.

That night, when he went into his dressing-room to get ready for bed, he found Jenny folding up the navy-blue uniform and putting it away carefully.

'What are you doing with that?' he asked. 'We should chuck it out – I shan't be needing it any more.'

'Perhaps not. But I'm very fond of this uniform... You were wearing it on the day you asked me to marry you: I couldn't bear to throw it away.'

'Sentimentalist!' He kissed her, then began to undress. 'I must say – it's going to seem a bit odd, being a civilian again.'

'It's going to seem odd not having to say goodbye to you at regular intervals. No more letter-writing on Sunday mornings, no more envelopes coming back covered in foreign stamps.'

Half-dressed, he took her in his arms, saying: 'You'll have me with you all the time from now on – day and night... Do you think you'll be able to stand the strain?'

'It's going to be wonderful.' She held him tightly. 'For me, anyway: how are you going to like being a farmer?'

'It will be fine. Pa's given me masses of tips on what needs to be done – I'll pick it up soon enough. In one way I'm glad this has happened. Do you realize I've never really lived at Crown House till now? First there was Oxford, then I went into the Navy – I've never spent more than a few weeks at a time here. This is my chance to get to know the old place; a chance to put down roots . . . I'm looking forward to it.'

She put her lips to his ear and whispered, 'You're a terrible liar. You're going to hate it at first, and we both know it.'

'Well – just at first, perhaps. But I'll soon get used to it. And we shall be together – that's the important thing.' Swinging her up into his arms, he carried her into the bedroom. 'We'll have a chance to start that family of ours at last.'

Their lives soon fell into the new pattern. Following his father's example, Nick rose early every day, and put in long hours at the farm office, while Jenny looked after Harry – and when Alex was not mastering the three Rs in the nursery she took both children for walks in the park. Alice was still in London, busy with a hundred and one tasks in the aftermath of the Gloucesters' wedding (like his brother George, Prince Henry had been granted a dukedom to mark the occasion) and Lord Minster spent a good deal of time on his own.

One afternoon, when he was dozing by the window, Polly came into his room. Finding him asleep, she pulled up another chair, and sat beside him. When he woke, he found her there, gazing at the view.

'Polly – my dear girl . . .' William stared at her. 'How long have you been there?'

'I don't know. I just looked in to see how you were. Do you mind?'

'Of course not. It's always a pleasure to see you.'

'Is it? There's no accounting for tastes. I looked in a mirror this morning, and I couldn't stand the sight of myself: I decided it was time for a change of company . . . But that doesn't mean you've got to make conversation,' she added. 'I'm quite happy not to talk.'

William smiled: 'So am I.'

They remained silent for some time, looking out over the garden. The leaves were falling fast, and the trees stretched out their branches to an angry sky. Presently Alex appeared, kicking up drifts of gold, and stooping every now and then to pick up a glossy chestnut. Behind him, Jenny followed with Harry in the pushchair.

'Good old Jenny,' said Polly, with a crooked smile. 'There she goes – doing my job for me.'

After a pause, William said, 'And I suppose Nicholas is in the farm office, busy doing *my* job.'

Polly turned and stared at him. 'Oh, no – Nick's trying to be Richard... But of course he never will be, not in a million years.'

The year ended in a minor key. The King and Queen went to Sandringham for Christmas; the usual family party had been planned, but then the Duchess of York caught influenze, which developed into pneumonia, and she was forced to stay at Royal Lodge while the Princesses travelled up to join their grandparents in Norfolk.

The King himself was far from well, and the little girls noticed the change in him; he tried to bark a greeting in his usual gruff manner, but succumbed to a fit of coughing, looking grey and haggard.

On Christmas Eve the Gloucesters joined the house-party, and Princess Elizabeth was enchanted by the two Scottish terriers her Uncle Henry had brought with him.

'We'll have to keep them well out of sight!' he warned her. 'So don't let me down... Your Grandpapa doesn't like us to bring our pets to stay, in case they pick a fight with *his* dog.'

When tea was brought into the drawing-room, the Scotties were concealed beneath the long tablecloth, and told sternly to 'Sit – and keep quiet!'

They might have obeyed – but when Princess Margaret followed the King and Queen into the room, she was in high spirits, racing round and round the table. This was too much for the excited animals, and one of them bit her leg. Margaret was about to burst into tears, but her elder sister gripped her hand and whispered sternly: 'Don't you dare cry. Grandpa will have the dogs sent away if he finds out!'

Poor Margaret, very red in the face, managed to choke back her sobs until she was able to slip away to the nursery for sympathy and first aid – and afterwards Uncle Henry rewarded her with a shining new half-crown for her act of heroism.

On Christmas Day, the King had his own ordeal to face: his broadcast to the nation, which had now become an annual event. He hated doing it, but he would not let his people down; despite his illness, he took his place at the microphone, while the engineers checked the sound-levels and made some last-minute adjustments.

One of the BBC emissaries had been recalled from his duties at Alexandra Palace especially for the occasion, since he had been responsible for all the previous Christmas broadcasts.

'Good afternoon, Mr Weyman,' said the Queen, offering Paul her hand.

'Good afternoon, Your Majesty.' Paul bowed, then said: 'May I present someone who is here to assist me unofficially? She is not a member of the BBC staff, but a personal friend – Lady Caroline Gaunt.'

Caro dipped a curtsey, and again the Queen extended her hand.

'Lady Caroline?' she repeated, pleasantly surprised. 'Then you must be Alice's daughter – she has spoken to me of you so often...'

The Royal Family were renowned for their excellent memories, and suddenly the Queen stopped short, then resumed in a different tone: 'I believe you do not live at Crown House any longer?' She turned to give Paul a long, glacial stare, before adding: 'I'm sure that must be a great disappointment to your dear mother.'

And without another word, she moved away to join His Majesty in the makeshift studio under the staircase. The King liked to know she was close at hand, and when the engineers gave him his cue to speak, he squeezed her hand, before beginning his Christmas message:

'...It is this personal link between me and my people which I value more than I can say: it binds us together in all our common joys and sorrows...'

When it was over, and the technical staff were packing up their equipment, unplugging the microphone and rolling up yards of cable, an equerry presented each member of the team with a signed photograph of the King and Queen, inscribed: 'With best wishes – December 15th, 1935.'

It was a kindly gesture – but there was one photograph missing, for Paul Weyman appeared to have been overlooked.

'Oh, well – never mind,' he said to Caro, when he realized he had been left out. 'I expect someone must have made a mistake... Are you ready, darling? Shall we go?'

'Yes – let's go,' said Caro quietly, as he helped her into her coat. 'But I don't think it was a mistake.'

14

MONDAY, 20 JANUARY TO TUESDAY, 28 JANUARY 1936

'You will forgive me for being such a terrible hostess, won't you?' said the Duchess of York. 'Only the doctor insists that I must stay in bed until I'm completely well again.'

'Of course – you've had 'flu *and* pneumonia – it would be madness to take risks after that,' Alice reassured her, sitting back in her armchair and settling the supper tray on her lap.

They were in the Duchess's bedroom at Royal Lodge; a beautifully light, airy room on the ground floor which commanded a view of the rhododendron garden. On this winter evening, it was cheerfully cosy. A fire crackled in the grate, and the leaping flames shone on the silk coverlet of the bed – blue, with pleats of lemon-yellow. The walls were a subtler shade, between blue and dove-grey – Elizabeth's favourite colour.

The Duchess sat up in bed, supported by a heap of pillows, and picked at a plate of cold duck and salad.

'Are you sure this will be enough for you?' she asked anxiously. 'After that long journey up from Kent, you must be ravenous.'

'No, really – this is delicious.'

'It's very noble of you to come all this way, to visit the sick!' Elizabeth smiled. 'We had such a depressing Christmas... How was yours, at Crown House?'

'Oh – very traditional; we have the same old rituals every year. Of course Martin and Miranda are much too old for stockings now, but they refuse to give them up! Luckily they both sleep late, so I was able to slip into their rooms at the crack of dawn, and hang bulging stockings at the ends of their beds.'

'You had the whole family with you? How lovely.'

'Well – almost... Caroline wasn't able to get down this year, unfortunately.'

'Oh, what a shame. She's still with the *Argus*, is she? I suppose she was on duty over the holiday?'

Alice tried to change the subject. 'It was the same when Nicholas was in the Navy; they used to draw lots for Christmas leave. At least that's one problem we don't have any more.'

'It must be a great comfort, having him at home for good. And your husband's so much better now. No wonder you had a happy Christmas.'

Alice said nothing. She couldn't go on lying – but she couldn't blurt out the truth and say: 'I had an absolutely beastly Christmas. I hated every minute of it.'

The children had been tiresome; Martin and Miranda seemed to do nothing but squabble or sulk, for no apparent reason. As for William – according to Sir Cuthbert Wandell he was making excellent progress, but Alice could only see him as a shadow of his old self. He looked ten years older; he read, and he dozed, passing his days in a sort of dream. He wasn't the only one: Polly was still in a world of her own, and although she spent a good deal of time with her father-in-law, they did not talk much, but were content to sit in companionable silence – together, but alone.

Nicholas and Jenny were quiet too: they were both behaving splendidly, yet Alice sensed they were not happy. Nick had taken on the running of the estate willingly and dutifully, just as Jenny had taken over the care of Alex and little Harry. Certainly she loved the children, and they occupied all her time and attention. Nick devoted himself to her, and to his responsibilities; they were a model couple – and yet Alice knew something was wrong. Something was lacking in their marriage, though she could not put her finger on it.

And then there was Caro.

The worst thing that happened was the letter Caro had sent to her mother; written on Boxing Day, and posted the day after, it arrived on the breakfast table the following morning like a bombshell.

Jenny recognized the handwriting on the envelope, and said casually: 'Thank-you letters already? Caro's putting us all to shame – I shall have to make a start on mine today.'

Intent on peeling an apple, she did not see Alice's face as she read her daughter's words:

...I didn't tell Paul, and I'm sure he never suspected you had been gossiping to the Queen about us – but I knew immediately, from the way she looked at Paul. I could not have believed you would do such a thing, and I can't begin to tell you how angry I am – or how disillusioned. Please don't reply to this letter, or attempt to get in touch with me again. If there should be a change in Daddy's condition, I would prefer to hear any news through Nicholas. That is all I have to say...

Caroline.

Alice made some excuse about a bad headache, and slipped out of the room, so she could give way to her tears in private. There was no one with whom she could share her grief; she dared not burden William with this new misery, and she would never confide it to anyone else. She wished with all her heart that she had never told the Queen anything at all; even though she had not identified Paul Weyman as the man involved with Caroline, Her Majesty must have guessed as soon as she saw them together – though Caro would never believe that.

Alice was convinced that she had lost her daughter for ever.

It would have been a comfort to pour out the whole story to Elizabeth – she was a wise and sympathetic listener – but that was impossible. Alice knew she had to suffer alone, and in silence.

Now Elizabeth put her supper aside, scarcely touched.

'That's the worst of being in bed all the time – I never get an appetite... And I'm so cross with myself for being ill!'

Alice tried to smile: 'I don't imagine you did it on purpose.'

'No, but I could have shaken off the 'flu as soon as it began, if only I hadn't been so silly. I've got a pet remedy, and it never fails; the minute you feel it coming on, you must have a raw egg beaten up in coffee – only be careful to take out all those nasty stringy bits – the egg has to be really well-beaten. And if you don't fancy it in coffee, try a glass of port or sherry instead: that works wonders! If only I hadn't been in a rush the first day, I'd never have had all this fuss.' She plumped up her pillows, punching them into shape as if she were working off her frustration. 'It couldn't have come at a worse time, either. I couldn't go up to Sandringham, so Bertie stayed here with me. Mind you, we weren't the only absentees – David was off winter-sporting in St Anton with the Baltimore Belle! But when His Majesty got so dreadfully ill, the Queen sent for Bertie – and David flew home as well. I gather his friend wasn't best pleased at having her ski-ing holiday cut short . . .'

There was a knock at the door, and the two Princesses appeared in their dressing-gowns to say goodnight.

Margaret flung her arms round her mother's neck and gave her a smacking kiss, before announcing proudly: 'We've been playing Happy Families – and I won!'

Princess Elizabeth looked troubled, and asked: 'Is it all right, when Grandpapa's so ill? Ought we to play?'

'Of course, darling.' The Duchess turned to the nursery-governess, and said: 'Take Margaret with you – Lillibet will be along in a moment.'

When Margaret had gone out, swinging gaily on Miss Crawford's hand, the Duchess drew her eldest daughter a little closer.

'Try not to worry about Grandpa, sweetheart. We must simply pray hard that God will make him better, very soon.'

Lillibet said gravely, 'Yes, but do you think He will? The day we left Sandringham, Grandma took us in to say goodbye to Grandpa, in his bedroom. He looked awfully tired . . . I think she meant it really was goodbye – only of course I didn't say so to Margaret; she wouldn't understand.'

Elizabeth hugged her. 'You're a good girl . . . We must just leave it up to God, and hope for the best. Goodnight, darling.'

Lillibet said goodnight to Alice, and went out. As the door closed behind her, Elizabeth added: 'It's so difficult to know what to say. I don't want to depress them any more than I have to – they're still so young.'

They tried to talk of other things, but Alice knew that the Duchess's thoughts were with her husband and his parents. Presently Elizabeth said: 'Alice dear – would you mind turning the wireless on? I'd like to hear the news bulletin.'

There was a portable set on a side table – though 'portable' was something of an exaggeration, as Alice discovered when she tried to move it; it contained two wet batteries in heavy glass jars, and seemed to weigh half a ton.

'We may be a little too early, but never mind – they often have one of the dance-bands on at this time of –'

She broke off. These were not the familiar strains of Jack Payne or Harry Roy; the measured cadences of 'Jesu, Joy of Man's Desiring' had an elegiac quality. When they came to an end, there was silence for several moments, and then the BBC announcer said that this concert on gramophone records would be interrupted for a special bulletin from the royal physician, Lord Dawson, and they heard the words: '...The King's life is moving peacefully towards its close...'

Elizabeth turned her head aside, and said in a muffled voice, 'Thank you, Alice – you can turn it off now. I don't want to hear any more.'

Alice retired to the guest-wing soon afterwards, and tried to get some sleep; at some time in the small hours she woke to the sound of a telephone bell ringing.

Next day, a maid brought her early-morning tea, and said, 'Excuse me, my lady, but Her Royal Highness would like to see you as soon as it's convenient.'

When Alice entered the Duchess's room, she was startled to find her up and dressed. Elizabeth took both her hands, and said, 'I hope the telephone didn't disturb you... Bertie rang to tell me – His Majesty died just before midnight. I'm going to Sandringham this morning; would you be a dear and drive up there with me?'

'Oh, but – your doctor said –'

'I don't care what the doctor said – I must be there. I've asked them to bring the car round in half an hour – I'll be well wrapped up, and just as warm and comfortable as if I were in bed... But I'd love you to come with me – if you can bear it?'

They reached Sandringham by two o'clock, and were taken immediately to a morning-room that looked out on to a bleak garden, partly covered with patches of snow. The Duke of York stood up to greet them, shaking hands with Alice, then putting his arms round Elizabeth.

'I have missed you,' he said.

'I thought of you all the time.' She looked into his face, shadowed by anxiety. 'It must have been such an ordeal.'

'It was very moving,' he said. 'We were all with Papa at the end. And when it was over, Mama turned to David, and knelt down to kiss his hand. She has been magnificent – as always.'

'How is David?'

'Absolutely shattered. I hadn't expected him to be quite so upset – his nerves must be in ribbons. After Mama had gone to her room, George offered to sit up and draft the telegrams that had to be sent to our relatives, all over the world – and there was a bit of c-c-confusion at first, because no one was quite sure whether the death had taken place before or after midnight . . . Because of the c-c-clocks, you know.'

Seeing that Alice looked puzzled, the Duchess explained: 'The clocks here are half an hour fast – "Sandringham time", they call it. It began when old King Edward wanted to get his shooting parties off to an early start, and King George kept up the old custom.'

'David's always been irritated by that, and last night when nobody quite knew what the real time was – or even what day it was – he suddenly flew into a rage and shouted: "I'll fix those bloody c-c-clocks!" . . . He insisted on dragging in a man from the village, then and there, and the poor chap was busy for hours, setting them right all over the house.'

'Where is David now?' Elizabeth asked. 'I mean – where is the King now?'

'In his room – telephoning Mrs Simpson, I believe.'

After a brief pause, Elizabeth said, 'We should like to see the Queen – if that's possible. But of course we won't disturb her if she would prefer to be alone.'

'I'm sure Mama will see you. She will want to do whatever is right.'

They found Her Majesty in her own drawing-room; she was wearing black, but her face was carefully masked by powder and rouge, and seemed quite unchanged. She held out her hand, and in turn the two ladies curtseyed and kissed it. Then Elizabeth said gently, 'We must be thankful that he can rest at last, Ma'am . . . And that when his rest came, it came so quietly. No man ever deserved it more.'

The Queen lowered her head; she did not want anyone – even her dearest friends – to see her tears.

On Wednesday, the King's coffin, which had been resting in the little church at Sandringham, was taken to the railway station at Wolferton, escorted by estate workers and tenants, and mourners from the village: the King's white pony Jock was led by a groom, while the Royal Family followed in closed carriages.

In London, King Edward VIII was proclaimed at St James's Palace. Traditionally, the monarch himself never attends this ceremony, but King Edward had a particular reason for wishing to do so.

A sharp-eyed press photographer managed to get a blurred picture of the new King at a window overlooking the Friary Court; at his side was the shadowy figure of a dark-haired woman.

On Thursday morning, when Alice telephoned William from Eaton Square, he mentioned the photograph which he had seen in his morning paper.

'Who was the lady with His Majesty?' he wanted to know.

'I can't be sure, but I imagine it was his American friend.'

'Hmph!' William grunted, and Alice couldn't help smiling; he sounded so much like his mother. 'And how was your journey down from Sandringham?'

'Very slow – and very cold. The train got in to King's Cross early, so we all had to hang about on the platform. I felt sorry for the Queen – and for the Duchess of York. She hasn't really thrown off her 'flu yet, and I'm sure she was feeling wretched. They had to wait for the crown to be brought over from the Tower, and fixed to the lid of the coffin; then the procession set off at last. The King and the royal Dukes walked behind the gun-carriage – and on the way to Westminster, the most extraordinary thing happened.'

'What was that?'

'The big Maltese cross on top of the crown got loosened – I suppose it was all the jolting and bumping up and down – and one big square-cut sapphire dropped out and fell on to the road. Apparently the King swore under his breath: "Christ! What's going to happen next?" ... And one of his Ministers overheard and whispered, rather too loudly: "That will be the motto of the new reign" ... Not a very good beginning, was it?'

'What happened to the sapphire?'

'A sergeant-major in the Grenadiers was marching beside the carriage, and he picked it up and slipped it into his pocket, without even breaking step. I think he deserves a medal!'

William reverted to the subject that concerned him most. 'When will you be coming home, my dear?'

'Next week. The lying-in-state at Westminster Hall goes on until Monday night; on Tuesday the coffin will be taken to Windsor for the funeral in St George's Chapel. I must stay with Her Majesty until then, William.'

'I suppose you must. You will telephone as often as you can?'

'Of course – every day ... How is Miranda?'

'She's feeling better, I think. Dr Parry says she will be well enough to go back to school in a few days.'

There had been a lot of influenza about that winter, and when Miranda should have gone back to Roedean for the new term, she had been laid low. Martin, who escaped the infection, was highly indignant that she had managed to extend her holiday, and departed for Eton in a bad temper.

Not that it had been much of a holiday for Miranda. At first she felt too ill to enjoy her unexpected freedom, and when her temperature went down, and she was able to get up and about, she felt very lonely.

Today she wandered down to the farm; the weather was too bad for the cows to be turned out into the meadows, so she went into the cowshed and talked to the beasts in their stalls, stroking their velvety muzzles and letting them lick her hand.

One of the cowmen was trying to muck out, and when Nicholas came in to check the supplies of cattle-cake, he asked Miranda to leave.

'This isn't a zoo, you know. We have work to do, and we can't get on with it while you're in the way!'

'Yes – sorry, Nick . . .'

She drifted off, wondering why he was always so grumpy these days; he never used to be like that. She remembered him coming home on leave, bringing presents for the whole family, looking so dashing in his uniform . . . But then everyone was different lately. Daddy, most of all – but that was understandable, because he'd been so ill. And Polly, who used to be such fun, once upon a time – when Richie died, the life seemed to go out of her too.

Even Martin had changed. She missed him when he was away, but she couldn't honestly say she had enjoyed his company at Christmas. He behaved as if being a young man was all that mattered, and girls didn't count at all; he showed off dreadfully, and he would keep telling her jokes with words she didn't understand but which were obviously rude.

Sometimes she felt as if everyone in the world was going away and leaving her behind. She longed to have someone to talk to – someone of her own . . .

Leaving the farm, she made her way back to the house by way of the garages. Grandmama's car stood in the yard, and Norman Brooks, in a moth-eaten jersey and corduroy trousers, was washing the paintwork.

He hadn't seen her yet; her first instinct was to back away. She had scarcely spoken a word to him since that day beside the lake when Martin caught him spying on them. She was about to retreat, but he raised his head and looked round.

'Oh – hello, miss,' he said awkwardly. 'Your ladyship, I mean...'

'Hello.' She strolled over to him, trying to think of something to say. 'That must be a chilly job, on a day like this.'

'It weren't too bad when I begun, 'cos I'd got some hot water from the kitchen – but now it's cooling down like...' He wrung dirty soapsuds out of the chamois leather and plunged it into the bucket again. 'You've had a nasty cold, they say? I hope you're on the mend now?'

'It was influenza – but I'm much better now, thank you. I shall be going back to school next week.'

'School!' Norman grinned suddenly, and Miranda decided that he was quite nice-looking when he smiled. 'Seems funny, don't it?'

'What's funny about it?'

'A grown-up young lady like you – going to school... That's for kids, that is.'

Miranda laughed: 'I'm not grown-up yet – I'm only sixteen.'

'Most of the girls I know left school when they was fourteen. If you wasn't a ladyship, you'd be in service by now – or working in a shop, or some such.' He shot a sidelong look at her. 'Besides – you look grown-up to me, all right...'

His eye ran over her slim waist and the curve of her blouse; he remembered how she had looked, climbing out of the water with her wet bathing-costume clinging to her... Suddenly he reddened, and she knew at once what he was thinking.

'I'd best get on with this,' he mumbled. 'Her ladyship wants the car this afternoon, to go into Medford.' He turned away, continuing to polish the bonnet with strong, firm, strokes. Impulsively, she touched his arm.

'I never told you – I wanted to say I was sorry – about what happened, last summer,' she said.

He glanced back over his shoulder, surprised. 'Sorry? For what?'

'For the way my brother spoke to you. You didn't mean any harm – he shouldn't have been so nasty.'

Slowly, Norman began to smile again. 'Thanks,' he said. Then he looked up, and his smile vanished as the first heavy raindrops fell on the car. 'My flamin' luck!' he exploded. 'It always happens when I've washed it – 'scuse me, miss...'

He reached inside and released the handbrake, then put his shoulder to the car, propelling it backwards through the open garage doors, as the heavens opened and the rain pelted down. Miranda lent a hand, helping to push; then took shelter within the doorway.

'You be careful you don't get wet – you'll be took poorly again,' the boy warned her. 'Here – tell you what – why don't you hop in? There's a rug to keep you warm.'

He opened the back door of the car. She hesitated. 'Do you think Grandmama would mind?'

'What she don't know won't hurt her. Come on.'

Miranda climbed into the back seat and unfolded the plaid lap-rug, pulling it up around her.

'That's the idea.' He stooped to look in, then added, 'If you was to budge up a bit, there'd be room for two in there.'

Obligingly, she moved over, and he scrambled in beside her.

'That's more like it!' he exclaimed, delighted at his own bravado. 'Snug as a bug in a rug, as they say – you'll be OK now, your ladyship.'

She found herself smiling back at him. 'Don't call me that – it sounds ridiculous.'

'All right then – what d'you want me to call you? Miranda?'

'If you like... And you're Norman.'

Greatly daring, he held out a hand. 'Pleased to meet you, Miranda.'

'Hello, Norman.' Laughing, they shook hands, and she found that he was shivering. 'You're cold too – why don't we share the rug?'

She held up one corner, and he slid beneath. They were very close now, and when she turned her head, she saw the whites of his eyes gleaming in the half-light, and heard him breathe a little faster.

'Do you know why I was watching you – that day – by the lake?' he asked huskily.

'No. Tell me.'

'It was because I thought you looked so lovely,' he said. 'And now I know – you're every bit as lovely as you look...'

Norman was breathless with anticipation. It was a long time since he had been so close to a girl. His attempts at courtship with Eileen Fennell had been irregular at best; once he began work at Crown House, he saw her less and less often, for Lady Beatrice kept him on a very tight rein. Not surprisingly, Eileen had soon got bored with this arrangement, and looked about for another admirer – so by now Norman's need for female companionship was becoming desperate.

Miranda's nearness was overwhelmingly exciting; he fumbled for her hand and stroked it. She said nothing – her heart pounded, and she could not speak.

'You feel lovely too,' he whispered, bringing his face closer still: and then his mouth was on hers, and his tongue between her lips. His hands moved over her, exploring her body, and she responded instinctively; her arms went round him, and she could feel that he was naked under his jersey. Quite suddenly she found herself thinking of Martin – she wondered what he was doing at this moment.

'Love me –' Norman panted urgently. '*Love me –*'

And then they heard a man's voice calling from the house: 'Brooks? Brooks! Her ladyship's sent for you – you're wanted!'

'Oh, damn...' he groaned. 'Damn it all... Damn...'

He pulled away from her; it was all over.

Tuesday was the day of King George's funeral, and the whole nation stopped to mourn his passing.

Princess Margaret was too young to attend the ceremony, so Miss Crawford stayed with her, trying to divert her enquiring mind from the event; but it had been agreed that Princess Elizabeth, nearly ten years old, should be present in St George's Chapel.

The Royal Family were to accompany the cortège from Westminster Hall to Paddington, and then continue by train to Windsor. The Duchess of York asked Alice if she would bring Lillibet to meet them at the station.

They reached Paddington too early, and had to wait on 'the Lawn', as the concourse is inaccurately named; it was a raw, cheerless morning, and Lillibet kept warm by skipping from one foot to the other. Alice noticed some photographers gathering, and put a warning hand on the girl's shoulder; it would never do for pictures of a dancing Princess to appear in the popular newspapers.

'Oh, yes – I'm sorry.' Lillibet was contrite. 'Mummy told me I must be specially grown-up today... I was allowed to stay up late last night, too.'

'Were you?' Alice smiled at the solemn little face beside her. 'Why was that?'

'They took me to see Grandpa lying in state. I had this black coat on, and my black velvet tammy – so nobody noticed me among the crowds. There were heaps and heaps of people there.'

'I'm sure there were. We all loved your grandfather very much, and we wanted to pay our respects to him.'

'Daddy was one of the officers standing round the coffin, but it was hard to recognize him in his uniform, under that big hat. And Uncle Henry and Uncle Georgie were there with him – and Uncle David –' She stumbled over the words, and corrected herself: 'The King, I mean. He never moved at all – I was watching all the time – not even an eyelid!'

Alice heard whispers breaking out among the assembled onlookers, and a moment later the royal party arrived.

The Queen appeared first; like the ladies in attendance upon her, she was heavily veiled, but there was no mistaking her walk; upright and erect as ever. Alice knew she was accompanied by the Duchesses of York, Kent and Gloucester, though it was hard to tell them apart under the deep black veils. Then one lady moved away from the others, holding out her hand to Lillibet.

'*Mummy* . . .' She breathed a sigh of relief and moved across to her, resisting a natural inclination to break into a run. She held her mother's hand, staying close beside her throughout the train journey, and the long funeral service in St. George's Chapel.

When the ceremony was over at last, and the mourners began to disperse, the Duchess praised her daughter.

'Daddy and I were very proud of you. You behaved beautifully – and for such a long time, too.'

'Yes, it did get a bit boring sometimes, but then I tried to think about poor Grandpa, and how I shall miss him.'

'I know.' Elizabeth turned to Alice, and her eyes shone with unshed tears. 'I was his daughter-in-law for twelve years, and in all that time he never said one unkind word to me . . . I shall miss him dreadfully.'

The Kents and the Gloucesters were getting ready to leave. Lillibet watched them getting into their cars, then looked back at the King, who stood apart from all the rest: a solitary figure, dwarfed by the huge stone walls that surrounded him.

'Poor Uncle David too,' she said. 'We're all going back to our families – but he hasn't got anybody waiting at home for him. It doesn't seem fair.'

When Alice got back to Crown House that evening, William welcomed her with open arms.

'It's so good to have you home again – you seem to have been away so long,' he said as he kissed her. Then he remembered Polly, sitting beside him, and added quickly: 'Though I can't complain – I've been very well looked after in your absence. Polly kindly agreed to read to me: I don't know what's wrong with the light in this room, but I find the small print seems very blurred lately.'

Polly smiled. 'When he asked me to read, I jumped at it – I thought it'd be a chance to do some acting again, after all this while. I quite fancied myself doing a bit of *Jane Eyre* or *Bulldog Drummond*... Only it turned out those weren't the sort of thing he had in mind.'

She held up the book on her lap, and Alice read the title: *Alpines for the Temperate Garden – Their Care and Cultivation.*

'The trouble is, I can't always get my tongue round the Latin names,' Polly admitted ruefully.

'Nonsense! You're a great help. I've been making notes for the spring planting,' William explained.

Alice left them to it, and went to find the rest of the family. Nicholas was in the Chinese drawing-room with Jenny, pouring sherry before dinner.

'You just missed Miranda,' Jenny told Alice. 'She only went back to school yesterday.'

'Never mind, she'll soon be home again for half-term.' Alice turned to Nick and asked: 'How's the farm?'

'The farm's doing splendidly, thank you.' Nicholas filled another glass and handed it to his mother. 'Everything's under control. Now I've got the hang of things, I'm really enjoying it.'

That night, while Nick was brushing his teeth before bed, Jenny followed him into the bathroom.

'Why didn't you tell the truth?' she asked, putting her arms round him. 'It breaks my heart to hear you pretend you enjoy what you do – why don't you admit it's driving you mad with boredom?'

'It isn't just the job,' he said. 'I could cope with that – oh, all right, it's dull, and there's never any let-up – I hate to think I'll be doing the same old things next year, the year after, ten, twenty years from now... But it's not only that.'

'You still miss the sea, don't you? The Navy was your life; I know what it meant, having to give it up.' She put her cheek against his; he went on staring at his reflection in the mirror.

'It's not that either,' he said – so quietly, it was as if she were listening to his inmost thoughts. 'It's being in his office – doing his job – trying to step into his shoes...'

'You mean your father?' But even as she spoke, she knew he was not thinking of William.

'*No*!' Angrily, he broke away from her. 'I mean Richard... He's still here – he always will be... I can never forget him, and neither can you.'

He walked out of the room, without looking at her.

15

WEDNESDAY, 29 JANUARY TO SATURDAY, 25 APRIL 1936

Some time before dawn, Jenny touched Nick's arm. 'You're awake too, aren't you?' she said softly.

'Can't you sleep either?'

'I've been dozing, on and off.'

'Me too. I wonder what the time is.'

'Shall I put the light on?'

'No, don't.' He stroked her hand. 'I'm sorry about last night.'

'I know. I felt as if we'd been quarrelling – but we hadn't.'

'It was my fault, as usual. I was being stupid . . . I do love you.'

'I love you too.'

They turned to each other, and he began to caress her. Needing the assurance that only their bodies could give, they clung to one another, and rediscovered the mystery of physical love: the passionate rite which always followed the same course, and yet was transformed into something startlingly new and different, every time.

Afterwards they lay in an exhausted embrace; for a little while, at least, they were at peace.

'I can see a sort of glimmer in the sky,' Jenny said at last. 'It must be nearly time to get up. I'd better go and see to the children.'

He drew a long breath, and let it go in a sigh. 'They're good kids . . . I just wish they were ours.'

'We'll have a family of our own, some day.' She pushed back the covers and got out of bed. 'Perhaps this time . . . You never know.'

'It's probably something to do with me: maybe the chemical thingummies aren't right. I suppose I ought really to see a specialist . . .' He shut his eyes against the sudden glare of lamplight as she pressed a switch. 'I do hate all that...'

'It's much more likely to be something to do with me – Dr Parry said the last time –'

'I bet it's not you. I bet if you'd married Richie, you'd have had a whole nursery full of babies by now. *He* never had any difficulties in that department...' The hard, bitter tone was creeping back into his voice already. Jenny pretended not to hear, and went quickly into the bathroom, turning on both the taps.

Later that morning, she sat with Alice in the drawing-room, helping her to plan menus for the weekend: it took a long time, because they kept getting side-tracked, talking of other things.

'Where had we got to? Oh, yes – I thought perhaps an old-fashioned stew for Saturday, with onions and dumplings,' Alice suggested. 'William always enjoys that – and Nick adored suet dumplings when he was little. Does he still like them?'

'I don't really know,' Jenny smiled. 'I don't think the subject has ever come up.'

'Oh, dear – I might be getting muddled. Now I come to think of it, I believe it was Richie who had a passion for dumplings, and I seem to remember Nick wouldn't eat onions... Or was it the other way round?'

'I really couldn't tell you.' Jenny turned away. 'I'm sorry.'

Alice looked up quickly: 'My dear – what is it? Have I said the wrong thing?'

'No, of course not. It was only – I've been rather worried about Nick lately... He's so unhappy.'

'Unhappy? Why is that?'

Jenny bit her lip. 'He's probably tired – he's been under a lot of strain... I think the work is getting him down.'

'I don't understand. Only last night, he was saying how much he's enjoying it –'

'I'm afraid that wasn't true. He does the job because he thinks it's his duty, but he hates it really. It was different for Richie – he took to it like a duck to water. But Nick isn't cut out to be a farmer... He'd be furious if he knew I'd told you.'

'I'm very glad you did – I had no idea.' Alice put down her notebook and pencil; the menus could wait. 'The trouble is – if William finds out Nick isn't happy to run the estate, he'll try to take it on again, and that would be asking for trouble. I'm beginning to think Mama was right: we shall have to bring in an estate manager.'

'Nick would never agree to that; it's a point of pride with him now. If you hire someone else, he'll feel he's let you down.'

'Yes... That's why we're going to have to be diplomatic about it.'

They began to discuss ways and means. Eventually, Alice told William that although Nick was making a valiant attempt to run the estate, he really needed professional assistance; only they mustn't hurt his feelings by telling him so. Then she went to Nicholas and said she was afraid that her father was planning to take over the reins again, and that the only way to prevent this was to appoint a manager to share the day-to-day running of the farm. If this could be arranged, William would realize that he was not needed, and relax.

Nick thought it over, and finally said, 'Well... If you think it will put Pa's mind at rest – I wouldn't object to that... There's only one snag, as far as I can see. Where are we going to find the right man for the job?'

'I don't know – yet.' Alice looked thoughtful. 'But I have got a vague idea at the back of my mind; would you like me to make some enquiries?'

The cheerless winter at last gave way to spring; and Alice had a longstanding engagement to spend a weekend with the Yorks, at the Royal Lodge. William had been invited too, and as he was feeling a good deal stronger, he decided that he could not refuse the invitation – even though the prospect of such an upheaval rather appalled him. Luckily, the weather was kind, and he found he was actually enjoying the car journey.

'I've spent so much time looking at one particular view, it's a refreshing change to watch some scenery that moves,' he told Alice.

They reached Windsor Great Park in good time for tea, and the Duke and Duchess gave them a whole-hearted welcome.

'Ever since you were k-k-kind enough to show us round the gardens of Crown House, I've looked forward to returning the c-c-compliment,' said the Duke. 'I know you mustn't do anything too strenuous, but I shall take you for a leisurely stroll through the rhododendron dell. They're at their best this weekend.'

As the two men wandered off, immersed in horticultural discussion, Elizabeth pressed Alice's hand.

'I'm so glad William was well enough to come with you,' she said. 'And Bertie's absolutely delighted – they'll be comparing notes about

Agapetum and Microleucrum for hours! Let's go indoors; we can have a good old gossip while we're waiting.'

In the Tent Room, a round table was already laid with lavender-blue china on a lace cloth. As Alice settled in an armchair, she said, 'I've been hoping to ask your advice about something. Is this a good moment?'

'Of course – what's the problem?'

Alice explained that they were looking for a manager to run the farm and estate, adding, 'I heard that His Majesty is reducing the staff at Sandringham. I wondered if there was anyone there who might be looking for another job.'

'Oh, my dear – it's not only the staff David has reduced; he's got a bee in his bonnet about economizing in all the royal residences. He's even cut down the beer-money they used to pay the men-servants – which didn't go down at all well, since they know he orders cases of champagne to be sent to Mrs Simpson!'

When Bertie returned with William after their tour of the garden, Elizabeth enlisted her husband's assistance.

'What was the name of that nice man who gave in his notice at Sandringham? When he heard they were going to cut down the staff, he volunteered to give up his job – I think he had some personal reason for wanting to leave, didn't he, Bertie?'

'I believe there was a young lady in the village – a broken engagement or something of the sort. She threw him over for someone else, and he decided to save embarrassment all round by bowing out... It was a great pity, because he's an excellent chap; he'll be very much missed.'

'Well, there you are then!' Elizabeth's eyes sparkled, and she raised a forefinger. 'The very thing – he wants to make a new start somewhere else – and he's been very well-trained. But I can't remember his name. Did it begin with an S?'

'Stubbs.' The Duke plucked the name out of the air. 'I'll write to him tonight, and ask him to get in touch with you.'

'We should be very grateful,' William began: but then the tea tray was brought in, closely followed by the two Princesses, who greeted Alice like a long-lost friend. They were a little shy with William, for they had only met him once before when they visited Crown House – and that had been five years ago; Lillibet could barely remember him, and Margaret not at all.

A jug of orange juice was put on the table for the girls, but the family tea-party was interrupted as soon as it began.

An American station-wagon – virtually unknown in England – drew up outside in a fusillade of flying gravel, and they all rose to their feet as two uninvited guests made an informal entrance through the french windows.

'I say, you've got people to tea – sorry about that... I suppose I should have rung up first,' said the King, grinning like a schoolboy. Then he recognized Alice: 'Good Lord – the Duchess of Dillwater, as I live and breathe! Wallis, I don't think you've met –?'

Mrs Simpson, cool and self-possessed in lime-green shantung, held out a hand. 'Oh, but we have... I know your sister-in-law – she's from Baltimore, too – am I right?'

'Quite right. Gina introduced us at a fashion show, and then we met again at Thelma Furness's party, the night my daughter was presented at court... May I introduce my husband? William – Mrs Wallis Simpson...'

William had already bowed to the King, and now shook hands with his elegant companion.

'But I'm a little confused right now, David,' Wallis rattled on, in her flat Maryland drawl. 'Did I hear you say – Dillwater?'

The King burst out laughing, and winked at Alice. 'An ancient and honourable title – it goes back a long way... No, I'm pulling your leg, my dear. It's an old joke, and it began on the day this young lady was christened, if I remember rightly.' He stroked Lillibet's fair hair affectionately. 'I haven't seen you for ages, my pet... Or you, you little monkey!' he added to Margaret.

'You never come and play with us now.' Margaret tugged at his sleeve. 'You said you were going to take us up in your aeroplane, but you never did.'

'I will – I promise – one of these days. But I have had a few little things on my mind lately, you know.' The King turned back to his sister-in-law. 'Look here – we mustn't interrupt your tea-party –'

'I'll ring for more cups,' said Elizabeth. 'Do sit down.'

'No, no – we can't stop. I was just taking a trial run in the new buggy, and I thought Bertie might like to see it. Come and drive it around, old man – it's terribly easy to handle.'

He led his brother outside, eager to show off his latest acquisition. Wallis laughed: 'He's just like a kid with a new toy. I know it's terrible of us, gate-crashing like this, but he absolutely insisted.' She flashed a brilliant smile at Elizabeth. 'And I must admit I was curious to take a look at your beautiful home. I've heard so much about it.'

'Perhaps you'd like me to show you round, after tea?' asked the Duchess, politely.

'Oh, we won't be staying that long . . . But I'm in love with it already – so much cosier than Fort Belvedere.' She moved across to the windows. 'And such a lovely garden, too . . . Though I must say if it were mine, I'd have those big trees cut down. Don't you think it's a shame, the way they spoil the view?'

The Duchess of York continued to pour tea, without comment; there was a marked drop in the social temperature. William and Alice struggled to make conversation, but it was a relief when the King returned to collect Mrs Simpson. Once again he made his apologies with the utmost charm, and then they drove away.

As the sound of the American car faded into the distance, Lillibet asked: 'Mummy, who *is* that lady?'

Her parents exchanged glances, and the Duchess said smoothly, 'Just one of Uncle David's friends, dear. Now, would you like another sandwich, or an iced cake?'

Afterwards, when the girls had gone back to the nursery, she told Alice privately, 'We can thank our lucky stars it happened this weekend . . . The Queen is coming to spend Easter with us. Can you imagine if they'd dropped in while she was here? It doesn't bear thinking about . . .'

Martin and Miranda would be home for Easter; just in time to celebrate their joint birthday, on 9 April.

Roedean broke up a few days earlier than Eton, so once again Miranda found herself on her own, waiting for her brother to return. She had not gone anywhere near the garages; she had seen Norman Brooks a few times, lifting her grandmother in or out of the car. He had seen Miranda too, but with the old lady in his arms he dared not speak to her. He gave her a long, meaningful look, but Miranda turned away, pretending not to understand his message.

It wasn't that she disliked him: in fact she had found him exciting and disturbing. At the same time, she knew that if she gave in to him again, she would be swept away on a flood of emotion, and the idea frightened her as much as it attracted her. So she avoided him.

Today she had gone out to pick some primroses. The woods were full of them, like patches of sunshine among the roots of the trees. Their scent was heady – too strong for such pale, delicate flowers.

She moved deeper into the woods, dropping to her knees each time she saw a particularly rich cluster. Soon she would have enough to fill the crystal bowl in the drawing-room.

'Hello again,' said a rough voice behind her – and a hand gripped her shoulder.

Norman was standing over her, still wearing his chauffeur's uniform with its gleaming brass buttons. She looked up, shielding her eyes; the sun was behind him, dazzling her.

'You made me jump . . .'

'Did I?' he asked. 'Why ain't you been to see me?'

'I – I've been busy.'

'Busy picking flowers!' he scoffed, and threw himself down beside her on the carpet of green moss. 'You could've found time if you'd wanted. Don't you like me no more – is that it?'

'Of course not. You know I like you, but – it's so difficult . . .'

'It ain't difficult – it's easy.' His hand closed round her wrist, and he drew her towards him.

Taken off guard, she lost her balance, tumbling towards him. He grinned, and pulled her closer. 'Give us a kiss,' he said. 'I'll show you how easy it is . . .'

Her mind told her that this was madness, but her body yearned for him. He knew she was excited, and began to play with her, tickling and teasing, as she laughed and protested: 'No – stop – we mustn't –'

'You like it – go on, say you do –'

And then, without any warning, everything changed. Suddenly she knew she had to get away: something else, something or someone stronger than Norman Brooks, had taken possession of her.

'I must go,' she gasped, pushing him with all her strength. Unprepared, he fell back, and she scrambled to her feet.

'Please don't go. What's the matter with you? Come back here – *Miranda!*'

But she was already running; the flowers she had picked were scattered and forgotten. She had to escape . . . Someone else was calling to her – someone else wanted her – and she had to find him.

Martin was sitting on the fence at the end of the kitchen garden. He looked up as she approached, with a strange smile.

'Where were you?' he asked. 'And what have you been doing?'

'In the woods – picking primroses,' she told him, out of breath.

'Don't tell whoppers. You were with somebody . . . I expect it was that lout Brooks, wasn't it?'

She stared at him, unable to reply, and he continued, 'I knew it. I knew the first time it happened – months ago. I'd just gone back to school – you were supposed to be ill. One afternoon I was doing my algebra prep and all of a sudden I knew what you were up to . . . It was a weird feeling – as if I were inside your head, sharing the same feelings. It took my breath away. What did he do to you? You didn't let him actually –' He broke off, and demonstrated with an obscene gesture.

Miranda reddened angrily. 'Of course not – don't be so beastly . . .'

'But I bet he tried to, didn't he? He's a randy-looking devil . . . Don't worry, I won't tell anyone; only you must tell me all about it – what he's like when he's undressed, how big his –'

'*Stop it!*' She backed away from him. 'You're disgusting! I'm not going to tell you anything. Anyway, you're quite wrong; there's nothing to tell.'

'Now you're fibbing again. My dear girl, you really should be more careful. Otherwise you'll finish up pregnant, and then there'll be all hell to pay.'

'Shut up, shut up, I won't listen to you – leave me alone!'

She turned and ran away, into the house and upstairs to her room, but even as she lay weeping on her bed, she knew that Martin was still laughing.

The next day was the twins' birthday, and Miranda found it hard to conceal the fact that she and Martin had quarrelled. Everyone took it for granted that they were as close as ever; Nicholas and Jenny offered to mark the occasion by taking them both out to dinner at the George Inn – the nearest thing to a first-class restaurant Medford could provide. Their mother wanted to give them a joint treat too, and suggested they might like to go up to Eaton Square one weekend during the holidays to do some shopping and see a show.

'I hear *Tonight at 8.30* is very good – you get three short plays in one evening. Most of them are funny, though some are more romantic – perhaps that wouldn't appeal to you . . .'

Martin and Miranda glanced at one another; she looked away quickly, unable to meet his mocking smile. He turned to his mother and said: 'As a matter of fact, I don't think I can make it, Ma – but thanks anyway. J. T. has asked me down to Devon, for the rest of the vac, if that's all right with you? We thought we could do some revision together, before next term's exams.'

J. T. – or to give him his full title, the Honourable James Travers – was Martin's classmate and best friend; he had stayed with the Travers family during the Christmas holidays.

'Well, of course, if that's what you want...' said Alice. 'Though I'm afraid it's going to be rather dreary for poor Miranda.'

'Oh, I don't mind,' Miranda broke in. 'Actually I've got heaps of reading to do myself. We have exams as well, you know.'

Alice smiled. 'Goodness what conscientious children! By the way, Grandmama has asked you both to go up and see her; I think she has something for you. And the post's just arrived – you've got plenty of birthday cards, by the look of it.'

They began opening envelopes; as soon as their mother was out of earshot, Martin remarked. 'Stingy blighters, our dearly beloved relatives – sending us measly cards. You'd think they might shove the odd cheque in, as well.'

Miranda tried to ignore him, though this was difficult as some of the cards – even more economically – were addressed to them both. Martin tore open one large envelope and exclaimed, 'Good old Caro – she's turned up trumps, anyhow! She's sent a couple of fivers – one each. And there's a letter as well.'

Caroline had written to them from an address in Primrose Hill, saying:

...I feel terrible guilty that I've neglected you for so long. I expect you've been told that I'm too busy to get down to Crown House these days, but the truth is I'm not on very good terms with Mother and Father. If I did come down, we should only have endless rows, so it's better to stay away. Is there any chance of you both getting up to town? Please try – though you'd better not mention it to the parents. They don't approve of me, and might try to talk you out of it. If you want to see me, you can always reach me at this address. I think of you very often...

Martin shrugged. 'I might look in on her some time – I could easily get up from school on a half-day exeat – it's no distance to Paddington... But more difficult for you from Brighton, I suppose; still, if you have any spare time, I expect you'd rather spend it with your bucolic swain... What a pity he isn't a gamekeeper – have you read *Lady Chatterley*? One of the men at school had a copy; just your cup of tea, I should think.'

Miranda lifted her chin and said coldly, 'I certainly haven't time to listen to any more of your rubbish. I'm going up to see Grandmama.'

Martin chuckled, and followed her upstairs.

Lady Beatrice was waiting for them in her sitting-room; her jewel-cases lay open around her, and the sunlight flashed and sparkled on the precious stones. She put up her cheek to be kissed, and wished them many happy returns of the day.

'I didn't know what to give you, so I decided I should pass on some of the family heirlooms... Miranda, I thought these fire-opals might suit you, with your fair complexion. They'll give you a dash of colour.'

Miranda caught her breath as the old lady held up the necklet: the creamy opals seemed to be alive with inner flame. 'They're beautiful, Grandmama – you shouldn't give them away.'

'Only the necklet, mind! There's a matching bracelet and a brooch as well, but I think I'll hang on to those a little longer. I don't approve of young girls wearing too much jewellery. And as for Martin...' She opened a velvet-lined box, showing him a set of dress-studs and links of yellow topaz. 'These belonged to your grandfather. They should look well with your straw-coloured hair.'

'Thank you.' Martin nodded a casual acknowledgement. 'Very kind.'

When they were out of the room, he said to Miranda, 'She's an old skinflint too. I'd rather have a spot of pocket-money, instead of these old-fashioned sparklers. Nobody wears stuff like this nowadays. I wonder how much a pawnbroker would give me for them?'

'Oh! You're so hateful about everybody and everything – you make me sick!'

'Do I indeed?' Martin stopped and stared at her. 'You think I wasn't grateful enough? Perhaps you're right; maybe I should go back and grovel a little. There's no sense in getting on the wrong side of the old girl.'

With an enigmatic smile, he went back to knock at his grand-mother's door. Miranda said crossly, 'You can do what you like. I love my fire-opals – I'm going to show them to Mummy.'

Lady Beatrice was surprised and pleased when Martin returned to say how much he appreciated her gifts; he promised he would treasure them always. She was less pleased when he lounged on the arm of her chair and began to talk about Norman Brooks... Did she really think he was a suitable person to be her companion? Was he altogether to be trusted? Wouldn't it be better to replace him with someone older, and more responsible?

Indignantly, Old Bea began to defend Norman; he was a good enough lad, strong and dependable – what did Martin have against him?

'You put me in a difficult position, Grandmama,' Martin sighed. 'I do hate telling tales, but there's something I feel you should know about young Master Brooks. He has a reputation as a ladies' man and he doesn't care who the ladies are, either.'

'If you mean he's been chasing some of the parlourmaids – well he's young and lively, and I dare say the silly creatures encourage him.'

'I've no objection to him pursuing the maids; but when he steps out of line and starts molesting my sister, I think it's time to call a halt, don't you?'

Old Bea's jaw dropped. 'Norman Brooks – and Miranda? You mean to tell me he had the effrontery to – to –' She choked on the words, and spluttered: 'Why didn't she tell me herself?'

'I think she was embarrassed. And perhaps she felt sorry for him – Mandy's terribly soft-hearted, you know. But I'm afraid if he's not put in his place once and for all, he might try his tricks again... That's why I think it would be better if you dismissed him, Grandmama.'

The old lady gripped her ivory-handled cane and ground it into the carpet, muttering; 'You may leave him to me. I shall deal with him – never fear.'

Twenty minutes later, when Norman came in to be given his orders for the day, he found Lady Beatrice surrounded by her jewel-cases. He stared: it was the first time he had seen the jewellery since the night he broke into this room. What was she up to now?

'I have been trying to decide whether I should send for the police and ask them to test these cases for fingerprints.' Her voice was as hard and as sharp as steel.

'No, my lady, you wouldn't do a thing like that...'

'It's what you deserve, isn't it? I've been far too lenient with you. You should have been charged with attempted robbery long ago. And now I hear you're guilty of attempted rape as well.'

Stunned, he gasped, 'No, it's not true – I never done nothing like –'

'Are you calling my granddaughter a liar? Are you telling me you did not force your attentions upon her?'

'Well – no – but it weren't like that... It wasn't – what you said...' He was stammering with fear. 'I never meant nothing wrong.'

'You're a contemptible creature, not fit for the society of decent people.'

'Please, my lady – I'm begging you...' His legs seemed to give way, and he dropped to his knees; grabbing her bony hand, he pressed it desperately. 'I'll swear I'll never do it again – as God is my witness!'

She felt the pressure of his fingers grasping her own, and the warmth of his palm upon hers; looking into his eyes, she realized with surprise that she had become quite fond of the boy during the past eighteen months.

'Well...' she growled at last. 'You're asking me to give you another chance? How do I know I can trust you?'

'I'll never do it again – I promise I won't!'

'I believe you... Because if you ever break that promise I'll have you in prison before you know it! All right – you can go.'

Light-headed with relief, he shuffled to his feet. 'You – you don't want to go driving today, my lady?'

'I'm not in the mood for joy-riding now. Go on – get out of my sight.'

'Yes, my lady.' He rushed off at top speed before she could change her mind. She watched him go and smiled grimly. She would have no more trouble with Norman.

Easter came upon Crown House like a blessing; the daffodils opened under blue skies, and for the first time there was real warmth in the sunshine.

Encouraged by the fine weather, William ventured out into the garden, and took a leisurely turn round the grounds, with Polly at his side.

'I feel as if I'd been shut up in a box for a long while,' he said, looking about him. 'I feel like a prisoner let out of gaol.'

'You're looking a lot better,' Polly assured him. 'Only don't forget what the doctor said: don't go mad, and try to do too much. You've still got to take things easy.'

'I shall do my best to remember that.' But there was a new light in William's eye, and as he gazed over the drifts of yellow blossom between the trees, he threw back his head like a young man.

'Jenny said you had to be at the house by midday to meet somebody. He's coming about a job on the farm, I think.'

'That's right; some fellow from Norfolk – Stubbs, I think the name is. Nicholas has gone to the station to meet him.'

Nick was already driving Mr Stubbs back from Medford; the short journey gave them an opportunity to get to know each other.

Not that it was easy to get Mr Stubbs to talk about himself; reserved and quiet by nature, he answered most of Nick's questions as briefly as possible. He had been employed on the various estates at Sandringham for more than twenty years, ever since he left the local school. Rising forty now, he had worked his way up from the youngest cowman until he was in charge of the dairy herds at Wolferton and Appleton.

'I worked under the head keeper for a spell, rearing the game-birds – and the old King, he was very keen on pigeon-racing. I used to look after the Royal Lofts when he was alive. But times change – and the new King, he takes no interest in such things. He prefers hunting to shooting, so there's been a lot of cutting down on that side. Maybe he'll build up the stables instead. It's hard to say what His Majesty has in mind for the old place.'

'They say he's cut down on staff too?'

'True enough, sir. But that's not why I'm looking for a new place. I had personal reasons for wanting to make a move.'

'I see. And no family ties to keep you in that part of the world?'

'No, sir.' Mr Stubbs hesitated as if he were about to enlarge on this, then repeated, 'No, sir – I'm a free agent, as you might say.'

'Fine. Well, you've had plenty of experience that will come in handy, though I'm afraid we don't go in for pigeons! But my brother built up a herd of Friesians, and there are the pigs and the poultry – and a few acres of land under cultivation, as well as the grazing. Mostly cornfields – the rest are root-crops... We've been talking about the possibility of flax –'

'Two years back we tried putting a couple of acres down to flax, but it didn't do; it wasn't economic.'

'Ah – that's worth knowing.' Nick pulled on the wheel, and the car swung round the side of the house, on to the farm track. 'Here we are – those are the stables, right ahead – and the farm office next to them... And there's my wife, waiting for us.'

They pulled up at the five-barred gate, and Jenny came forward to meet them. She shook hands with Mr Stubbs who said, 'Pleased to meet you, my lady.'

She corrected him gently.'I'm Mrs Gaunt. My mother-in-law is Lady Minster; she's up in London today – but you'll meet Lord Minster presently.'

They set out on a tour of the farm, and he said he liked the look of it. Nicholas and Jenny smiled at each other; they liked the look of Mr Stubbs. Nick took him into the office to run over the daily routine, and Mr Stubbs made some intelligent suggestions about dividing the work between them. Then Jenny reminded them that Lord Minster would be waiting, and they walked back to the house.

William had enjoyed his walk round the garden, but was feeling a little tired by now; he and Polly sat on the terrace, enjoying the unaccustomed sunshine. They looked up as Nicholas approached with the newcomer.

'This is Mr Stubbs, father; he seems to approve of us – and I'm sure he can set us to rights.' Then Nick remembered Polly. 'Oh, I beg your pardon, my sister-in-law – Mr Stubbs.'

Polly shook hands; she saw a round-faced man of medium height, with a weather-beaten complexion and hair that was beginning to recede. He seemed a little awkward, and smiled stiffly, as if smiling did not come naturally to him. Rather a dull little man, Polly thought; but pleasant enough in his way.

William asked him if he were interested in gardens, and Mr Stubbs said that in Norfolk he had cultivated a small plot of his own, behind the tied cottage he lived in – 'But it was nothing compared to this, of course. You've got a showplace here, sir, and no mistake.'

William warmed to him immediately, saying, 'Although the gardens won't be your responsibility, Mr Stubbs, if you have any thoughts you'd care to pass on, I'd be most interested to hear them.'

Nicholas added, 'I'm afraid we don't have any tied cottages to go with the job, but we have found you somewhere to live –'

'That's if you like it,' Polly cut in. 'The lodge has been redecorated, so it's all neat and tidy ... I hope it will be comfortable.'

'It hasn't been lived in since my sister moved abroad,' William explained. 'Polly, why don't you take Mr Stubbs to see if it will suit him?'

'I'll send the housekeeper to meet you with the keys, shall I?'

suggested Nicholas. 'Then you can tell her if there's anything that needs to be done.'

So Polly escorted Mr Stubbs across the lawn and down the gravel drive to the lodge cottage. They walked in a silence broken only by a chorus of birdsong from the treetops – until Mr Stubbs felt impelled to make some effort towards sociability, and said, 'I beg your pardon, ma'am, but I haven't sorted out all the names yet – if you're Mr Gaunt's sister-in-law, would you be another Mrs Gaunt?'

'I might have been, only my husband was the eldest son: that's why I'm called Lady Ebony. But don't let that bother you; it's a load of nonsense really. Mostly I'm called Polly.' She smiled at him. 'What's your first name, Mr Stubbs?'

'Kenneth,' he said shyly, then continued, 'I believe Lady Minster is away from home. Would Lord Ebony be in London too?'

'I'm afraid not. He was the Viscount; but he died, more than two years ago.'

'Viscount Ebony?' He stopped short. 'Of course – I should have realized – it was in all the papers.'

'So they told me,' said Polly flatly.

'I am sorry, my lady, I'd never have said anything if I'd known –'

'It's not your fault; don't worry, I'm not offended.' She changed the subject. 'Look – there's Lilian Brooks, the housekeeper, coming down the path. She has been quick.'

They met at the front door of the lodge, and Mr Stubbs was introduced all over again. Lilian produced a bunch of keys and let them in.

Certainly the cottage needed cleaning, but the new tenant seemed very pleased with the accommodation, and Lilian promised that by the time he moved in, she would have everything in apple-pie order.

'It's a bit on the small side, I'm afraid,' she apologized. 'And the second bedroom's not much more than a box-room.'

'That's no problem,' he said. 'I've no one but myself to bother about – it'll do very well as bachelor lodgings.'

'What about cooking?' Lilian asked. 'You're more than welcome to take your dinner and tea in the servants' hall, but as for your breakfast –'

'I can manage to fry myself an egg and a rasher of bacon. But I'll take advantage of your hospitality for the other meals, Mrs Brooks.' He moved away unrolling a tape-measure.

'We'll be glad to see you,' she said, then lowered her voice to add, 'and it's Miss Brooks, by the way...'

Polly turned to her; Lilian's plain, homely face was pinker than usual. She was staring at Mr Stubbs, who made notes on the back of an old envelope, muttering to himself. 'Four foot seven – yes, I've got a bedstead will fit in there nicely... But how about the bookcase?'

He did not see the look in Lilian's eyes, and if he had done so, he might not have understood it. But Polly recognized it at once; that was how it happened sometimes: all in a moment, Lilian had fallen in love.

She felt oddly moved, and perhaps a little envious, trying to remember how it had felt... Such a strange emotion, so long ago.

As the school holidays came to an end, Miranda realized she hadn't spoken to Norman Brooks for weeks; perhaps he was keeping out of her way deliberately. It would be hardly surprising, after the abrupt way she left him last time. She felt a little guilty about it, and decided to try and put things right between them.

When she went round to the garages, the bonnet of the Lanchester was open, and Norman's legs were sticking out from beneath the car.

'Hello,' she said.

He wriggled out on to the cobblestones, looking up at her; there was a black smudge of grease across his face.

'What do you want?' he asked, suspiciously.

'Nothing – I just came to say hello. I won't interrupt, if you're busy.'

'Blockage in the petrol-feed...' He sat up, wiping his face with a grubby rag. 'You'd better not hang about; someone might see you.'

'What does that matter?' she asked, puzzled by his truculent manner.

'Don't be daft,' he said. 'If her ladyship finds out I been talking to you, I'll be in real trouble.'

'What do you mean?'

He frowned. 'You know what I mean. What did you want to go and tell her for? I'd never have believed you'd do a thing like that – telling lies about me, and all... I didn't do nothing wrong.'

Miranda was shocked. 'I don't know what you're talking about –'

'There you go – telling lies again. You said I tried to – to interfere with you . . . Bloody near got me the sack, you did!'

She gasped, 'Norman, I didn't – I wouldn't –'

But he wasn't listening; hearing footsteps approaching, he interrupted her fiercely, 'I'm fed up with you and your tricks. Push off – and don't come back no more!'

He disappeared beneath the car, as Dennett, the senior chauffeur, crossed the yard, touching his cap to Miranda.

Overwhelmed by frustration and injustice, Miranda made her escape. She wanted to assure Norman she would never have betrayed him to her grandmother – but what was the use? He wouldn't believe her now.

She walked round to the front of the house, and found one of the Medford taxi-cabs ticking over at the foot of the steps. Martin was paying off the driver while one of the footmen carried his luggage indoors; two suitcases and a pair of tennis-rackets. As the taxi moved off, Martin turned to greet his sister.

'Are you the welcoming committee? Where's the red carpet?' He kissed her lightly on the cheek. 'Actually, this is hello and goodbye – I'm off to school again tomorrow. Did you enjoy your hols? Devon was glorious; J. T.'s people have asked me again for the long vac, so I'll be going back at the end of July –'

'Thank goodness for that.' As he tried to put his arm round her, Miranda pulled free. 'I wish you'd go away for good.'

'Good Lord!' He began to laugh at her angry face. 'What's brought this on? What have I done now?'

'I've only just found out what you did – going to Grandmama and telling her about me and Norman.'

'Oh, that . . .' He brushed it aside. 'My dear girl, *somebody* had to put a stop to it. It was for your own good.'

'I hate you, Martin, I really do.' She walked up the steps, then turned to look back at him. 'I'm glad you're going away tomorrow. I hope you never come back.'

Martin smiled. 'But that wouldn't make any difference, would it? Even when I'm not here – we're still together. We'll always be together . . . You know that.'

16

SUNDAY, 4 OCTOBER TO FRIDAY, 11 DECEMBER 1936

LONDON on a Sunday evening: at Primrose Hill, everything was deceptively quiet, although in other places – near and far – the world was beginning to crack up and change its shape.

Sitting by the fire, Paul Weyman browsed through the *Sunday Times* and *Observer*, and listened with half an ear to Caroline, who was taking a long telephone call in the hall.

'All right', he heard her say at last. 'I'll see you in the office tomorrow... But I warn you – if they'd don't give me the Jarrow story, there's going to be one hell of a row.'

There was a 'ting' as the receiver went down, and then Caro came back into the sitting-room. Paul glanced up, and saw she was frowning.

'Trouble?' he asked.

'It's so damned unfair!' she burst out. 'Why don't they ever think of me as a serious reporter? Why do I always get the stupid society rubbish?'

'What's happened now?

'That brute Mosley took his bully-boys out on another march today – all in their black uniforms, shouting slogans and deliberately stirring up trouble. They were supposed to go from Tower Hill to Victoria Park, only it didn't work out like that. I've been talking to Bob Kendall; he was sent to cover the march, and only just got back. He said he was lucky to get home in one piece.'

'More riots, I suppose?'

'The police must be mad – they let them march through the East End, shouting jolly little slogans like "The yids, the yids, we've got to get rid of the yids"... By the time they got to Cable Street they had a full-scale battle on their hands; people were throwing bricks and bottles, hitting each other over the head. Gosh, I wish I'd been there!'

'I'm very glad you weren't. I heard you mention Jarrow – that's up north somewhere, isn't it?'

'Near Newcastle. Ellen Wilkinson's leading a protest march to London; they're setting out tomorrow.'

'Not *another* march?' Paul groaned.

'This one's totally different. Did you know there are thirty-five thousand people in Jarrow, and most of the men have been out of work since they closed the shipyard? I'm going to ask Fred Binns to send me up to meet them – I want to join the march. That would be a story worth writing.'

'I'm not sure I like the idea of you going on a protest march. Besides, I need you here to look after me. You can't go off and leave me all alone!'

He stretched out a hand; she went over to the fireplace and curled up at his feet on the hearthrug.

'I doubt if you'll even notice I've gone,' she said. 'You're always at the television studio nowadays. I hardly ever see you.'

'Well, it's bound to be a bit hectic at present – we start on the second of November,' Paul reminded her. 'Perhaps you could persuade your news editor to let you write about us instead?'

'Mmmm..' She didn't sound enthusiastic. 'That's exactly the kind of job he gives me – the latest craze for a few rich women – something to fill up their time between luncheon-parties and cocktails...'

'You're in a fierce mood this evening.' Paul began to stroke her hair. 'What's the matter?'

'Oh – I don't know... I just hate my job sometimes... No, it's not the job – it's because I'm who I am – nobody takes me seriously... I wish I could go away and change my name, and start my life all over again!'

He put his arm round her shoulders. 'I wouldn't let you. I could never let you go.' He bent his head to kiss her, expecting her to lift her face to him; but she was staring into the heart of the fire, and did not look up.

The Bowyers' flat in Curzon Street did not have an open fire, but the radiators gave out a stuffy heat. As Sir Charles handed Alice a gin and tonic, she said, 'Could I have some more ice in mine, Charlie? You keep the flat so warm – don't you ever have the windows open?'

'Too much traffic noise, old girl – can't hear yourself think . . . Cheers!'

She raised her glass. 'What time are you expecting Gina?'

'Heaven only knows. When she's off with her Fascist chums, she's liable to stay out till all hours. If she's not back by eight, we'll begin supper without her.'

He lowered himself into an overstuffed wing-chair, with a little grunt. Alice watched him, and thought how much older he was looking these days.

'You ought to take more exercise,' she said. 'You're putting on weight.'

'I do take exercise: I walk to the Club practically every day – and back again . . . unless it's pouring with rain, of course.' Sir Charles changed the subject; he did not like being criticized. 'I saw that bounder Weyman in the smoking-room last week – he doesn't come in very often these days – he's working at some extraordinary place in Muswell Hill . . . But it's still extremely awkward when he does look in; I can't exactly cut the fellow dead, but I never know what to say . . . He goes on about this damned television most of the time.'

'Does he ever mention Caro?' asked Alice quietly.

'Oh – yes – I generally ask how she's getting along. He says she's very happy.'

'I'm glad.' Alice sipped her drink. 'I suppose as long as she's happy, that's all that matters.'

A silence fell. Charlie put his glass down on the front page of the *Sunday Express*, where it made a damp circle round a picture of the King.

'I see His Majesty's been to open some new aircraft factory . . . It's about time he buckled down to work, after all that gallivanting round the Mediterranean on a yacht . . . They managed to keep Mrs Simpson out of the newspaper photographs – but everyone knew she was there . . . I can't understand Simpson letting his wife carry on like that – the fellow's made himself a laughing-stock.'

'I think he realized the marriage was over, long ago. That's why he's giving her a divorce.'

'I never met the lady – Gina usually kept her smart friends to herself – but judging by her photos, she's not exactly a beauty, is

243

she? I can only suppose she must have a very striking personality –'

He broke off at the sound of the front door opening, and Gina's voice calling out: 'Hi! I'm back!'

The door slammed, and she burst into the room, her red hair in vivid contrast to her blackshirt uniform. She took off her leather coat and flung it over a chair, swooped on Alice to kiss her, then embraced her husband, keeping up an excited babble.

'I'm not late, am I? Alice, you're looking simply heavenly, darling – Charlie, be an angel and fix me a drink – I'm absolutely exhausted; Tom had to call the march off in the end, under orders from the police commissioners. Would you believe it? Those filthy reds had barricaded some of the streets, and the cops did nothing – they were too scared of the Jewish rabble... But the big news is, I've got to start packing – Tom's off to Germany tomorrow, on a secret mission. He's taking a few of his very closest friends, and he's particularly asked me to go along – I'll be back some time Thursday, or Friday at the very latest – I knew you wouldn't mind – isn't it too thrilling for words?'

Some time in the small hours of Thursday morning, Gina lay awake in a wide, old-fashioned bed in a Berlin hotel.

She could not sleep; the feather quilt lay heavy on her, but the night was too chilly to throw it off. She stared at the pattern of light thrown across the ceiling from the street-lamps, and tried to piece together the events of the past few days.

The reason for Sir Oswald Mosley's trip to Germany was not political but personal, and he had gone to great lengths to keep it secret. His wife had died three years earlier, and for some time he had been living with Diana Mitford, the ex-wife of Brian Guinness: now he had decided to marry her. Secrecy was essential, as Sir Oswald feared Diana might become the target for violent attacks from his enemies.

He could not risk marrying her openly, in England: but German regulations permitted foreign nationals to be married before a German registrar, not at their Embassy: this was the reason for the sudden journey abroad.

The morning after the Cable Street battle, Sir Oswald slipped quietly out of London together with Lady Diana and his best man, an ex-Hussar and an old friend. They were accompanied by Roland

Voss, in charge of all the arrangements, and Lady Diana's travelling companion, Lady Gina Bowyer.

Gina had been sworn to secrecy. She could not even tell her husband about the wedding; she simply said that Tom would be holding some discussions with high-ranking officials in the German government.

Just how high-ranking those officials were, even Gina did not know until she reached Berlin.

The wedding took place in an office at the Reichs Chancellery; and the German witnesses were Herr Goebbels, the Minister for Propaganda, and his wife Magda, a personal friend of Diana's. The best man and the bride's sister, Unity Mitford, were the English witnesses. Roly and Gina took no official part in the ceremony, though Gina held Diana's bouquet while she signed the register.

Afterwards they were all driven back to the Goebbels' house beside the Wannsee, for lunch – and were welcomed by yet another guest.

Gina saw him coming towards them across the polished floor of the entrance-hall, and caught her breath; she had seen him a hundred times in photographs and newsreels. Frau Goebbels presented them: 'Lady Gina Bowyer – Mr Roland Voss .. Our Führer, Herr Adolf Hitler.'

Smiling, he shook hands with them both. Gina decided that the British press had been very hard on him: he was an absolute charmer.

It was clear that Unity Mitford thought so; throughout the evening, she never took her eyes off him. She hung on every word he uttered, looking very lovely, with her blonde hair and pink-and-white complexion – though Gina thought it was a pity she kept her mouth slightly open as it made her look simple-minded.

During luncheon, the Führer turned to Gina and enquired after the King. 'They say he hopes to marry a lady from your country – is this true?'

Gina thought fast. 'I used to know Wallis Simpson pretty well, sir, when she first came over from Baltimore, but I don't often see her these days. I'm afraid I can't tell you what the King is planning to do.'

Herr Hitler nodded, then said, 'He should marry her. I think she will make a very good Queen of England.'

Unity hooted with laughter, and Herr Hitler smiled politely – though Gina was not altogether sure he had intended it as a joke.

She noticed too that although the Führer was very affable towards the English guests, he kept his distance from Oswald Mosley.

Later, when she went into Frau Goebbel's bedroom to repair her make-up, she found Unity sitting at the dressing-table, spraying herself with her hostess's scent, and they got into conversation.

'Doesn't Herr Hitler like Sir Oswald?' she asked. 'He seems to be avoiding him.'

Unity giggled: 'He daren't side openly with the BUF because it might put the British politicians off, and he's still hoping to win them round... Between you and me, Tom irritates him a bit. He told me once – "The trouble with the man Mosley is, he will try to imitate me!"...' She laughed, then bit her lip, like a naughty child telling tales out of school.

When the party broke up at last, Roly took Gina back to their hotel. For the sake of appearances they were booked into separate rooms, but as they went up in the lift, she whispered, 'Just give me time to have a bath, angel... I'll leave my door unlocked.'

He kissed her swiftly and said, 'It'll be rather longer than that. I've arranged to meet those two SS officers; I presume they were Hitler's bodyguard... We're going to compare notes about the situation, here and in London.'

'Oh, no – must you?' she pouted, as the lift door slid open.

'It's all good for international relations. I'll get back as soon as I can, I promise.'

'I'll be waiting...'

And here she was hours later, still waiting. She rolled over, punching the soft pillows; how could Roly be so mean, leaving her alone like this? They were going back to London tomorrow, so this would be their last chance to spend a whole night together...

At some point she must have dozed off, because when she opened her eyes again it was almost morning. Roly was standing in the first light of dawn, pulling off his dress-shirt.

'Hey – what time do you call this?' she asked indignantly. 'Where in hell have you been?'

'They dragged me off to some sordid little night-club. They wouldn't take no for an answer.' Naked, he climbed into bed and embraced her, but she held him at arm's length.

'You smell of cheap face-powder and there's lipstick on your cheek... What have you been up to, you rat?'

'Oh – we had to dance with the girls there – and some of them turned out to be boys dressed up. It was all pretty foul... I got away as soon as I could, I promise you...' Stopping her mouth with a kiss, he began to make love to her, and she forgave him immediately.

'Did you watch the new television broadcasts?' asked the Duchess of York.

'No, I was at home when they began; we can't receive television in our part of Kent,' said Alice.

They were having tea at 145 Piccadilly, on a grey afternoon in the middle of November. Rain trickled miserably down the windows, but the drawing-room was as welcoming as ever, with an arrangement of glowing autumn leaves that picked up the gleam of firelight.

Elizabeth buttered a crumpet, and said, 'We watched it, on the first afternoon; it's all very wonderful, of course, but I can't honestly say I was enthralled. They had a little variety show with a singer, and some coloured gentlemen from America called Buck and Bubbles, and a lot of Chinese jugglers spinning plates on sticks... Lillibet and Margaret were rather taken with them, and had to be dissuaded from practising on the nursery tea-things.'

Alice smiled. 'Will the Princesses be joining us for tea today?'

'I'm afraid not – this is one of the days when they have their swimming lessons; and afterwards Crawfie takes them out to tea, with lots of sponge cake – it's known as "swimming-cake", and has very special properties.'

Seeing that Alice looked blank, the Duchess laughed: 'Well, that's what Miss Daly says – she's the swimming instructor. Sponge, you see – full of air, so it keeps them very buoyant in the water, and they don't need rubber rings! I know one shouldn't deceive children, but it's like Father Christmas – it seems a shame to disillusion them.' She dabbed at her chin. 'Oh, dear – I do love crumpets, but the melted butter goes everywhere... Anyway, I took your advice about waiting to start them off at the Bath Club, and now I'm very glad I did. They simply love it, and it's helped to take their minds off – other things...' Her tone changed, and the light dimmed in her bright blue eyes.

'Other things?'

The Duchess sighed. 'It's impossible to deceive them over anything really important. They know there's trouble in the family; of course we never talk about it in front of them, but they seem to understand that we're living through a difficult time... It's been such a dreadful summer.'

'You mean the King, and –' Alice hesitated.

'I mean the transatlantic typhoon that blew in from Baltimore...' Elizabeth let her tea grow cold as she looked back over the past months. 'First there was David's cruise on board the *Nahlin* – he should never have gone; he upset so many people – and the foreign papers were full of it... "The English King and his inamorata" – it was simply frightful... Her Majesty knew quite well what was going on, though we never discussed it.'

'She told me once that it must be an infatuation, so it would eventually burn itself out.'

'I'm sure she prayed that it would. The Duke of Kent is convinced that it's witchcraft! He says Mrs Simpson has cast a spell over David – that's why he's so besotted about her.' Elizabeth laced her fingers together, and continued, 'August was bad enough but September was even worse, as far as we were concerned, anyway. He invited her to stay at Balmoral, and once she'd settled in, she behaved as if she owned the place. We were in Scotland ourselves, at Birkhall, so of course we had to go and visit them: I found out he had given her his mother's bedroom. I'm afraid that made me very cross. And she insisted on marching in to the kitchens and telling the cook how to make what she calls a "three-decker sandwich"...'

'She's a lady who likes to have her own way, certainly.'

'And David gives in to her every time... If she leaves her compact in her room, she sends him to fetch it – she treats him like a lapdog! What I resented most was that he made Bertie take on one of his public duties – opening the new hospital in Aberdeen, which had all been arranged ages ago. The official pretext was that the King was in mourning for his father, but that was absurd because Bertie was in mourning too, and anyway David had been sunning himself on the Mediterranean a few weeks earlier! No, the real reason was that he wanted to drive to Ballater station to meet Wallis off the London train, the day she arrived. Everyone knew that; and I'm sure the good people of Aberdeen aren't going to forget it in a hurry.'

'And now Mrs Simpson has got her divorce.'

Elizabeth shut her eyes for a moment. 'Don't – I can't bear to think about it...' She opened them again, and looked at Alice. 'Do you know Alex Hardinge – the King's Private Secretary?'

Alice was puzzled. 'I've met Lord Hardinge. I can't say I know him.'

'He's a good man, loyal and dependable... Last week he wrote David a confidential letter. He warned him he mustn't expect the British press to keep up this discreet silence much longer; once the story gets into the papers, the country will be in an uproar. He advised the King to send Mrs Simpson abroad – back to America, anywhere at all, as long as it's a long way off. That might keep the gossips quiet for a while.'

'What was the King's reply to that?'

'He threatened to sack Alex Hardinge... He summoned the Prime Minister and told him that he intends to marry the lady; he gave Mr Baldwin an ultimatum: either there will be a wedding or there will be no coronation.'

Alice could not help noticing that Elizabeth's eyes were red; her voice was choked as she fumbled for her handkerchief. Helplessly, Alice could only murmur, 'I'm very sorry: this must be a nightmare for you.'

'Don't worry, I'm not going to dissolve in floods of tears!' The Duchess forced a smile. 'But I'm afraid I may be starting my annual bout of 'flu – so tiresome...'

'How about your never-failing remedy?' Alice reminded her. 'The egg beaten up in coffee?'

'I tried that already, but somehow I don't think it's going to do the trick, this time.'

The Duchess was quite right; once again she was laid low, and as soon as she was strong enough to travel, she and her family retired to Scotland in search of peace and quiet.

But the constitutional crisis grew worse; at the beginning of December she had to cut short her convalescence, and they returned to London on the overnight train.

As they were getting into the waiting car at King's Cross station, Lillibet noticed a newspaper placard, and read it aloud: 'Oh, look – "The King's Marriage"... What does it mean?'

A little crowd had gathered on the forecourt, and they raised a loyal cheer as the royal party drove off. For once, the Duchess was too appalled to wave or smile in response. She looked at her husband; he held Margaret's hand and his other arm was round Lillibet's shoulders, but his face was like a death mask. Her heart turned over.

She knew she would never be able to forgive Wallis Simpson for this, as long as she lived.

The newspaper silence had been broken at last, and a larger crowd blocked the pavement when they reached Piccadilly.

'You'd better take the g-g-girls in,' said the Duke, speaking with more difficulty than usual. 'I must go to Mama at once.'

He remained in the car, driving straight on to Marlborough House, where he found his mother in the first-floor drawing-room. She had an embroidery frame on her lap, and looked up as he entered.

'Bertie – you are early – that's good. How is Elizabeth?'

'She hasn't quite recovered from her influenza yet, Mama. I wish she could have stayed in Scotland for another week, but – as I had to come back to London, she wanted to be with me.'

'Of course. Please give her my love and best wishes; I hope she will very soon get well.' The Queen put aside her petit point. 'I have been trying to do some needlework, but I can't give my mind to it.' She looked at the clock on the overmantel, and frowned. 'David should be here by now. You came all the way from Scotland, and managed to be here in good time; he has only to travel a few hundred yards along the Mall, but he always seems to find the journey difficult...'

She tried to make light of it, but the pain in her voice betrayed her. After her husband's death, Queen Mary had moved out of Buckingham Palace, and her son had moved in – but he had not been to visit her very often.

A bustle in the corridor told them that the King had arrived, and a moment later he joined them, his face lined with anxiety. He kissed his mother's cheek, nodded to his brother, then said, 'Well – here I am.'

'Thank you, David; I am very grateful. I felt I must talk to you both, especially after those upsetting items in this morning's papers. You are my eldest sons, and it is time we had a family conference.'

'Quite.' The King cleared his throat. 'I hope you didn't imagine that I had been deliberately neglecting you, Mama?'

'I did not imagine anything. I realize you must have many other things to do.' She looked round the large, shadowy room, and sighed. 'How strange – the last time we met in this house, ten years ago, we had a disagreement. I tried to persuade you then that you must take your future role – your responsibilities – more seriously, and you accused me of interference... I hope we shall not fall out again today.'

He inclined his head slightly. 'I hope not... Perhaps you think I should have consulted you about this situation – but I had no wish to bring the family into it... It's something I had to handle alone, to decide for myself.'

There was a brief pause, and then the Queen asked: 'And have you reached a decision?'

'Yes... I know now that I cannot live alone, as the King of England; and that I must marry Wallis Simpson.'

A long silence followed. The Queen glanced at her second son, and saw the tic of a muscle twitching in his cheek. At last she said, in a voice that was little more than a whisper: 'You are determined to abdicate?'

'Yes, Mama. I shall not be the first King to give up his throne to marry the woman he loves. Not so long ago, King Carol –'

The Queen interrupted with a flash of anger: 'Really, David! This is Great Britain, not Romania!'

Bertie's throat was dry, but he managed to utter the words: 'What are you g-g-going to do?'

'Today, I'm going to Fort Belvedere. Wallis has left the country – she is in France by now; I have to decide on my next move. Come and see me at the Fort tomorrow, Bertie.'

When the Duke of York returned home, Elizabeth did not have to ask what had happened; his white face told her everything. All he said was: 'I don't understand... The King of England c-c-cannot abdicate... I'll never understand it.'

A miserable weekend followed. On Friday, Bertie rang his brother to ask what time he should see him, but David put him off, saying: 'Come tomorrow instead.'

On Saturday, the Yorks went down to Royal Lodge as usual, and Bertie rang him again.

'Come and see me tomorrow night,' said David. 'I'll talk to you then. I'll tell you my decision as soon as I've made up my mind.'

On Sunday evening Bertie tried again, only to be told that the King was in conference, and would return his call later. He sat up until very late, but the call never came.

On Monday he telephoned the Fort and insisted on speaking to the King, who told him: 'I might be able to talk this evening – I'll let you know.'

Bertie waited all day, and at ten to seven the King rang back, saying; 'Come round and see me after dinner.'

'No, David.' Bertie stood his ground. 'I've waited long enough. I'm coming to see you right away.'

Within ten minutes he had reached Fort Belvedere. The King came to meet him, looking years younger; the lines of worry had gone from his face, and he said simply: 'I have decided to go . . . It's up to you now.'

The long wait was over.

On Thursday evening, Paul arrived home late, and when he walked into the flat at Primrose Hill, Caro looked up enquiringly: 'Bad day?'

He nodded. 'That's putting it mildly. I thought for a while we'd have to cancel tonight's *Picture Page* altogether.'

'Why? You weren't doing a feature about the King, surely?'

He stared at her as if she had gone mad. 'The King? What are you talking about?'

'The Abdication.' Now it was Caro's turn to look mystified. 'Don't you know he signed it this morning? Fleet Street was thrown into a complete frenzy. I thought that's what you meant.'

'Oh, that – yes, we put out an announcement at the start of the day's programmes; that was perfectly straightforward. No, the real trouble was Camera One – it was playing up all through rehearsals, and just before we went on the air tonight, Camera Two packed up altogether. It was touch and go all the way, I can tell you.'

Caro smiled to herself; crises in the television studio had their own scale of priority.

Paul poured himself a drink, and stretched out in his easy-chair by the fire; almost at once, the telephone rang in the hall. Caro stood up. 'I'll go; it's probably for me.'

But she was wrong; a carefully modulated voice that only just succeeded in concealing its agitation asked to speak to Mr Weyman.

'This is Sir John Reith's office, at Broadcasting House . . . It's a matter of extreme urgency.'

'All right – I'll call him.'

She passed the telephone over to Paul, wondering what new catastrophe might have occurred; and at the same instant the doorbell rang. 'Oh, help – *now* what . . . ?'

Caro opened the door, and was astonished to find her younger brother standing on the mat.

'Martin – what on earth –?'

He looked pale and tired, though he tried to carry off his surprise entrance nonchalantly. 'I know it's rather late for a social call, but you did say I could come here any time, so I hoped you wouldn't mind if –'

Then he saw Paul, involved in his telephone conversation further down the hall, and exclaimed: 'Uncle Paul! I haven't seen you for ages – hello!'

Paul sketched a gesture of welcome, with the abstracted look of a man listening to two people at once, and gestured apologetically at the instrument.

'He's talking to his boss at the BBC', Caro explained. 'I think it's something important. Anyway, come in and sit down.' She led Martin into the sitting-room, wondering how much she should tell him about their domestic arrangements. But that could wait: the first thing was to find out why he was here.

'Shouldn't you be at school?' she asked. 'This isn't half-term, surely? No, it can't be –'

Without answering her question, Martin threw himself into the chair Paul had vacated, and looked round. 'It's nice here,' he said. 'This is what I'd like – a flat of my own.'

'Well, it's not exactly my flat,' she began. 'I sort of share it.'

'Oh, really? Well, it's jolly comfortable...' Through the closed door, they could still hear Paul on the phone, and Martin added: 'I can't remember the last time I saw Uncle Paul. What a coincidence he's here this evening.'

Caro decided to take the plunge. 'Not really. You see – he's the person I'm sharing with. This is his flat.'

Martin stared at her. 'You mean – you – and Uncle Paul...? But – but he's old as Pa –'

'No, he isn't. He's years younger. Anyway, what difference does that make? We love one another.'

'I see...' He was still staring. 'Is that why you never come home nowadays?'

'That's why. The parents have been very stuffy about it.'

'I did wonder.' Martin grinned suddenly. 'In that case, I'm jolly glad I came here. I expect they'll be pretty stuffy about me too, when they find out.'

'But what's wrong, Martin? What's happened?'

He looked down at the carpet, unwilling to meet her eye, and muttered: 'I've left school ... I'd had enough of it.'

'What? That's ridiculous!' She was bewildered. 'I always thought you were so happy at Eton – you're in your final year –'

'There's been some trouble – it's all a bit grim. It's not just me – several of my chums got caught too, after lights out – mucking about ... You know.'

She didn't understand at first; then she saw he was blushing. Suddenly he stopped looking like a worldly-wise young man; he was a shamefaced and scared little boy. 'J. T.'s got expelled – they sent for his people to come and take him away. I think they were going to do the same with me, but I didn't wait to find out. I ran all the way to the station – it was a good thing I had enough cash on me to buy a ticket ... Only a single – I'm never going back.'

The door opened, and Paul came in, saying wearily: 'Sorry about that, Martin – everything's been rather chaotic today, I'm afraid.' He turned to Caro. 'Apparently the King – or the ex-King, or whatever he's called – is going to broadcast to the nation tomorrow night. Even though I'm in television now, Sir John has decided I ought to handle it, since I've been in charge of all the royal broadcasts so far, and I know the form ... I suppose it's rather an honour, in a way – but it's a damn nuisance as well. I shall have to go down to Windsor tomorrow with the engineers, to fix it up.'

He moved automatically towards his armchair, then found it was occupied. Martin stood up quickly. 'I'm sorry – is this your chair?'

'Well, yes – no – I mean, I was sitting there, but it doesn't matter ...' Paul looked uncertainly at Caro.

'It's all right,' she said. 'I've told Martin we're together. We don't have to keep any secrets from him.'

'Oh ... Well, Martin – I'm glad to see you after all this time. You've certainly grown up since our last meeting. How's the world treating you? Is this your last year at Eton?'

Martin slumped back into the chair. 'Yes – it was.'

'He's got into some trouble,' Caro explained. 'He was afraid they would expel him – so he's run away.'

'I couldn't go home; Ma and Pa would be horrified.' Martin began to blush again. 'I couldn't face them – it's all a bit rotten, actually ...'

'What sort of trouble? What have you been –' Paul broke off, then said quietly, 'Oh – I see ... Caro – could you make us some coffee? I think Martin and I should have a talk on our own – do you mind? And you'd better make up the spare bed for him, as well.'

An hour later, when they had lent Martin a pair of pyjamas and settled him in the guest-room, Paul told Caroline, 'I tried to talk some sense into him. He feels like a criminal at the moment, but I explained this is just a phase he's going through. He'll be all right. It's difficult for a chap, being shut away at school without any female company. I wanted to quote that bit of Keats, about the time between boyhood and manhood, when the clear stream turns muddy and – something or other – but I couldn't remember it . . . I went through a similar sort of thing myself at his age; it's nothing to worry about.'

Caro looked doubtful. 'All the same – shouldn't we telephone home and say he's here? Suppose the school rings up and tells them he's disappeared? They'll be frantic.'

'The school will try to find him first. I'd leave it tonight, if I were you. It's very late; I want to talk to him again tomorrow, and then decide what to do . . . I'd like to help him, if I can.'

'Well – if you think that's best . . .' Caro yawned. 'It *is* late. We'd better go to bed as well. You're going to have a very busy day tomorrow.'

As it happened, Alice was still in London on Thursday night, and on Friday afternoon she made her way to Piccadilly, hoping to see the Duchess of York before returning to Crown House. Outside number 145, the street was packed with people, waiting for news or hoping to catch a glimpse of the new King. When Alice got out of her taxi, she heard shouts of: 'God save the King!' and 'Long live King Albert!'

The butler opened the front door, and ushered her in quickly; she was surprised to find the Princesses, in outdoor clothes, waiting in the hall.

'Hello, Lady Minster,' said Lillibet. 'We're on our way to the Bath Club – this is one of our swimming days. Crawfie will be down in a minute.'

She came closer, as if she were about to impart a great secret, and lowered her voice: 'Look!'

A pile of letters and telegrams, which had been arriving all day, were stacked neatly on a console table; the one on top was addressed to HM the Queen.

'That's *Mummy* now, isn't it?' said Lillibet, in an awestruck whisper.

Alice nodded, and felt very touched. She wondered if the eleven-year-old girl understood, even now, that she had become the heir to the throne.

Margaret, not to be outdone, joined in the conversation; she had a grievance, and was determined to air it.

'I mustn't sign my name "York" any more,' she complained. 'And I've only just learned to write "York", too . . . It's not fair – I can't spell "Margaret"!'

Miss Crawford hurried down the staircase and greeted Alice, then turned to the girls. 'I'm afraid your mother says we can't go swimming today, after all.'

'Oh! Why not?' They were both very disappointed. 'We always go on Fridays.'

'We can't drive to the Bath Club, because your father has taken the car, and we mustn't walk – the streets are so crowded. We'll have to go another day; take off your hats and coats, and we'll go back to the nursery. Would you like a game of Snakes and Ladders instead?'

When Alice was shown into the drawing-room, Elizabeth wiped her eyes quickly, and held out both hands. Alice curtseyed to her Queen: then the two friends embraced, and Alice felt the trace of tears upon her cheek.

'So – it's happened,' said Queen Elizabeth with a catch in her voice. 'They telephoned from the Houses of Parliament during lunch to tell Bertie he had just been proclaimed King . . . Of course we were expecting it, but even so – it was still hard to accept, when it actually happened.' Holding on to Alice's hand, she took a deep breath. 'There are going to be great changes in our lives. We must take what is coming to us, and make the best of it.' Pulling herself together, she continued, 'May I ring for tea? You don't have to dash away, do you?'

'Not yet. I am going back to Crown House later – but I'd love some tea before I go.'

'That's good. Bertie's driving down to Windsor; he's having dinner at Royal Lodge tonight, with his brothers – and Queen Mary . . . But he has to call in at Fort Belvedere first.'

The Fort was in a state of upheaval when Bertie arrived; there were suitcases and crates in the hall, packed and ready to go; a manservant took his coat, saying, 'Good evening, Your Majesty. His Royal Highness is in his room. I will tell him you are here.'

For a moment Bertie thought it had been a slip of the tongue, and that the man must have confused their titles – then realized with a shock that he had not.

His cousin Dickie Mountbatten came to meet him, and said: 'David's still not finished his packing. You should see the state of his bedroom – telegrams everywhere wishing him good luck or begging him not to go, dozens of photographs of Mrs Simpson being wrapped in tissue paper and shoved into suitcases, and in the middle of it all the man himself: bright as a button, having his corns done... Anyone would think he was going off on holiday – quite incredible!'

Bertie tried to smile, but could not. Struggling for words, he burst out, 'This is terrible, Dickie... I never wanted this to happen – I'm quite unprepared for it. David has been trained for it all his life; I'm only a naval officer – it's the only thing I know about.'

His cousin said cheerfully, 'Exactly! You were trained in the Navy – you couldn't have a better preparation for being a King.' He patted Bertie on the back, adding, 'George and Henry are both here; they're having a drink. I suggest we go and join them.'

At eight o'clock, the four brothers left the Fort and drove to Royal Lodge, for a very subdued dinner-party. Queen Mary was there, together with her brother and sister-in-law, the Earl and Countess of Athlone; they had always been David's favourite uncle and aunt. Bertie was surprised to find his mother dressed in bright colours; it was the first time he had seen her out of mourning since his father died. If she hoped to lighten the prevailing gloom, she was disappointed; there were long, uncomfortable silences round the dinner-table.

The meal had not finished when Sir Walter Monckton arrived to say that the car was outside, to take His Royal Highness to Windsor Castle.

At twenty minutes to ten, Paul Weyman waited at Prince Edward's private suite within the Augusta Tower; during the afternoon, the sitting-room had been converted into a makeshift studio.

Sir John Reith, the BBC's Director-General, ushered the Prince in and presented Paul, who presented his technical staff. Everyone spoke in low tones, though the Prince himself seemed to be quite untroubled and smiled easily.

The microphones stood on a table, facing the single chair; Paul asked the Prince if he would be good enough to read a few words from the evening newspaper, to check his voice level. The Prince obliged by reading out a passage from the sports pages, which happened to refer to the new King as 'an excellent tennis-player'.

The Prince chuckled: 'They'll like that!' Then he looked at his watch. 'How much time have we got?'

'Just a few minutes, sir.'

'Right.' He nodded. 'In that case...' And he disappeared into the nearby lavatory. When he came out, he was smiling. 'Funny to think it's the last time I'll ever go in there.'

Half a minute before ten o'clock, Paul said, 'Thirty seconds, please,' and Sir John Reith sat at the table. When the red light flashed, Paul gave him the signal to speak.

'This is Windsor Castle. His Royal Highness, Prince Edward.'

Sir John moved out of the chair, and the Prince took his place, then began, 'At long last I am able to say a few words of my own...'

At Primrose Hill, Caroline and Martin had switched on the wireless. When Prince Edward said that he could not continue to bear the burden of kingship 'without the help and support of the woman I love', she felt tears pricking at her eyes — and for some reason found herself remembering her own parents. She was sure they would be listening together at Crown House.

Looking across at Martin, she wondered whether his school had been in touch with the family yet, to say he was missing... The thought of their anxiety seemed suddenly unbearable.

When the broadcast was over, she slipped from the room, and went to the telephone in the hall.

Alice and William had been listening to the wireless set in Lady Beatrice's room; they were deeply moved – even Old Bea had sniffed a little, though she could not forgive the Prince for rejecting his throne and his people.

'Sentimental balderdash!' she snorted, blowing her nose. 'It would never have happened in my day. Look at his grandfather, the last Edward. We all knew he had a mistress as well as a wife, but he kept up appearances, and we respected him for it!'

When the Minsters returned to their own drawing-room, the telephone was ringing, and Alice went to answer it.

'Hello, yes? *Caro!*' Her face lit up. 'Oh, darling – it's so good to hear you...' But as Caroline went on talking, the light died from her face. 'Run away? But he's safe? ... With you? ... No, this is the first we've heard of it. I can't imagine why the school didn't let us know... Anyway, he'd better come home tomorrow; I'll send a car to meet him at the station, if you tell us which train he's on... Hold on a moment, will you?' She put her hand over the mouthpiece, and reported rapidly to William, 'Martin's got himself into some sort of scrape at Eton, and he's run away... But he's perfectly safe – he went to stay with Caro, thank goodness.'

'You mean he's at Weyman's flat?' William asked sharply.

'Oh... Well, yes – I suppose so... I didn't stop to think...' Alice resumed her phone call. 'Is Paul there too? ... At Windsor – yes, I see. But he'll be coming back presently?'

William crossed the room to her, cutting in, 'I don't want Martin to stay there. Tell Caroline to order a car and send the boy home – right away.'

'Your father's just saying – he wants you to send Martin down to us now – tonight –' Alice began.

At the other end of the line, Caroline exclaimed, 'But that's silly – it's much too late. Anyway, I think Martin would rather be here. I know Paul wants him to stay; they had a long talk this morning; Martin finds it easier to talk to Paul than anyone else.'

Alice's lips were trembling, as she blurted out desperately: 'No! No, Caro – this is nothing to do with Paul. I don't want him to talk to Martin... Paul's taken you away from us already – he shan't take Martin as well –' Then she broke down in tears, unable to continue. William took the telephone from her and replaced the receiver without another word.

When Paul walked into the flat, just before midnight, he found Martin and Caroline waiting up for him. Martin began immediately, 'You'll never believe what Caro did. I think she's trying to get rid of me – she rang Ma and Pa! She knows I don't want to go home!'

Pale and shaken, Caroline said, 'I had to tell them – I was afraid they might be worried. Mummy took it very well at first – until I said Martin wanted to stay here, and talk to you... Then she went completely to pieces; I've never heard her so upset about anything...'

Slowly, Paul took off his overcoat and hung it up. 'I wish to God you hadn't spoken to her,' he said.

'I told Caro – she's only made things worse, and stirred up more trouble. I told her she should have waited!' Martin went to Paul, and appealed to him: 'You're not going to chuck me out, are you? Let me stay here – please!'

Side by side, they turned to look at Caro; both of them anxious and reproachful: two fair heads, two troubled faces, with the same expression, the same accusing lift of the chin...

And then Caroline understood.

17

SATURDAY, 12 DECEMBER 1936 TO SUNDAY, 17 JANUARY 1937

IT was after midnight, and Caro and Paul had gone to bed, before she was able to ask him the question that tormented her.

'Goodnight, my love.' He kissed her, then turned the light out and was about to settle down to sleep when she stopped him.

'Paul... I've got to talk to you – about my mother.'

After a brief pause, he said, 'What about her?'

'I told you how upset she was tonight. It wasn't just because Martin had run away – it was because he came *here*... She couldn't bear the thought of him being here – with you.'

There was a longer pause. 'Your parents have never forgiven me, since they found out about us. I suppose it's understandable.'

'It was more than that. You told me once that you loved my mother. I didn't quite understand then, but now I think I do. You had an affair with her, didn't you?'

Now there was a very long silence. She felt him moving restlessly in the bed, and at last he answered: 'Yes... It was just before the end of the war. I was home on sick-leave – I'd been sent back to hospital in England; your father was still out there, fighting. She hadn't had any news of him for weeks. He might have been dead, for all she knew... She was lonely and unhappy, and so was I – I loved her very much... Then the armistice was signed, and your father came home, and – that was the end of it.'

'Was it really the end?' Caro lay beside him, still and tense. 'I don't think so.'

'What do you mean? What did she say to you tonight?'

'It was nothing she said. It was when I saw you and Martin

together; he's so like you, Paul. I don't know why I never thought of it before, except I suppose it was unthinkable . . . Martin is your son, isn't he?'

'Oh, God . . . I hoped you would never know. Caro, darling, it was all so long ago –' He turned to her, trying to put his arms round her, but she would not let him.

'Does my father know?' she asked. 'Did she tell him?'

'Not then – he never suspected anything. When the twins were born, everyone thought they were premature . . . But years later, he found out.'

'So that's why he hates you . . . That's why he didn't want Martin to stay here.' Again he tried to embrace her, and she held him off. 'No, Paul – please don't . . .'

'Caro . . . This doesn't make any difference to us. It can't –'

'Of course it does. Everything's different – don't you see? This changes everything . . . I've got to think.'

'There's nothing to think about. I love you – you can't blame me –'

'I don't blame you. I don't blame anyone. I only know I – I don't want you to touch me . . . I'm sorry, Paul.'

'Don't – don't do this to me . . .' He gave a cry, as if her name had been wrenched from him in a spasm of physical pain: '*Caroline!*'

'Be quiet – Martin will hear you.' She rolled over, away from him, staring into darkness. 'We'll talk tomorrow.'

A long way off, in Regent's Park, they heard a lion roaring. Once that had been a favourite joke; Paul would have said, 'Wild beasts on the loose again. That settles it, you can't go home tonight, I'm afraid . . .'

Now there were no more jokes.

The next morning when Paul woke up, he saw she was already dressed, packing clothes into a suitcase.

'You said we would talk –' he began.

'There's nothing to talk about, Paul. It's over; there's no more to be said.'

'How can you be so hard?'

'I'm not hard. I just feel – dead . . . Don't try to talk me out of it; I shan't change my mind.'

She explained that she would look for somewhere to live: she was not going back to Eaton Square – that was equally impossible. As soon as she had made other arrangements, she would come back to

Primrose Hill for the rest of her belongings, and return his front-door key. Then she would start again, on her own. In her heart of hearts, she knew that their parting was inevitable; it had been coming for a long time. She was too old for teddy bears now; she had grown up at last.

By the time Martin woke, Caroline had already left the flat; he found Paul making breakfast in the kitchen.

'But where has she gone?' he asked.

'Oh – she had to go out early – on a job, I think. These newspaper folk keep strange hours...' Paul was putting slices of bread under the grill. 'I shall see that you get home safely.'

'Home? No, I don't want to –'

'It's the best way, old lad. You can't stay here indefinitely; you've got to go back to your family, and say you're sorry you made such a mess of things. I shall take you to Charing Cross and put you on the Medford train; there will be a car to meet you at the other end.'

'I thought I was staying here, with you... You said you would help.'

'This is the only thing to do, believe me; you can't keep running away. I'm sure that if you own up and face the music, the school will take you back... Damn!' He burnt his fingers on the grill-tray, filling the toast-rack.

As he brought it over to the kitchen table, Martin asked, 'I say – Uncle – are you all right?'

'Yes, of course. Sorry the toast's a bit black. I'm not very good at it; that's usually Caro's job...'

'I didn't mean the toast. You look sort of – I don't know... Didn't you sleep well?'

'Not particularly... Help yourself to marmalade... What was I saying? Oh, yes – about going back to school. It won't be as bad as you think; the important thing is, you have to take what's coming to you, whatever it is. That's a lesson we all have to learn, sooner or later.'

It seemed he was right; Martin found, when he reached Crown House, that his parents were so relieved to see him again, safe and sound, that they did not dwell upon the reasons leading up to his escapade.

From first to last, Paul Weyman's name was never mentioned.

His mother seemed to direct most of her grievances against the school authorities: 'If it hadn't been for Caroline, we shouldn't have known you'd disappeared! When I rang your housemaster to tell him you were here, he said he was under the impression that you'd gone to your friends in Devonshire; he'd asked the Travers family to let him know when you turned up... Have you ever heard anything so absurd? I told him you wouldn't dream of arriving at somebody's house without an invitation!'

At first William said very little, but as soon as they were alone, he gave his son a dressing down that made him sweat with shame and humiliation. Martin wanted to say he was sorry, but was afraid that if he opened his mouth he might break down in childish tears. Realizing this, William put his hand on Martin's shoulder, saying, 'All right, my son... We'll say no more about it. We've all been tempted, now and then; we've all done things we're ashamed of afterwards. Just remember what I've said – and try to have a bit more self-respect in future.'

There was another telephone call from Ebony to Eton. Martin's housemaster said that the whole thing had been extremely regrettable, but that the ringleader had now left the school, and he felt sure there would be no further trouble. Since there was less than a fortnight till the end of term, it was agreed that Martin should stay at home until the holidays were over. On his return, he would be appropriately disciplined, and then a veil would be drawn over the sorry business.

The rest of the family were informed that Martin had 'fallen into bad company', but had learned his lesson.

When Miranda came home from Roedean, she asked her brother outright what he had been up to. He was sprawled on a sofa with his feet up, and a catalogue from Harrods on his lap, trying to decide what he wanted for Christmas; he pretended not to hear her.

'Something nasty and piggy, I suppose,' she said scornfully. 'That's why you won't tell me about it.'

He refused to enlighten her; all he would say was that it was jolly thick on poor old J. T. 'He did ask me to go down to Devonshire with him; I rather wish I had, in a way. It would have been a bit of a lark if they'd sacked both of us... It was stupid to call him the ringleader – there wasn't any ringleader – they just wanted someone to put the blame on... As for learning my lesson – the only lesson I've learned is to take bloody good care I don't get caught, another time!' With a superior smile, he flicked over the pages of the catalogue; Miranda snatched it from him.

'When I heard you'd got into a row, I actually felt sorry for you. But now I don't feel sorry at all. You're not even ashamed!'

Martin laughed. 'Why should I be ashamed? It was only a bit of fun – everyone does it. Do you know what I found out while I was in town? Caro and Uncle Paul are living together; they've been going at it like rabbits, only they had the sense to keep quiet about it.'

'You're lying again – you're a filthy liar –'

'All right, you don't have to believe it if you don't want to. Why don't you run away and leave me in peace? There's a good girl.'

Downstairs in the main hall, Jenny was asking Polly, 'Have you seen the Harrods catalogue anywhere about? It was here on the hall table this morning.'

'I think Martin took it upstairs. Shall I go and ask him?'

'No, don't bother; I'll get it later. It's just that Alice is going up to town again tomorrow, and I want her to put in an order for us. We need some new decorations this year; the old ones are falling to pieces – and some fairy-lights for the tree, and crackers for the Christmas dinner table... I must write out a list.'

They looked up into the echoing spaces of the hall, which rose to an impressive height above the main staircase.

'It takes a lot of decorating to make this place look Christmassy,' said Polly.

'But it's worth the effort, don't you think?'

'Oh, yes, that's how I remember it best – the first year I was here... Christmas Eve, with the kissing-bough hanging up, and green leaves and flowers everywhere, masses and masses of flowers.'

They were both silent for a moment. Jenny wished she had not brought the subject up – she remembered why there were so many flowers, that Christmas Eve; it was Polly and Richard's wedding day... At the time she was still in love with Richard herself, and she had thought her heart would break.

'Yes, I was the one he married,' said Polly softly, as if she were reading her mind. 'But in the end, you were the lucky one... How are you and Nick these days? As happy as ever?'

'Of course, very happy.' Jenny moved away. 'I must ask him to cut some holly and mistletoe for the house.'

Polly pulled on a thick tweed coat, and knotted a scarf round her throat. 'I'll tell him. I'm just going out for a breath of air; I can easily call in at the farm.'

'Oh, don't go to any trouble –' began Jenny.

'It's no trouble. I'll be glad to stretch my legs.'

Jenny guessed that this was probably the first time Polly had gone near the farm since Richard died. It was a good sign; perhaps she was beginning to get over it.

The sun had gone down now, and in the west the sky was fading to green and indigo. It took some courage for Polly to walk down the farm track and open the five-barred gate leading into the stable yard. She could see a light in the office window, and braced herself for the inevitable pain; her whole body ached with longing to see Richie sitting at his desk, when she walked in: she must not feel cheated when she found Nick there instead.

She opened the door, and had a momentary shock of surprise. It wasn't Nick either; the estate manager glanced up, then rose to his feet. 'Good afternoon, your ladyship.'

'Good afternoon, Ken; I was looking for Nicholas.'

'I'm afraid he's not here just now; he's driven in to Medford, to stock up with cattle-cake. By all accounts, it looks like being a hard winter.'

'Have you been listening to the forecasts?'

'I generally tune in for the news and weather – and the fat-stock prices. I've fixed up a wireless set in the lodge now.'

'That's nice. You've settled in comfortably, have you?'

'I have indeed, ma'am. You must drop in some time for a cup of coffee.'

'Thank you – I'd like that.' She held out her hands to the old iron stove, which gave off a warm glow. 'So – it's going to be a cold winter?'

'So the forecasts say. And they may be right; there's plenty of berries on the holly this year – that's generally a bad sign.'

'Holly – thank you for reminding me: could you give Nicholas a message? We shall need some holly and mistletoe and all that stuff to decorate the house, and a big Christmas tree to go at the bottom of the stairs. Could you ask him about it?'

'No need to bother Mr Gaunt; I'll see to it myself. How tall a tree do you want?'

'Oh, I don't know. Six foot? Eight, perhaps?'

Behind her, the door opened again, and Lilian Brooks entered.

'Oh, beg pardon, your ladyship – I didn't know you was here,' she said, a little flustered. 'I've brought your flask of tea as per usual, Mr Stubbs.'

'That's very good of you, Miss Brooks.' He glanced at Polly. 'You see we're well looked after here – tea provided every afternoon!'

Lilian unscrewed the thermos and began to fill the bakelite top which served as a cup. Polly broke in: 'Lilian, I'm sure you can tell us how big the Christmas tree ought to be – the one that goes in the hall.'

'Oh, yes, ma'am – it's generally twelve or fourteen foot.'

'I guessed wrong – it's a good job you came in. Will you be able to find one that tall, Ken?'

'I dare say; you'd better give me some idea how much green stuff you need, as well.'

Lilian added shyly, 'While you're at it, you might cut a bit extra for the servants' hall, Mr Stubbs.'

'With pleasure. What will you be wanting? Holly and ivy, I suppose?'

'And a bunch of mistletoe, p'raps,' she said, in an off-hand way.

'I believe there's some growing on the poplar trees down by the water meadow; I'll see what I can do.'

'It's all a lot of nonsense, but it amuses the young folk.' Lilian turned to go. 'Don't forget to bring back that thermos when you come in for your supper, will you?'

She disappeared, and Polly smiled to herself. She had a shrewd idea that afternoon tea had not been regularly provided at the farm office until Mr Stubbs came to work there.

When Alice went up to London a few days later, she was invited to call at 145 Piccadilly.

The Queen was writing a letter at her desk, but she put it aside when Alice was shown in.

'How lovely to see you! I've got a thousand things to do, but I don't care – I'm going to stop and talk. That's why I asked you to come at eleven, so we can both have coffee; do sit down, my dear.'

Alice had brought a shopping-bag crammed with packages, and she unloaded them on to the coffee table, one by one.

'I've brought some presents for Lillibet and Margaret; I hope you don't mind. They're very silly really, but I thought they might like them... Pink sugar mice, chocolate money in gold foil in little net purses, peppermint sticks, wire puzzles, miniature playing-cards, crystallized fruit, and tangerines in silver paper...' The little hoard of treasures grew larger as she continued: 'It suddenly struck me that you wouldn't be able to go out and buy things like this – and I thought the Princesses might be disappointed if they don't find stockings by their beds on Christmas morning.'

'Alice, you're simply brilliant! It's true – they'll have plenty of big presents, but I'd never have managed to get little things for the stockings...'

'It's much easier for me; I found most of these in Ebony, at the village store.'

'Goodness, I envy you. I wish we could go and live in a little country village. In fact I wish we could live anywhere except the Palace! We're supposed to be leaving here early in the New Year, and moving into that great barracks of a place. I'll never make it feel like a home.'

Alice sympathized: 'It will be very different from this house.'

'It will be horrible; vast and draughty and gloomy – and damp! It's never been modernized – it's not even been kept in a decent state of repair. They say it's crawling with vermin, too. Do you know, there's a permanent rat-catcher on the staff? and he's kept fully employed! But it's no use grumbling – we're expected to live "above the shop", and that's that.'

'How do the Princesses feel about all these changes?'

'Oh, they don't want to leave here. Bertie tried to cheer them up by pretending that once we settle in, he'll have a tunnel built underneath Green Park, so we can all slip away from the Palace whenever we feel like it, and come home again... But they know he's only joking.'

'It must be difficult for them; there have been so many changes in their lives, in such a short time.'

'My dear, our lives have changed completely. The minute David signed away the throne, our whole world changed. It was like an iron door clanging shut behind us... Bertie had to get used to a new name; he was horrified when his advisers suggested he should become King George – he felt as if he were trading on his father's reputation. But he had to agree; King Albert sounds so old-fashioned, and King Bertie would hardly –' She stopped in mid-sentence as the doorbell rang, and glanced at her watch.

'Now we're going to be interrupted,' she said. 'I have an appointment with a gentleman from the BBC; but don't run away – he won't stay very long.'

Alice's heart sank; and her fears were realized when the door opened and Paul Weyman was shown in. He bowed over the Queen's hand, then turned to Alice. The Queen introduced them, and they shook hands: neither of them admitted that they had met before.

'If it's about the Christmas message, Mr Weyman, I'm afraid His Majesty has not changed his mind,' the Queen began. 'He has never made a wireless broadcast, and he feels he could not do so without a lot of rehearsal, and since time is so short –'

'I understand that, Ma'am; that's why I ventured to trouble you again. How would it be, if we recorded His Majesty in advance? Then there would be an opportunity for him to have more than one attempt at it, and we could edit out any slight...' He chose his words with care. 'Any slight pauses...'

'Yes, I see. That might make a difference, I suppose.' The Queen looked troubled. 'Perhaps I should go and speak to His Majesty, and see if the idea appeals to him. He's in his study; I shan't be long... Alice – may I leave you to entertain Mr Weyman for a few moments?'

When she had gone, Paul said awkwardly, 'I'm sorry... If I'd known you would be here –'

'It can't be helped. As long as you're involved in these royal broadcasts, I suppose it's inevitable that our paths will cross occasionally.'

'I won't be involved in future; my real job now is in television. I've only been sent this time because there's no one else to do it. Everything's happened so quickly, in the last few weeks.'

He moved to the window, looking out at the traffic in Piccadilly. Finally Alice broke the silence by asking, 'How is Caroline?'

'I don't know.' He swung round. 'Hasn't she spoken to you?'

'Not since that trouble about Martin... What do you mean?'

'I thought perhaps she would have told you. I haven't seen her since then; we're not – together – any more. She left me.'

'Left you? Why? Where has she gone?'

'I don't know that either. She told me she has moved in with some colleague of hers, on the *Argus*. She didn't give me an address, or a telephone number; she asked me not to try and get in touch with her.'

'Oh...' Alice felt he was holding something back. 'May I ask why she left you? Is there – someone else?'

'No, it's nothing like that... There were some problems – things that came between us...' He wondered if he should tell Alice what Caroline had discovered, but found it hard to confess; certainly not here, where they might be interrupted at any minute. 'It's difficult to talk now,' he concluded. 'Perhaps – if we could meet some other time –'

'I don't think so,' said Alice. 'I prefer that we should not meet again.'

She rose as the door reopened, and they were joined by the King and Queen. Paul was presented to His Majesty, who said: 'I'm g-g-grateful to you, Mr Weyman, for your suggestion about recording the message in advance, but my father established it as a live broadcast – I'm sure the people have c-c-come to expect that now. I don't feel I'm ready to speak over the air just yet; later, perhaps – but not yet.'

So that was the verdict Paul had to carry back to Broadcasting House. He bowed to the King and Queen, said that it had been a great pleasure to meet Lady Minster, then left the room.

The King relaxed at once, clasping Alice's hand; he asked after her family – and particularly enquired about Nicholas and Jenny. 'Please give them our very best wishes for C-C-Christmas – and say I hope to see them again, one of these days. Though g-g-goodness knows when that will be – we've abandoned all hope of a normal social life. There's always so much to be done – people to see, letters to write – the telephone never stops ringing –'

As if on cue, a telephone bell rang shrilly in an adjoining room and they all laughed. Then the King's Private Secretary appeared in the doorway, to say that it was a long-distance call from Austria; the Duke of Windsor was on the line. The King and Queen exchanged glances, and he excused himself, leaving the two ladies together.

Her Majesty turned to Alice, and sighed: 'Those telephone calls! David talks to Bertie every single day – sometimes several times a day. At first he rang up to discuss the arrangements for storing his furniture and so on; he left so much stuff at the Fort, and in the Palace ... But now he calls about other things too – Bertie's public duties, the political issues, that kind of thing. I suppose he's trying to be helpful, but he's putting a lot of extra pressure on Bertie, as if he hadn't enough on his mind already. Quite honestly, I'd be inclined to tell David that the King is too busy to come to the telephone, but Bertie is still so loyal to his brother, he'd never let me do such a thing ...' She shook her head. 'I just wish he'd leave us in peace.'

Caro had been lucky. The day she moved out of Paul's flat, she went in to the *Argus* office, and Fred Binns, the news editor, found her scouring the local papers, looking for somewhere to live. She explained that she had decided to leave North London 'for personal reasons'.

Fred, who was no fool, cocked an eyebrow and went off to make a phone call. He came back five minutes later and said: 'I just talked to the wife. We've got a room going begging at our house, if you want something to tide you over – just till you get somewhere better. It's nothing special, but it's warm and it's clean – and since Freda's in the family way again, she's had to give up her job at the Town Hall, so she'll be glad of a bit extra to make up the house-keeping.'

The Binns already had four school-aged children and lived in a shabby Victorian terrace in the unfashionable part of Chelsea, near the World's End.

Caroline accepted the offer gratefully, and managed to cram all her worldly goods into one room on the second floor, with a view of identical grey slate rooftops, and not a tree in sight. It was a far cry from the civilized comforts of Primrose Hill, but she would never go back on her decision.

She was on her own now; independent for the first time in her life – and proud of it.

The family were friendly enough, though the evenings tended to be rather noisy, as Freda liked to keep the wireless going at full blast, and the children squabbled at the tops of their voices, even when they were supposed to be doing their homework.

Caro generally retired to her own room, and lay on the bed, reading; when she felt like a change of scene, she would go for a walk along the Kings Road, and drop in at the Six Bells. It was a cheerful pub, with an arty, Bohemian reputation. Most public houses would frown upon a single girl coming in on her own, but the Six Bells took it as a matter of course; there were nearly always one or two young ladies, wearing carelessly buttoned blouses and too much make-up, on the look-out for prospective clients.

A few days before Christmas, Caro bought her usual half-pint of mild and bitter, and admired the crêpe-paper frills and festive bells that the guv'nor had pinned up above the bar. Two ladies in Salvation Army uniform made their way through the crowd, selling copies of the *War Cry*; a young man in a threadbare overcoat moved out of their way, and collided with the table where Caro was sitting. Her glass rocked and nearly fell over, slopping a little puddle of froth across the table-top.

'Oh – sorry –' said the young man.

'That's all right; no harm done,' said Caroline. 'I only spilled a few drops.'

He stared at her through thick-lensed spectacles, and screwed up his eyes.

'I know you,' he said. 'I recognize that voice – you're Lady Caroline Gaunt.'

She looked at him blankly: 'Yes, I am – though I'm afraid I don't remember –'

'We only met once, at Invergordon,' he said. 'Carpenter's the name, miss – Don Carpenter.'

Then it all came flooding back; five years ago, she had gone up to Scotland, to cover the so-called 'mutiny' at the Naval dockyard: Nicholas was involved in the dispute, and Wireless-Telegrapher Carpenter had helped her to get the story on the front page of the *Argus*.

He insisted on buying her a drink, and then she bought him one; they sat in the pub until closing time.

He told her he had always worn spectacles, since he was a kid; but his sight had deteriorated during the past five years, to the point where he had been discharged from the Service on medical grounds. Over the last twelve months he had drifted from one dead-end job to another; but that was all over and done with now. He knew where he was going next.

Rather diffidently, he said, 'You'll be shocked when I tell you I'm a Communist – you being a ladyship and all that.'

'Nothing of the sort!' Caro said indignantly. 'I think it's splendid – my trouble is, I'm not sure Communism is the answer to all life's problems, though I agree it solves a lot of them. If I were totally convinced, like you, I'd join the party tomorrow.'

His face lit up 'Is that a fact? I knew you were all right, the first minute I saw you. I've been a CP member for over a year now . . . And tomorrow – I'm going to join something else.'

'Something else . . . ?'

'The International Brigade. They're taking chaps on, to go to Spain.'

Quickly, he filled in the details. Since King Alfonso abdicated, Spain had been a Republic, swinging violently between opposing

272

parties. The Popular Front had been in power since February of this year, but after only a few months General Franco had led a military revolt against the government, and the country had been split by civil war; the right-wing Nationalist forces against the left-wing Republicans. By the end of July, Socialist and Communist sympathizers from all over the world were flooding into Spain, to form the new International Brigade, pledged to save the country from Franco and his Fascist militia.

Caroline's sympathies were always with the left, but the idea had never appealed to her as strongly as it did now; she listened as Don told her why he was ready to leave his humdrum life in London to go and fight for the Republican cause.

'The war-lords in Germany and Italy are on Franco's side,' he said. 'This is the testing-time. Everyone has to choose now: it's freedom for the people – or world dictatorship.'

Carried away by his enthusiasm, Caroline said, 'You're absolutely right! It's no good sitting here comfortably, talking politics. We ought to be out there *doing* something! I try to tell myself I'm helping, writing about Mosley's hateful meetings – but half the time they don't print what I write... It's all watered down, in case it offends somebody. I wanted to do a piece on the hunger-marchers, but they wouldn't let me... Now I want to write about the war in Spain, and the International Brigade.'

That night, she told Fred Binns she was on to a really big story, and he gave her permission to go and meet Don when he went to sign up, next morning.

The recruiting centre was the Communist Party office in King Street, behind Covent Garden market; a narrow building, squeezed in between two vegetable wholesalers. She picked her way through over-ripe oranges and squashed cabbage-leaves, then climbed a rickety staircase to a series of offices leading out of one another like a maze. She found Don sitting on a bentwood chair, waiting.

'Don't say you're from Fleet Street,' he told her in a low voice. 'They get suspicious of newspapers – and no wonder, when you see the lies they print.'

'If anyone asks, I'll say I'm your sister, come to see you off,' said Caro.

Don grinned. 'In that case you'd better keep your mouth shut – you don't sound much like my sister!'

Two more recruits arrived during the next half-hour, and were also told to wait. Eventually someone called Comrade Smithers asked the men for their names and addresses. Then he told them grimly, 'This isn't going to be any picnic. This war's going to be a proper bastard.' He looked at Caroline, to see her reaction, but she didn't turn a hair. 'You're going to be short of food, short of medical supplies – you'll be bloody lucky if you get enough arms and ammunition to defend yourselves. If you think you're going out there like heroes in shining armour, you can pack up and leave right now, because it's not that sort of fairy-tale... I can't make you any promises – except one. You're going out to fight against Fascism... Has anybody got any questions?'

Don raised his hand and said, 'I was invalided out of the Navy on account of my eyesight – do we have to go through a medical examination?'

Comrade Smithers looked him over, then said, 'You look strong enough – are you fit and healthy, apart from that?'

'Yes, I am.'

'Right – I'll take your word for it.'

That was the medical examination. The three men were given twenty-four hours to make their personal arrangements before leaving the country, and told to report back at the same time tomorrow morning.

When they left the office, Caro said to Don, 'I'll be here as well. I've made up my mind – I'm coming with you.'

At Crown House, Christmas came and went placidly enough. Alice heard nothing from Caroline; she told William that their daughter was no longer living with Paul, but she did not know her new address. They would have to wait until she felt like getting in touch with them.

Then, early in the New Year, they had news of her from an unexpected quarter. Norman Brooks knocked at the drawing-room door, to pass on an urgent summons from Lady Beatrice.

'Her ladyship would like to see you as soon as possible,' he said, adding, 'She's a bit put out about something.'

William and Alice wondered what had upset Old Bea this time: was the rain seeping through her bedroom windows again? Had her breakfast egg not been boiled for the correct length of time? They went upstairs to deal with the problem, whatever it might be.

The Countess was sitting in her usual chair, with a pair of spectacles on the end of her nose; at eighty-four, she had been forced, much against her will, to admit that she could no longer read without them. She still resented the fact, and was continually putting her spectacle-case down the side of her chair and losing it among the cushions; Norman was convinced she did it on purpose.

'What is the meaning of this?' As soon as her son and daughter-in-law appeared, she brandished a newspaper. 'How many more times must I tell you? I won't be overlooked!'

'What seems to be the trouble, Mama?' asked William patiently.

'I am still a member of this family, I hope? Am I not to be kept informed when my granddaughter leaves the country and goes off to war?'

'What are you talking about? Who's gone to war?' said Alice.

'Caroline, of course ... And there's not been a word about it on my wireless; I had to pick up the news from the gutter press ...' She thrust the copy of the *Argus* at them accusingly. 'You should have told me. I have a right to know!'

Alice took the newspaper; in a box on the front page, the chairman of the Hathaway Press announced that Lady Caroline Gaunt, one of the most valued members of his staff, had left England *en route* for Spain, and would be sending back regular despatches on the progress of the Civil War, exclusively for *Argus* readers.

Alice could not read any more; the newspaper shook in her hands, and William said, 'My dear, don't upset yourself –'

'I'm all right ... I just – I think I'd like to sit down for a minute ...'

It had all happened so suddenly.

Fred Binns had passed Caro's request on to the editor-in-chief, who in turn passed it along to the chairman, Sir Perkins Hathaway. Sir Perkins, who was a blatant snob, was graciously pleased to grant Lady Caroline this favour, and within twenty-four hours she was at Victoria Station, with a press pass, a return ticket to Paris – the first stop on the journey – and all the money she could immediately raise, stuffed into her bag.

Don Carpenter and a dozen other young men, all recruited at the King Street office, were on the platform; silent and anxious, wearing their best suits, and looking as if they were going to a funeral. On board the channel steamer, the nervous strain and the fear of sea-sickness drove them into the saloon, where they drank too much; by the time they reached Calais, they were in a sorry state, and Don said he was ashamed of them.

The major obstacle was that none of the men spoke any French. Caroline had hazy memories of lessons with 'Madame', who had been imported into Crown House for a time as a governess; and she found herself in charge of the party.

On Don's advice, she was still concealing her connection with the *Argus*. The other recruits assumed that she was Don's girlfriend; he told them she was sympathetic to the Republican cause and would be helping behind the lines – cooking, washing, mending clothes or even doing a little nursing if anyone happened to fall ill. At this stage, nobody mentioned the possibility of being wounded in action.

Caro wondered how she would get her little band across Paris – but that proved to be no problem. The taxi-drivers at the Gare du Nord, Communists to a man, identified them at once and offered free transport to the Gare d'Austerlitz, where they were to board the 'Red Train'.

The daily departure of this train carrying volunteers of all nationalities to Perpignan near the Spanish frontier had become one of the sights of Paris, and there were large crowds waiting to see them off, waving banners with goodwill messages, and throwing flowers. By the time the train pulled out, they were feeling like heroes.

The overnight journey, in crowded, unheated carriages, was a severe anti-climax; but worse was to follow.

At Perpignan, the recruits were marched off to temporary quarters in an inhospitable, semi-derelict château, which served as a transit-camp; there they would have to wait before proceeding on the next stage of the expedition, to the Republican stronghold of Barcelona.

But the château catered for members of the Brigade only; there was no accommodation for women.

Caroline told Don she would join him when she reached Barcelona, and booked in to the cheapest *pension* she could find. She made representations to the Spanish Consulate in Perpignan, and showed her press pass, and a letter signed by Sir Perkins Hathaway himself.

This did not seem to cut any ice. Too late, she realized that the Spanish authorities had no wish to co-operate with the capitalist press of western Europe, and she was told politely to go away and 'return another day'.

The International Brigade moved out, and she was left behind, with the words of the nursery-rhyme running through her head: 'Rain, rain, go away. Come again another day...' As one grey day followed another, it seemed that the sun would never shine; each time she presented herself at the Consulate, she was received with gleaming, golden smiles and shakes of the head. Her entry permit to cross the frontier had not yet been processed; she must come back another time.

At last she realized she would never be allowed to enter Spain through the official channels.

Coming out of the Consulate after one more frustrating interview, she stood in the windy street, and looked up at the blue-grey Pyrenees marching along the skyline, dominated by the peak of Mount Canigou, crowned with snow. Spain lay beyond those jagged walls.

The next day was a Sunday, and the sound of church bells rang in her ears, summoning the faithful to Mass. A thin, wintry sunshine broke the clouds as she packed her luggage and sewed all her remaining cash into the lining of her skirt. Then she paid her bill and set out, leaving no forwarding address.

18

MONDAY, 18 JANUARY TO MONDAY, 15 MARCH 1937

'Look at us – two orphans of the storm!' exclaimed Alice. She shook out her umbrella, then kissed her brother on the cheek as she as she joined him under the Ritz arcade.

They had met by chance; Alice had been shopping in Bond Street, and Charlie was on his way home from the club when the heavens opened. Now they stood and watched the waterlogged traffic crawl by, and waited for the weather to improve.

'I haven't seen you for ages,' Alice said. 'Such a pity you couldn't get down to us for Christmas.'

'Gina's political activities take up so much of her time – and I didn't like to leave her in town on her own . . . I tell you what: why don't you come back now and have some tea with us? I'm sure she'll be pleased to see you; it might cheer her up.'

Alice was puzzled. 'Does Gina need cheering up?'

'Well, yes – I'm afraid so. She's been rather out of sorts lately; I don't know why.'

'That doesn't sound like Gina at all.' Alice peered out at the sky. 'I do believe it's stopping. Shall we make a dash for it?'

It was only a brisk walk to Curzon Street, but they were both very wet by the time they reached the Bowyers' flat. As the parlourmaid helped Alice off with her coat, she said, 'I'll hang this up in the kitchen, near the cooker, ma'am – it'll dry out before you go.' She took Sir Charles's overcoat as well, adding, 'Will you want tea straight away, sir, or will you wait for Lady Bowyer?'

'Oh – isn't she here?' Charles frowned. 'She didn't say she was going out.'

'She left about twelve o'clock, sir; I thought she'd be back by now.'

'We may as well have our tea; I don't expect she'll be long.'

'Very good, sir... Oh, there was a telephone message for her ladyship, just after she left; Dr Lennard's receptionist rang to change the time of her ladyship's appointment tomorrow.'

'Did you say "Lennard"?' Sir Charles looked mystified.

'Yes, sir. I've written it down on the telephone-pad.'

As they settled themselves in the living-room, Alice said, 'I hadn't realized Gina was seeing a doctor?'

'Nor had I.' Charlie took off his glasses, which were still speckled with raindrops, and began to polish them. 'As I said, she's been rather low-spirited, but this is the first I've heard about a doctor... He's not our usual chap, either.'

He replaced his spectacles and cast about for another topic. Seeing a copy of the morning's *Argus* on the table, he picked it up and asked, 'Any more news of Caroline?'

'Not really: the paper has only printed two brief reports from Perpignan – and of course she never writes to us, not so much as a postcard.'

The maid brought in a tea-tray, and Alice took charge of the teapot. A moment later she heard Gina's voice in the hall, and said, 'There she is. I'll pour another cup.'

She was shocked to see how much older Gina looked. She was dressed as immaculately as ever, but under her make-up, the lines of strain showed in her face. Greeting Alice, she exclaimed, 'Isn't this weather simply ghastly? I can't imagine why we put up with it – we should all go and winter in Antibes or somewhere.'

As Alice passed her a cup of tea, Charlie remarked, 'There's a message for you from a Dr Lennard. Apparently he wants to change the time of your appointment tomorrow – it's on the pad.'

For a second, Alice thought Gina would drop the cup; some of the tea slopped into the saucer, but she managed to put it safely on the table. Then she pulled out a pack of Chesterfields; the flame of her lighter trembled as she lit the cigarette.

'You never mentioned you were seeing a doctor?' Charlie pursued. 'Who is this Dr Lennard?'

'He's supposed to be simply brilliant.' Gina flung herself on to the sofa, and inhaled deeply. 'Thelma swears by him.'

'Why didn't you tell me you were feeling ill?'

'Oh, for heaven's sake, Charlie!' Her temper seemed to be near breaking-point. 'You know I haven't been too good lately. I'm getting so many headaches – maybe it's blood-pressure... I just want him to give me something for my nerves, that's all.'

'But why didn't you say –'

'Because I didn't want to worry you! And because I didn't want to be cross-examined like this – that's why!' With an effort, she switched on a brilliant smile and turned back to Alice. 'Darling, it's so good to see you – I'm just longing to hear all your news. How's your divine family? Do you hear any word from Caroline?'

It was not raining in the Pyrenees; high above the frontier post of Le Perthus, the snow fell in thick, wet flakes that covered Caro's footprints on the stony track almost immediately.

She brushed the snow from her eyelashes and stumbled on, trying to keep up with the two goatherds who led the way. They could have followed the route blindfolded – which was just as well, for snow and darkness blotted out the landscape.

Caro was very tired, but she dared not slacken her pace for fear of being left behind. The bag she carried grew heavier at every step, but there had been no suggestion that either of the men might help to carry it, so she gritted her teeth and ploughed on.

So far, she had been lucky; she had made discreet enquiries at the last village before the frontier, if it could be called a village – a handful of cottages and a little store that also served as a bar. Over coffee and cognac she got into conversation with these two men: goatherds who had brought their flocks down from the high pastures just before the hard weather set it. She decided to trust them, and explained that she must get across the border, to join her friend in Spain.

The men grinned and winked: 'He is your lover, this friend?'

'He is a soldier in the International Brigade, fighting for freedom.'

They did not seem impressed; they preferred to think of her as a passionate heroine, yearning for her sweetheart. But they struck a deal and agreed to guide Caro over the mountains and into Spain, at a price.

She had to wait until after midnight before they would set out; it was too risky earlier, they said – there might be frontier-guards on patrol. So they sat in the little bar by a dying fire for some hours; everyone else had gone except the *patron*, who dozed in a chair in a neighbouring room, waiting for them to leave so he could lock and bolt the door.

The men eyed her speculatively, muttering to one another in a Catalan argot she could not understand. But she could guess what they were saying, and she felt a tremor of unease. It they were to assault her now, who would ever know? Tired as she was, she forced herself to stay awake, on her guard. At about one in the morning, the older man rose and walked towards her; she tensed up, but he merely said, 'We go now.'

Then they set out, into the black night; and the snow began to fall.

She lost all count of time, but guessed it must have been two hours or more before the men stopped walking. She caught up with them, and began: 'How much further is it to –'

They silenced her instantly, with a warning gesture, and the older man whispered: 'This is as far as we go. Walk straight ahead; the path leads downhill. Within a kilometre you will find a small house ... Tell them Pepe sent you.'

She had not expected this; the prospect of continuing her journey alone was terrifying. But she could not turn back now.

Her luck held, for after she had gone another hundred yards the snow stopped, and she could see more clearly. A half-moon broke through the clouds, and ahead of her she saw the path twisting and turning downhill, as she had been told.

Looking back, she had a brief glimpse of the way she had come – and her heart missed a beat. The track she had followed ran along the edge of a ravine; beneath the ribbon of white, a sheer drop fell away into a void.

She trudged on without another backward glance, and at last a darker shape reared up against the snow; a rough shack, with an oil-lamp burning in the window. She screwed up her courage and knocked at the door.

It was opened by a young woman in an old-fashioned nightgown, a shawl wrapped round her shoulders. Beyond her, Caro saw a man sitting at a table – and she recognized the colours of the Republican armband that he wore. She took a deep breath and managed to say, 'Pepe sent me ... I am a friend of Spain. I need your help.'

The man stood up. '*Pase usted*,' he said, and welcomed her in.

It was the end of her first journey, and the beginning of many more. Next morning, the man changed her French francs into pesetas, and took her with him to the nearest village where she could catch a bus to Gerona, and from there a train to Barcelona.

Travelling was difficult, for she knew very few words of Spanish, although she picked up a smattering of the language as she went along.

At Barcelona she found a cheap hotel and booked a room; then she set to work, writing her first impressions of life in the Republican city. By now the country had been divided by the Falangist Army: Madrid was still a loyalist stronghold, though it was completely surrounded by Franco's men and in a state of siege. Barcelona fared a little better, but not much.

Posters and banners with political slogans plastered the streets; at every public building, sentries armed with rifles stood on guard, looking for Nationalist spies. Some shops remained open, though there was very little on sale; a few cafés and restaurants carried on normally. Food was not, at that time, in short supply, though bread was almost unobtainable.

The city was drab and grim, yet there was a feeling of optimism in the air; the citizens were convinced that the Fascists would soon be defeated, and that a better and brighter world awaited them. The bulletins Caro sent back to London reflected this mood of euphoria.

She had not yet managed to trace Don. She made enquiries at the barracks of the International Brigade, and learned that a party of British volunteers had passed through recently and were now on their way to the front line, where reinforcements were urgently needed. She tried to send a message to him, but was not certain it would get through. Still, that didn't matter; she felt sure she would see him again very soon. The mood of the Spanish people was so determined, and they were so united against the Nationalists – the war could not last much longer.

This was the theme of the copy she sent back to the *Argus*. It was not to the taste of Sir Perkins Hathaway.

The next time she telephoned London, and got through to the news-room – no small feat in itself for telephone communication was notoriously unreliable, and the line was apt to go dead at any moment – Fred Binns told her there had been a change of policy.

'The chief doesn't care for the stuff you've been sending us,' he told her. 'It's too left-wing – practically Communist propaganda, he says. So he's dropping your articles; you're to come back as soon as possible.'

Caroline was outraged. She had barely begun yet; she was hoping to get nearer the front line, and report on the actual fighting. There had been air-raids on unprotected civilian targets with horrifying casualties, Franco's war-planes were backed up by German and Italian reserves, there was so much she had to tell the *Argus* readers –

Fred interrupted her, his voice thin and distorted: 'Sorry, dear – orders is orders; you're to come home at once – OK?'

'That's ridiculous!' she exclaimed. 'I won't come home. You can't make me!'

'Don't be daft – you don't want to get the sack.'

'Sir Perkins can't sack me – I'd sooner resign!'

Through a storm of crackling, Fred yelled: 'What? I can't hear – the line's breaking up. What did you say?'

'Tell Sir Perks to keep his rotten job – tell him to go to hell!' And she slammed down the phone.

Outside the Central Post Office, the street looked grey and bleak, and she began to realize what she had done. On the corner, a man was selling hot potatoes from a brazier; roasted in their jackets, split open, and flavoured with a little salt and olive oil. She bought one, eating it as she walked along. It tasted delicious. Slowly, her spirits began to rise again.

This war was not going to be won by journalists. She would offer her services to the International Brigade; she knew volunteers were needed in the administration offices. She would not be a reporter – an onlooker – any more. She would be one of the fighters.

On the first Sunday in February, Polly seized gratefully upon a break between showers to walk into the village. She wanted to buy the Sunday papers, to read the notices of the new Cochran show; she was on her way back, with a bundle of newspapers under her arm, when the rain began again. Looking round for somewhere to shelter, she saw the lodge cottage and ran across to knock at the door.

When it opened, she apologized: 'Sorry to disturb you – can I come in till the rain gives over?'

'Of course,' said Ken Stubbs. 'I told you you're always welcome. Are you going to have that cup of coffee I promised you?'

'Why not?'

He disappeared into the kitchen, while she sat in an armchair by the fireside and leafed through the papers, finding the notices for the new revue.

'*Home and Beauty*,' she read aloud, when he came back with two cups of coffee on a tray. 'Strange sort of name, don't you think?'

'I beg your pardon?'

'The new show at the Adelphi – it's set in an English country house,' she said. 'The notices are what you might call mixed, though they're all good for Binnie Hale.'

She realized that he was staring at her as if she were speaking Chinese, and laughed: 'Sorry – that's the worst of being in the business – you think everyone else is as potty as you are.'

'The business?'

'Show business – the theatre. I used to be on the stage, before I got married – didn't you know? And the last show I did was a Cochran revue, like this one. Funny really. Cockie came down here to give me away at the wedding, on account of me not having a father – and he fell for Crown House in a big way. I remember, he told me he was planning a show set in a place like this... He's certainly taken his time about it!' She put aside the newspapers and took the cup he offered her. 'I'm chattering on – tell me to shut up.'

He sat in the chair at the other side of the grate, and put a log on the fire. 'I shouldn't dream of such a thing. It's a pleasure to have some company; I don't see many people.'

'No?' She sipped her coffee. 'I don't know why not – you certainly make your visitors welcome.'

After a moment, he said, 'I'm afraid I don't make friends easily.'

'That's a shame. You ought to get out more.'

'What – the village pub? whist-drives? that kind of thing? Perhaps I'm not a very sociable sort of chap.'

'Well, you could go into Medford. They have shows at the Corn Exchange sometimes – and dances... And there's always the Picture Palace.'

He shook his head. 'It's not much fun going on your own. It might be different if I had someone to go with.'

In the silence that followed, the log settled in the grate. Then Polly said, 'Would you mind if I made a suggestion?'

'Of course not – what is it?'

'Tell me to mind my own business, but – you know Lilian? Lilian Brooks? She doesn't get out much either; living in like she does, she hardly ever gets away from Crown House. I think she'd enjoy a trip into Medford sometimes – an evening at the flicks would do her good – take her out of herself. So if it's company you're wanting...'

He nodded his head, but seemed a little depressed. 'Yes... Thanks for telling me. It hadn't struck me, but now you mention it – yes, that might be an idea.'

Polly smiled and drank her coffee, happy to think that she had done her good deed for the day.

Caro was happy too. She felt she had turned her back on her old life for ever. The shallow society gossip the *Argus* expected her to contribute was a thing of the past; she was in touch with real life at last. She was working for something worth while, and devoting every minute of her day to a cause she believed in.

She had gone to an office run by the British Communists in Barcelona which acted as an information bureau and clearing-centre for the International Brigade. She explained her situation frankly to the man in charge. Shaggy and truculent, he regarded her with suspicion: his beard bristled at the mention of the *Argus* – a well-known organ of the decadent capitalist press – but he relaxed when she told him how she had disobeyed orders and thrown up her job in order to stay in Spain and work for the Loyalists.

She explained that she could do shorthand and typing, and would be happy to write press releases or do public-relations work. All she wanted in return was a minimum wage, enough to pay for her board and lodging.

Stroking his beard, he decided to take a chance on her. He said she could start right away, though he warned her to say nothing about her connection with Fleet Street, as the party leaders were convinced that Fascist spies were being infiltrated into the ranks of the Brigade. But it was essential to keep up morale by giving the volunteers regular and frequent news-bulletins on the progress of the war, and it would be Caroline's job to produce a news-sheet which could be duplicated and distributed to the front line.

She enjoyed the work, though she soon found out that as the only woman in the office she was also expected to act as unofficial secretary to everyone else, sending off letters and cables, and doing her best to deal with such things as shopping, simple cookery on an antiquated stove and, of course, the washing up.

From time to time she acted as hostess too, for the office provided tours of the combat zones for distinguished visitors with left-wing sympathies. She would go to the station and meet celebrities such as Stephen Spender, W. H. Auden and the photographer Cartier-Bresson. They usually spent an hour or two at party headquarters, where Caro made endless pots of coffee and they were given an up-to-the-minute report on the battle fronts. Then they would climb into an old and unreliable Mercedes to be driven off towards beleaguered Madrid, while Caro stayed behind to wash up the coffee-cups and empty overflowing ashtrays.

A few weeks later, the situation changed.

The next visiting celebrity was an American writer, Mr Ernest Hemingway, and Caro took an instant dislike to him. He was big and hearty, with a swaggering manner, and he called her by her first name immediately. Unfortunately, he misheard the introduction, and addressed her as Carole all the time he was there; she tried to correct him once or twice, then gave it up as a bad job.

'Hey, listen, Carole – let me tell you something,' he said. 'I'm reporting on this war for the newspapers back home, and I'm keen to get down to the American Hospital at Villa Paz – that's near the scene of the fighting, right?'

'Yes, I believe so.'

'Great – that's what I want to see. Frankly, I'm in need of a secretary right now; I brought a girl along, but she got sick with some goddam bug – I told her shouldn't drink the water round here, but would she listen? She'll be laid up for the next day or two, and I can't type my own stuff – so how'd it be if you come with me to take her place?'

Caro was torn; she had no wish to become Mr Hemingway's travelling companion, but on the other hand this was the opportunity she had been hoping for – a chance to get to the front-line troops, and perhaps make contact with Don Carpenter. Finally she agreed, and a few hours later she set out with the great man, in the battered Mercedes. This time somebody else could wash the cups and empty the ashtrays.

The journey was slow and uneventful; and when they reached their destination, nothing much seemed to be happening. They were escorted to a makeshift pillbox, fortified by sandbags, with dug-out trenches running off at either side across empty farmlands, now barren and riddled with shell-holes.

Mr Hemingway inspected the machine-gun post, and enquired about the location of the enemy lines. The officer in charge pointed vaguely into the distance, but there was no sign of any activity, so the great man sat behind the machine-gun, and demonstrated how to feed it with a belt of ammunition.

'I know how these damn things work – I had plenty of experience with them, in Italy,' he said casually. 'OK if I loose off a couple of rounds?'

'If you want,' said the officer, rather surprised.

'Fine, fine . . .' He prodded the machine-gun shield with an exploratory finger. 'I guess this stuff is bullet-proof – in case they happen to feel like returning fire? OK Carole, you'd better stand well back and take cover.'

She moved away, behind a wall of sandbags, and covered her ears as he pressed the trigger. He seemed to be enjoying himself, for he did not stop after a couple of rounds, but carried on until he had used up the entire ammunition-belt.

'Betcha that scared the pants off them!' he said, laughing.

Seconds later, the enemy responded with a mortar bombardment which exploded around the dug-out, rather too close for comfort; and Mr Hemingway decided it was time to withdraw from the battlefield.

As soon as things quietened down, he said to Caro: 'I guess we should head for that grey stone farmhouse we passed a mile or two back, then I can dictate my article before I move on: you can work on it while I go visit the hospital. I'll leave you my portable typewriter. You can bring it with you when you join me at Villa Paz – right?'

She never finished typing out the copy he dictated. She never saw him again, nor did she return the typewriter, for shortly after he left the war-zone, the fighting broke out once more – and this time it was deadly serious.

Caro waited at the deserted farm, wondering how long she would be marooned there, and hoping that Franco's artillery would not overshoot their targets by accident, and land a direct hit on the building. She was not very frightened, for she did not feel she was in any real danger; she could not believe this was really happening. It was like a scene in a film: curiously unreal, so that she was able to observe the uncomfortable and disagreeable experience with detachment, and wait for it to stop.

But the battle continued for several hours, and when there was a lull in the bombardment at last, she saw through the broken windows that a handful of soldiers were making their way towards the farm – keeping close to the ground, darting from one patch of cover to the next.

For a moment, she was afraid they might be an advance party from the enemy – then recognized some of the volunteers she had seen in the dug-out. They tumbled into the farm, panting, sweating, muddy and bloodstained, amazed to find the visiting Englishwoman already there.

'You picked the wrong day for your little outing, miss,' said one of the men, a thin-faced cockney. 'Seems like our bloody stupid officers decided to try and attack Franco's lot. They want to break through their lines and open up the road to Madrid... But they haven't got a hope in hell. We've been sent here to get the place ready as an emergency dressing-station; they're going to start getting our blokes back on stretchers. You'd better push off while things are quiet. This is no place for you.'

Caro longed to get away, yet she heard herself saying, 'No – I'll stay... I might be able to help.'

Afterwards, she never knew how she had managed to cope with the wounded bodies that were carried in and laid out on the dirt floor. The sight and sound made her want to be sick – or to run away – yet she went on working automatically, washing away blood and filth, helping the single medical orderly to clean up raw flesh and apply primitive dressings and bandages.

And then she saw Don.

He had been very badly hurt; she knew at a glance that his wounds were too severe for the simple first-aid treatment which was all they had to offer. His glasses had disappeared – probably blown to pieces when a mortar had exploded directly in front of him, and the jagged shrapnel had ripped away part of his face... He was almost blind, but when she took his hand and spoke to him, he knew her immediately.

'Caroline... I'll be OK now,' he said.

Incredibly, he did not appear to be in much pain; the shock had been so great, he seemed to be almost numbed by it.

'What's going to happen next?' he asked. 'Where do we go from here?'

Her thoughts raced; she knew he had to have skilled medical attention as quickly as possible. Then she remembered Villa Paz.

'Don't worry,' she told him, trying to sound calm and reassuring. 'I'm going to get you to hospital.'

As Polly walked across the entrance hall at Crown House, something caught her eye: a piece of paper broke up the geometric pattern of black and white tiles. She stooped to pick it up, and turned it over. It was a drawing in brightly coloured crayons, and she realized that it was the work of her son. Alex must have brought it down from the nursery to show Jenny, then lost interest in it when something else caught his attention.

She studied it carefully, feeling a twinge of sadness. It wasn't bad for a nine-year-old; two grown-up figures – a standing man and a seated woman, holding a tiny child on her lap – and beside them a boy holding a red balloon on a string. The four figures were identified with painstakingly printed labels: '*Jenny ... Harry ... Nichlaos ... Me*'.

'Good morning,' said a gruff voice, and Polly looked up, startled. Ken Stubbs had come through the door from the servants' quarters, shrugging into his overcoat.

'Hello!' she said. 'This is a nice surprise. Are you on your way out, or can I return your hospitality and offer you some elevenses?'

'No, thank you, ma'am – I've had mine already. I've got a message for Mrs Gaunt, from her husband. He says to tell her he could drive her in to Medford after all, if she can hang on for ten minutes or so.'

'Oh – you're just too late; Jenny took the children on the half-past-ten bus.'

'Ah – sorry about that. I'll tell him I missed her.'

Polly held out the drawing: 'This is Alex's latest masterpiece – a family portrait.'

'Very good. Is that meant to be you, sitting down?'

'Oh, no.' She turned it towards him, so he could read the lettering. 'I'm not in it.'

The green baize door under the staircase opened again, and Lilian Brooks appeared, holding a tweed cap. She bobbed an acknowledgement towards Polly, then addressed Ken: 'You left your hat behind, Mr Stubbs. Don't you go getting a cold in the head now – it's a nasty treacherous day.'

'Thanks.' He took the cap from her, slightly embarrassed, and turned it round in his hands. 'And thanks again for the coffee.'

'My pleasure, Mr Stubbs. It was the least I could do.' She smiled at him, and for a moment her heavy features were transformed; she looked almost pretty. Then she glanced back at Polly, saying, 'Excuse me, madam,' and returned to the servants' hall.

Ken Stubbs hovered for a moment as if he were reluctant to leave, and said awkwardly, 'By the by, I followed your advice. I took Miss

Brooks to the Picture Palace the other night... I think she enjoyed it; we had a very pleasant evening.'

'I'm so glad.'

Polly rolled up Alex's drawing, and thought wistfully how nice it would be to go into Medford and see a film, to have a drink in a pub or a meal at a café. It was a long time since she had been able to do that. Since Richard's death, she had barely set foot outside the grounds of Crown House, unwilling to face the curious stares of people who might recognize her, or to hear them whispering behind her back: 'She's the one – Lady Ebony... She used to be a chorus-girl before she got married – and a fat lot of good it did her, 'cos the Viscount went and got himself shot, carrying on with another man's wife – scandalous, it was...'

Dismissing these thoughts, she concluded lightly: 'Lilian's very lucky – I quite envy her.'

Ken looked thunderstruck. He opened his mouth to say something, but changed his mind, and a slow flush spread over his face.

For a second Polly was bewildered, and then she realized how thoughtless she had been: the poor chap must have thought she was trying to flirt with him! Hot with embarrassment, she added quickly, 'I mean – I envy her, because she's got a life of her own; I wish I had a job like that, running the house... I wish I had something to do – anything at all – but I'm absolutely useless...'

Ken frowned: 'Don't say that. I'm sure there must be plenty of things you could do, if you put your mind to it.'

'Like what? I'd be no good as a housekeeper – I'm not the domestic type. I can't offer to help you and Nick at the farm; I never had any training for office work. All I ever learned was to sing a bit and kick my legs up – and I'm too long in the tooth for that, these days! Oh, well...'

Smiling brightly, she said goodbye and went upstairs, escaping to her own room.

Villa Paz was not very far from the scene of the Jarama battle, but it could have been a different world: a comfortable and prosperous estate, set in a rolling landscape broken by wooded hills and sparkling rivers. Once it had been a royal palace, and the residence of the Spanish Infanta, but it resembled a rambling farmhouse, built round two huge courtyards.

The Americans had converted it into a hospital with beds for a hundred patients, a fully equipped operating theatre, pathology laboratories and staff accommodation.

At present they had very few patients, and when Caro arrived with Don in an ambulance, which she had requisitioned through a mixture of flattery, bribery and brow-beating, the matron – a brisk, practical woman called Freddy Martin – was understanding and co-operative.

Caroline introduced herself, and mentioned her tenuous connection with Mr Hemingway, hoping this might be a point in her favour, but Freddy smiled: 'Mr Hemingway didn't stay here more than a couple of hours. It was what you might call a flying visit. Let's have a look at your patient; I can't tell you anything till we've examined him . . . Is he asleep?'

'Yes – I gave him some pain-killers to get him through the journey, and they've knocked him out for the moment.'

The matron called one of her nurses, and they peeled off the bandages and the dressing. Then she said quietly: 'Jesus . . . You did the right thing. We must get him into the theatre – and fast.' She gave instructions to the nurse, then told Caro, 'Strictly speaking, this unit caters for American casualties only, but this poor guy needs treatment right now, so the hell with rules and regulations. I'm certainly not going to turn him away.'

The operation took some time, and when at last they wheeled Don back to his bed in a small side ward, he was still unconscious.

'How is he?' Caro wanted to know. 'Is he going to be all right?'

'In my job, I don't give guarantees,' said Freddy Martin. 'With a bit of luck, I reckon he'll pull through. But it's going to take time. Don't expect any overnight miracles.'

'That's all right,' said Caro. 'I'm not going anywhere.' Then she added, 'As long as I'm here – I'd like to make myself useful, if you'll let me. I don't know much about nursing, but I can learn.'

'Good girl.' Freddy touched her hand. 'Things are quiet now, but we never know when we're going to be busy. I'll fix you up a bed in the nurses' quarters; you look as if you need a good long rest.'

'Thank you. For the time being, I think I'd rather stay here. I'd like to be with him when he comes round.'

Freddy nodded and went away. Some time later a little nurse with ginger hair and a Bronx accent brought Caro a cup of coffee with a shot of Spanish brandy in it. After she had drunk it, she dozed off.

The room was almost dark when she woke up; for a moment she had no idea where she was, but then she heard Don's voice.

'Caroline? Where are you?'

'I'm here.' She reached out and held his hand. There was a faint light from the doorway, and she could just see the bedclothes stirring as he turned towards her. 'You're safe now, in hospital. Try to rest.'

'I can't – I can't see you –' he blurted out; she heard the panic in his voice.

'Your eyes are bandaged; they had to operate on you. But it's going to be all right.'

His hand gripped hers very tightly, and then he said, 'You won't go away, will you?'

'Of course not. I've told matron I want to stay here and work in the hospital, so I can be with you. Don't worry.'

He sighed with relief. After a moment he said, 'I've been lucky. If it wasn't for you, I reckon I'd be a goner. But I knew you'd be here when I needed you. I suppose it was fate, really – meeting you in the first place and then finding you again... It was meant to happen, wasn't it?'

'I suppose it must have been.'

'Yeah – it was fate, all right... I've been in love with you from the first minute I saw you. You know that, don't you?'

She wanted to interrupt – to stop him, to say he was making a mistake – but she could not find the right words to tell him so, and he went on talking.

'We were meant for each other, you and me... Now you've found me – and you've given up your job to stay with me – everything's going to be all right... We're going to be so happy...'

His voice trailed off, as he sank back into an exhausted sleep. Caro said nothing: what could she possibly say?

'These letters are ones I think you will want to see, Your Majesty,' said Alice, putting a little sheaf of papers down on the table. 'The others can all be passed over to the Palace.'

Queen Mary sighed. 'It becomes so complicated, doesn't it? I'm very grateful to you for sorting things out, my dear.'

They were in Queen Mary's sitting-room. Outside in St James's Park, the daffodil buds were beginning to fatten up, and some were already showing traces of yellow. Soon it would be the first day of spring.

Alice had just begun another fortnight of waiting upon the Queen; her duties were less frequent now, for Her Majesty had moved away from the centre of the royal scene when she took up residence at Marlborough House.

'I am glad that the pressure of work upon me has been lightened, but of course there are still a great many calls upon my time. I should not wish to withdraw from public life altogether,' she told Alice.

One area that might have led to difficulties was the Queen's association with various charities. There were so many of them, and in some cases she had been graciously pleased, as Queen of England, to accept the title of 'Patron'. When Elizabeth became Queen, she had automatically become Patron of these charities; but in some instances Queen Mary had been active President as well, and these were causes with which she still wished to be connected.

'Elizabeth has been wonderfully helpful and understanding,' the Queen continued. 'She discussed the situation with me, and we went through the list together. Between us, we decided which organizations should pass to her, and which might remain with me.'

'I'm sure Her Majesty would do all she could to fall in with your wishes, Ma'am; she is always so thoughtful.'

'Oh, yes – always. There could have been problems too in the Royal Household: naturally Elizabeth and Bertie wished to make some appointments of their own, but she has been so diplomatic in the way she kept everyone happy, fitting the new people in with the old guard so cleverly... I have nothing but admiration for her.'

'Moving into the Palace must have been difficult for them, I imagine.'

'They never grumbled about it; they just accepted it. Bertie said to me one day: "The people have had a lot to put up with in the past year; I want to try and make amends to them for what has happened." He has a very strong sense of duty.'

Her face clouded for a moment; perhaps she was comparing Bertie with his elder brother. Alice ventured to say, 'Her Majesty told me the King talked to his brother every day – on the telephone.'

'Those dreadful telephone calls! Yes, but they have stopped now, thank goodness. David had begun to make demands for money, insisting that the financial settlement from the sale of his estates must be paid immediately and so on. Matters came to a head one evening when Bertie telephoned Schloss Enzesfeld, and was told that the Duke of Windsor was at dinner, and that he should call again later . . . Such impertinence!' Queen Mary flushed with anger, drumming her fingertips upon the arm of her chair. 'Elizabeth urged Bertie not to subject himself to any more slights of that nature, and a message was sent to inform David that their telephone conversations must cease . . . And high time, too.'

'I'm sure it must be a welcome relief,' Alice agreed.

'The King and Queen have too many other things to deal with. Why, their Coronation Day is only two months away, and there is so much to be done before then . . . I trust that you and your dear husband will be present at the Abbey?'

'I sincerely hope so, Ma'am; I know that William won't want to miss such an important occasion. I'm just praying that his health continues to improve.'

'Of course he must follow the advice of his doctors; it would be foolish for him to run any risks.'

'But on the other hand, it may do him good. It's given him a goal to work towards; he says he's determined to be well enough to travel to London by then – and that's half the battle.'

'Quite so; please give him my very best wishes . . . And now, my dear, I think we should make a start on these letters, or the morning will be gone before we know it.'

At the end of the day, when Alice returned to Eaton Square, she was surprised to find she had an unexpected visitor.

Sir Charles Bowyer put down his tumbler of whisky as she entered the drawing-room, and came towards her with his arms outstretched. When she kissed him, he held her very tightly, and she knew something must be wrong; her brother was not given to displays of affection.

'Charlie – how are you?' she began.

'Not too well, I'm afraid. I've had rather a bad day.'

'Oh, I am sorry.' She looked round. 'Isn't Gina with you?'

'No . . . She's not.'

'What a pity. I hoped you could both stay to dinner.'

'As a matter of fact, I should like to stay rather longer than that . . . I've brought a couple of suitcases with me; do you mind if I move in here for a while? If it's not inconvenient?'

'Charlie, what's happened? Where is Gina?'

'I left her at Curzon Street.' His voice was unsteady, and his eyes red-rimmed. 'I shan't be seeing her again.'

'What?'

'I found out today that she's been deceiving me... We had a terrible row... Our marriage is over; I shall apply for a divorce.'

19

MONDAY, 15 MARCH TO WEDNESDAY, 23 JUNE 1937

'Sit down, Charlie... Tell me about it.' Alice led her brother to the sofa and sat beside him. As he picked up his tumbler of whisky, he tried to control his shaking hand.

'I don't like talking about it. You'll think I'm such a fool.'

'Of course I won't.'

'Yes, you will – and you'll be right. I've behaved very stupidly.' He knocked back the rest of his drink, then said thickly, 'It was one of those damned Fascists; somebody called Voss – Roland Voss. I met him a few times; I never liked the fellow. You remember when she went to Berlin last year? They went together, of course – I suppose I should have guessed.'

'How did you find out? Did she tell you?'

'She did – in the end.' Suddenly he looked at Alice suspiciously. 'Did you know about it? Did everybody know? Were you all laughing at me behind my back?'

'Don't be silly – I knew nothing whatever. How could I have known?'

'It just struck me; you didn't seem particularly surprised.'

'Well – no. I suppose I've never thought of Gina as being very trustworthy – but never mind that. Tell me what happened.'

'You remember she'd been seeing a doctor – Dr Lennard? And she was rather secretive about it; I must admit that made me curious, so I made some enquiries at the club – we've got several Harley Street chaps there. And when I mentioned that my wife was seeing this fellow Lennard, one of them smiled and congratulated me... Dr Lennard's speciality is gynaecology.'

'You mean she's pregnant? Oh, no!'

Charlie frowned: 'It's not impossible, you know; she's only forty-two, and I'm not altogether in my dotage. That's why – at first – I was quite delighted. I even . . .' He glanced unhappily at the decanter. 'Would you mind if I help myself?'

He refilled his glass, then continued: 'On my way home from the club that afternoon, I stopped at a florist and bought an armful of roses. I thought perhaps she was too shy to tell me about the – the happy event – and I wanted to make it easier for her. I even opened a bottle of champagne. When she asked what it was all about, I told her it was an old English custom, to wet the baby's head . . . That was when she began to laugh.'

Alice saw the misery in his eyes, and her heart went out to him. 'There wasn't any baby?'

'There never had been. Dr Lennard is also an authority on the – um – related ailments of women – sexual complications and so on . . . Sexual – diseases . . . Gina laughed hysterically – she couldn't stop. She asked if I'd ever heard of syphilis? That was why she consulted Dr Lennard; her lover had contracted a venereal infection, and she was afraid she might have caught it.'

A knock at the door startled them. Automatically, Alice said, 'Come in.' The housekeeper entered the room, a notebook in her hand.

'Excuse me, my lady – Cook was wondering if there would be any change in the menu tonight – if Sir Charles will be dining –?'

'Oh – I'm not sure – could you come back later, Miss Kendall? I'll ring for you when we have decided.'

'Very good, my lady.'

The housekeeper left the room, and Charlie asked anxiously, 'Do you suppose she heard?'

'No, I'm sure she didn't . . . I'm sorry – please go on.'

'There's not much more to tell you. Gina had been very worried, waiting for the result of her blood test – although ironically enough, it turned out to be negative. But she admitted everything; she said I bored her. She realized she had made a mistake in marrying an older man. When she met Voss, she couldn't help herself – it was love at first sight, she said. I shall get a divorce; there's nothing else for it.'

'And Gina? What will she do?'

'I've told her she can stay on at Curzon Street until she finds other accommodation; I imagine she will join her lover.'

At the same moment, Gina was walking into Roland Voss's bedroom in Maida Vale.

'I've been trying to call you for hours – why don't you answer your telephone?' she asked. She was smiling – a forced, bright smile – but her voice sounded desperate.

'I only got in half an hour ago,' he said. 'What's the matter? You seem rather upset.'

'Do I?' Her laughter was brittle and unconvincing. 'I can't imagine why – I'm feeling terribly good. I just told my husband exactly what I thought of him...' Then she saw the open suitcase lying on the bed, with a pile of clean shirts and underclothes beside it, and her laughter stopped abruptly.

'What are you doing?' she asked.

'Packing. I'm going away for a while.'

'What? Why didn't you tell me?'

'It happened quite suddenly; I've been invited to Germany.' He went on putting clothes into the suitcase. 'I talked it over with our Leader. He's very keen for me to go.'

'You were going away without even telling me?'

'Of course I was going to tell you. I should have rung up – or left a message at party HQ –'

'You bastard! You can't do this to me. I won't let you!' Suddenly she threw herself on to the bed, knocking the case on to the floor, and scattering the tidy heaps of socks and underpants. 'If you go to Germany, I'm coming with you...'

He stared at her: 'That's impossible – your husband would never stand for it.'

'That's what I'm trying to tell you. He's not my husband any more; he wants a divorce... Isn't it divine?'

'I don't understand –'

She knelt up, pulling him towards her; he lost his balance and tumbled on to the bed, and she threw her arms round him, saying between kisses, 'Sweetheart, it's really very simple... Charlie and I had a hell of a row. He found out about us, and he's walked out on me...' She held his face between her hands. 'Why don't you look happy? ... This is what we wanted all along, isn't it?'

'How did he find out?' Roland asked.

'What does it matter? He'd been prying and nosing around – so

298

I finally told him. I couldn't be bothered to go on lying; I wish I'd told him ages ago.'

Roland pulled free and stood up, smoothing back his ruffled hair. 'If I'm cited as co-respondent, the Leader will be furious; you know how he feels about bad publicity for the party –'

'Tom can't say anything; he'd moved in with Diana years before they were married... Anyway, we'll sort it out somehow. The important thing is, I can come to Germany. How long are we going for?'

'Gina... I don't think this is a good idea. I'm going on party business – setting up a liaison group with the SS... It was all Heinrich's idea originally –'

She sat up. 'Who the hell's Heinrich?'

'You remember Heinrich Gessler? He was at the wedding: he's one of the Führer's right-hand men. I'm going on a tour of the main SS units. I'll probably be living in barracks most of the time; honestly, you'd much better stay here. Perhaps I can send for you later.'

As he stood by the dressing-table mirror, straightening his tie, she came up behind him, slipping her arms round his waist and holding him tightly.

'Just tell me one thing, honey-lamb... Do you love me?'

'Well, yes – of course – you know I do.'

'That's OK then, 'cos I'm still crazy about you, in spite of everything – and I'm telling you here and now, I am definitely coming to Germany.'

'Yes, but I'm still having treatment – until I get a final clearance from the doctor, we shan't be able to... Well, you know.'

'This Heinrich Gessler... Would he be the little charmer who took you to that stinking night-club, by any chance?'

He turned to face her, protesting, 'You can't blame Heinrich because I got a dose – it wasn't his fault! That was later on, when I went back with one of the –' He broke off, and began again: 'If I hadn't been drinking, it would never have happened.'

'Maybe, but I'm not taking any more chances. We are going to Germany together, my precious, and this time I'm not letting you out of my sight!'

The worst time for Caro was when Don started having nightmares. She had volunteered for night-duty, because Don found it hard to sleep; it made the nights more bearable if she was within call. After she had done her rounds, she used to sit by his bed, and he would talk drowsily for hours on end.

Once she said to him, 'You sound tired; try to sleep.'

'I want to, but – something seems to stop me... I get bad dreams; perhaps that's why I won't let myself fall asleep.'

When he dozed off eventually, the nightmares began. The first time it happened, Caro was in the little cubby-hole which served as ward office, kitchen and medical store. She heard him cry out in agony, and ran to him, switching on the light. She found him sitting up in bed with a look of terror on his face, and his eyes shut – fast asleep.

When she woke him, he clung to her, saying brokenly, 'Oh, God... Oh, my God – I thought I was back there. I thought I was in the dug-out.'

Bit by bit, he told her about his experiences in the front line. The food was terrible, and the men were half-starved most of the time. The meals were usually the same – a thin stew with lumps of gristle, potato and turnip floating in a watery gravy; it was tasteless, and practically cold by the time it reached them – but it allayed their hunger for a while.

Then there were the lice. Water was scarce, as it all had to be brought to the trenches in buckets, and there weren't any spare men available to carry it. They eked out the meagre ration: water was essential for drinking, and for cooking; there was never enough left for them to wash themselves, let alone their clothes.

'They kept saying reinforcements were on the way, and that we'd be sent back to base-camp for a rest, but it never happened. I was stuck in that filthy hole for nearly two months, and we all stank like pigs... Our clothes were crawling with lice; the only way to kill 'em off was to run the seams of your jackets and trousers through a candle-flame, listening to them pop and shrivel up.'

Lowering his voice, he confessed: 'At first I thought I was doing my bit for the cause of freedom – but after a while I was just trying to stay alive, hoping I'd get out of that hell-hole in one piece, before a shell landed on top of me and blew me to kingdom come... I wish to God I'd never come to Spain...'

His nightmare was always the same: he dreamed he had recovered from his injuries, and he was being sent back to the front line to go through it all again... Caro knew he would never go back into active service, and tried to tell him so, as gently as possible.

'Do you suppose they'll send me home again?' he asked, with longing in his voice. 'Just think – you and me – getting on the boat to England – getting off the train at Victoria . . . Walking along hand in hand – everyone looking at us, knowing that you're my girl – that's what I'd like . . . You and me, together – in a little place of our own . . . I love you so much, Caroline.'

Then he would start to make plans, building fantasies about a little cottage with a garden – a few flowers and some trees . . . 'Wimbledon, p'raps – somewhere near the Common. Do you know Wimbledon at all?'

She shook her head, forgetting he could not see her face.

'Caroline? Are you still there?' he asked sharply.

'Yes – I'm here . . . I'm afraid I don't know Wimbledon.'

'It's a pretty sort of place; I'll take you round and show it to you when we get home . . . We'll find somewhere to live – it's going to be bloody marvellous – you wait and see . . .'

Caro put her hand on his forehead, and he sighed contentedly, thinking of the golden future that lay ahead. He was still running a high temperature; the surgeon had said he was concerned about Don, for he was not making a good recovery. When Caro changed his dressings, she saw that the wounds were not healing as they should. There was some talk of a deeper infection, and the possibility of a second operation.

She had never felt so miserable: she pitied Don with all her heart, but she did not love him – and she felt guilty because he trusted her completely, and she could not tell him the truth.

Though he was nearly blind, his ears missed nothing, and he asked Caro quietly, 'Is it right they're going to carve me up again?'

'They might. Nothing's really been decided yet,' she said carefully.

'You tell them from me – the sooner they patch me up, the better. I don't care what they do to me. I just want to get out.'

A week later, they took him back into the theatre.

Without any real training, Caro could not assist in the operation. She spent the afternoon scrubbing the floor of an empty ward, and making up beds; there had been another battle, further down the line, and the hospital was standing by to receive heavy casualties.

The sun had gone down when Freddy Martin came to find her. Sitting in the little office, Freddy lit a cigarette, then said, 'He never came round from the anaesthetic . . . He'd been through so much; in the end, his heart just gave up the struggle. He can't have known anything about it; he looked quite peaceful.'

After a long silence, Caro said huskily; 'At least he got away – that's what he wanted... I just wish I'd been with him when he – when it –' She gulped, and Freddy produced a small bottle of brandy, pouring a generous measure.

'Get this inside you... You must have loved him very much.'

Caro swallowed some brandy, then said, 'No... But he thought I did – that's what mattered.'

'What will you do now?' Freddy asked. 'Go back to Barcelona?'

'I don't know. It seems a bit pointless, somehow.'

'Back to England, then?'

'That's pointless too. There's nothing there for me. Nobody needs me, in England.'

The noise of approaching vehicles interrupted her, and they looked out of the window as a convoy of field-ambulances rumbled into the courtyard.

'Right.' Freddy stubbed out her cigarette. 'I got to go – looks like it's going to be a busy night.'

'I'll stay on and help, if you want me to,' said Caro. 'I'd sooner be here than anywhere else.'

As the weeks went by, the preparations for the Coronation were in full swing, and all over London the decorations were going up: huge wooden stands sprang up like mushrooms along the processional route, providing seating for those fortunate enough to be specially invited.

Queen Mary, on an afternoon drive with her lady-in-waiting, Lady Flora Kelso, shook her head in disapproval: 'Really too ugly – the poor daffodils had only just come out, and now they're all squashed and hidden underneath.'

Lady Flora demurred, as tactfully as possible: 'Surely, Ma'am, you must be glad to know the people are so enthusiastic? There's a feeling of such love and loyalty – of real excitement.'

'Oh, yes – it's most gratifying. That is why I have decided to attend the ceremony myself; it is important for us all to be seen there – together, as a family.'

Traditionally, the widow of a King never appeared at his successor's coronation; it was considered to be unlucky. But after discussion with Bertie and Elizabeth, Queen Mary had chosen to defy superstition: now that the upheavals of the last twelve months were over, the Royal Family wished to demonstrate that there would be no misunderstandings and no more false starts: the monarchy was established more securely than ever.

For this reason, the King and Queen included their daughters on several public occasions; the little girls appeared at an afternoon party in Buckingham Palace, and just after her eleventh birthday, Princess Elizabeth accompanied her parents on a river trip to Greenwich, for the opening of the National Maritime Museum. But the forthcoming Coronation would be the most exciting event of their lives, and they could hardly wait for 12 May.

Originally, it was suggested that Princess Elizabeth should wear her first full-length dress to the Abbey, under a robe of purple velvet, with a gold circlet on her head; while Princess Margaret would be in a short dress, with white socks and shoes, as usual.

Margaret soon put a stop to that. She said it was not fair, and that she was a Princess too, just as much as Lillibet, and she wasn't going to wear a short dress and horrid white socks for anybody – so there!

A nursery feud developed, and was resolved by the King, who announced that in the interests of family harmony, they should wear identical dresses and identical robes – even their trains should be the same length.

Lillibet thought this was taking equality altogether too far, and was prepared to argue the matter, but her father put his foot down.

'Oh, well...' She gave her sister a baleful glance. 'I just hope she won't disgrace us all by falling asleep in the middle. After all, she is very young for a coronation...'

At Crown House, William and Alice were also discussing what they should wear.

'Knee-breeches and silk stockings?' William exploded, when Alice reminded him that they would have to put on their full regalia for the Abbey. 'With half a ton of moth-eaten old velvet and ermine – and that blasted coronet? I shall suffocate!'

'Oh, dear...' Alice sighed. 'So you don't think you'll be feeling strong enough to go to London after all?'

He looked up indignantly. 'I didn't say that. I'm perfectly well – never felt better.'

'Yes, but those heavy robes... If it's going to be too much for you, we should send a note to explain and apologize. I'm sure they'll understand –'

'Nothing of the sort!' snapped William. 'I'm going to take my place in Westminster Abbey – nothing will stop me.'

Alice tried to hide her smile, but William saw her expression, and grumbled: 'You know very well I wouldn't miss it... Stop teasing.'

'I'm sorry, darling. I wanted to make quite sure you wouldn't turn up at the last minute in your old gardening jacket!'

Alice had asked Nicholas and Jenny if they would like to stay at Eaton Square during Coronation Week and join in the festivities, since they were personal friends of the King and Queen. They discussed the possibility one morning when Jenny dropped in at the farm office. She had brought both children down to the stables; Alex had gone out for a riding lesson, and little Harry was being taken to see a foal that had recently been born, so she had a few minutes to herself.

'Am I interrupting anything important?' she asked, perching on the corner of Nick's desk. 'Tell me to go away if I'm being a nuisance.'

'Don't be silly.' Nick put down his pen. 'I'm always glad of an excuse to stop doing these wretched accounts.'

'I can finish them off, if you like, sir,' Ken Stubbs offered, from his desk at the far end of the office.

'No, thanks, Ken,' said Nicholas crisply. 'I'll see to them myself. I'm not totally incapable, you know!'

'No, sir.' Ken accepted the rebuff, and bent his head over his work.

Jenny continued: 'I wondered if you'd thought any more about going up to town for the Coronation?'

'I can't decide what to do. I quite like the idea of a few days' holiday – after all, Ken's perfectly capable of running the entire operation without me, we all know that...'

Jenny shot her husband a warning glance; he spoke lightly, but there was an edge to his voice, and she felt sure Mr Stubbs must be aware of it.

'On the other hand,' he went on, 'it seems to be rather a lot of fuss for nothing. It's not as if we'd get within miles of Their Majesties; it would be different if we were actually going to see them.' He balanced a ruler on his fingertip, watching it see-saw as he added ruefully, 'It's odd to think that a year ago we were spending a weekend with them – and now I don't suppose we shall ever meet them again.'

'It's nobody's fault – that's the way things happen,' said Jenny. 'I think you're probably right; there's no real reason for us to go to London . . . I shall be quite glad in one way – I was worried about leaving the children.'

The ruler toppled on to the desk with a clatter, and Nick exclaimed angrily, 'For heaven's sake! Don't talk as if we were tied to them, Jenny – they're not our children –'

'I know, but –'

'They're *his* children . . . !'

She looked into his face, and saw for the hundredth time the ghost that still haunted him.

'Nick . . . please,' she said quietly.

He had the grace to look ashamed. 'I'm sorry,' he said. 'Perhaps I'd better get on with these damned accounts after all. We'll talk later.'

Jenny nodded, and went out to look for Harry; at the other end of the room, Ken Stubbs continued his work, without looking up.

On 12 May, Princess Elizabeth was out of bed by five a.m. She had had a restless night, for there was a continuous noise outside; the troops had been arriving to line the streets, and shouts of command pierced the night air. At three, the loudspeakers on the lamp-posts, which would relay the ceremony from the Abbey, were switched on, and a harsh metallic voice boomed out: 'Testing – one, two, three –' over and over again.

Then the band of the Royal Marines struck up, rehearsing under the windows of the Palace – and Lillibet abandoned any idea of sleep.

She sat in the window-seat with an eiderdown wrapped round her, watching the stands in the Mall filling up.

As dawn broke, people studied the sky; they were praying for fine weather, but the forecast was 'changeable'; unbroken cloud gave no hope of sunshine, but at least the rain was holding off, so far.

The West End was soon jammed with sightseers; many people had arrived the day before, to bag their places, and had spent the night on the pavements, wrapped in rugs and sleeping-bags. Only the streets remained empty of traffic.

In Parliament Square, a solitary dog, out for an early morning stroll, broke through the police cordon, and received a friendly cheer from the crowds; and a policeman on a bicycle got an ovation.

Then the nobility began to arrive at Westminster; a few drove up in their own State coaches, and this touch of pageantry was greeted with rapturous acclaim.

Dennett, the Crown House chauffeur, stopped the car exactly at the edge of the red carpet leading into the Abbey; the chrome and bodywork were polished to a dazzling sheen, but as she climbed out, Alice murmured to William, 'I do wish we had a horse-drawn carriage – it seems so out of place to turn up in the dear old Daimler...'

William did not reply; he was too preoccupied with his coronet, which kept slipping down over his ears. He told Dennett to drive on, and gave Alice his arm. Acknowledging the cheering crowds, they walked up the long red carpet and into the building, to take their places. They had a very long wait ahead of them.

Inside Buckingham Palace, Queen Elizabeth was worried; Bertie looked so pale, and the muscle along his jaw had already begun to twitch. He said he couldn't face breakfast; he'd hardly slept a wink all night, and he was feeling queasy.

This state of affairs was made even worse later when, in their coronation robes, they climbed into the golden coach, drawn by eight grey horses, to join the long procession to the Abbey. The coach was very pretty, with its painted panels and gilded cherubs, gods and goddesses supporting the crown; but it was also ancient and extremely uncomfortable, with uneven iron wheels and no shock absorbers.

The little Princesses were ahead of their parents in the procession; a specially raised seat brought Margaret up above the level of the windows, so she could see out – and the people could see her. The two girls smiled and waved, and the crowd roared affectionately, like a friendly lion.

At Crown House, Polly and Jenny were invited into Lady Beatrice's sitting-room to listen to her wireless set.

Norman Brooks had tried to persuade her ladyship to go up to London to see the procession, saying, 'Remember how you enjoyed yourself last time, my lady, when we went up for the Jubilee?'

'I remember very clearly that you lost your way, and we never saw the King and Queen at all,' Old Bea retorted grimly. 'But this is totally different. I've seen coronations before – twice! – but this is the first time a coronation has ever been relayed by wireless. I shall stay here and listen to it in comfort.'

So Norman had to content himself with the celebrations to be held in the servants' hall later; in the evening, many of the staff would attend the Coronation Dance in the village hall, next to the church.

'I'm told Lilian is going with Ken Stubbs,' said Polly, settling down near the loudspeaker.

'Yes, isn't that nice? They seem to have struck up a real friendship,' said Jenny. 'I'm very glad.'

'So am I.' Polly smiled. 'I think I can take a little bit of the credit, too – it was my idea in the first –'

'Sssh!' Old Bea rapped her cane angrily on the floor. 'What's the use of having the wireless on if you girls keep chattering all the while? Do be quiet!'

The BBC commentator was saying in reverential tones: 'Here, inside the sacred precincts of the Abbey, I can see Her Majesty Queen Mary, sitting in the Royal Box, overlooking the nave and chancel. She is accompanied by various members of her family – now she is leaning across to speak to her granddaughters. Their Royal Highnesses look deeply impressed by the dignity of this wonderful occasion.'

In actual fact, Queen Mary was reminding them that they must not fidget, since everyone would be watching them.

Lillibet said at once, 'Don't worry, Grandmama, I'll look after Margaret.' Turning to her little sister, she added firmly, 'Margaret, don't keep swinging your legs like that –'

But her words were drowned as a fanfare of trumpets rang out, echoing under the high, vaulted roof, as a signal that the King and Queen had entered the Abbey.

In the long ceremony that followed, two moments stood out above all the rest. The first was when the Archbishop of Canterbury lifted the St Edward crown high, then placed it upon the King's head – drums rolled, silver trumpets sounded, and the Westminster boys shouted lustily: 'God save the King!' The second climax occurred almost an hour later, when the Queen was crowned, and the bare arms of the assembled peeresses rose in a single movement like a wave breaking, as they put on their coronets. Watching Her Majesty, Alice felt there was a physical change in her appearance: she seemed to lift her head with a new assurance, and there was a calm radiance in her expression which Alice had never seen before.

The long day wore on, and the weather held until after lunch;

when the royal procession returned to the Palace, the first rain began to fall – but by then the crowds were too happy and excited to care about getting wet.

That evening, Alice had been asked to attend upon Queen Mary at the Palace, and Her Majesty had particularly requested that she should bring Lord Minster, whom she had not seen for so many years. William felt a little more comfortable once he had shed his ceremonial robes, but he fingered his white tie and complained to Alice in an undertone that his collar was too tight.

Waiting in an anteroom, they heard the sound of lively chatter in the corridor; a moment later the King and Queen came in with their daughters, followed by the rest of their family, all talking over the day's events.

'...As for that bishop standing behind me, I could have k-k-kicked him!' said His Majesty cheerfully. 'At the very moment the c-c-crown was placed on my head, the silly duffer was standing on my train, pinning me to the floor – I told him to get off pretty smartly, before I fell down...!'

Princess Elizabeth looked up at her mother, saying, 'I thought Margaret was very good really – I only had to nudge her once or twice when she played with the prayer-books too loudly.'

Lady Flora Kelso touched Queen Mary's arm, pointing out Lord and Lady Minster, who stood to one side, waiting; Her Majesty came over to them immediately, so that William might be presented to her. As soon as the King and Queen saw Alice, they crossed the room to join them, and William was presented again.

Alice noticed a red mark on Queen Elizabeth's forehead, where the heavy crown had rubbed it, and said. 'You must be very tired, Ma'am.'

'Not a bit – we don't look it, do we?' asked the Queen, with a smile. 'We're trying so hard to do it well!'

Then the Royal Family moved out on to the floodlit balcony, and the roar of the crowd rolled over them like thunder.

Some time before eight o'clock, an equerry reminded the King that it was time for him to make his broadcast to the nation, and he went away to a small private office. It was a great ordeal, even though the Queen had gone over his speech with him, revising the words here and there to avoid any awkward consonants. But the job had to be done; his people expected it.

He took a sip of water, and when the signal was given, he began:

'It is with a very full heart that I speak to you tonight. Never before has a newly crowned King been able to talk to all his people in their own homes, on the day of his Coronation...'

The first paragraph alone had three unavoidable hurdles – 'crowned', 'King' and 'Coronation' - but he took a deep breath and cleared them all triumphantly. As the speech continued, his voice became clear and confident, and he reached his final words safely: '...I thank you from my heart – and may God bless you all.'

When the King returned to the anteroom, Elizabeth threw her arms round him, and congratulated him: 'You did it splendidly – we all thought so.'

His Majesty smiled shyly, looking almost boyish, and said, 'You must thank Mr Weyman – I couldn't have got through it without his help.'

William stiffened and looked at Alice as Paul followed the King into the room. His Majesty insisted that he deserved a glass of champagne for his efforts, saying, 'This poor chap's been slaving away all day – just like us. He was in charge of the television broadcast this afternoon, and then they dragged him away to come and steer me through this evening's little effort.'

By now the noise of the crowds outside was almost deafening, and he added, 'I think they're trying to tell us it's time for some more waving... Come on – let's go!'

Queen Elizabeth hung back for a moment, saying to Paul, 'I'm sorry we have to desert you, Mr Weyman – we shan't be very long. If you are hungry, there are plenty of sandwiches – do help yourself.' Seeing Alice at the other side of the room, she said, 'I'm leaving you in good company – I think you met Lady Minster, at our old house in Piccadilly...' then she followed the others on to the balcony.

The Minsters were left alone with Paul. After a long silence, he went over to them and said, 'I suppose it would make things easier if I simply walked out, but I can't very well do that. I'm sorry.'

'You said you wouldn't be responsible for any more royal broadcasts,' Alice reminded him.

'I shouldn't have been; but His Majesty specially asked for me, since I was the only BBC man he knew. I've been working flat out, ever since the crack of dawn, supervising our television unit at Hyde Park Corner.'

'I hope it went off well?' said Alice politely.

'Very well, thank you. The Director-General was delighted. He's here tonight, I believe; you'll probably meet him.'

William had said nothing, and they were very conscious of his silence. At last he cleared his throat and asked Paul, 'Have you heard from Caroline?'

'No, not directly. As far as I know she's still in Spain.'

'We were getting rather anxious. There haven't been any bulletins from her in the paper for weeks,' Alice said.

'That's because she's not working for the *Argus* any longer – didn't you know? She threw up the job, apparently; but she stayed on in Spain. I don't know what she's doing now.'

'How did you hear that?' William asked.

'I have contacts in Fleet Street – I made enquiries.' Paul put down his champagne glass. 'Whatever you may think of me, I still love her, you see. I always will.'

'I still don't know why you quarrelled –' Alice began.

'We didn't quarrel. You might as well know ... She found out – about the twins ...'

William drew in his breath as if he were in pain. 'You *told* her?'

'She saw me – and Martin – together ... She recognized some sort of resemblance, and guessed the truth. After that, she didn't want anything more to do with me ... I thought you should be prepared, the next time you see her.'

Alice said huskily, 'After what you have told us – I don't imagine she will want to see us.'

William clenched his fists, and Alice put a restraining hand on his arm as the french windows reopened and the royal party returned.

Queen Mary came towards them, smiling, 'It has begun to rain again, but nobody seems to mind – they are all so happy tonight.' Then her expression changed to one of concern. 'Why – Lord Minster – what is the matter? Are you not feeling well?'

Before he could speak, Alice cut in quickly, 'William is rather tired, Ma'am – I think, if you will be kind enough to excuse us, we should go home now. It has been a long day for all of us.'

Time stood still for Caroline. Life went on at Villa Paz, and one day followed another without any variation.

Was this really why she had left home – had thrown up her job in England – just to go through the numbing drudgery of hospital routine? She felt completely helpless, and for the first time in her life she did not know what to do; she did not even know what she wanted to do any more.

Spain had shown her another side of the fight for freedom, and she did not like what she had seen. Though her political ideals were as strong as ever, she no longer believed that the revolution would be brought about by this grim, relentless war which dragged on and on; in her heart she knew that the men who claimed to be in charge of the Brigade were liars. The whole thing was out of control now – and there was nothing she could do about that. At least she was of some use at Villa Paz; she tried not to think about the future, but carried on with her daily chores. She slept, she worked, she ate, she slept again – and she scarcely noticed the months going by.

'It's midsummer tomorrow,' said the red-haired nurse from the Bronx, as they worked together in the linen-room.

'Is it? How do you know?'

'On account of there's some kind of party tonight in the village – dancing, bonfires, plenty of hooch. Most of the girls are going. How about you?'

'I don't think I'll bother.'

'Jeez – it's better than staying here all the time. We'll have a few laughs, maybe – why don't you tag along?'

'Perhaps. I'll see how I feel.'

The truth was, she felt nothing. After Don's funeral, life seemed to have no meaning whatever.

They shook out another freshly laundered sheet, and began to fold it between them – sides to middle, once, twice, and then they moved towards one another, doubling it twice more, as if they were following the pattern of an ancient ritual. Suddenly Caroline noticed an elaborate crest at one corner, embroidered in white silk.

'Where did these sheets come from?'

'Search me. They're a new lot some guy brought in the other day. Most of the big houses round here are empty now. Someone broke in and took them, I guess.'

Caro traced the fine silken crest with her finger, imagining the family it had once belonged to – and remembering another family, back in England. For the first time, she felt a pang of homesickness. With a sigh, she put aside the folded sheet, and took up the next one.

As they went on with their work, footsteps clattered along the passage, and Freddy Martin, unusually formal in a stiffly starched uniform, ushered in a stranger. She introduced him to the girls; his name was Darrell, and he was a member of a political commission organized by the British Communist Party, on a tour of inspection.

Caro had heard rumours that the International Brigade, dismayed after a series of defeats at the hands of the Falangists, were putting the blame on traitors within their ranks. No doubt this inspection was part of a general enquiry.

Mr Darrell had a thin, pencil-line moustache, and a sallow complexion; he seemed to be in a bad temper.

'Why do you keep such a big staff here, Matron?' he asked. 'Why not break them up into smaller groups and send them into the battle zone?'

'We couldn't send enough supplies and equipment with them,' Freddy pointed out. 'It makes more sense to keep this hospital fully staffed, ready for any emergency.'

He sniffed, unconvinced, and began to question the girls. As soon as he heard Caro's accent, he pounced.

'*You're* not American,' he said accusingly. 'Where do you come from?'

'From London,' said Caro. 'I was working at the International office in Barcelona. Then I volunteered to help the staff here, instead.'

'Who gave you permission to come here?' said Mr Darrell. 'What's your name?'

'Gaunt – Caroline Gaunt.'

He looked deeply suspicious, and said, 'Show me your passport.'

She opened her handbag and gave it to him. Too late, she remembered that it still had her press pass inside it.

'*Lady* Caroline Gaunt,' he read aloud. 'Very impressive, I must say... I notice you have no entry visa. How did you get into Spain? Which frontier-post did you come through? When was that?'

'Le Perthus,' she lied. 'It was some time in January... I don't know why they didn't stamp my passport – there was some sort of muddle. May I have it back please?'

He ignored her, flicking over the pages, and then came across the press pass. 'The *Daily Argus*? So you're a journalist?' His eyes narrowed. 'You were sent out to spy on our activities. Everyone knows the *Argus* is a pro-Franco publication. You're here under false pretences!'

Freddy Martin tried to intervene, but he waved her aside. 'Leave this to me. This woman is a member of the British upper classes, and a paid informer of the capitalist press. I shall take her back with me to the Karl Marx barracks in Barcelona – for questioning.'

20

THURSDAY, 1 JULY TO SATURDAY, 31 JULY 1937

THERE was a crack on the wall above the iron bedstead. Caro had thought at first that it was a spider's web. She rather hoped there might be a spider still resident in it: at least that would give her a living creature as a cell-mate. Looking closer, she discovered that it was only a patch of damp which had seeped through the wall, cracking the paint into small, delicate flakes, curling up from the plaster: so even that chance of companionship was denied her.

Perhaps it was an exaggeration to describe the room as a cell: it had been used as sleeping-quarters for a sergeant in the International Brigade. There were no bars at the grimy window, but as the room was on the fourth floor, with a sheer drop to the parade-ground below, there was no possibility of escape that way; and the door was always kept locked.

Caro was let out of the room to go to the lavatory, across the corridor; there she took a shower once a day, under primitive conditions. The only other time she left the room was when she was taken to Mr Darrell's office every afternoon.

Darrell soon discovered that she had lied about entering Spain at the frontier-post; she admitted she had been refused an entry-visa, and had simply walked across the mountains, though she pretended she had made the journey alone as she did not want to involve anyone else.

Apart from that, she had told the absolute truth; from her first visit to the Communist Party office in Covent Garden to the moment when she had been removed from Villa Paz and brought to the Karl Marx barracks.

Darrell refused to believe her, and kept asking the same old questions again and again, to which she gave the same replies. They had reached deadlock.

She was beginning to feel frightened, for she could see no way out of this routine; the days and nights dragged by hopelessly.

After she had been there a week, the door opened one morning, and Mr Darrell walked in, accompanied by a stranger: a youngish man, bearded and red-haired, who spoke with an American accent.

The beard was unfamiliar, but the voice was not: she leaped to her feet, exclaiming, '*Scott!*' and burst into tears.

Scott Hanson put his arms round her, saying quickly and quietly, 'OK, honey – leave this to me.' Then he turned to Darrell, and said, 'This is outrageous. How dare you treat Caroline Gaunt as an enemy? She's loyal to the cause and always has been. She worked for me at one time – I can vouch for her.'

'That's all very well...' Darrell scratched his jaw. 'We knew nothing about her, except that she comes from a titled family –'

'Hogwash! I'm telling you Caroline's OK; I'm taking her out of this dump right now.'

'I'm afraid it's not as simple as that, Mr Hanson. I haven't the authority to release her. I shall have to apply to Head Office for instructions.'

'Ye gods – is that really necessary? OK – you call Head Office. I'll stay with Caroline till you get back.'

Darrell hesitated, then said, 'I warn you, this may take some time. The telephone system has been very unreliable lately.'

'We'll wait.'

Darrell went out, closing the door behind him. Caroline dried her eyes, and said shakily, 'What are you doing here? How did you find me?'

'I'm reporting on the war for the magazine – and I send despatches back to the States. I went to Villa Paz, and Freddy Martin told me what had happened – but we can't talk now. Let's get going.'

'What? You said we'd wait until –'

'I was lying. I know these bureaucratic little jerks. He could take all day getting through to Head Office – and when he does, there's no knowing what they'll decide. I'm not taking any chances.'

'But I haven't got my bag – my passport – they took them away when I was brought in.'

'Forget it – come on!'

As an international journalist of the left, Scott Hanson had authority and influence: they walked downstairs and out of the building without being stopped. At the main gates, two sentries sprang to attention, giving the clenched-fist salute. Scott returned it, then took Caroline to the cab-rank at the end of the street. One old taxi waited there, its driver sitting on the running-board, picking his teeth. At their approach, he sprang up and opened the door.

'*Estacion Francia*,' said Scott, as they climbed in.

'Where are we going?' asked Caro.

'The railroad-station, to catch the next train. I'm taking you out of this country before you land yourself in any more trouble, so don't argue!'

'There's the shopping-list – and don't forget the toilet-rolls, whatever you do,' Lilian Brooks concluded. 'The stores will have everything ready for you, but you'd better check the items.'

'Anybody'd think I was a perishing errand-boy,' grumbled Norman.

They were in the servants' hall, and Norman was wearing his chauffeur's uniform, ready to drive Lady Beatrice into Medford for her daily outing.

'You might just as well pick up the shopping while you're there. It saves Dennett having to go,' Lilian pointed out. 'Lady Beatrice said it was all right.'

'She would... She don't care what she makes me do. I wish I'd never taken this blasted job –' He broke off sheepishly; Jenny had joined them, overhearing his last remarks.

'I'm afraid there's one more errand,' she said. 'A jar of cod-liver oil and malt, for the children – would you add it to the list, please?'

'Yes'm,' he muttered sulkily.

Jenny felt a little sorry for him. At twenty, Norman was a strong, well-built young man; small wonder that he found his post as dogsbody to Old Bea unsatisfying.

'Cheer up,' she added. 'If you're so fed up, why not give in your notice and take a job somewhere as a mechanic?'

'I can't,' he said. 'Her ladyship'd never let me go.'

'Don't let her bully you, Norman; it's a free country.'

'I wish it was,' he muttered. 'She'd stop me all right – she's got ways... I'd better go; she don't like being kept waiting.'

As he walked out, Lilian clucked disapprovingly: 'He should think himself lucky! But there – he always was a difficult boy. Was there anything else, madam?'

'Perhaps we could go through the weekend menus with Cook, if this is a good moment,' Jenny began – then said in a different tone, 'Why, Lilian – what a beautiful ring... I never saw you wearing that before.'

Lilian blushed and smiled. 'No, madam... We only got it yesterday – it's an engagement ring. Mr Stubbs has asked me to marry him.'

The news soon went round Crown House. At lunchtime, Jenny told Polly – and after lunch Polly called at the farm office. She found Ken on his own, totting up the monthly milk-yield.

'I won't hold you up if you're busy,' she said, 'but I had to come and congratulate you.'

'Never too busy to talk to you, ma'am – you know that.' Ken pulled out a chair for her. 'What's all this about congratulations? Don't tell me we've won a prize for our pigs at the show, after all?'

'I meant your engagement. I only just heard – I'm so pleased.'

'Oh – that.' He turned away, and seemed a little discomfited. 'Yes – me and Lilian have got an understanding, as you might say. But it's going to be a long engagement. We're neither of us the type to rush into things.'

'I'm really glad. I had a hunch things might work out for you both.'

'Yes, well – it was you put the idea in my head in the first place – we owe it all to you really.' Ken moved to the window and threw it open; summer sunshine lay across the fields, and somewhere a blackbird was singing. 'Anyhow – they've got a nice day for the show. Mr Nicholas has gone to enter a couple of our pigs for the judging.'

'Yes, Jenny told me. She's taking the children over this afternoon, to help him carry home the silver cup!'

'I don't know so much about that; we might manage a rosette, perhaps.' Ken gave Polly a sidelong glance. 'I'm surprised you didn't go with them.'

She shrugged. 'I didn't feel like it. I don't go out much.'

'So I noticed. Funny, really – you were the one who encouraged me to get out more.' She said nothing, and he went on quietly, 'I'm sure your children would have liked it too. They don't see a lot of you, do they?'

'Oh, they're very happy with Jenny; she's marvellous with them.' Now it was Polly's turn to feel uncomfortable. 'I'm hopeless with kids. In fact, I'm pretty useless all round! I told you that, ages ago.'

'I wish you wouldn't keep running yourself down like that,' he said. 'I still think you'd be happier if you found yourself a job to do... You're bright enough, goodness knows. You'd soon pick it up, whatever it was.' He looked abashed. 'I hope you don't mind me speaking my mind.'

'You don't seem to realize – I'm no good at anything.'

'You're good with people,' he told her. 'You're very understanding – look how you helped me and Lilian.'

'Yes, but you can't make a living out of –' She stopped dead, as an extraordinary thought occurred to her.

'Yes?' He urged her on.

'Nothing really... It's just – I think p'raps you've given me an idea, Mr Stubbs,' she said. 'I wonder...'

The journey from Barcelona to the French border took several hours, and it was dusk by the time the train pulled into the station at Port-Bou. Most of the passengers were going on to France, and stayed on board while the frontier police and customs officers went through the train.

'What shall I do?' asked Caroline. 'I've got no passport; suppose they send me back to Barcelona?'

'Let me do the talking,' said Scott.

Two Spanish officials in peaked caps came into the compartment, checked Scott's passport, and gave his suitcase a cursory examination. Then they turned to Caroline. Before she could say anything, Scott took charge of the situation.

'This is Lady Caroline Gaunt,' he said. 'I am escorting her back to England. She has been robbed: her luggage was stolen in Barcelona, and the thieves also took her handbag and her passport. We are now on our way to London, where we shall make the strongest possible protest, through the Foreign Office, to the Spanish Ambassador.'

The two officials looked at one another. 'This lady will please come with us. You will kindly leave the train.'

'This lady is staying right where she is,' said Scott.

He proceeded to make a long and impassioned speech, gradually working himself up into a towering rage. He pulled out copies of his articles in *Tomorrow* magazine, and some American newspapers with his photograph printed beside the by-line. He explained that he had readers all over the English-speaking world, who would be furiously indignant at the humiliations which had been heaped upon Lady Caroline Gaunt. He repeated that he was taking her ladyship to London immediately, and that they must not leave the train, or they might miss their connections in Paris and on the Channel ferry: he went on to describe in detail the noble lineage of Lady Caroline's family, and spoke reverently of her parents, the Earl and Countess of Minster – both of whom happened to be close personal friends of the King and Queen of England. He stressed that unless her ladyship were permitted to continue her journey without further interference, there would be an international crisis which would result in the severing of all diplomatic relations between Spain and the United Kingdom. He wound up this tirade by saying that those responsible for insulting the British Royal Family – or their intimate friends – would be made to suffer; and hinted that heads would undoubtedly roll.

By the time he had finished, the officers were sweating profusely; they backed out of the compartment, touching their caps.

'Tell the engine driver we can't wait any longer!' Scott shouted after them; and the train moved majestically on, into the tunnel that separated Port Bou from Cerbère, on the French side of the border.

Caroline did not know whether to laugh or cry. She turned on Scott reproachfully: 'You're supposed to be a Communist. How could you be such a terrible snob? I've never been so embarrassed in my life!'

'Honey – I would have said anything to get you out of that jam,' he retorted. 'I was prepared to say you're a direct descendant of Queen Isabella *and* Christopher Columbus... But I warn you – the French may not be quite so impressed. They got rid of their royalty a long time ago.'

When they reached the railway station at Cerbère, Scott adopted very different tactics. He explained concisely that Lady Caroline's luggage and passport had been stolen, and that the Spanish authorities had taken full responsibility for this outrage, which was why the frontier-guards had waived the usual formalities, and permitted Lady Caroline to leave the country. He offered them all cigarettes, and made little jokes; he was charming, unruffled and totally at his ease.

The French guards looked suspicious, and asked them both to

wait, saying they must telephone their Spanish colleagues in Port-Bou for further details of this unfortunate incident.

Then they trooped into the passport office, and could be heard arguing amongst themselves.

'What's going to happen?' asked Caro.

Scott looked along the platform, which was deserted. By now, even the station staff had gone into the office to find out what was happening; everyone was enjoying the unexpected crisis, which promised to enliven an otherwise boring evening. Beyond the open ticket-barrier, the lights along the sea-front began to twinkle, one by one.

'I think,' said Scott cautiously, 'this would be a good moment to get the hell out of here . . .'

He picked up his suitcase, and they walked out of the station, into the night.

Cerbère was not much more than a village, but because of its situation on the border, it contained several hotels. Scott led the way to an area just off the waterfront, where the cheapest hotels were huddled together in a maze of narrow streets. Two or three girls lounged under a street-lamp, talking and laughing.

'This will do,' said Scott.

Five minutes later they were upstairs in a back room, with a tin basin on the washstand, and a tin *bidet* underneath it; and one double bed with brass knobs at each corner. An elderly chambermaid showed them in, and gave a knowing smile as she left them together.

'Is this a brothel?' asked Caro, interested.

'Something damn near it. I knew they wouldn't ask for our passports in a place like this,' said Scott. 'You have the bed – it's not exactly de luxe, but it looks comfortable . . . I'll take the armchair.'

'Why?' asked Caro.

'I'm being chivalrous,' he explained. 'Otherwise I'd suggest we toss for it.'

'You're being very silly,' Caro told him. 'It's a nice big bed – don't you think there's room for two of us?'

'Well . . . this has been a pretty exhausting day,' he said. 'OK, then – I guess we both need a good night's sleep.'

That night, Nicholas held Jenny in his arms. She surrendered to the urgent demands of his mouth upon her, and his hands moved over her body.

'Mmmm... You smell of Pears soap,' she said.

'I'm not surprised – I had to scrub myself clean. Think yourself lucky I'm not still smelling of pigs!' he said, nuzzling her ear.

'I'm not complaining,' she whispered. 'I remember when your lips tasted of the sea – salty and exciting.'

He grunted. 'Don't remind me... A day at an agricultural show isn't exactly a thrill a minute, is it?'

'Your best boar won a prize,' she said. '*That* was exciting.'

'Second prize,' he corrected her. 'Oh, Lord – I suppose one day I'll get used to all this.'

'Used to all what?'

'Going to work in a little office, coming home for lunch every day, adding up columns of figures, and ordering cattle-cake... I never thought my life would end up like this.'

'End up?' She tried to laugh him out of his mood. 'You're talking like an old man!'

'Sometimes I feel like an old man.'

'What nonsense! You're only thirty – we've got our whole lives ahead of us.'

'A lifetime of account-books and cattle-cake? Thanks very much.' He shifted restlessly. 'I wish I could make you understand... When I left the Navy, I thought I'd done the right thing – because of Pa's heart attack – but it was a big mistake. Look at Ken Stubbs. He knows a hundred times more about estate management than I ever will; he could run the farm on his own. I wish we'd looked for someone like Ken years ago, after...'

She finished the sentence for him: 'After Richard died?'

'Yes... Everything comes back to Richard, doesn't it? That's when it all started to go wrong.'

'Nick – I do understand. But you're overlooking one thing. When you were at sea, you never came home for months on end. This way, we're together all the time: that counts for something, doesn't it?'

He gripped her tightly, beginning to make love to her: 'Yes... Yes, I suppose it does...'

'You know it does.' She responded to him willingly. 'This is the best thing of all – the very best...'

'Is it? Is it really?'

Something in his voice sent a chill through her. His movements were mechanical, his words hard and unloving.

'Am I the very best, Jenny? Or do you lie in my arms, trying to imagine I'm someone else? Trying to pretend he's still here?'

'No! Don't say that –'

'Tell me the truth... You still think of him when we make love, don't you? I know you do – I can tell – afterwards, I can see that look in your eyes, and I know you're remembering... What did he do that was so special? Tell me all about it, show me what he did... Teach me how Richard made love, then perhaps one day I'll be as good as he was – show me how you like to –'

'*Stop it!*' She pulled away from him. 'Nicholas – don't say things like that; it's not true. None of it's true... How can you think of anything so horrible – so hateful?'

'Horrible and hateful – is that what I am? ... Well, now we know.' He turned away from her. 'Perhaps we'd better get some sleep.'

At the hotel, Scott and Caroline were talking in the dark. Neither of them had any night-clothes – Scott never wore pyjamas anyway – so they had gone to bed in their underwear: Caro wore a plain cotton slip, and Scott a pair of shorts and an undershirt. They lay on their backs, leaving a space between them, taking care not to touch one another accidentally.

They had been talking for a long time about the Civil War, and the Spanish situation. Scott had become increasingly disillusioned as he toured the battle areas; Franco's Army, backed up by reserves from Germany and Italy, was incomparably stronger and more efficient than the gallant, disorganized Brigade.

'There's no real leadership,' he said. 'Don't get me wrong – I'm as convinced as ever that Communism is the only answer – but we're no match for the warmongers. They're trained to kill for what they want – and we're not. They're properly disciplined and equipped; for every man we send into the front line, there are a dozen back at base, arguing with one another, trying to wage war by committee, and it doesn't work... I never said this to anyone else, but – the Republicans haven't got a hope in hell. The Falangists are running our guys ragged; eventually they'll wipe us out.'

Caroline agreed sadly: 'Don told me things – when he was in hospital, in the weeks before he died – he made me see what a mess it was. I used to think we were on some glorious crusade, and so we were, in a way. But now it's turning into a glorious failure.'

'Madrid can't hold out much longer. Then it's only a matter of time before Barcelona collapses as well. We were right to get out;

we couldn't have done any good by staying on.'

They lay side by side, thinking unhappy thoughts. At last Scott said: 'Funny – I thought I'd fall asleep the minute my head hit the pillow, and here we are, still talking.'

'I'm wide awake too,' said Caro. 'I suppose it's because there's so much to say – and we haven't seen each other for so long.'

Scott asked tentatively: 'This guy Don Carpenter... You met him after you left Paul Weyman – right?'

'Yes, I did, though I first met him five years ago, in Scotland.'

'Sure – you said. But you never told me if...'

'If what?'

'Maybe I don't have the right to ask, but – were you and Carpenter – I mean, did you ever –'

'Were we lovers? No, it was never like that.'

'Ah...' He gave a small sigh. 'Thanks for telling me.'

'Did you imagine I jumped into bed with every man I meet?' she asked.

'Of course not.'

'You might have thought so. That time you came to Eaton Square, I behaved very badly.'

'No... I was sorry I – I couldn't go along with – I mean –'

'I thought I was in love with you, and I assumed you must be attracted to me too. But I'm not such a fool now; don't worry – I shan't throw myself at you again.'

The bed-springs creaked, and she felt him roll over to face her.

'One thing you didn't realize,' he said. 'I didn't chicken out that night because I wasn't attracted... I was – very much. But you were nine years younger than me, and so innocent. It wouldn't have been fair.'

She turned to face him: 'Are you trying to tell me you *wanted* to...?'

'Of course I did. I wanted you like hell. I guess I was trying to do the honourable thing.'

'Oh, Scott – you idiot...' Her mouth felt dry; she asked in a whisper: 'Do you still want me?'

He did not reply: suddenly she was in his arms, and he was kissing her. They could not speak; for a long time they held one another, they they began gently to undress each other, and when at last they found the words to say, the words were completely banal – and it didn't matter at all.

'I love you, I love you,' they repeated, again and again; and they began to laugh at the absurdity of it all, and the joy and the wonder.

'Those sweet-williams are really lovely,' said Edith.

On her knees beside the flower-bed, Grace pulled out another weed, saying, 'Yes, they're doing well. But then everything does well in this climate – the weeds are thriving too!' Looking up at Lady Edith, she scolded her gently: 'You're not wearing your hat. If you sit out here with nothing on your head, you'll be getting one of those headaches again.'

Obediently, Edith crammed the straw hat on her head, pushing back the long, loose grey hair that fell to her shoulders. 'Very well, dear. I thought I'd make some preliminary sketches for a little picture of the garden; it looks so wonderful, this summer.'

Grace sat back on her heels, looking over the display of flowers with quiet satisfaction. 'Isn't it strange? I never took much interest in gardening before, but now I've grown quite fond of it.'

Edith smiled. 'You're a gardening fanatic, like my brother! I always think of him when I see the sweet-williams; that border reminds me of home.'

They had chosen to create an English garden under the white-washed walls of Mas-Lou. Only a shaggy palm tree, the flourishing mimosa, and a clump of aloes, their tall seed-heads rearing up like telegraph-poles above fleshy jungle leaves, were native to the Catalan landscape; the herbaceous borders had been grown from seed ordered by post, the seedlings planted out lovingly under the Mediterranean sky – clarkia and alyssum, zinnias and candytuft, and sweet-smelling double stocks.

'You're not getting a wee bit homesick, perhaps?' Grace suggested.

'Oh, no – never. I think about Crown House sometimes – and the family – but I'd never want to go back. We've been so happy; I didn't know what life could be, till we came here.'

It was three years since they first stumbled upon Mas-Lou. It had been a long, difficult quest – tracing the owners of the tumbledown property and making an offer for it, and the interminable wrangles with the estate agents, the local authorities and a series of notaries. At last the deeds were handed over; and then the next stage began: the struggle to restore the semi-derelict cottage and reclaim the patch of land from the wilderness.

They were fortunate to find an ally in the person of Maria, a plump, nut-brown widow with shining black hair, who came in to help with the back-breaking work. Maria had an extensive family in the village; there was always a handy brother-in-law or a second cousin to open up the old well, and supply them with water, to knock down a broken wall and build a new one, to replace lost tiles and re-hang the doors.

At last the little house was ready for them to move in. Three days a week, Maria cooked and cleaned for them; the rest of the time they fended for themselves. They were never bored; they never got tired of each other's company; and they were never lonely. When they walked down the stony path into Collioure, the shopkeepers and fishermen hailed them as friends. They were known as the 'English misses' – undoubtedly mad, but pleasantly harmless.

As Edith set up her easel and opened her box of water-colours, they heard Maria calling them from the house. A moment later she appeared in the arched doorway, her face alive with excitement.

'*Qu'est que c'est?*' asked Grace.

Before Maria could explain that they had visitors, Scott and Caroline emerged from the dark interior and stood blinking in the sunlight.

For a moment, Edith did not recognize her niece. Then she gave a cry of delight and sprang to her feet, upsetting the jar of paint-water and scattering her brushes.

'Caroline!'

She ran up the path, and hugged her joyfully; Grace followed more slowly.

'Aunt Edith – Grace – it's so good to see you. You're both looking so well! You remember Scott, don't you? Scott Hanson?'

'Of course.' They shook hands; but with a hint of reserve. The ladies could not quite forget that Scott was Gina's brother, and the memory of Gina's attempt to disrupt their domestic situation still rankled, after all these years.

'But what are you doing here?' Edith asked Caro. 'The last time William wrote, he said you were in Spain. We were so worried; one hears such dreadful things about the air-raids...'

'I was in Spain until yesterday; Scott helped me to get away – I've no money or passport or anything. Last night we stayed at a hotel in Cerbère...' She glanced at Scott, then went on: 'I don't know what I'd have done, if he hadn't rescued me... And this morning, when we left the hotel, I saw a signpost that said "Collioure – twenty kilometres", so we caught a bus, and here we are!'

'We're lying low at present,' Scott explained, 'on account of Caro crossing over into France illegally. I guess we'll have to come clean and tell the authorities sooner or later, but for the time being –'

'For the time being, you'll stay here,' said Edith firmly. 'There's nothing to worry about. Tomorrow I shall take Caroline to meet the British Consul in Perpignan; such a nice man – he's always been very helpful whenever we've had any little problems.'

'But tonight we shall celebrate – you're the first real guests we've had, since we moved in,' added Grace. 'I shall tell Maria we want a very special dinner.'

'And I'll show you to your rooms,' said Edith. 'It's a small cottage, but there's one spare bedroom ... Scott, perhaps you won't mind if we make up a bed for you on the sitting-room sofa?'

'Of course – that's perfectly OK,' he said, with a quick look at Caro.

As they made their way into the house, she asked, 'Do you hear from Daddy often? How is he? and Ma – and everybody?'

'They're very well. Your father seems to be making a good recovery; he says he's begun gardening again – that's a good sign.'

That night Maria made a huge bouillabaisse, and Grace opened two bottles of rough, red wine from the nearby Corbières hills, which suited it very well: she offered to fetch a third bottle from the cellar, but the visitors said they were sleepy already, and took themselves off to their respective beds.

Grace and Edith shared the principal bedroom, overlooking the garden; as Edith sat in her nightdress at the dressing-table, brushing her hair, Grace gazed out at the stars, and smelled the night-scented stocks beneath the window.

'They're so much in love,' she said.

'Caro and Scott? What makes you think so?' Edith asked.

'You mean you'd not noticed? Didn't you see the way they look at each other? It's written all over their faces.' Grace sighed. 'I'm glad to say he doesn't take after his sister. Imagine her leaving Sir Charles like that, and then running off to Germany with some young man. She always was a flighty creature; she'll come to no good, mark my words ... But Scott's a different kettle of fish altogether. I hope he'll make Caroline happy.'

'You can't be sure they're in love,' Edith objected.

'You think not? Ssh! Listen...'

They both heard the sound of the stairs creaking at the far end of the landing; a door swung softly open, then closed again as quietly.

'Now do you believe me?' said Grace.

'I suppose so... How very nice. Our first visitors – happy together – just like us.' Edith put down the hairbrush and stood up.

'Lady Edith, you take my breath away! There was a time you'd have been shocked at such goings on,' Grace teased her.

'Well – I've learned a good deal since those days.' Edith turned back the sheets of the big double-bed. 'But then... I had a very good teacher.'

William spread out a sheet of graph-paper, and said, 'Now we can begin.'

He was sitting on the terrace with Jenny, their chairs drawn up at a white iron table: a pile of gardening catalogues was at his elbow, and a box of coloured pencils at his right hand.

Seeing the pencils, Alex and Harry had pestered their grandfather to be allowed to join in, until Jenny diverted them with a game; now they were off on a treasure-hunt, to see how many different petals they could find – no more than one from each plant – with a promise of lollipop prizes if they brought back more than fifty. She watched them flitting like butterflies from one clump of flowers to another, down the long walk, and smiled. 'At least we should have a few minutes of peace and quiet.'

'We'll need more than that,' William told her. 'It wasn't till I started making the list yesterday evening that I realized how many different herbs there are.'

He had decided that Crown House needed a herb-garden; and he had enlisted Jenny's help. The real work wouldn't begin until the autumn, when the beds could be dug and the soil prepared for planting out in the spring. But these were the preliminary stages, and he was full of ideas.

'I'm going to draw a plan,' he explained. 'A circular pattern, with wedge-shaped beds radiating from a sundial in the centre, like the spokes of a wheel. To start with, I'd like you to read out the different species, and I'll try to find places for them all... You're sure you can spare the time, Jenny? I don't want to impose on you if you're busy.'

'I shall enjoy it,' she said truthfully. 'It's a long while since we sat and planned the garden together.'

'It'll be like the old days ... Now Martin and Miranda are home for the holidays, I thought of asking them if they'd care to help. But I don't really think gardening appeals to them. Anyway, they won't be here next year, to see the plan come to life.'

The twins had made a good showing in their final exams at school. Their future had been decided: Martin was to follow in his Uncle Nicholas's footsteps and go to Oxford in October, taking up a place at Wadham – and Miranda would be sent to a finishing-school in the French Alps.

'Time goes so quickly nowadays.' William screwed up his eyes, watching Alex and Harriet playing in the sunshine. 'It's hard to remember the twins are nearly grown-up; I still think of them as children ... But it's a mistake to look back – we must think ahead, and make plans. What are the first names on the list?'

Jenny read aloud: 'Angelica ... balm ... basil ... bay.'

'Angelica – I know nothing about that, except Cook sometimes sticks it on top of fancy puddings, and it's rather sickly. I've no idea what it looks like in the raw! Balm – that's in the garden already – lemon-balm, anyway. I might take some cuttings ... Basil – that will be in the vegetable-garden, along with mint and parsley and sage, for cooking purposes; but they deserve a place in the new plan. And I believe rosemary makes an effective hedge – I shall definitely want some rosemary. Make a note, will you?'

'We haven't got that far down the list,' Jenny pointed out.

'Sorry – my mind jumps from one thing to another these days; I'm getting absent-minded, I'm afraid. All the more reason to plant rosemary – that's for remembrance, isn't it?'

Jenny put a ring round the word 'rosemary' further down the page.

'Sometimes remembrance can be dangerous,' she murmured. 'You were right – we mustn't look back at the past ...'

William was aware of something in her tone, and tried to interpret it: 'You sound as if the past made you unhappy?'

'It does, sometimes.'

'Yes ... When we think of people we loved, who have gone ... Your mother – and Richard –'

'Please don't talk about Richard!' Jenny exclaimed, before she could stop herself.

The words broke from her with such feeling that William put

down the coloured pencils, and said, 'I'm sorry. Have I upset you?'

'It's not your fault...' Jenny choked back her tears, determined not to cry. 'It's only – I try not to think about Richie... But Nicholas never lets me forget him.'

'Nicholas?' William frowned. 'I wasn't going to say anything, but I couldn't help noticing – you and Nicholas don't seem as close as you were... Is there something wrong?'

Jenny felt she was being disloyal to Nick, but William had always been wise and comforting – and she needed desperately to confide in somebody... Averting her face, she answered, 'Nick has never got over the fact that – before I loved him – I loved Richard.'

William put his hand upon hers. 'My dear...'

'It's something we have to work out for ourselves. I keep hoping we shall. I keep thinking it will get better as time goes on, but it doesn't: it seems to get worse. Nicholas is so jealous of Richard – and there's nothing I can do about it. I can't go back and wipe out the past. I wish I could: and I can't make him understand how much I love him.. Richard was the first – and he can never forgive me for that.'

'But surely, he must understand –'

She interrupted him: 'The children are coming back – I shouldn't have told you. Promise me you won't say anything to Nick: it would only make things worse.'

'Very well,' he said reluctantly. 'I promise.'

Then the children ran up the steps, laughing, their hands full of brightly coloured petals – and the moment was over.

Gina pushed the plate of cream cakes across the table. 'Go on, spoil yourself, honey. Have another one.'

Unity Mitford giggled. 'Do you think I should? Oh, well – perhaps just one more. But then I must positively stop – it would be simply too shaming if I started getting fat... The Führer disapproves of big girls.'

She bit deeply into an éclair, not realizing that it left a smudge of chocolate and whipped cream on her cheek. Gina was about to tell her so, but Unity chattered on without pausing for breath.

They had met for lunch at a little café on the Unter Den Linden; Unity said it was the most heavenly place in the whole of Berlin – all her very dearest friends went there. Gina did not particularly enjoy Unity's company, but she had so few English-speaking friends in Germany – and anything was better than another day in that dreary hotel, all by herself.

Her German holiday with Roland Voss had not been as successful as the previous trip. He had warned her he would be staying in the SS barracks, so she could hardly complain that she did not see him often. His work occupied most of his time; he seemed to be getting on well with Ober-Leutnant Heinrich Gessler: they were hammering out a policy of international co-operation between the British Fascists and the Nazi Party.

Occasionally Roly had some time off, and then he and Gina would spend the night together. Sometimes they went away for a long weekend, once to Munich and once on a river-boat up the Rhine. It was very pretty and romantic, yet Gina felt something was lacking.

Today she was on her own, so she had arranged to meet Unity; after lunch they were going shopping – Gina wanted some new summer dresses. She was bored with the ones she had brought from England, and she had seen a little two-piece in black and white silk that was absolutely stunning... 'What do you think?' Unity had asked her a question.

'I'm sorry – would you mind saying that again?'

'You're not listening,' said Unity reproachfully. 'I was telling you about the Führer's plans. He's got to meet that ghastly man Mussolini who's arriving on a State Visit – but then the Duke and Duchess of Windsor are coming as well. Will you still be here?'

'I thought they were on their honeymoon?' said Gina. 'I had a letter from Wallis. They're staying at some castle in the Austrian Tyrol –'

'I mean after the honeymoon. The Führer's really looking forward to meeting them both; he says if Baldwin hadn't been so stupid and stuffy, he would have been welcoming the King and Queen of England... And that might have been the start of a new understanding between Great Britain and Germany. He'd much rather have that than this Axis thing with Italy. Between you and me, he can't *stand* Mussolini... I told the British Ambassador so – in strict confidence, of course.'

Gina wondered if Herr Hitler planted nuggets of information with Unity – in strictest confidence – when he particularly wanted them to get back to the British Foreign Office. But she said nothing.

Unity looked at her watch. 'Heavens – is that really the time? I must fly – I've promised to meet Magda Goebbels at three; it's just possible the Führer may be there as well . . .'

'I thought we were going on a shopping spree –?'

'I can't miss a chance like this; he's so busy these days, poor lamb, I don't often see him. You can get Roly to take you instead. You might even persuade him to pay the bills.'

'I asked him to come, but he couldn't manage it: he's working with Heinrich Gessler today.'

Unity pursed her lips. 'Don't you think perhaps Roly is seeing a bit too much of that creepy Herr Gessler? Quite frankly, I wouldn't trust him – and poor Roly gets so carried away . . . But I mustn't stay here talking. Thanks for lunch, angel – I must dash.'

Blowing a kiss, she disappeared. Gina resented her criticism of Roland, and was glad she had not told Unity about the chocolate cream on her cheek. She hoped it would still be there when she met the Führer.

Irritably, she asked the head waiter to call a taxi; she didn't feel like shopping by herself. She drove back to the hotel, intending to put her feet up and have a rest before she met Roly for dinner.

When she asked the desk-clerk for her key, she was told that Herr Voss had already taken it; he was upstairs, in her room. Smiling, she hurried to the lift; what a lucky coincidence that he should have arrived early today.

She opened the door of Room 303, then stood rooted to the spot.

There were two men in the room. Roland was on the bed, half-dressed, with another man: she had a startling glimpse of naked flesh and black leather. They stared at her, transfixed. Then Roland said thickly, 'Shut the door, for God's sake.'

Heinrich Gessler stood up, grabbing his uniform from a chair, then disappeared into the bathroom and slammed the door.

'What exactly is going on?' Gina asked at last.

The question was idiotic; not bothering to reply, Roland began to get dressed.

Suddenly she felt cold – and very frightened. She had not known fear for such a long time; she had forgotten how to deal with it. When she put her hand on the back of a chair to steady herself, she found she was trembling and had to sit down.

Without looking at her, Roland said:

'You may as well know. I'm taking a job here; Heinrich has found some work for me – confidential work, for the party . . . He's taking a flat; I shall move in with him. And I'm going to become a German citizen: I shall never go back to England.'

She said nothing... How could she have been such a fool? Those endless meetings at S.S. Headquarters – those boisterous drinking-parties that often went on all night – above all, his recent lack of interest in her... All the signs had been there – God, she must have been blind.

She knew that she was trapped in this situation; helpless, and utterly alone. Maybe Unity would take her in for a couple of nights, but –

Suddenly she remembered Unity's cryptic warning about Gessler; could she have known something already? Gina decided not to turn to Unity for help. She couldn't face that sweet, pitying smile.

But London was out of the question; Charlie would never take her back now... If only her hands would stop shaking...

What the hell was she going to do? Where could she possibly go?

21

FRIDAY, 1 APRIL TO FRIDAY, 27 MAY 1938

In the field of world politics, 1938 began badly, and soon became worse. Hitler assumed supreme command of Germany, becoming an absolute dictator. On 11 March, he moved into Austria, claiming it as part of the German Reich, and was welcomed by hysterical crowds.

Britain prepared for war. Everyone hoped it might still be averted through the diplomacy of the Prime Minister, Neville Chamberlain; but air raid precautions were put into operation throughout the country: gas masks were distributed, and four hundred thousand Anderson shelters were manufactured.

And yet, on an April morning, it was hard to believe that anything could go badly wrong. At Crown House, the family welcomed another spring day, and went on with their various activities.

Nick worked at the farm office with Ken as usual; Jenny spent the morning with William, planting out seedlings in the new herb garden. After her moment of confession last year, she had never spoken to him again about Nicholas; and he refrained from asking questions. He hoped that time would heal the breach between them; she did not tell him that they were further apart than ever.

Two members of the family were missing; Alice was in London, finishing another spell of duty at Marlborough House, and Polly was in Medford.

Polly had been spending a good deal of time in Medford, over the past six months. She planned to set up a little business there; she had consulted her bank manager and her solicitor, and cleared any financial or legal obstacles out of the way before she began – but she had not discussed it with the family at all.

They were pleased she had broken out of her solitary shell, and welcomed the idea that she should begin to rebuild her life; if she did not choose to tell them exactly what she was doing, they were too polite to pester her. Jenny had heard through Lilian – whose uncle worked in an estate agency – that Lady Ebony was renting some business premises in the main shopping street of Medford, and guessed she might be opening a little dress-shop; Polly was always interested in fashion, and had a professional eye for cut and design.

Then she heard that the premises were on the first floor, to be used as offices; and Polly set off day after day, in an old jumper and skirt, returning each evening with smears of paint on her clothes, face and hands.

'Buttercup yellow,' she said brightly, as she ran upstairs to wash. 'Well, it's a lot more cheerful than that awful old chocolate-brown . . .'

They heard that she was interviewing girls for a shorthand-typist's job; an older woman was taken on to answer the telephone and do the book-keeping.

'But what exactly *is* this business she's running?' Old Bea asked, with her mouth full.

Nicholas had brought his grandmother a sample of full-cream cheese from the dairy; one of Ken Stubb's innovations at the farm had been an experiment in cheese making.

'Well, Grandmama? What do you think of it?'

'Too mild for my taste. You should try a blue cheese – something with some bite to it,' the old lady pronounced. 'But I dare say it will please the others; most people have no palate nowadays.' She wiped her lips with a lace handkerchief and continued, 'You haven't answered my question: what is Polly up to in Medford?'

'We don't know. She did say something about an agency – I think she's trying to start an employment agency, but that's only a guess on my part.'

'Why should she do that?' demanded Lady Beatrice. 'I hear on the wireless that industry is booming. There are plenty of jobs about, aren't there?'

'Thanks to the war-scare,' commented Nick drily. 'There's nothing like a good crisis for boosting the national economy. And if war should come, the young men will find themselves in other occupations.'

'Going into the Army, you mean?'

'Or the Air Force or the Navy ... Lucky devils.'

She eyed him narrowly: 'You still miss it, don't you?'

'Is that so obvious?'

'You used to be a bright, lively lad; now you moon about the place like a sleep-walker. Any fool can see you're not happy.'

'Well ... Let's say I wasn't cut out to be a gentleman-farmer. I've got salt water in my veins, and I get restless when I've been ashore too long ... Sometimes I hope there will be a war, so I can get back into uniform and –' He pulled himself up. 'Sorry – I'm talking too much.'

'Hmph!' She cocked her head on one side, like an old parrot. 'What does Jenny have to say about all this?'

'Jenny? I haven't discussed it with Jenny.'

'Surely you talk things over with your wife –'

'We don't talk much these days. Perhaps that's part of the trouble.'

There was a knock at the door, and Polly walked in. She wasn't wearing paint-spattered clothes today; she had on a tailored suit in charcoal grey, with an open-necked shirt and a red silk scarf at her throat; and she carried a bunch of spring flowers.

'A present for you,' she announced, handing them to Old Bea.

'For me? What have I done to deserve presents?'

'I felt like celebrating. I bought some new clothes, and once I started spending, I couldn't stop.'

'I thought I hadn't seen that outfit before,' said Nick. 'Very smart.'

'That's the idea. Does it make me look like a respectable business woman?'

'Attractive, I'd say, rather than respectable.'

'Oh, lor' – that's the chorus-girl in me coming out. Let's hope the clients are impressed.'

'What clients? What are you talking about?' asked Old Bea.

'My office opens for business,' said Polly. 'There'll be a piece about it in tomorrow's *Gazette*, but I thought I'd better tell you first ... I'm starting a marriage-bureau.'

They stared at her. The Countess began to make choking noises, and clutched at her throat. 'What? I never heard of such a thing. You can't! Remember who you are – Lady Ebony, my grandson's widow –'

'Don't worry, dear; I'm not going to drag the family through the mud; I'll be using my professional name ... "The Polly Harvey Bureau" – that's what it says over the door.'

'It's outrageous!' spluttered Lady Beatrice. 'Nicholas, you must do something, put a stop to it at once!'

'Why shouldn't Polly go ahead, if there's a demand for that sort of thing?' Nick asked. 'I hope she makes a go of it ... Good luck to her.'

The old lady snorted impatiently: 'It's out of the question ... It – it's improper!'

'That's where you're wrong,' said Polly. 'Oh, I know there are a few seedy little agencies already – adverts in the papers for single ladies looking for unattached gents and all that – but my bureau's going to be very different. I won't take anyone on my books unless they're genuine about getting married – no hanky-panky!'

The rest of the family were not worried: Jenny said she admired Polly's initiative, and wished her well; and if William had private reservations about his daughter-in-law going 'into trade', he kept them to himself.

One person who didn't approve was Ken Stubbs. He had been supervising the birth of a new calf, and when Polly talked to him, he was in his shirt-sleeves, washing his hands at the pump in the yard.

'Yes, I heard some talk about it, in the servants' hall,' he frowned. 'It gave the girls something to gossip about.'

'I thought you'd be pleased I'd found a job,' she said.

'You've got a job already,' he retorted. 'You have two children to bring up; you can't expect Mrs Jenny to spend the rest of her life mothering your family ...'

She flinched, as if the reproof were a physical slap in the face, and he went on quickly, 'I'm sorry – I shouldn't say that – it's no business of mine.'

He dried his hands and forearms on a rough huckaback towel, then turned away, rolling down his sleeves and fastening his cuff-links.

'You're the one who told me I ought to find something to do,' she reminded him.

His jacket was hanging over the shafts of a hay-wain, and she held it up for him, automatically.

'Well, yes ...' He was momentarily disconcerted as she helped him into his coat. 'Thank you ... I suppose what really concerns me is that – this particular job doesn't seem very suitable – for a lady in your situation.'

She tried to smile. 'You're as bad as Lady Bea! She gave me a ticking-off – she says it's "improper"! I tried to explain, it's going to be very respectable.'

'If you're running it, I'm sure it will be. And I've no doubt you'll make a success of it... You could make a success of anything you put your mind to, I reckon.' He turned to face her. 'No doubt it will fill a need; the world's full of lonely people.'

'And I've had some practice already! It was introducing you and Lilian that gave me the idea...' Polly remembered to ask: 'By the way, have you fixed the date for the wedding?'

'Not yet. We want to find somewhere to live; the lodge isn't really suitable. Lilian's set her heart on a modern bungalow... The trouble is, there's nothing like that this side of Medford. But we'll go on looking; there's no hurry.'

That evening, Alice returned from London. She found William in the garden room, tired but happy, after a satisfactory day in the herb garden.

'The new rosemary bush has taken very well; and the bay is flourishing like – well, like a green bay tree!' Then he remembered he had family news to pass on, and told her about Polly's business venture. 'It will be good for her to develop a new interest, though I can't help wishing she'd hit on something rather less...' He realized that Alice was not giving him her full attention. 'My dear – what's wrong?'

'I have some news for you as well – and I'm afraid it will come as rather a bombshell... This afternoon, as I was leaving Marlborough House, Queen Mary said, "At last I can fulfil a promise I made you some time ago. I had been planning a visit to old friends at Badminton, but now there is illness in the family, it must be postponed – so as I have a blank space in my engagement-book, I thought this might be an excellent opportunity for me to come and stay at Crown House instead"...'

William's eyebrows shot up: 'Her Majesty – coming *here*?'

'I know it's going to be a dreadful upheaval, but what could I possibly say? I told her we should be honoured and delighted... I'm very fond of her; she's always been so kind – but I must admit that the thought of entertaining her as a guest fills me with absolute terror!'

To call it an 'upheaval' was putting it mildly. The entire family was thrown into a frenzy, and the staff were run off their feet. For a fortnight they turned the house upside-down – spring-cleaning, scrubbing, sweeping and polishing every inch of space, until it was fit for a Queen.

Her Majesty would be accompanied by Lady Flora Kelso – since Alice could not act as hostess and lady-in-waiting at the same time – together with an entourage of maids, footmen, private detectives and her ageing and eccentric chauffeur, Mr Humphries.

'And I shall have to go round, removing all the portable *objets d'art* beforehand,' said Alice.

'Good heavens – you're not suggesting that Her Majesty is – um – light-fingered?' William exclaimed in mock dismay.

'Ssh! Don't be naughty... But she sometimes takes a fancy to various little ornaments, and when she particularly admires something, one is expected to make her a present of it when she leaves.'

'In that case, I suggest we display Great-Aunt Mabel's Venetian-glass epergne in a prominent position; I've always loathed the damn thing.'

This was the least of their problems. It was more difficult to pacify the staff, who had to be shuffled round the servants' quarters, much to their indignation, doubling up and sharing rooms in order to accommodate the Queen's retinue.

'Oh – and there's another thing,' Alice instructed Lilian Brooks. 'At the dinner table, you must leave at least two feet between Her Majesty and the people on either side; she likes to have plenty of elbow-room.'

Lilian looked grim. 'It's not like the last time, when the King and Queen came to stay – the Duke and Duchess of York they were then. I remember how easy and friendly they were with everybody; we didn't have all this fuss and carry-on.'

'Well – Queen Mary comes from a different generation; she's rather set in her ways,' said Alice.

When the great day arrived, a little procession of cars purred up the drive. Mr Humphries, in the royal Daimler, managed to over-shoot the turn at the corner, leaving tyre-tracks across the lawn and the edge of a flower-bed: William, waiting at the foot of the steps, gritted his teeth and went on smiling.

When the Queen alighted, William bowed over her hand and

Alice dropped a full curtsey, as they welcomed Her Majesty to Crown House.

'What a charming spot,' she said, looking about her. 'I particularly want to see the gardens. I have heard so much about them.' Then she pointed her parasol at the south wall, adding sharply, 'But I'm surprised to see that you let ivy disfigure the building... It's not only unsightly, it damages the structure so badly; don't you know it pulls out the cement between the bricks?'

William swallowed and said, 'The gardeners will see to it at once, Ma'am.'

When they retired for the night, after a gruelling afternoon and evening, Alice confided to William: 'I think she's getting bossier as she gets older.'

'I must say I rather resented her comments on the grounds; she was complimentary enough about the gardens, but she was very critical of the parkland... She kept pointing to the brushwood under the trees, and saying: "That will have to go – much too untidy"... Tomorrow she's going to organize what she calls a "wooding party", to clear it all up!'

'She has very strong views about nature; she feels it should not be allowed to get out of hand.'

'I can see we're in for a difficult week.'

'It's all right for you; you can keep out of her way. Flora and I have to be on call right round the clock. And she wants to make some expeditions to other houses in the area; they're going to get a nasty shock when I ring up and say: "Guess who's coming to tea this afternoon"...'

'You'd better warn them to hide the silver candlesticks at the same time.'

'William, it's not funny!' Alice began to laugh despite herself. 'At least she's found a kindred spirit in your Mama. They were getting on like a house on fire, at dinner... Two of a kind, I'm afraid!'

Certainly the Queen and Lady Beatrice struck up an immediate friendship, and when the weather was warm enough, they had tea together in the garden.

Norman carried Old Bea outside, and settled her in a wicker armchair; then Lady Flora escorted the Queen to the summerhouse, where the tea table awaited them.

'Such a pleasant view.' Queen Mary gazed down the long vista towards the lake.

'It's a pity you weren't here a week or two ago, Ma'am, when the daffodils were out,' said Lady Beatrice. 'By the edge of the lake, under the trees.'

'Really?' Her Majesty sounded unconvinced. 'I know that's the modern notion – it's meant to look natural, but to my mind, flower-beds are the proper place for flowers.'

'You must talk to Minster about that – he's the gardener. I can't abide the land, neither could my husband ... And I'm afraid young Nicholas takes after him.'

'Your grandson? But I understood he left the Navy in order to manage the estate?'

Pouring cups of Earl Grey, Lady Beatrice explained that Nicholas had resigned his commission, feeling it was his duty to shoulder the family burdens; and now he was regretting it.

'How strange ... There was a parallel situation within my own family.' The Queen sipped her tea thoughtfully. 'I hope poor Bertie does not suffer similar regrets ...'

'I'm sure he does not, Ma'am', said Old Bea firmly. 'His Majesty knows there was no other course open to him; it was more than his duty – it was his destiny, and I've no doubt he will be a worthy successor to his father ... It's different for my grandson; he has an excellent manager now, to run the farm – his father has made a good recovery from his illness – so Nicholas feels he has sacrificed his career for nothing.'

'Dear me, most unfortunate. Life plays cruel tricks upon us ...' Her Majesty changed the subject. 'I understand you sometimes make excursions in your motor, round the district? Where do you recommend me to visit?'

The following afternoon, as she drove back from a call upon a startled neighbouring family, Her Majesty said, 'Such hospitable people ... And so generous – just look at this dear little *famille rose* box: I happened to say how pretty it was, and they positively insisted upon my having it – really *too* kind ...'

Alice and Flora made suitably admiring noises, and tried not to look at one another.

As the car approached Ebony, they passed some boys and girls on their way home from the village school. Speechless with wonder, the children shrank back into the hedge, as the Queen raised her hand, graciously nodding and smiling.

"*Cheer*, little idiots, can't you?' she said under her breath, as they drove by; but they were far too awe-struck to respond. 'Dear me – these country children are so slow; did you notice they all had their mouths open? Adenoids, I expect.'

The royal visit eventually came to an end, and the Queen prepared to return to London.

'It's all been quite delightful, every moment,' she told Alice and William as they said goodbye on the terrace. 'And your grounds look so much better, now you have cleared them up and got rid of that nasty ivy.'

Taking Alice's arm, she descended the steps to the Daimler. 'I must tell you a little secret, my dear. I had a special reason for wishing to visit your lovely house. You see, it has been decided that if war breaks out – of course we all pray that it won't, but if it should – I had better remove myself from London, and stay with friends in the country for the duration of hostilities. And that is why I visited you – and why I am about to visit Badminton very soon; I have to decide where I should go.'

Alice heard herself say in a high, strained voice, 'You thought – this house might provide a suitable refuge –?'

'It had crossed my mind. But I want you to know, Alice dear, that I only decided against it in the end on advice from Whitehall. They pointed out that in the event of air-raids, this part of Kent would be directly in the path of the enemy aeroplanes, so it looks as if I shall settle upon Badminton instead. I shouldn't want you to think I had rejected Crown House for any other reason. You do understand, don't you?'

'Oh – yes, Ma'am . . . I understand perfectly,' said Alice, feeling quite faint with relief, and hoping it didn't show. 'Thank you for telling me.'

Shortly after this, gilt-edged cards arrived from Buckingham Palace. Lord and Lady Minster, and the Hon. Nicholas and Mrs Gaunt, were invited to attend a Royal Garden Party, to be held on the last Thursday in May.

Nicholas asked Jenny if she thought she might be able to tear herself away from the children for one day – and she replied coolly that she looked forward to going to the Palace. Only William declined his invitation; the jaunt to London last year had been more than enough, and he hoped Their Majesties would excuse him, on grounds of ill-health.

'You're an impostor!' Alice scolded him. 'You're looking better than ever.'

'Well, I can hardly tell the truth and say I'd rather get on with my herb garden, can I?' said William. 'This is a good time for gardening; not too hot or too cold, and God willing, not too wet either.'

So it was decided that Alice, Nicholas and Jenny should go; they would stay at Eaton Square on Wednesday night, giving themselves plenty of time to get to the Palace on Thursday afternoon. Alice warned them to allow for the usual traffic problems in the Mall, but even so, despite Dennett's valiant attempt at a detour through Birdcage Walk, they found themselves in a solid jam of immovable cars.

Alice found herself remembering the last time this had happened to her; on the night of Caro's presentation at Court, almost seven years ago... Thank God she had survived the terrors of the war in Spain – Edith's letter had been like an answer to a prayer. At least they knew now that Caro was alive and well, and apparently travelling all over Europe with Scott Hanson, working for his left-wing magazine. But Alice could not help wondering if she would ever see her daughter again – and tried to suppress a sigh.

Nicholas glanced at her, misinterpreting it.

'Come on, Ma – let's walk the rest of the way,' he said. 'We'll be here all day at this rate.'

They finished the journey on foot; Jenny hoped the hem of her long dress wouldn't trail in the dust, and Alice held on to her hat, for a gusty breeze sent the clouds scudding across the sky.

'I do hope it doesn't rain,' said Alice. 'Two years ago, there was an absolute cloudburst, and everyone got soaked to the skin. To make matters worse, the King decided it was too wet to carry on, so he walked away from the receiving-line and called the whole thing off... The girls who'd been standing in the pouring rain, waiting to be presented, were simply furious.'

'That doesn't sound like His Majesty,' frowned Nicholas. 'He's usually very thoughtful.'

'Two years ago, darling, we had a different king,' Jenny reminded him.

'Good Lord... It seems longer than that: everything's happened so fast.'

At first the rain held off and things went according to plan, though Alice admitted privately: 'Don't expect too much, will you? Royal

Garden parties are usually an anticlimax; most of the guests never get anywhere near their Majesties – and the refreshments aren't exactly sumptuous.'

There was a tea tent, where tea or lemonade was provided, together with rather dull sandwiches and little iced cakes. Outside, a brass band from the Brigade of Guards played selections from Gilbert and Sullivan, while the guests strolled across the lawns in morning suits and floral dresses. The men wore grey toppers, and the ladies had broad-brimmed straws in pastel shades, trimmed with veiling or ostrich feathers.

The Minster family were directed to a separate area, enclosed by pipe-clayed ropes; here, Alice explained, they might snatch a few words with the King or Queen if they were very lucky; but it would take far too long for Their Majesties to speak to everyone.

'Where do all these people come from?' asked Nick.

'Oh – they're civic dignitaries – retired officers and their wives, worthy citizens who have helped some charitable cause or other,' Alice replied. 'An invitation to a Garden Party is a minor accolade.'

'But we're none of those things,' said Jenny. 'How did we get on the list?'

'I suppose it's a kind of thank you for Queen Mary's visit to Crown House.'

As it turned out, there was another reason for the invitation. When the King and Queen emerged from the Palace with the Princesses, the favoured guests flocked to the ropes round the enclosure, and the Royal Family made a slow progress, stopping to chat every few yards. Then the Queen caught sight of the Minsters and made straight for them.

'Alice – how lovely to see you... And Nicholas and Jenny – so glad you could come.' She touched her husband's arm, drawing his attention to them. 'I believe you wanted a word with Nicholas, darling?'

King George shook hands with Nick, saying, 'Indeed I do... But not here. C-c-could you spare a few minutes, later on? I'll send someone to find you.'

'Yes, of course, thank you, Sir.' Nicholas watched the little group move away, and wondered what it was all about.

He soon found out. Half an hour later, when the Royal Family had done the rounds, a liveried footman appeared at Nick's elbow and escorted him to a small ante-room in the Palace, where the King was loosening his tie and unbuttoning his collar.

'I never enjoy these bun-fights,' he said. 'Too many people – most of them go away disappointed. Still, I'm very pleased to see you, Nicholas; I have something to ask you ... sit down, there's a good chap.'

Mystified, Nicholas obeyed, and the King continued, 'I shall be appointing some new equerries in the near future. And in view of the international situation, I decided that my personal staff should be members of the Armed Forces ... I wonder whether the idea might appeal to you at all?'

Nick was bewildered. 'I – I don't quite understand, Sir; I thought you knew – I resigned my commission when my father was taken ill –'

'I was told you were having second thoughts about it now. That's why I hoped I might persuade you to re-enlist in the Navy. I don't think the Admiralty would raise any objection ... How about it?'

'It's a very tempting thought, Sir,' began Nick. 'But might I ask how you knew I was having second thoughts?'

The King grinned; he was so relaxed, even his stammer had disappeared. 'Your grandmother and my Mama put their heads together recently; you know how old ladies talk ... This would give you an opportunity to get out and about. We're making a State Visit to France this summer – and if the worst should happen, and we find ourselves plunged into this damned war, you'll probably get the chance to travel further afield.'

'I don't know what to say, Sir; you've taken my breath away.' Nicholas hesitated; 'May I have some time to think it over? I must talk to Jenny before I decide.'

At that moment, Jenny and Alice were in the refreshment tent; storm clouds were gathering, and many of the guests had decided to take shelter.

'The tea's not very nice, I'm afraid,' whispered Alice. 'They make it in urns, and it never tastes quite right.'

As they took their cups back to the serving-table, Jenny kicked over a pretty umbrella, propped against a folding-chair. Picking it up, she apologized and handed it back.

Its owner was a lady in early middle-age; once she had been very pretty, and she still had beautiful, wide-set eyes.

'Thank you so much –' she began; then stopped, staring at Jenny with absolute amazement.

344

Vaguely aware that she had seen her before somewhere, Jenny began: 'I'm so sorry – I'm sure I know you, but I can't quite –'

The lady moistened her lips, and said in a low voice, 'No – I don't think so.'

Her companion, an older gentleman in black with a clerical collar, said, 'I don't believe we have had that pleasure. Perhaps we may introduce ourselves; my name is Ernest Walden, and this is my wife, Helen.'

They shook hands, and Alice said, 'Our name is Gaunt; this is my daughter-in-law, Jenny –'

Jenny smiled. 'Are you quite sure we haven't met before? Your face is so familiar, and yet –'

'No, never... Ernest, don't you think we should make a move? It looks as if it's going to pour, any minute.'

A sudden lightning flash made everyone jump, and the reverend gentleman said, 'You may be right, my dear; it does look rather ominous.'

Jenny looked into the lady's face – and saw unmistakable terror in those wide eyes. Then, as the first heavy drops began to fall, a stream of guests hurried into the refreshment tent, and they were swept apart by the crowd.

Minutes later, Jenny saw the pretty umbrella which the stranger had left behind in her haste to get away. She picked it up; it was white silk, with a pattern of blue polka-dots... And then she remembered where she had seen her before.

'We'd better hand it in to one of the attendants,' said Alice. 'She may come back for it.'

'No, leave it to me,' said Jenny. 'I'll see she gets it.'

In the car, on their way back to Crown House, Nicholas told his wife and his mother about the proposition the King had put to him. 'It's a great honour,' he said. 'And of course it would give me a chance to get back into uniform, though I don't imagine I'd go to sea very often. Still, it would mean plenty of travelling, with His Majesty.'

'You'd love it – you know you would,' said Alice.

'Well, yes – but I'm thinking about the family.' He turned to Jenny. 'How would you feel about me being away from home so often?'

Jenny was looking out of the car window at the countryside flashing past; but all she saw was a girl's face... a frightened girl, in

a dress with blue polka-dots . . . She pulled herself together: 'Sorry –
I was miles away.'

'Oh, no – I'm the one who should apologize; I'm obviously boring
you,' said Nicholas heavily. 'I was only asking your opinion about
my future career; it's not particularly interesting.'

'Nick, I am sorry – I had something else on my mind.' She turned
the umbrella round and round in her hands. 'Of course your career
is important. And if His Majesty has asked you to join his Household,
I don't see how you can refuse . . . But it's up to you, naturally.'

'In other words, you don't really give a damn whether I'm at
home or not . . . No – I don't suppose it will make much difference
to you.'

Alice broke in: 'Nick – Jenny – please . . . Surely we can discuss
this quietly and sensibly, without getting upset?'

'There's nothing to discuss. Jenny doesn't care either way, so it's
up to me to decide . . . I said I'd give His Majesty my answer after
the weekend.'

Next morning, when Nick came back from the farm before lunch,
he found his mother in the Chinese drawing-room.

'I've made up my mind. I want to do the job; I want to rejoin the
Navy. You never know; I might manage to get to sea, now and
again.' He looked at his reflection in the old mirror above the
overmantel, supported by the twisted tails of golden dragons; and
he thought of the China Sea . . . 'I won't wait till next Monday – I'll
send a message this afternoon.'

When he turned to face her, Alice thought that he looked like
a boy again; as eager and excited as when he first went off to
Dartmouth.

'I'd better tell Jenny,' he said. 'Where is she?'

'Oh – didn't you know? She's gone to return that umbrella she
found after the Garden Party.'

'I don't understand –'

'Nor do I; it was rather odd. She asked me to ring the Palace and
find the address of the Reverend Ernest Walden – so I did. He's the
vicar of a village in Hampshire, somewhere outside Basingstoke.'

'But that's ridiculous! It will take her all day to get there and back.
Why did she take the wretched thing anyway? She could have sent
it by post.'

'I suggested that, but she said she had to take it back to Mrs

Walden herself . . . I don't know why.'

The drawing-room at the vicarage was used as a study by the
Reverend Ernest Walden, and his roll-top desk, stuffed with papers,
tended to dominate it; so did a photograph of a school group,
yellowing with age, above the bookcase.

Mrs Walden had made little impression on the room, Jenny
thought. The chintz-covered armchairs and sofa were anonymous;
the *Church Times* and *Punch* occupied the magazine-rack – there was
no sign of *Good Housekeeping*, or *Woman's Own*.

The door opened, and Helen Walden came in; she looked very
pale, and clasped her hands to stop them trembling.

'Good afternoon,' said Jenny. 'I came to return your umbrella.'

'It's good of you to go to so much trouble.'

'I also wanted to talk to you.'

'Yes . . .' Mrs Walden gave a little sigh, and sank into a chair. 'So
you remembered, after all . . .'

'I only saw you for a moment, three years ago – the day Richard
died. I thought at the time you were one of the picnic party who
came into the grounds by mistake; but yesterday I saw you were
terrified – and I realized.'

'I'm frightened of thunderstorms –'

'No. You were afraid of me – afraid I might recognize you. Before
you married Mr Walden, you were Mrs Helen Morrissey, weren't
you?'

'Yes . . .' The answer came in a whisper.

'You didn't appear in court; you were too ill by then, in a nursing-
home – so I never saw you in public. But yesterday I discovered you
were at Crown House at the time of Richard's death . . . Not Mr
Morrissey – you.'

Jenny had lain awake during the night, trying to puzzle it out;
Lady Edith, who first saw the picnickers, had said there were two
men and two women in the group. By the time Jenny reached them,
one woman had vanished – and when they met Helen Morrissey on
her way back from the stable yard, Jenny assumed she was the fourth
member of the party. At that moment Edith was absorbed in her
own problems, and probably she had not looked closely at the
trespassers: so the girl in the polka-dot dress had never been referred
to again – during the police investigation, at the inquest, or in the
years that followed.

347

'What were you doing at the home farm, that day?' Jenny continued.

'Richard had written me a letter, saying it was all over; he wouldn't see me again – and Joe found it. There was a terrible row, but I didn't care about that; all I cared about was Richard – I had to see him, to try and make him change his mind. We went up to the stable-loft, where we could be alone. He had his gun with him, and when he got angry and told me to get out, I threatened to shoot myself. I grabbed the gun, and he tried to get it away from me – and it went off... It was an accident, a terrible accident.'

Jenny remembered the note that Richard had sent her; the stable-boy had been unable to find her immediately, so it was some time before she went to the farm office. Perhaps Richard had wanted to tell her that he had followed her advice, and decided to break off his relationship with Helen Morrissey.

She wondered now what would have happened if she had received the note sooner; she might have been with him when Mrs Morrissey arrived – the quarrel could have been avoided, the tussle with the gun, the accident...

But had it really been an accident? Looking into those wide, frightened eyes, she asked herself: had Helen Morrissey, in a moment of passionate despair, pulled the trigger and killed the man who had thrown her aside? No-one would ever know.

'As soon as I realized he was dead, I panicked. I wiped my fingerprints off the gun, and I ran away – that's when you saw me... Then I went home, and told Joe... We tried to decide what to do; I suppose I should have gone to the police and confessed, but that would have meant the whole thing coming out in court... I couldn't face that, and neither could Joe. He knew by then that our marriage was over – there was no hope for us. That's why he wrote the letter that night, then walked out of the house and killed himself. He let everyone think he had shot Richard: it was a sort of farewell gesture...'

'And – that's when you collapsed?'

'I was in the nursing-home for a long time. Ernest was the curate of a nearby church; he used to come and visit the home, and he took an interest in me. I was desperate; I had nobody else to turn to, and nowhere to go. When Ernest asked me to marry him, it was a blessed relief. I thought I'd make a fresh start, in a new place, where nobody knew me. I hoped I could turn my back on the past and begin again... But you can never do that.'

'You mean you can never forget?'

'How could I? Ernest will always be here, to remind me... He forgave me, of course; he's very good at forgiveness – that's his job – and he's gone on forgiving me, every day since he married me. He's a man of strong moral principles; everyone admires him for that.'

'Does he know you and I had met? Did you tell him who I was?'

'Oh, no; that would have made him angry. It's lucky he's out this afternoon, visiting the almshouse. He doesn't like anything to bring back the past; we never mention it now. He forgives me, but we don't talk about it.'

There was a long silence, and then Mrs Walden asked, 'Now you know, what are you going to do?'

'Nothing. What would be the point? We can't change what happened.'

'You won't tell anybody – that I did it?'

'I won't tell anybody.'

All the way back to Kent, Jenny tried to analyse her own feelings. What did she feel about this woman – this total stranger, who had once been Richard's lover, and who might have killed him deliberately? Should she have agreed to keep silent? Should Helen Morrissey – Helen Walden – be allowed to escape the consequences of her action?

But nothing would bring Richard back. And perhaps Helen had brought a worse punishment upon herself; a lifetime of imprisonment in an unhappy marriage, ruled by a husband who made a profession of forgiveness... Better, she thought, to let sleeping dogs lie.

When she reached Crown House, Nick was waiting for her in the library.

'Where have you been?' he asked. 'What's going on?'

'Didn't your mother tell you? I went to return the umbrella that was left behind at –'

'Yes, but why? In God's name, why go half across England, to see this woman? Ma says you thought you'd met her before. Is that true?'

'Nick, it really doesn't matter; and I'd rather not talk about it. I must go and bathe and change before dinner; I'm late enough already.'

She tried to escape, but he grabbed her by the shoulders. 'You're hiding something ... Tell me the truth – who is this woman?'

Looking him full in the face, Jenny replied: 'She's Helen Morrissey. I didn't realize at first, but then I guessed. She was the woman Richard had been seeing, before –'

A sudden uncontrollable rage swept over Nicholas, and he flung her away from him – so violently, she lost her balance and fell to the floor.

He stood over her, his face contorted with anger. 'So that's it ... That's why you had to go and find her again; you had so much in common. How lucky for you, to be able to share those happy memories – comparing notes on darling Richard – how handsome and strong he was – and so wonderful in bed –'

Blindly, she scrambled to her feet and opened the door, as he shouted after her: 'I suppose you'll be meeting regularly from now on – perhaps she'd like to come and stay here? Then you can both put flowers on his grave, and weep over your lost lover ...'

Jenny went upstairs to the bedroom; she took some clothes from the wardrobe, removed everything of hers from the bathroom, and packed a suitcase. Then, without seeing anyone or leaving any message, she walked out of the house.

It was over. She never wanted to see Nicholas again.

22

FRIDAY, 27 MAY TO THURSDAY, 21 JULY 1938

'How are you getting on at your bureau?' Alice asked.

Polly thought hard. 'I don't really know ... All right, I suppose. At least we've been busy, ever since we opened. I had a dreadful feeling that once I'd taken on my helpers, we'd just sit and look at each other all day long, but the letters keep rolling in, and people ring up all the time – so I suppose we've made a good start. I don't know how we're doing on the money side; Mildred keeps the books. She used to work in the Borough Treasurer's office, and she's a wonder with figures.'

'How much do you charge your clients?'

'Five guineas to join – that's after I've interviewed them. If they're really hopeless cases, I tell the poor souls I haven't got anyone for them at the moment, but I promise to get in touch if anyone suitable turns up. The others pay their five guineas, and fill up a form, and then they go into our card-indexes – one box for men, one for women. If two people actually get married, they have to pay the second half of the fee; that's another ten guineas each... Nobody's taken the plunge so far, but it's early days yet, and we live in hopes.'

The drawing-room door opened, and Nicholas walked in. His face was pale and expressionless, and Alice braced herself for bad news.

'I thought I'd better tell you –' he said, then stopped and began again: 'Jenny's gone.'

'Gone? What do you mean?'

'She walked out, about an hour ago. We had a row – I said something that upset her... She went upstairs and packed a bag;

nobody's seen her since... She's left me.'

He took his car and drove through the village, then circled the country lanes; but there was no sign of her.

When he returned, the family spent a miserable evening, hoping the telephone might ring, and wondering what to do. They tried to think where Jenny might have gone; she had no close friends of her own.

'She's always been a solitary person,' Alice said, as they sat in the drawing-room after dinner.

'That's because of being an outsider,' remarked Polly. 'When she got married, she lost touch with the people she'd known before; and she never made any new friends – not really. I know; I've been through it myself.'

'But there must be *someone* she'd go to... Perhaps if we ring round some of the local people –' Alice began.

'I don't think so,' said William. 'She may come back tomorrow – it would be embarrassing for her if we tell the neighbourhood she's disappeared.'

'She won't come back,' said Nick. 'Not now.'

When they went to bed, Alice told William, 'I suppose I half-knew there was something wrong, but – one doesn't want to interfere... If only I hadn't been away so much – if I'd been closer to Jenny, she might have talked to me.' She climbed into bed beside William. 'Shall I turn out the light?'

'No – leave it on.'

As a rule, Alice was the one who kept the bedside light on, reading a chapter of a book before she settled down; while William usually closed his eyes and fell asleep at once. Tonight, he wanted to talk.

'I did know,' he said.

'Know? Know what?'

'Something of Jenny's problems. She confided in me once, when we were working in the garden. She never mentioned it again, and I hoped that things were getting better... Obviously I was wrong.'

'When you say – Jenny's problems –'

'She told me they were beginning to drift apart; and she told me why. Nicholas is obsessively jealous of Richard.'

'Because Jenny had an affair with Richie, all those years ago? That's absurd!'

'Absurd or not, it's destroyed their marriage.'

'But it's not as if she'd been unfaithful to Nick. Since they fell in love, she's never looked at another man.'

'There's such a thing as retrospective jealousy . . . I discovered that myself,' he added quietly.

Alice turned to look at him. 'That was completely different. You had every reason to be jealous – and angry.'

Paul Weyman's name hung upon the air, unspoken; they never mentioned him now.

'Did I really? Twelve years after the event? Oh, I admit I was very hurt when the truth came out, but – you can't go on nursing a resentment for ever. It's the present that matters, not the past.'

She put her hand on his for a moment, then continued: 'Jenny loves Nick so much – it's terribly unfair. Did you tackle him about it? Try to make him understand?'

'She made me promise not to. In any case, I doubt if that would have helped.'

Next day there were two empty places at the morning-room table. Jenny had not returned, and Nicholas had not come down for breakfast.

'Shall I ask Lilian to give him a call?' suggested Polly. 'Perhaps he's overslept.'

'If he had a bad night, it'll do him no harm to have an extra hour or two,' said William. 'Better leave him.'

'Still no news of Jenny, I suppose?' Polly went on. 'The children are going to wonder where she is. What shall we tell them?'

'We can't keep it a secret,' Alice pointed out. 'It must be the talk of the servants' hall by now. That means it'll be all round the county by lunchtime. Don't worry about the children; I thought I'd take them down to Folkestone. It looks like being a sunny day – they can go on the beach.'

'There's no need for you to do that,' said Polly.

'I was only thinking – Jenny usually takes them, and you'll be going to work –'

'Not today. The bureau doesn't open on Saturdays, thank goodness. I'd like to have them. It's about time I did something for my own kids.'

It wasn't going to be easy. She had avoided them for so long, they were like strangers. When she went up to find them, they were playing on the hearthrug; Alex was laying out his train set, and

Harry tried to help by putting their farm animals between the rails; but her chubby hands were clumsy, and she kept knocking things over.

'Can't you leave things alone?' complained Alex, as Polly came in. 'Jenny, tell her not to –' Then he saw it was not Jenny. 'Oh ... hello, mummy.'

The nursery-governess came forward, saying, 'Good morning, my lady. Is there something I can do for you?'

'No thanks. But you can go and have your elevenses, if you like; I'll look after the children this morning.'

The governess looked startled but merely said, 'Very good, my lady,' and left them together.

'Where's Jenny?' Alex wanted to know.

'I'm not sure,' said Polly. 'She's out somewhere, so I'm here instead. We might go for a walk, p'raps.'

'No, thank you,' said Alex politely, busy with a complicated level-crossing.

'Well, we can't stay here all day,' said Polly. 'How about going out in the car? We could drive down to the seaside and go paddling. Would you like that, Harry?'

Little Harriet said nothing, but stared at her mother in astonishment.

'Jenny says the sea's too cold for paddling yet,' said Alex.

'All right then – I know what we'll do!' Polly had an inspiration. 'We'll go exploring indoors. Have you ever been right up to the top of the house – into the attics?'

Alex turned and looked at her; now she had caught his interest. 'We're not allowed ... Could we really?'

'Of course we could.'

They went up two flights of stairs to the attic floor; apart from the water-tanks, it consisted mostly of box-rooms with sloping ceilings and small grimy windows, tucked away under the roof. They opened one door after another, discovering a bizarre collection of old furniture and family relics: a dressmaker's dummy with a half-finished ball-gown pinned to it, a gilded bird-cage, a hip-bath, a solar topi, a selection of rusting swords and assegais, and luggage everywhere ... all kinds of luggage, from steamer-trunks to hat-boxes.

In one corner was a huge wicker basket which Polly recognized immediately.

'That's mine!' she exclaimed. 'My old skip – I'd forgotten all about it ... It must have been put up here when I moved in, donkey's years ago.'

'What's a skip?' Alex asked.

'That's what we called it – it's a dress-basket really. I used to travel round the country with that old skip, on tour. I kept all my costumes and props in it; let's have a look.'

When she lifted the lid, the smell brought it all back instantly; powder and greasepaint, size, canvas, sweat and spirit-gum, hot, stuffy dressing-rooms, and the draughty spaces backstage ...

'It's still got my make-up in it.' She opened a black japanned box. 'Funny to think I used to slap this on my face once upon a time.'

'But what's it *for*?' Alex and little Harry crept closer, peering at the contents of the black tin box.

They didn't know their mother had been on the stage; Harry had never seen a theatre, but Alex had been to a pantomime at the Medford Corn Exchange; and once he went up to London for a matinée of *Peter Pan* – a magical, unforgettable occasion.

Now they listened spellbound, as Polly tried to tell them about it. Getting carried away, she sang snatches from some of her old numbers, and demonstrated some of the dance-routines. They wanted to copy her, and she pulled out some costumes, improvising a glittering dress for Harry from a sequinned blouse, and fitting Alex into the navy-blue tunic and sailor hat she'd once worn for *All the Nice Girls Love a Sailor*. She daubed their faces with greasepaint, turning them into clowns, and taught them a few simple dance-steps. They got into a hopeless muddle, and finished up on the floor, shouting with laughter; she put her arms round her children, and they all laughed together – and Polly knew that if she didn't stop laughing soon, she would start to cry.

Nicholas had not overslept. Alice found him in the yard behind the garages; the bonnet of his car was open, and he was tinkering with the engine.

'What are you doing?' she asked.

'I don't know.' He straightened up. 'I don't know what to do. I thought about going out again to look for her. But I'd never find her now ... Anyway, what's the point? She doesn't want me to find her. She doesn't want me at all – she never did.'

'Have you had any breakfast?'

'I had some coffee when I first came down. I don't know what time that was; it must have been early – they were starting work in the kitchen, and Cook made me some.'

'Come indoors and have something to eat. You won't make things any better by starving yourself.'

'I'm not hungry.'

'Well, come in anyway. I've got something to say to you.'

The maids were busy in the drawing-room, so they went into the library, where they would not be disturbed. Nick said bitterly: 'Very appropriate. This is where it happened.'

'What?'

'The row. This is where I shouted at her, and she walked out.'

'Nicholas – sit down . . . We must talk.'

They took the two wing-chairs on either side of the fireplace; a vase of brilliant wallflowers stood in the empty hearth, and their sweet, piercing scent filled the room.

'What's the use of talking?' he asked. 'It was bound to happen, sooner or later; she never really loved me – I know that.'

'How can you be such a fool?' Alice looked at him with pity. 'She loved you with all her heart; I never saw anyone so much in love.'

'Yes, you did . . . Remember how she looked when she was with Richard? She couldn't take her eyes off him. She was head over heels –'

'Of course she was – she'd never known love before. She was still very young; she had so much love to give, and when Richie came along, he swept her off her feet. But it didn't last.'

'Only because my dear brother was such an oaf he couldn't be satisfied with one girl. When she found out, it nearly broke her heart . . . She married me on the rebound; you know that.'

'I know nothing of the sort. She'd grown up by then; she loved you: it wasn't infatuation, it was true love, the kind that lasts a lifetime. That's why she still loves you – ten times more than she ever loved Richard.'

'I suppose that's why she ran away from me?' he asked ironically.

'Of course! She couldn't stand the pain any longer; she wanted you – nobody else – but you wouldn't have that. You kept dragging Richard in between you and at last you drove her away.'

There was a long silence. Then Nicholas said, 'I can't help it, Ma. How can I help being jealous? She loved Richard first. I can never forgive her for that.'

Alice stood up and walked away; looking out of the window because she could not face her son.

'Please listen to me,' she said. 'If you really loved her, you could forgive her anything. That's what love means. That's how much your father loved me... I only hope that's how you love Jenny.'

'I don't understand – what's Pa got to do with it?'

'Just this... He knows about forgiveness.'

As simply as possible, she told Nicholas about her own infidelity twenty years earlier, when she was already a happily married woman with three children. She told him how loneliness and unhappiness had drawn her into a brief love-affair, which resulted in the birth of the twins – and how, long afterwards, William had discovered the truth. He had learned to bear the pain, and to forgive her; and their love had grown deeper and more precious than before.

'It was hard for me to tell you – but I want you to understand that love and forgiveness are the same thing.'

She stared out at the garden, wondering if she had made a terrible mistake, unable to turn and look at him.

She heard him stand up, and she was afraid he would walk out of the room. Instead, he came towards her. He did not speak; he put his arms round her and kissed her.

He had to find Jenny. He had wasted so much time: where should he begin? He ran to his car and drove to the village store; that was the centre of information in Ebony. It would be humiliating to have to talk about Jenny, but humiliation was a small price to pay. As he entered the shop, the little bell above the door tinkled cheerfully.

Old Mr Wilkinson was behind the grocery counter, slicing bacon. Seeing Nick, he stopped and said, 'Good morning, Mr Gaunt, sir. What can I do for you?'

'I'm afraid I'm not a customer; I want to ask you something. Did you see my wife yesterday evening, by any chance?'

'I may have done,' Mr Wilkinson admitted, cautiously.

'She had a suitcase with her when she left Crown House, but as far as I know she didn't order a taxi. By that time, the last bus would have gone, so I'm fairly sure she set out on foot. I wondered if you knew which way she went?'

'Well, sir, there's not much I miss, being right in the middle of the village... Yes, I saw her; she stopped to speak to young Alf Ramsden, him what works at Ramsden's timber-yard. He'd got his

Dad's car for the evening – going to the dance at the Medford Palais, he was.'

'How do you know that?'

'He had his best suit on, and his hair slicked down; he generally goes dancing, Friday nights. Your lady wife asked him for a lift, and he told her to hop in – then they drove off together.'

'You think he took her into Medford?'

'Certain sure of it. When he come in to pick up his *Daily Mirror* this morning, I asked him straight out: "Where was you off to with Mrs Gaunt last night?" I said – and he told me he dropped her at the railway station.'

'Ah ... Thank you.'

Driving to Medford, Nick could imagine the gossip that must be buzzing round the village; but he didn't care. He was trying to think where Jenny might have gone.

The booking-clerk in the station ticket-office was obliging, but not very helpful.

'Yes, sir, I know Mrs Gaunt – well, that's to say, I know her by sight ... Yes, she did come in last night; she asked for a single ticket to Charing Cross. But it was a bit awkward-like, 'cos when she opened her bag, she found she hadn't got enough money in her purse. So she changed her mind: she said she was sorry she'd troubled me, and she turned round and went out again. That was the last I saw of her.'

Nick walked out of the station, his head full of conflicting thoughts. Why did she want to go to London? Whom did she know there? At least she hadn't gone by train. Could she have got another lift, from a helpful motorist? If so, his task was hopeless; how would he ever find her?

On the other hand – when she found she had no money, she might have decided to stay in Medford.

Looking up, he saw the half-timbered bulk of the Medford Arms facing him across the street, just as it must have faced Jenny, when she left the station, wondering where to go. They had often been to the hotel together; at cricket-club dances, or cosy suppers for two when they felt like an evening on their own ... At least it was worth trying.

The receptionist behind the desk wore rather too much make-up, and suspiciously auburn hair; she had a corsage of lilies of the valley and a refined accent.

'Mrs Gaunt...? Ay really couldn't say, ay'm sure... We're not permitted to divulge information about our guests – ay'm sorry.'

She glanced down the hotel register, open in front of her, and made a move to close it, but Nick was too quick for her.

'Don't bother,' he said. 'I can recognize my wife's signature, even upside-down. So she stayed here last night?'

The receptionist raised a pained, plucked eyebrow. 'She may have done.'

'Look ... I expect you think I'm the villain of the piece, and you're doing your best to help my wife – I appreciate that. But actually I'm trying to put things right: I want to apologize to her. Is she in her room now?'

'No, sir. Mrs Gaunt is not on the premises.'

'You mean I've missed her – she's already left?'

His disappointment and his sincerity were obvious, and the lady softened slightly.

'Her luggage is still upstairs; she's retaining her room for another night... But she went out, first thing.'

'I don't suppose you know where she's gone?'

'Well... She did ask me what time the Copper Kettle opens in the mornings. It's a tea-shop at the other end of the –'

'I know it. You think she was dropping in for morning coffee?'

'It seems unlikely, when she'd only just had breakfast... But that's where she was going.'

'I see. Well – thanks very much.' Nick pulled out his wallet, and produced a couple of notes, but the receptionist looked shocked.

'That won't be necessary, sir. Ay'm only too glad to have been of assistance. And...' she leaned forward with a conspiratorial smile, 'if ay may say so, ay do hope it turns out all right.'

It was only just after ten when Nick entered the Copper Kettle. He seemed to be the first customer; there was no sign of Jenny. He wondered if she might be in the smaller, more secluded tea-rooms upstairs, but a sign on the staircase stated that the upper floor was closed.

Trying to decide what to do next, he sat down and ordered coffee and biscuits. 'Just the one, is it?' asked the waitress, smothering a yawn.

'Yes –' Hearing a door open, he looked up, and his face changed. 'No ... Coffee for two, please. My wife may be joining me.'

Coming out of the manageress's office, Jenny stopped short. Nick stood up, and pulled out a chair.

'I've ordered for both of us,' he said.

She walked up to him and said in a low voice, 'Please don't make a scene.'

'I've no intention of making a scene. Shall we sit down?'

Reluctantly, she took the chair he offered, then asked, 'How did you know I was here?'

'Someone at the Medford Arms told me. I knew you hadn't gone to London, because you were short of money.'

'I left in such a hurry – I didn't stop to think... Of course the bank won't be open till Monday; but the hotel said I could pay by cheque. I'll move out as soon as I find somewhere cheaper.'

'For God's sake – you know you don't have to worry about money –'

'I don't want to be a burden to you. That's why I came here – to ask about getting a job. I haven't got any training, except as a housekeeper, but I thought I might learn to be a waitress. The manageress was very helpful; one of the girls is leaving to get married, and I can start the week after next.'

'Jenny...' He reached out and took her hand. 'I came to tell you I'm sorry... And to ask you to forgive me... I love you very much, and I can't let you go. Last night was the worst night of my life – and the loneliest. I realized how stupid I'd been, and how cruel, and I want to try and make it up to you... if you'll let me.'

At that moment, the waitress returned with their coffee and biscuits, and Jenny pulled her hand away. Nicholas managed to control himself, and thanked the girl politely. As soon as they were alone again, he turned back to Jenny: 'Will you give me another chance?'

Pouring cream into her coffee, she said thoughtfully, 'This is where you met me one afternoon, years ago – do you remember? You'd just joined the Navy; I hardly recognized you, in your uniform.'

'Of course I remember; we were upstairs, in one of the cosy corners – you were waiting for Richard... That was when I realized how you felt about him.'

'Yes, that was when it began. I was desperately in love with him, and he broke our date to be with another girl. You sat opposite me, looking hurt and disappointed... You were jealous – even then.'

'Not any more. I think I've been a bit crazy, but it will be different from now on. No more jealousy, I promise.'

'Oh, Nick...' She looked into his face, and her heart went out to him. 'I wish I could believe that.'

'It's true. I need you, Jenny. I think we need one another. Nothing else matters...' Suddenly he remembered something. 'Except –'

'Except what?'

'Last night, when you wanted to go to London, who were you going to see?'

She nearly got up and walked out, all over again. But then she began to laugh instead; a moment later, rather shamefaced, he laughed too. 'I'm sorry... I shouldn't have asked –'

She shook her head. 'It's all right... If you want to know, I thought I'd go and see your Uncle Charlie... Sir Charles has always been kind to me; I know he's on his own now, and I thought he might understand...' She added gently, 'But I'm glad I didn't go to London.'

He smiled. 'So am I. Can we try to start all over again?'

'If you really want to.' She stirred her coffee, watching the cream swirl round in the cup. 'I kept thinking of you last night; I didn't sleep very much. I believe I know why you were so unhappy about Richard... You compared yourself to him: you couldn't believe I really loved you because you don't like yourself very much. When you start the new job, perhaps you'll learn to like yourself a bit more. Then it will be all right.'

He squeezed her hand. 'I'll try – only there isn't going to be any new job.'

'What? But – the King's equerry –'

'I shan't do it. I won't do anything that takes me away from you. We'll stay at Crown House, together.'

Turning to him, she said urgently, 'Nick, you mustn't turn it down. It's what you want... To get back into the Navy, to live your kind of life – you can't give that up.'

'But if it means travelling –'

'We'll be together as often as we can. I might be able to come with you sometimes – and if not, I'll write to you, just like I used to. That's how we got to know one another, writing letters, backwards and forwards. This will be a chance to get to know one another all over again.'

On a July afternoon, Polly took Alex and Harriet for a walk in the garden, as she did every day when she came home from the bureau. The children could see their grandfather working at the far end of the long herbaceous border, and ran towards him; they dodged round an ornamental urn brimming with geraniums and lobelia, and nearly collided with Old Bea on the other side, where she sat in the shade, propped up with cushions in a wicker chair.

'Good gracious me – this is not a race-track!' she protested. 'Can't you look where you're going?'

They halted, abashed, and Polly said hastily, 'Sorry about that – we didn't see you there . . . Alex – Harry – don't bother your Great-Grandma.'

'Quite right; go and bother your grandfather instead,' said Old Bea.

William was waving at the children; they squeaked with delight and rushed off again.

'Not you!' Old Bea put out a bony hand, arresting Polly. 'Stay and keep me company; I haven't seen you for a very long time.'

'I know . . . I've been busy.'

'Too busy to come and visit me?'

'Well, I wasn't sure I'd be welcome, after I started the bureau and brought disgrace on the family.' Polly settled herself at Lady Beatrice's feet. 'Are we still speaking, then?'

The old lady pursed her lips. 'I may have been a trifle hasty . . . Alice tells me you're making a success of it; I had no idea matrimony could be such a profitable business. There was nothing of that kind in my young days.'

'I'm sure you didn't need it!' Polly twinkled at her. 'The men must have been falling over themselves for you.'

'I certainly had my chances . . .' Lady Beatrice smiled reminiscently. 'But I wasn't thinking of myself; a marriage bureau would have been invaluable for some families I could name – gawky lumps of girls, all unmarried and likely to remain so, driving their parents to distraction . . . They'd have paid any price for an eligible bachelor.'

'I can't work miracles; some people aren't the marrying type.'

'They tell me you've had some triumphs already. I hear you paired off a pork-butcher with the daughter of a titled family. Is that true? Perhaps he married her for her money?'

'No, it was love at first sight. As a matter of fact, he's richer than she is – he's got a chain of shops.'

'Really? Is the girl anyone we know?' But before Old Bea could ask any more questions, she was interrupted; Norman Brooks came up the path, and she sat back crossly. 'This really is too bad. Am I never to be left in peace? I thought this was your afternoon off, Norman; what are you doing here?'

Looking very pleased with himself, the young man replied, 'I just been to sign on, my lady; that's what I come to tell you. I'm handing in my notice.'

'*What*?' Old Bea's face darkened. 'Impossible! I don't wish you to leave – you know that perfectly well. I won't let you go.'

She gave him a meaning look, toying with the string of pearls around her scrawny throat, but Norman stood his ground.

'I'm sure you won't stand in my way, ma'am; I'm leaving for patriotic reasons. I've just signed on to join the Army – volunteered, I did, for King and country.'

'Congratulations, Norman!' Polly shook him warmly by the hand. 'That's marvellous. We're all very proud of you, aren't we, Lady Beatrice?'

The old lady's jaw sagged; for once she was lost for words.

'Can't let that chap Hitler have it all his own way – we got to show him we mean business!' Norman explained. 'Anyhow, I thought I'd better tell you – I'll be leaving the end of next week, and I'm off to training camp the Monday after . . . All right?' And he marched away, whistling.

Old Bea mumbled irritably, 'I suppose it's only to be expected. All the young men will be enlisting if this wretched crisis goes on . . . The boy may be right. Hitler's an odious little man: he must be put in his place.'

Polly tried to look on the bright side. 'I'm sure you'll soon find another chauffeur.'

'Yes, I dare say, but I dislike chopping and changing . . . Nothing seems to last any more; even the family is breaking up . . . Martin at Oxford, Miranda in France at that finishing-school, I haven't seen Edith for years, and Caroline seems to have disappeared altogether. Nicholas and Jenny spend more time at Eaton Square than they do at home –'

'Well, they have to, now he's at Buckingham Palace.'

'Alice tells me they're going to France, with the King and Queen, accompanying Their Majesties on a State Visit, if you please! Nicholas shouldn't leave Mr Stubbs to run the estate single-handed . . .'

'I'm sure Mr Stubbs has got everything under control,' Polly assured her. 'He's a very good organizer.'

'How can you say that? The man couldn't even organize his own wedding!' snorted Old Bea. 'Lilian tells me the engagement is off – she'll be the next one to give in her notice, I shouldn't wonder.'

Polly looked blank. 'The engagement's off? Lilian and Ken Stubbs? Are you sure?'

'She told me so herself. I tell you nothing lasts, everything keeps changing, all the time... Now where are you going?'

Polly had scrambled to her feet. 'I've got to see someone. Tell the children I won't be long; they'll be all right with their Grandpa for ten minutes... Excuse me –' And she set off briskly, towards the home farm.

When she walked into the office, Ken was at his desk, discussing the dairy herd with one of the stockmen. He stood up, greeting her cheerfully: 'Good afternoon, ma'am. Where's the family? Isn't Harriet coming for her pony-ride today?'

'They're in the garden, with his lordship... I wanted a word with you.'

'Certainly.' He nodded. 'All right, Johnson; we'll talk later.'

The man went out, giving Polly a sidelong look. Ken sat down again, saying, 'The children are always welcome here, you know that. They're growing up well and happy. They do you credit.'

'I don't give them as much time as I'd like to; I never see them between breakfast and teatime.'

'You're here when they need you,' he told her. 'I take my hat off to you – running a business and bringing up children. It takes some doing.'

'Yes, well – I'm still learning,' she said. 'But that's not what I came to talk about... I just heard about you and Lilian – breaking off your engagement.'

'Oh – that.' His smile faded. 'Yes, I'm sorry about it – but it wouldn't do. We weren't cut out for one another, not really.'

'But you were getting on so well –'

'We had our disagreements. We wanted different things from life, I dare say. Better to find that out now than later.'

'Yes, but – surely you could have sorted it out between you?'

'No.' He looked at her squarely. 'If you don't mind me saying so, it's a personal matter. We had our ups and downs, and we finally decided to call it off. That's all there is to be said about it.'

'I feel sort of responsible ... I brought you together.'

'Oh, I see.' A faint smile touched his lips. 'You think we're a poor sort of advertisement for your marriage bureau, eh? Are you afraid we'll put the other customers off?'

'Of course not! It's nothing to do with the bureau – it's just – I don't like people to be unhappy ... People I care about.'

After a pause, he said quietly, 'All right, then. I'll tell you something I never even told Lilian. I couldn't marry her; I'm not free to marry.'

'What do you mean?'

'I'm married already. You know I had some trouble, up in Norfolk?'

'You said there was a girl – she threw you over for someone else.'

'I didn't tell you the whole story. The girl was my wife. We'd only been married a year when she took up with another chap, someone her own age. They've been living together ever since.'

She stared at him. 'You got engaged to Lilian – knowing you couldn't marry her?'

'I thought I'd get a divorce. But there's difficulties about that too; besides, when I thought it over, I realized I didn't want to tie myself to Lilian for the rest of my life. She's a good sort, but I don't love her.'

'Then why did you –'

'She was lonely, like me. And you were so dead set on pairing us off; I suppose I did it to please you, more than anything ... I'd do anything for you – don't you know that?'

Then she realized she'd known it all along, but had never admitted it to herself. 'Oh, Ken – I'm sorry ... I mean, I'm very flattered and all that, but ...'

He finished the sentence: 'But you don't feel the same way about me. No, I never thought you did ... I hoped, I suppose; but it was only a sort of dream.' He cleared his throat. 'Don't be embarrassed. You can forget we had this conversation; it won't happen again.'

He behaved perfectly, and she was able to leave the farm office without any feeling of awkwardness. All the same, as she walked back to find the children, she decided she must be more careful in future; without being obvious about it, she would avoid seeing Ken on his own, so there need be no embarrassment for either of them ... As to forgetting about it – that might not be quite so easy.

The good weather continued, and a week later William was on his knees in the garden, wrestling with some particularly stubborn dandelions, when Alice came out with a tumbler and a jug.

'I've brought you some lemonade; it's so warm today. You've been hard at it ever since lunch – remember what Dr Parry said about not overdoing things.'

'Just ten minutes more; I must grub out these little blighters first.' He took the glass from her, and tasted it. 'Mmmm... Very refreshing.'

Alice sat on the grass and watched him, as he went on with his work.

'I wish I could do something to help, but I'm hopeless at gardening... I expect you miss Jenny, don't you?'

'I miss them all when they're away.' He looked back at the house, shimmering in a heat-haze, and shaded his eyes. 'Who's that, coming towards us? Don't tell me we've got visitors!'

'I sincerely hope not... Your old gardening trousers are an absolute disgrace...' Alice peered at the young couple walking across the lawn. 'It's no good; I haven't got my glasses.'

'It couldn't be Nicholas and Jenny, could it?'

'They're still in Paris – I told you.'

'And Martin and Miranda don't come home till next weekend... They must be strangers – I'm off!' He pulled himself up, heading for the shrubbery.

'Don't you dare – they've seen us now. It would be very rude.'

Side by side, they watched the visitors approach. Suddenly William said under his breath, 'Good God... It's Caro.'

Caroline and Scott walked up to meet them; Scott was smiling, but Caro looked nervous. For a moment, no one knew what to say; then the two men shook hands, and William said, 'You took us by surprise – we thought at first you were strangers.'

'I suppose that's what we are – practically,' said Caro, and she held out her hand uncertainly.

'Never!' said Alice; she caught Caro's hand, pulled her close, and kissed her. 'Oh, darling – what a wonderful surprise...'

'We heard from Edith after you'd been to see her,' William told Scott. 'But that was some time ago... And of course we lost touch with Gina altogether.'

'Yes – my sister made a real mess of things. That guy in Germany ran out on her, and in the end she went back to the States. I haven't had any news of her since then,' said Scott. 'But we've been travelling round Europe; observing, writing, taking the pulse –'

'Trying to guess what's going to happen,' added Caro, and suddenly hugged her father. 'It's lovely to see you, Daddy.'

'How long will you be here?' Alice wanted to know. 'Are you staying?'

'Just till Saturday; we're off again at the weekend,' she replied. 'We have to pick up visas from the Czech Embassy, then we're flying to Prague. Scott is hoping to get an interview with President Benes.'

'You think Hitler intends to make trouble there?' asked William.

'I'd say it's more than likely.' A shadow crossed Scott's face. 'After Austria, he fixed his sights on the Sudetenland, and if he doesn't get what he wants – he's liable to kick up one hell of a row . . .'

'You mustn't start talking politics now,' Alice broke in. 'I've got so many questions to ask – it's been so long –'

'Too long.' Scott put his arm round Caroline. 'That's why we had to drop by and say hello; even if it's only a flying visit. Maybe this is none of my business – but I know you've had your problems, and I thought it was about time we got things straight . . . OK?'

'There's nothing we'd like better,' said William, and Scott continued: 'I had another reason for coming down here today. If it's all right with you both – I'd like to ask for your daughter's hand in marriage . . .'

Caro turned on him indignantly. 'You never told me that! Of all the sneaky things to do –'

'I even surprised myself,' he agreed. 'I guess deep down I must be pretty conventional, after all.'

The State Visit to France had been a triumph, though it was nearly cancelled at the last minute.

The Queen's mother, Lady Strathmore, had been ill for some time, and a week before the date of their departure, she suffered a fatal heart attack; the King and Queen were with her when she died. President Lebrun was quick to send a message of condolence, adding that all preparations for the State Visit would of course be stopped immediately.

But Their Majesties knew how important it was in the current political situation for Britain and France to be seen as firm allies, closer than ever before; and they decided they must proceed with their plans, only postponing them for three weeks.

367

An immediate problem was the question of royal mourning; the Queen's dressmaker, Norman Hartnell, who had prepared a brilliant collection for Her Majesty, was asked for his advice.

'Surely, Ma'am – black and purple aren't the only possible colours?' he suggested. 'Isn't white the prerogative of royal mourning too?'

Within a fortnight, every dress in the collection had been copied in white.

On the last night of the Paris visit, Queen Elizabeth was radiant in a Winterhalter-style crinoline of white Valenciennes lace, sparkling with silver. The press anounced that the French people had taken the Queen to their hearts, adding, 'At last we have a monarchy again!'

'You look breathtaking,' whispered the King, as they left the final reception at the Quai d'Orsay, and returned to the private apartments that had been set aside for them, throughout their visit, on the upper floors of the French Foreign Ministry.

As the door closed behind them, the Queen gave a sigh of relief.

'Thank goodness that's over!' she exclaimed. 'Home tomorrow – I can hardly wait.'

Nicholas was in attendance upon the King, who had invited Jenny to join them for a few moments at the end of the evening.

'Can I get Your Majesties a drink?' asked Nick. 'I expect you could do with a nightcap.'

'Anything as long as it isn't champagne – in the past four days, I've had enough to last me a lifetime.' The Queen sank on to an elegant Louis XIV sofa, her crinoline billowing round her like a cloud. 'What I'd *really* like is a nice cup of cocoa, but that's too difficult at this time of night; I'll settle for a gin and tonic instead.'

As Nicholas poured the drinks, Jenny said sympathetically, 'Has it been such an ordeal?'

'It's been damned hard work,' replied the King. 'They kept us on the go from the moment we arrived; the State Banquet, the Hôtel de Ville, the Opera Gala and today we had a trip to Versailles *and* a farewell dinner with a cabaret afterwards.'

'Maurice Chevalier was enchanting,' said the Queen. 'In fact it's all been absolutely wonderful – and absolutely exhausting.'

'You've had a pretty strenuous year, one way and another.' The King put his hand gently on his wife's shoulder. 'And I dare say the year ahead isn't going to be easy, either – for any of us.'

'Nothing worth having ever comes easily,' said the Queen, taking the glass Nick handed her. She looked up at her husband. 'But there will always be good times as well as bad – so let's drink to the future. A new beginning, perhaps.'

They raised their glasses: 'A new beginning.'

Then the King crossed the room, taking a printed sheet of paper from the writing-desk.

'This arrived today, in the diplomatic bag,' he told Nicholas. 'That's why I asked you both tonight. I wanted you to have it as soon as possible; they kept you waiting long enough.'

It was the formal confirmation of Nicholas's appointment, from the Lord Chamberlain's office:

> ... *To certify that the Hon. Nicholas Gaunt is by the King's command hereby appointed into the Place and Quality of a Lord in Waiting to His Majesty.*
>
> *To have, hold, exercise and enjoy the said Place: together with all Rights, Profits, Privileges and Advantages thereunto belonging.*
>
> *This Appointment to be during His Majesty's Pleasure and to become void on the death of the Sovereign.*
>
> *Given under my Hand and Seal this fourteenth day of June, 1938, in the second year of His Majesty's Reign* ...

The King shook hands with Nicholas, and the Queen kissed Jenny, saying, 'I'm so glad – I feel as if you're both part of the family now.'

It was after midnight, but the street outside was still packed with people, and through the general tumult they could hear shouts of '*Vive le Roi – vive la Reine!*'

'They're hoping you might make one more appearance on the balcony, Sir,' said Nick. 'I suppose it's too late for that?'

'Well ... I don't know what our hosts would say; they're very strong on security and protocol. Still, we are leaving tomorrow, so – what do you think, my dear?'

Elizabeth smiled at him mischievously. 'Why not?' she said.

She took his hand, and they ran out of the room like two children, down the long hall and on to the balcony. The crowd went wild with delight, roaring their appreciation.

Nicholas and Jenny looked at one another. He had never loved her so much and they had never been so happy.

'I think we should go back to our hotel,' he said.

Jenny looked into his eyes, and smiled. 'Our last night in Paris.'

'Our second honeymoon,' said Nick, taking her in his arms. 'And a new beginning.'